Visit us on the Web! rhcbooks.com

Educators and librarians, for a variety of teaching tools, visit us at RHTeachersLibrarians.com

Library of Congress Cataloging-in-Publication Data
Name: Gallicano, Todd Calgi, author.
Title: The selkie of San Francisco / Todd Calgi Gallicano.
Description: First edition. | New York : Delacorte Books for Young Readers, 2018. | Series: A Sam London adventure ; 2 | Summary: "When a selkie appears in the San Francisco Bay, Sam London and the guardian Tashi are summoned by Dr. Vance Vantana of the Department of Mythical Wildlife to help track the creature down. Except unbeknownst to them, other forces are at work and the secret that mythical creatures exist and live amongst humans is in even bigger danger than ever before" — Provided by publisher.
Identifiers: LCCN 2017039046 (print) | LCCN 2017050295 (ebook) |
ISBN 978-1-5247-1371-3 (el) | ISBN 978-1-5247-1369-0 (hardback)
Subjects: | CYAC: Selkies—Fiction. | Animals, Mythical—Fiction. | National parks and reserves—Fiction. | Supernatural—Fiction. | San Francisco Bay (Calif.)—Fiction. | BISAC: JUVENILE FICTION / Action & Adventure / General. | JUVENILE FICTION / Legends, Myths, Fables / General. | JUVENILE FICTION / Fantasy & Magic.
Classification: LCC PZ7.1.G3478 (ebook) | LCC PZ7.1.G3478 Sel 2018 (print) | DDC [Fic]—dc23

The text of this book is set in 13-point Fournier MT
Interior design by Ken Crossland

Printed in the United States of America
10 9 8 7 6 5 4 3 2 1
First Edition

FROM THE FILES OF THE DEPARTMENT OF MYTHICAL WILDLIFE

THE SELKIE
OF SAN FRANCISCO

A SAM LONDON ADVENTURE

TODD CALGI GALLICANO

DELACORTE PRESS

THE SELKIE
OF SAN FRANCISCO

BOOKS BY TODD CALGI GALLICANO

SAM LONDON ADVENTURES

Guardians of the Gryphon's Claw

The Selkie of San Francisco

For Mongo and the kiddo

AUTHOR'S NOTE

The following account is based on a case file that originated with the Department of Mythical Wildlife (DMW). In an effort to inform the public of this previously unknown government agency, my sources have provided me with copies of files from the DMW archives. As far as I can determine, "The Selkie of San Francisco" is the department's second case involving Sam London.

DMW case files consist of witness interviews, investigative notes, research materials, and reports offering comprehensive explanations of the events that transpired. Due to the often dry, fact-laden nature of this information, I have created a dramatic interpretation of the file's contents. All the details have been maintained, but the narrative has been enhanced for the reader's enjoyment. I have also included several references to the source material within the text and have appended a legend of abbreviations, codes, and terms to assist in decoding the DMW's distinct classification system.

Since these files are classified, dates have been omitted and some names have been altered to protect the identities of witnesses and individuals still in the department's employ.

—T.C.G.

PROLOGUE

Lynnae of Russia's Lake Baikal had never seen a production of *Swan Lake,* but she felt a special kinship to the classic ballet created by Pyotr Ilyich Tchaikovsky in the late nineteenth century. In fact, she possessed a small advertisement for its famous 1964 London staging, which featured legendary dancers Rudolf Nureyev and Margot Fonteyn de Arias. She'd found the crinkled-up vintage poster on the shore of her home, a hidden inlet on the world's oldest lake. Likely left behind by a ballet-loving vacationer, Lynnae surmised. She often imagined living out the tale—particularly the part where the character finds her one true love. That was her favorite part of all. Lynnae had been told the fable as a child, and although she had never heard how it ended, she assumed the maiden and her prince lived happily ever after. Unfortunately, Lynnae would never have the chance to experience a love like this, since she was forbidden to interact with humans, or any creatures, for that matter. Lynnae was a swan maiden and was destined to live her life separated from the world that lay beyond the lake.

It was for this reason that it came as quite a shock when word spread that an outsider had arrived to speak to the Maiden Council—the maternal protectors of the swan maidens. Lynnae couldn't help entertaining the notion that this stranger would gaze upon her and fall madly in love, just like in *Swan Lake*. The possibility was too tantalizing to ignore, so Lynnae and two other curious maidens scurried off to the council's gathering spot to catch a glimpse of their unexpected guest.

"Do you think it's a human man?" Lynnae wondered aloud to her cohorts. They gasped, as if such a thought were unimaginable. Lynnae had to admit that it was highly unlikely. The council had established a boundary, which was guarded by the fearsome Baba Yaga, a forest-dwelling hag with supernatural powers and a penchant for devouring the souls of trespassers. She was under strict rules to never allow a human to pass, especially a male human.

When Lynnae arrived at the meeting place, she and her sisters hid behind a bushy row of blue-berried honeysuckle. They spied not one but two strangers standing in the clearing. The taller one was a monstrous creature, large in stature, with green skin, and antlers that sprouted from his head like bony vines. The other stranger was a woman with long, pitch-black hair who was dressed in a flowing white robe. She was stunningly beautiful but grim in her expression.

Lynnae watched as nine swans floated toward the shore. The long-necked, water-dwelling birds had orange bills and snow-white-feathered plumage. As these majestic creatures approached, they transformed in unison. Unlike Lynnae and her fellow maidens, who took on human forms for their work in the sanctuary, the Maiden Council always retained several aspects of their swan form, including their wings, which they kept tucked behind their bodies; a head of white feathers in place of their hair; and orange eyes with beady black pupils. The rest of their bodies were feathered, except their arms, faces, and necks, which were covered in skin that was as delicate as gossamer and shimmered when the glow of the moon reflected on the water's surface, like it did this night.

Uravasi, Caer, Melusine, Manto, Sibyl, Undine, Palatina, Melior, and Faye appeared calm and, as always, were radiant. For Lynnae, it was like having nine mothers. Though each was unique in personality and style, they all cared deeply for her and her sister maidens. The nine took up a position a few feet from the lake's edge in waist-deep water. The ever-curious Uravasi was the first to speak.

"This is an unexpected visit, Cernunnos," she said in a wispy, angelic voice.

"*Lord* Cernunnos," the dour woman corrected her. The nine maidens exchanged irritated glances; then the formal Melusine spoke matter-of-factly.

"Such titles are not honored by the Maiden Council. If this recognition is the reason for your visit, you may leave." And with that, the maidens began to recede into the waters.

"Phylassos has betrayed you!" the horned creature bellowed, his deep voice echoing throughout the inlet. The maidens paused. Sibyl, the most learned of the council, eyed the two discerningly.

"There are whispers that you are the creature who betrayed the gryphon, with the cynocephalus called Chase," she said with authority.

"If you heard these whispers, did you not also hear of the boy?" Cernunnos asked.

"Boy?" the formidable Faye replied inquisitively.

Cernunnos nodded. "Sam London. He was with the human Vantana. The gryphon appeared to Sam. The boy was the one who helped save the gryphon's claw."

"This would be a *violation*," Palatina, the chief maiden, observed. Cernunnos nodded once in agreement. The maidens turned toward each other and whispered fervently. Lynnae reflexively leaned forward to try to discern their hushed murmurings, but in so doing caused an ever-so-slight rustling of the bush that was helping to conceal her. The noise did not go unnoticed. The female stranger spun her head in Lynnae's direction.

"Are your maidens spies as well as swans?" she sneered.

The nine maidens of the council looked to the honeysuckle as Lynnae and her cohorts made haste back to their dens. Lynnae hoped she had not been identified by her mother maidens, but she prayed the punishment would be mild if she had. She hurriedly settled into her nest, which glittered with specks of the bioluminescent fungus known as foxfire. She tried to think of excuses she could give for her eavesdropping, but she couldn't stop wondering about what she had heard.

Whoever this Sam London was, he was known by the nine, Lynnae concluded. Yet his existence had also appeared to be a surprise to the council. Who was this boy, and why did he so concern her mothers? When Lynnae heard Caer approach, she slipped her *Swan Lake* poster beneath the twinkling foxfire-laden tree limb and pretended to be asleep. Avoiding the disciplinary maiden's wrath was more important to Lynnae than satisfying her curiosity. These questions, like so many others she collected over the years, would simply have to go unanswered.

Chapter 1
STUCK IN THE MIDDLE

Twelve-year-old Sam London believed the term "middle school" described the grades between elementary school and high school perfectly. These were transformative years that saw students grow from playful children into rebellious teenagers. Of course, in school, as in life, being in the middle of anything was never all that comfortable. In the middle meant you were neither getting started nor about to finish. You were trapped between two stages of life—old enough to know better, yet too young to be trusted with major responsibilities.

But for Sam London, middle school had taken on a whole new level of discomfort. Maybe it was all the fantastical things he had experienced just weeks earlier on his adventure to save the gryphon's claw. Perhaps it was the now-constant presence of the Guardian Tashi, who attended school with Sam and acted as his secret bodyguard. Maybe it was that Sam's new pet/companion was a shape-shifting raccoon-dog named Nuks who masqueraded as Sam whenever needed. Or it could be the fact that Sam's new teacher was an old friend reincarnated as a human being without any knowledge of his previous life as a mythical dog-man. Point being, life had recently been pretty exciting for Sam London, and now it was anything but.

School, homework, sleep, became wash, rinse, repeat. It was Sam's routine, day in and day out. He did have a small semblance of a social life in the form of birthday parties he was invited to or random activities his mom enrolled him in. As for simply hanging out with the boys, Sam had never been the type to have a large circle of friends to play video games with or just shoot hoops. Sam had classmates but no best friends. Most of the kids thought he was an odd duck, including the other odd ducks.

Sam's mom, Odette London—or Ettie, as people called her—was always encouraging Sam to make friends, and he had made a few lackluster attempts in the past. However, if making friends had been difficult for Sam before his adventure with Dr. Vance Vantana, now it seemed nearly impossible. How could he be friends with someone and not share the life-changing truth that mythical creatures are real and living among us, but a centuries-old gryphon's curse renders them invisible to human eyes? How could he relate to someone who didn't—and couldn't—know *anything* about this secret? This was why he hung out with Tashi so much, besides the fact that she rarely, if ever, left his side; after all, she had been sworn to protect his life with her own and was steadfastly committed to the cause. But at least she knew the truth and Sam didn't have to be so careful with his words around her. And besides, Sam's focus was not on friend-making; rather, it was on preparing for his next case.

Since returning from his first adventure, Sam woke up every day with an anxious excitement that today would be the day when he'd be called on to help the Department of Mythical Wildlife with a new investigation. In the days that followed, Sam started watching the news and scouring the internet for any hint of a potential assignment or any sign of the world that he knew existed, but he consistently came up empty. The secret remained quite secret. Of course, there were dozens of internet sites devoted to cryptids—creatures and plants that the scientific community didn't recognize as real. And there was even a television show that followed the exploits of Boone "the Wildman" Walker, a self-described monster hunter who traveled the world seeking proof of the existence of legendary creatures, but never found any evidence. As for the individuals who claimed to have seen bigfoot or a chupacabra, Sam figured they either had mythical DNA and didn't know it or their eyes were just playing tricks on them. So without any indication of recent sightings and no communication from Dr. Vantana, Sam had reluctantly settled into his humdrum life and started to quietly wonder if the call would ever come.

It was a Friday in spring when things finally changed. Sam awoke to find Nuks missing from his bed. A moment later, the raccoon-dog entered the room in Sam's form. It was still an odd feeling for Sam to stare at a duplicate of himself. He imagined it was similar to what twins experienced.

"Why are you—" Sam started, finding it strange that Nuks would be up and posing as Sam this early on a school day.

"Your mom is cleaning the house," Nuks explained, interrupting. "I thought I would help and that would help you."

"You don't have to do that, you know?" Sam said. "It's not your responsibility. Next time check with me."

"Oh yes. Yes, of course. I'm very sorry, Sam. So sorry," Nuks replied, instantly unnerved and jittery. Sam noticed.

"Nuks, you gotta stop freaking out whenever I tell you something," he told the raccoon-dog in his most pleasant tone. "I'm not going to send you away, okay? You'll always have a home here. *Always.*" Nuks softened and smiled.

Sam found himself having to constantly remind the creature that he wasn't going to abandon him over the slightest slipup. Nuks adored having a family and a roof over his head, and he would do anything to keep it that way. Normally, a shape-shifting raccoon-dog was prohibited from passing itself off as a human's pet, but Nuks had found a loophole and had become the envy of his kind.

In return, Nuks had grown into a loyal, trusted friend for Sam. The best part was he never complained and was eager to follow Sam's lead. In fact, when Ettie wanted Sam to do an activity he dreaded, Sam would send Nuks in his place—in Sam's form, of course. Tashi was critical of this, as she believed Sam was taking advantage of the creature's natural desire to please. But Nuks genuinely loved the opportunity to discover new things. Over the past few weeks, he had learned about the origins of folk music, taken a beginner's ballet class, done some woodworking, and even gone geocaching. The latter activity had proven problematic, as Nuks consistently relied on his nose to sniff out the hidden caches, instead of using the GPS device. This led to an awkward exchange between Ettie and the leader of the geocaching day camp, who was concerned about Sam's mental state but also wildly impressed with his canine-like olfactory senses.

"There's a bag of granola in my desk—help yourself," Sam offered to Nuks as a reward for his cleaning. The creature grinned broadly and walked toward the desk, but Sam put his hand up. "Not as me . . ."

"Oh, right. Of course," Nuks responded, transforming hurriedly back into his natural form and scurrying the rest of the way to the waiting granola.

Sam eyed the door to his room with trepidation. If his mom was up early cleaning the house, it could mean only one thing: Ettie's famous "spring thing." It was an annual tradition Sam dreaded, when his mom would clean the house from top to bottom. She became a tornado of tidiness, and Sam would inevitably get sucked into the storm. Although he didn't despise cleaning, he had developed a love-hate relationship with the "spring thing" because of a rule Ettie had instituted that said if something hadn't been used in three years, it was relegated to the donation pile. Sam was an unabashed pack rat and loathed this rule.

To work around his mother's unjust decree, Sam would

try to use everything in his possession within a three-year time span. That way, when Ettie asked, Sam could answer honestly. Of course, Sam defined the word "use" quite liberally in this instance—often meaning he simply touched the belonging in question. This worked for exactly two "spring things" before Ettie got wise to her son's ruse and began interrogating him.

"Did you actually use it, or just pick it up and put it back down, Sam?" she would ask. At that point, Sam would capitulate and admit the truth. More recently he had begun initiating a new tack when dealing with his mother's insistence on tossing his cherished possessions: he would purposely keep things he didn't want anymore. This had the advantage of satisfying his mom's thirst for getting rid of his stuff while allowing him to keep the things he really cared about. But he knew it was probably just a matter of time before she figured out his new scheme and began exacting more sacrifices.

Sam sucked in a breath and ventured into the hallway. What he found shocked him. The attic access door in the hallway ceiling was open, and there was a stepladder placed beneath it. Despite a repeated promise to clean the cramped, unfinished storage space during the "spring thing," his mother had always wound up getting too tired and would put it off for another year. The cramped unfinished storage space was chock-full of boxes, old vacuums, and who knew what else. And now it appeared that Ettie finally had the time to tackle it.

"Nothing short of a miracle, huh?" Ettie said, finding Sam frozen in the hallway. Sam nodded, still staring in awe. "Well, I wouldn't be able to get to the attic without your help this morning. I can't thank you enough. You're really such a good kid." As she spoke those last few words, she smiled lovingly at Sam and mussed his hair.

Sam couldn't help but feel guilty for taking the credit for Nuks's hard work. As a way of placating his conscience, Sam had begun responding to this sort of praise in an unusual manner.

"I'll let him know you said that," Sam replied, to which his mom grinned.

"Right, you do that." Ettie laughed. She seemed amused at Sam's new response and likely thought it was simply Sam being his goofy self. Sam didn't necessarily mind being thought of as goofy, especially if it meant he could rest easier knowing he wasn't stealing all the glory from his friend. "Oh, and while you're telling yourself thanks, also tell yourself you're late. We're leaving for school in ten minutes, not a minute more," Ettie added before slipping past Sam and heading for the stairs.

"Okay. I just have to get dressed and eat something," Sam replied.

"Eat something?" Ettie stopped and asked with surprise. "You polished off all the doughnuts, and you're still hungry? With the amount of sugar you ate, you should be able to run to school faster than I could drive you."

"Oh. Right. Of course. I was just joking," Sam said quickly, trying to cover his misstep as he turned back toward his room. There he saw Nuks curled up near the window.

"You didn't save *me* any doughnuts?" he asked after closing the door. The raccoon-dog lifted his head slowly.

"You wanted some?" he replied with a genuine innocence.

"Of course. But you helped clean—you deserved them. I'll just have to settle for some of that granola," Sam said with a shrug. Nuks's eyes widened in guilty surprise.

"You wanted some?"

* * *

It was not ten but twenty minutes later when Sam and Ettie finally emerged from the house, headed for school. Tashi was already waiting patiently by the car, as she had every day since Sam suggested to his mother that they give the new girl a ride to school. Ettie found the gesture sweet and interpreted it to mean that Sam had a crush. Sam's adamant denials only further convinced Ettie that this was the case. If there was one upside to his mother's false assumption, it was that she no longer referred to Nerida Nyx as Sam's future wife. Nerida was a childhood friend whose mother happened to be Ettie's best friend. Ettie teased Sam relentlessly about Nerida, so this was a nice, albeit annoying, change of pace.

"Sorry we're late, Tashi," Ettie said, out of breath as she scrambled for her keys and unlocked the car. "It's been a hectic morning."

Tashi climbed into the front seat while Sam jumped into the back. Although the passenger seat had always been Sam's spot, he had relinquished it after an incident on the first day of carpooling, when he had yelled "shotgun" to stake his claim on the front seat. Tashi, being unfamiliar with the term, thought Sam was shouting a warning. In response, the Guardian switched into full-on protection mode and tackled him. It took a few minutes to explain the phrase and calm Tashi down. Ettie wasn't sure what to make of it all until Sam convinced her it was a cultural misunderstanding—and that in Tashi's village, the passenger seat is relegated to the female.

As Ettie pulled the car out of the driveway with a light screech of rubber, Tashi glanced over at Sam's mother.

"Will you be late again on Monday?" the Guardian asked matter-of-factly.

"Excuse me?" Ettie replied, surprised by the question.

"We'll be on time, I promise," Sam piped in, trying to avoid an ugly situation. His mom looked back at him in the rearview mirror, and Sam gave her a shrug.

"That is reassuring," Tashi said. "It is neither honorable nor respectful to be tardy."

"Excuse me?" Ettie repeated, her voice clearly more irritated. Sam leapt back into the fray.

"It's cool, Mom. It's just a cultural thing," Sam explained, relying on his standard excuse for Tashi's odd behavior.

"Oh, right," Ettie replied. "Of course."

Tashi peered back at Sam. "I don't believe this to be—"

Sam glared at Tashi, pleading with his eyes and placing a shushing finger to his lips. Tashi caught on. She turned toward Ettie and attempted to calm the proverbial waters.

"Thank you for the ride, Ms. London," Tashi offered with her singular slight smile. "You look very . . . pretty today," she added awkwardly.

"Thank you, Tashi," Ettie said with a grin. Sam threw Tashi a secret thumbs-up, which she acknowledged with a small nod. Ettie continued, "You look pretty as well. Doesn't she, Sam?"

The relief he'd felt quickly vanished, and Sam fought to keep his cheeks from blushing. This was a typical Ettie ploy to force Sam into complimenting a female of his age. She used to do it constantly with Nerida, and it always led to an uncomfortable exchange. What could Sam do but agree?

"Yes, she does," Sam concurred.

Tashi immediately shifted her eyes to Sam. Her expression was one of surprise, and her signature slight smile grew less slight. Ettie caught Sam's eye in the mirror and winked, believing she was doing her part to help her son with his latest crush.

Sam managed to avoid any more forced compliments for the rest of the car ride, and once they arrived, he headed toward the school, with Tashi a step or two behind. He had come to accept the Guardian following him like this, as it was certainly better than when she'd been at Sam's side and everyone just assumed they were a couple. Sam had become sensitive to this notion ever since Nerida asked him about it. He would never admit this to anyone, but he didn't like the idea of Nerida thinking he had a girlfriend. Of course, he wasn't quite ready to admit to himself why he didn't like that.

Unfortunately, the few steps of separation between the pair didn't seem to eliminate all speculation.

"Sam and Tashi sitting in a tree . . . ," a trio of girls sang teasingly. Before they could finish their tired jibe, Tashi stopped walking and interrupted.

"Sitting in a tree?" the Guardian asked thoughtfully. Then she quickly added, "If you are speaking of my time living in a tree in the place you call Benicia Park, I can assure you that Sam—"

Before she had a chance to get out another word and embarrass both of them, Sam pulled her away. The Guardian was a formidable warrior, but she lacked any social savvy and as such remained completely oblivious to her tormentors' mean-spirited ways.

"Ignore them, Tashi," he told her. "They're just trying to upset you."

"Upset me?" she replied, appearing confounded.

"Yeah," Sam confirmed. "You know, make you feel bad about yourself. Hurt your feelings—"

"By using words?" she asked, clearly still not getting it. Sam nodded. "And they are not banshees?"

"No, Tashi, they aren't banshees," Sam replied, stifling a laugh. "Listen, don't worry about it. It's just one of those stupid human things."

Tashi nodded, as if suddenly understanding. "Ah yes," she said. "Like the girls who paint their faces for reasons other than going into battle."

"Sure . . . ," Sam said slowly. "Sort of like that." He was gradually coming to terms with the fact that there would be some aspects of his world that Tashi would never completely understand. But that was okay. There was plenty about Tashi's culture and the world of mythical creatures that Sam would likely never fully comprehend either.

"Did you hear from Dr. Vantana?" Tashi asked as they walked into the school.

"Not yet," Sam replied with disappointment, before leaving the Guardian to head to his locker.

"Be mindful of your surroundings," Tashi called out to him, like she did every day. He gave her a lethargic thumbs-up without turning around.

When Sam reached his locker, he was surprised—and a little disheartened—to see that Nerida wasn't there. She had the locker next to his and could always be found standing in front of it at the same time every morning. If it were any other student, it wouldn't be all that strange, but Nerida never missed a day of school. In fact, she had gotten the perfect attendance award every year for as long as Sam could remember. Maybe she was late or had just gone to class early, he speculated. He'd probably see her at lunch in the library, since he'd been spending his lunchtimes there researching mythical creatures in order to be at the top of his game for the next case, and Nerida could always be found in the library on Fish Fridays. She was apparently highly allergic to seafood and had to self-quarantine indoors for the whole period. Without Nerida to grab his attention, Sam grabbed his books and was quickly off to start the school day.

* * *

Sam's last class before lunch was English with Mr. Canis, who was the human reincarnation of Sam's cynocephalus friend, Chriscanis, the latter having returned to Gaia at the hands of the Beast of Gevaudan. Mr. Canis was halfway through the day's lesson when the unthinkable happened.

"Sam?" a muffled voice said, jolting Sam out of a daydream. He sat up straight and looked to his teacher attentively.

"Yes?" Sam answered.

"Yes, what?" Mr. Canis replied.

"You called my name," Sam said. The rest of the class broke out into a smattering of giggles.

"I did not," Mr. Canis said. "Perhaps you misheard me."

"Oh . . . sorry," Sam apologized, feeling embarrassed. He chalked it up to his daydream and focused back on the lesson.

"Sam?" the muffled voice called out again, this time sounding anxious. Sam suddenly realized it was not coming from his teacher or his daydream—it was emanating from the DMW badge in his book bag. He scrambled to find the device before the voice of Dr. Vantana spoke again. Unfortunately, he pulled it out just as the doctor decided to try once more.

"Sam London!" the doctor shouted, the button almost jumping out of Sam's hand. The anxiety in Vantana's voice had been replaced with irritation. Sam's classmates were now all staring at him. Most were shocked by the flagrant rule-breaking, while a few others watched excitedly for the imminent confrontation with Mr. Canis like the incident was some kind of spectator sport. Sam quickly brought the badge up to his mouth and whispered, "Hang on."

"Mr. London—is there a problem?" Mr. Canis asked as he walked around his desk and approached Sam.

"No, sir. But I was wondering if I might use the restroom."

"What's that in your hand?" the teacher inquired.

"My hand? Uh . . . n-n-nothing," Sam stammered.

"Let me see it," Mr. Canis demanded firmly. Sam felt a knot in the pit of his stomach as he handed the badge over, crossing his fingers and wishing for it to keep quiet. The teacher took the badge and examined it.

"It's just a toy. I must have forgotten to turn it off," Sam explained, hoping it wouldn't draw any further scrutiny. But Mr. Canis appeared intrigued by the item.

"A toy?" he wondered, as if not quite buying it. His eyes zeroed in on the inscription. "Department of—"

"Do you mind if I use the bathroom?" Sam interjected, fearing the doctor would call again at any moment. He whispered to the teacher, "I gotta go pretty bad. Number one, number two, and maybe even number three." This spurred a smile from Mr. Canis.

"Oh dear," the teacher whispered back. "You'd best get a move on, then. Grab the hall pass on the way out."

As Sam stood up, he gestured to the badge. "Can I?" Mr. Canis eyed his pupil with suspicion. "I promise you won't see it ever again. Second chance?" Sam added with a pleading smile. Mr. Canis considered it, then slowly handed the badge over.

"No third chances."

"I wouldn't think of it," Sam said with seriousness.

The second Sam reached the bathroom, he pulled the badge back out, pressed the shiny metal face, and spoke.

"Dr. Vantana? Are you still there? It's Sam London." A moment later the doctor answered.

"My apologies, Sam," Vantana said in his signature Southern drawl. "I forgot about school. Do you need me to ring you up later?"

Sam had already waited long enough to hear anything from the doctor—he wasn't going to wait any longer.

"No, sir. How can I help?"

"Well, we've got ourselves a bit of a situation," Vantana replied.

"What kind of situation?" Sam asked.

"The kind that's made its way into the news. We're on the case, kid, and I'm on my way."

Chapter 2
AN OLD FRIEND

Sam London was practically levitating with excitement. After finally hearing from Dr. Vance Vantana about a new case, it was time to spring into action. Vance had informed Sam that he'd pick him up at lunchtime, which was in only half an hour, and he was bringing Nuks with him, since the raccoon-dog's Sam London substitution services would be required. Sam would meet Nuks in the school library, where they would stealthily make the switch.

Although Dr. Vantana had mentioned that what they'd be investigating had made the news, Sam had no time to go online or find a TV to get a sneak preview. He still had to sit through the remainder of Mr. Canis's class without upsetting his teacher any further. So he sat up straight and did his best to listen—or, rather, pretend to listen. The suspense was making it nearly impossible for him to concentrate. After all, the last time an event involving a mythical creature had made its way into the news, it had been Sam's encounter with the gryphon. And that was because their meeting led to a chain-reaction collision and massive explosion.

When the school bell rang for lunch, Sam catapulted himself out of his chair and sprinted to his locker. As expected, Tashi was waiting for him. She always waited at Sam's locker at lunchtime so she could accompany him to the cafeteria.

"Vantana contacted me," Sam reported enthusiastically.

"A mission?" Tashi asked, intrigued. Sam nodded and stuffed his books into his locker.

"He said it was something that made the news," Sam said, then turned and headed for the library. Tashi followed closely. "He's picking me up in a few minutes. I'm meeting Nuks in the library so that he can—"

"The doctor is picking both of us up," Tashi interjected. Sam stopped.

"No, Tashi," Sam replied. "You can't leave campus without a really good excuse."

"I have a plan," Tashi said confidently, and she continued toward the library. Sam walked alongside her.

"If your plan has anything to do with faking an illness, you can just forget it," Sam informed her. "Our school nurse used to be in the Russian military. Kyle from gym said she was responsible for making sure the soldiers who faked injuries to avoid combat were sent to the front lines. She has a nose for it. Tim Nelson, an eighth grader, perpetrated this elaborate scheme where he convinced everyone, even his parents, that he had chicken pox, just so he could stay home for a video game tournament. Nurse Orlova not only logged in to the game to beat him, but she went on to win the title, then snuck over to his house and dumped a big bucket of soapy water over him to prove that his so-called chicken pox were just dots from a red marker." Tashi's eyebrow raised for a brief moment as she came to a halt in front of the entrance to the library.

"You believe this tall tale?" she asked.

"I've seen photographic evidence, and the point is, pretending to be sick won't work."

"I appreciate the warning, but it will not be a problem," Tashi asserted. "Now let's go meet Nuks. We don't want to keep the doctor waiting." She entered the library, and Sam sighed heavily before following her. *What does the Guardian have up her sleeve?* he wondered.

When Sam and Tashi entered the library, the librarian, Ms. Bryce, was in her usual spot at the checkout desk. She was in her midtwenties and always wore her hair tucked beneath a purple knit beret. Ms. Bryce looked over when she heard the door, and did a double take.

"Sam?" the librarian said, appearing confused. "Didn't I just see you come in?"

Sam realized Nuks must already be waiting for him. The raccoon-dog was supposed to adjust his face before entering the school so they could avoid these kinds of awkward situations.

"Uh . . . yes," Sam replied. "Yes, you did. And then I left to get something out of my locker."

"A new outfit?" she inquired, eyeing his clothes.

"Oh . . . yeah," Sam answered. "I spilled some juice on my shirt and had to change." Ms. Bryce nodded but didn't seem convinced. Sam was eager to avoid any more questions, so he added hurriedly, "I'll be in my favorite stack," before heading to the back of the library with Tashi in tow.

The folklore and mythology section was the predetermined spot where he and Nuks had agreed to meet whenever the time came for them to switch places. Besides the ironic nature of the aisle's subject matter, the section was well hidden and saw little foot traffic. Sure enough, Nuks was waiting exactly where he was supposed to. He had a book in hand and a duffel bag at his feet. He saw them approach and grinned.

"Sam! Tashi!" the raccoon-dog exclaimed. He held out the book proudly. "Look!" He pointed to an illustration of a raccoon-dog. The caption denoted the creature as a tanuki. Nuks continued excitedly, "It's *me*. Well, not *me*. But one of my kind. Isn't that cool?"

"Very cool," Sam concurred. "I thought we talked about you changing your face if you ever came here. Ms. Bryce is totally suspicious."

"I have to touch someone to do that," Nuks explained. "And I didn't have time."

"All right. We'll just be better prepared the next time we have to do this," Sam said.

"Definitely!" Nuks agreed, then greeted the Guardian with a smile. "Hi, Tashi."

"Nice to see you again, Nuks," she replied. "Did you bring what we discussed?"

"You two discuss?" Sam asked with surprise.

"When necessary," she said.

"Just like you wanted, Tashi," Nuks told her as he reached down to the bag at his feet.

"What's this all about?" Sam asked. "Dr. Vantana is waiting."

Nuks unzipped the duffel to reveal a raccoon-dog. This one had pinkish-red fur and a pink nose. When it gazed upward and saw Sam, its eyes fluttered.

"Is that—" Sam began.

"Her name is Nuiko. She is from Japan," Nuks explained. Sam had a sudden realization.

"Tashi," he said, turning to the Guardian. "You're not thinking you're going to—"

"You said it yourself, Sam London," she replied. "I cannot leave school on a whim, so I must have someone take my place. I took Nuiko in like you've taken Nuks in, and she's agreed to this arrangement. If Nuks ever got the call, he was instructed to bring Nuiko with him."

"But you live with a cat lady," he said. "An *actual* cat lady!" Sam emphasized, referring to the fact that the woman whom Tashi lived with was a child of Bastet, a creature that was half feline and half human. "Am I the only one who sees how that could be a problem?"

"Sam," Nuks said dismissively. "We all get along just fine."

"Besides, I checked with Miss Bastifal beforehand, and

she gave her approval," Tashi reported. "Now let's begin." She leaned down to pick up Nuiko, but Sam reached out and grabbed her wrist.

"Wait," he said in a loud whisper. "You can't just have her transform in here. What if Ms. Bryce turns the corner? Then what?"

"We do not have a choice. It must be done in here," Tashi told him. "You will create a distraction."

"I will? How?" Sam asked, unnerved.

"I do not know," Tashi responded as she touched Nuiko and the raccoon-dog began her transformation. "But do so quickly."

Exasperated, Sam stepped out of the aisle, his mind racing with possible distractions, all of which would likely get him detention. But it suddenly didn't matter, because Ms. Bryce was walking toward him.

"Hey, Ms. Bryce . . . ," Sam said, placing himself between the librarian and the aisle where Nuiko was currently shape-shifting into a duplicate of Tashi. "How have you been lately?"

"Good. Thanks for asking. I've been wanting to talk to you," she began, pulling to a stop only steps away from the aisle. "I'm assuming you didn't see the news yet?"

"No, not yet. Why?"

"Have you ever been to Pier 39?" she inquired in her library whisper. Pier 39 was a popular tourist destination in San Francisco that featured restaurants, shops, and other attractions. Sam didn't know where this exchange with the librarian was headed, but at least it was keeping her from walking into the folklore and mythology section and getting an eyeful.

"Sure," Sam said. "Lots of times."

"Do you know the sea lion colony?"

"Of course," Sam answered. "I love that place." Sam had stood at the railing with the other tourists to watch the creatures roll around in the sun and to hear them bark.

"Well," Ms. Bryce continued, "there was a news story I think you'll be interested to hear."

"Oh?" Sam said, intrigued. He deduced that this "story" was likely the case Dr. Vantana had called about. Sam's distraction of Ms. Bryce was not only fulfilling its purpose, but it might even prove to be informative. "What happened?"

"A bunch of tourists saw a man dressed in a seal costume climb onto one of the platforms," Ms. Bryce explained. "Someone got everything on video, and it's gone viral."

"Wow," Sam said. "That's pretty weird."

"That's all you have to say?" Ms. Bryce asked, surprised by his subdued reaction. "I figured you would have a crazy theory about how this guy was some sort of merman." Ms. Bryce knew of Sam's penchant for mythical creatures.

"You said he was a man in a seal costume," Sam pointed out.

"I know," she said. "But what if he wasn't? What if he was a seal in a human costume?" She raised her eyebrows, waiting for his response. Sam nodded slowly.

"Now I get it. That is interesting. . . ."

"Yeah," Ms. Bryce said as she continued toward the aisle

where Nuiko was transforming. "I think we should take a look at one of those reference books. See what we can find!"

"Wait," Sam said. "Can I see the video? So I know what to look for," he added hastily, worried the transformation hadn't been completed yet.

"Sure," Ms. Bryce offered, but she wasn't turning around.

"Wait," Sam said again, this time with more panic in his voice. The librarian paused and glanced back—

"What's wrong?" she asked, facing him.

"Nothing. I just thought we were going to watch that video." Sam shrugged, aiming for nonchalance.

"We will, but first I want to grab the book." Ms. Bryce smiled, disappearing around the corner and into the aisle. Sam's heart dropped, and it felt like it pulled all of the blood in his head with it. If she witnessed a transformation of a shape-shifting raccoon-dog, Sam's future with the DMW would be over, practically before it had begun. He was going to have to think quick to avoid a catastrophe.

"I can explain," Sam shouted as he rushed forward to catch her.

"Explain what?" Ms. Bryce asked. Sam looked past her at an empty aisle, then glanced back to an expectant Ms. Bryce.

"Explain . . . where the book is you're trying to find," he scrambled.

"I'm the librarian," she laughed. "I *think* I have a pretty good idea."

"Of course," Sam replied, relieved at the bullet—scratch

that, the cannonball he just dodged. "It's my helpful nature. It's like a reflex. Like when the doctor hits your knee and your leg goes up. Someone needs something, and I'm ready to help."

Ms. Bryce eyed him a moment, then turned to the books.

A "Pssst!" sounded from behind Sam and he peered back toward the front of the aisle. Two Tashis and a second Sam were peeking around the first stack. The original Sam frantically shooed them away, before pivoting back to Ms. Bryce, who was pulling a book off the shelf.

"Here it—" she began, but before she could finish her sentence, she sneezed. It was a substantial sneeze and one that took her by surprise. "Excuse me," she said.

"God bless you," Sam offered as Ms. Bryce continued to stare at the floor.

"What is—" She knelt down and poked at what appeared to be a pile of animal hair. Nuiko's hair, Sam concluded in horror. No doubt shed during her transformation. It was at this moment that Ms. Bryce erupted into a sneezing spree the likes of which no creature, human or otherwise, had ever witnessed. Sam lost count at twenty-three consecutive sneezes. They all started to blend together, and some didn't even finish before the next one began. It was such a violent fit that her signature purple beret flew off her head and revealed a bright purple head of hair. Sam was stunned at the sight but didn't have time to process it.

"I'm—allerg—ic to—dogs," Ms. Bryce stammered between sneezes. "But why would there be a—"

Sam helped her to her feet, then guided her to the end of the aisle and over toward the doors.

"Maybe you should go see the school nurse," he suggested, making sure to use his gravest tone. The librarian nodded. At least, it appeared to be a nod; Sam couldn't tell the difference between her head jerking back from sneezing and it bobbing in agreement.

"Yes—yes—I think I should," she was able to say in stops and starts, her nose now red as a beet.

"I'll stay here and keep an eye on the place until a teacher can come take over," Sam offered. Ms. Bryce nodded again as she sneezed her way out of the library.

When she was out of sight, Sam rushed back to the book stacks and found his friends one aisle over from the mythology section.

"Excellent distraction, Sam London," Tashi commended. "Very impressive."

"*Impressive?* That was a disaster!" Sam exclaimed. "The poor woman almost sneezed herself to death because of the hair *she* left on the carpet." Sam gestured toward Tashi's double. "It looked like Carl the bigfoot shaved his back in there."

At that, the Tashi that was Nuiko began to cry. Not just cry, but sob uncontrollably.

"Now you've upset her!" Nuks said, putting a hand on Nuiko's shoulder. Sam felt awful.

"I'm sorry," Sam said somberly. "I really am."

Nuks pulled Nuiko into a hug. It suddenly felt weird for

the real Sam to see a version of himself hugging Tashi, even if he knew they were both raccoon-dogs in disguise. Tashi similarly was confused and appeared downright mortified by the display. The hug wasn't what bothered her, though; it was the tears.

"You must not cry if you are going to masquerade as me," Tashi scolded. "Guardians *control* their emotions. You must control yours or you will not fool anyone." Nuiko sniffled and attempted to hold back her tears. The result was the sort of blubbering one would expect from a distressed toddler.

"She'll be fine," Nuks assured Tashi. "I will keep a close eye on her. You two should go."

"Right," Sam said, rearranging his thoughts from the hug to the awaiting doctor. "Just don't do anything crazy." He wasn't quite sure if the hug fell into that category, but there wasn't time to ponder the implications.

"You have nothing to worry about," Nuks told him. "I will be the best Sam London substitute yet!" he declared with a smile a block wide.

"I'm pretty sure I've never smiled that big in my whole entire life," Sam corrected him. Nuks quickly adjusted his grin. "A little less," Sam suggested, and Nuks diminished it further until it was barely a smirk. "Perfect," Sam reported. "See you two later."

Tashi retrieved her bag, and as they headed out of the library, Sam noticed the Guardian glancing nervously over her shoulder at a still whimpering Nuiko. He had never seen Tashi so apprehensive before, but he couldn't blame her. She had no idea what would be waiting for her when she returned. Sam just hoped Nuks didn't try out for any sports teams or make dozens of new friends.

Thanks to Tashi's stealthy instincts, the two slipped off campus unseen and found Dr. Vantana's government-issued SUV parked on a side street. The doctor was talking into his badge as Sam climbed into the backseat and Tashi took the front.

"I know it's strange for one of them to show up so far from home," the doctor said. "I've got a message in to Phylassos for his take. We'll get to the bottom of it. Gotta run. Sam and Tashi just arrived."

"Hi, Sam. Hi, Tashi," a voice called out over the badge. Sam recognized it as belonging to Redwood National Park ranger Penelope Naughton. "Trevor says hello."

"Hey, Penelope!" Sam exclaimed. "Please tell my good friend Trevor that we both said hello back. And that we miss him and value him as a friend." Trevor was a troll who lived in Redwood National Park, and like all trolls, he was obsessed with the number of friends he could claim to have.

"He'll be very glad to hear that," Penelope replied happily.

"I do not—" Tashi began, but Sam quickly shushed her.

"All right, enough pleasantries. Vantana out." The doctor touched his badge to power it off and caught Sam's eye in the rearview mirror. "Good to see you, old buddy. You too, Tashi."

"Same to you, Dr. Vantana," Sam said, grinning from ear to ear.

"I concur," Tashi chimed in, buckling her seat belt.

The doctor put the SUV into gear and pulled away from the curb.

"Any problems making the switch?" Vance asked.

"It could have gone a little more smoothly," Sam said. "Especially if Tashi had told me she arranged for her own tanuki to take her place."

"It wasn't important until it became important," Tashi asserted.

"Blame me, actually," Vantana said sheepishly. "I knew she wasn't going to leave your side, so I sent her a note to be ready when the time came." Sam looked at the Guardian, stunned.

"You had contact with Dr. Vantana and didn't tell me?"

"It was not about a mission," Tashi explained. "It was a recommendation that I found to be agreeable." Sam shifted in his seat and gazed out the window, displeased by her lack of transparency.

"Do you know where we're headed?" the doctor inquired.

"San Francisco," Sam replied. Vance nodded.

"Do you know why?"

"A seal in a human suit?" Sam posited.

Vance grinned. "Something like that. You saw the video?"

"I heard about it."

On the forty-five-minute drive to Pier 39, Sam questioned Dr. Vantana on what he had been up to these past few weeks that didn't require Sam's assistance. Vantana revealed he had been traveling the world, visiting national parks to communicate that things were back in order after news spread of the events in Hérault. There existed a great many creatures whose brethren were in the amphitheater the day the cynocephalus Chase exposed Phylassos as Dr. Knox and attempted to destroy the claw, which would have ended the concealment curse. Many of these creatures were worried they might be found guilty by association. Or as Vance put it, "They were as nervous as a bunch of long-tailed cats in a room full of rocking chairs." The doctor worked to alleviate these creatures' fears and made sure they knew there wouldn't be any repercussions. Some of the creatures were also deeply offended by Phylassos's ruse and felt betrayed when they'd learned he was masquerading as a mere human. That group sounded like it was a little tougher to handle, but according to Vance, "After a whole lot of listening and little talking, they were all as happy as clams in mud."

"That's a relief," Sam replied as he gazed out the car window and spotted the Fisherman's Wharf area of San Francisco. Vance pulled into the Pier 39 parking garage and parked. They all climbed out and Sam headed toward the sea lion colony.

"Where ya goin' there, partner?" the doctor asked.

"To Pier 39. That *is* where the incident happened, isn't it?"

"Yes, it is. But we have no need to investigate that," Vantana said. "It's all over the internet. What *we* need to do is talk to a witness."

"Oh . . . okay," Sam replied. "Like who? One of the tourists?"

"Not exactly," the doctor answered. "Most of the eye-witnesses spoke to the media already, except one. My guess is that this witness saw more than the others and isn't talking. I'm hoping a visit from us might change their mind."

Dr. Vantana led Sam and Tashi a few blocks from the pier to a narrow four-story stucco apartment building whose age showed only because it was crammed between brand-new condominiums. The three of them took the stairs to the third floor and walked to an apartment at the far end of the hallway. Vantana knocked, and a few moments later, the door opened to reveal the witness. It was the last person Sam London had ever expected to see again.

"I knew you would come," Gladys Hartwicke said with a smile. Then she peered beyond the trio and asked curiously, "Where's the gryphon?"

SL002-130-20
SUBJ: Hartwicke, Gladys
SOURCE: WS
DATE: ███████

Gladys Hartwicke knew when to hold her tongue.
After several weeks of being questioned—more like
interrogated—by a series of state psychiatrists, she
had been declared mentally fit and hadn't been bothered
since. Despite what she told the doctors, Gladys knew
the truth and she also knew to keep it secret. She had
seen a gryphon in Death Valley. It had saved her from

certain death. And that boy on the bus had been talking with it. Of all this she was certain. There was also the visit from that strange doctor at the hospital, who asked a number of questions and then wanted her to guess the card he was holding and point to the cup that had a quarter in it. She did surprisingly well on those tests at the time and started fancying herself a psychic. Unfortunately, when she attempted to demonstrate these abilities to her friends on bingo night, she only wound up looking foolish.

Nowadays, if asked about the gryphon, the boy, or the doctor, Gladys would laugh it away and attribute it all to a potent blend of exhaustion, dehydration, and the thrill of being in Death Valley. But that didn't mean she had forgotten what had happened. So it was particularly ironic that Gladys was at Pier 39 in San Francisco when another mythical creature chose to make an appearance.

It was a typical spring morning when Gladys left her apartment in the North Beach area of San Francisco and set out on her daily walk. She loved these walks, since they afforded her the opportunity to observe people and eavesdrop on the world around her. This helped satisfy her inherent curiosity, or, as some of her close friends and relatives dubbed it, *nosiness*. Gladys was the kind of person who loved to say hello to strangers she encountered on her excursions, ask them about their day, and find out where they were from. The latter would almost certainly spark a story from Gladys about how she shared a connection to their hometown. She called this little game Three Degrees of Gladys Hartwicke. She would reward herself with chocolate from a local fudge shop if she succeeded in connecting herself with a stranger's home in less than three steps, and she had yet to lose the game. Of course, the more people she met on her daily walks, the easier it became.

On this particular day, the city's legendary fog was still hugging the coast like a moist blanket. If it didn't dissipate by the time she reached her destination, it was unlikely she would meet any tourists. She usually timed her walks for the early afternoon so as to be sure that the area would be bustling with activity, but later that day she was scheduled to see one of her nephews, who had recently announced his engagement. Gladys was looking forward to talking with the young man about his fiancée—she had been preparing a list of questions ever since she'd heard the news. Things like how did they meet, did they share the same love of cats or dogs, and did they both floss and brush their teeth after every meal. Gladys was a firm believer that coordinated dental hygiene was critical to a successful union.

When she stepped onto Pier 39, Gladys found that the crowd was especially thin, no doubt due to the weather. So she headed to the one place where she always went when there weren't enough people to satisfy her social cravings. Gladys stepped around the corner of a row of stores on the western side of the pier and followed the railing to the end. It was lined with benches and coin-operated binoculars, for those who wanted to enjoy a view of San Francisco Bay or the other popular site: the famed sea lion colony.

Over the course of many years and a great many walks, Gladys had come to know every sea lion in the colony— she had even given them names. She had started by naming them after U.S. presidents, but when she'd exhausted that list, she'd moved on to other famous historical figures, and then famous fictional characters. Because she was so familiar with the members of the colony, she would quickly recognize any new visitors that shimmied their way onto the square-shaped platforms.

As Gladys approached, she saw that a few people were already standing at the railing, hoping to catch a glimpse of the sea lions and snap some photos. With their backpacks, comfortable walking shoes, cargo shorts with bulging pockets, and fancy cameras, Gladys was certain they were tourists. There was a couple who she concluded were newlyweds on their honeymoon; there were also a mom, dad, and young son speaking German. She was just about to engage the German tourists in conversation and play a round of Three Degrees, when something unusual caught her eye. The colony had a new member.

Gladys noticed that a seal had pulled itself onto one of the docks. From the time she'd spent volunteering at the Aquarium of the Pacific, Gladys knew based on the seal's wide nostrils and long snout that it was a gray seal, a rare pinniped found in the North Atlantic Ocean. What was it doing here in the Pacific Ocean? she wondered. This specimen was quite large, dark silver with light-colored blotches scattered about its body. She had never seen a seal in the sea lion colony before and wondered how the resident creatures might react. They did so in a rather peculiar way. Much to her surprise, the sea lions of Pier 39 made room for their new guest. In fact, not only did they move to accommodate their fellow pinniped, but they turned their bodies toward it and began bowing their heads up and down. It was as if they were genuflecting in the seal's presence, like he was royalty. This was strange, Gladys thought. But then things got a whole lot stranger.

The seal began to transform. It didn't appear to be a seal at all, but rather a human wearing an elaborate costume. The creature split apart down the middle, and a man emerged from inside. He was as naked as a jaybird. The tourists gasped in shock, parents blocked their children's eyes, and Gladys just stared, slack-jawed in amazement. Her desire to socialize with the tourists evaporated in an instant. There was a new traveler in town she wanted to question, and she grinned in anticipation. Today's walk would most definitely be one to remember.

Chapter 3

SEAL OF APPROVAL

The boy who had seen the gryphon was now seated across the woman who had also seen the gryphon. It was an improbable reunion, and one Sam London had never anticipated. But there they were, two human beings from different generations and backgrounds brought together, once again, by a mythical creature who had chosen to make a surprising appearance. Unlike with the Bakersfield incident, this time it was Gladys Hartwicke who held the answers Dr. Vantana sought. Sam was sitting next to Vance on Gladys's overly colored couch in her overly decorated living room. It was as if she had owned a large home and forgotten to downsize her furniture when she'd downsized her living space. The couch was comfortable enough, but Sam was certain the fabric incorporated every hue in the color spectrum. Gladys could have any shade of throw pillow, and it would have gone perfectly. The pillows she did have appeared to be handmade and were as colorful as the couch.

Gladys sat in a red velvet armchair and clutched a small porcelain cup of tea, which clinked and rattled each time she took a sip and placed it back on its saucer. Tashi stood off to the side and refused to make herself comfortable, as Gladys suggested repeatedly. Gladys kept glancing over at the stoic Tashi, reminding her every few minutes that she could sit down, but Tashi wouldn't budge.

"I am perfectly comfortable where I am, but I thank you for your concern," the Guardian told her each time the woman made the suggestion.

Gladys was kind enough to provide them with glasses of water and set out a plate of cookies. She explained at length that the latter were originally intended for her nephew and his new fiancée, but she had promptly rescheduled their visit following her experience on the dock that morning. She had a feeling that the strange doctor from Bakersfield might be paying her a visit.

"I'm not authorized to discuss the events at Death Valley. However, I can confirm that what you saw there was a gryphon and what you saw today was a selkie. They are both real and you're not crazy," the doctor assured her.

"I *knew* I wasn't," Gladys said with a relieved smile. "And what is a 'selkie,' *exactly?*" she inquired.

"A mythical sea creature of sorts," Vantana explained. Then he added cautiously, "Ms. Hartwicke, I can't prevent you from talking about this to anyone else, but I'd urge you to keep our conversation to yourself. For your own safety, of course."

"Of course," Gladys replied. "Who would believe me anyhow? They'd think I was a crazy person who was seeing things—just like last time." Then she added in a whisper, "But it's certainly nice to know the truth."

"Now . . . ," Vance began, "once that selkie dove back into the water, did you see where he went?"

Gladys nodded. "I did, indeed. I watched him in the water. He swam so fast. Like a torpedo. *Shoom!* Right to the boat slips. Everyone else was still staring at the sea lions, expecting him to pop back up, but I took off for the slips. I wanted to meet him!"

"And did you?" the doctor asked.

Gladys shook her head with disappointment. "I startled him. I do that to people sometimes. He stumbled and ran off, but not before he dropped something. I have it drying on the windowsill." Gladys stood and walked to the large picture window in her dining room area. Vance followed, along with Sam and Tashi. The afternoon sun beamed into the apartment through the double-paned glass as Gladys retrieved a wrinkled piece of paper that was propped against the window. She handed it to Dr. Vantana, who studied it. Sam craned his neck to get a better glimpse. It was a cover torn from a fashion magazine. The colors were faded and streaked, no doubt the result of being submerged in salt water. An odd thing for a mythical sea creature to be carrying, Sam thought.

Despite the cover's poor condition, Sam could see that

the model pictured had big blue eyes; porcelain-white skin; and light, almost silvery blond hair. She looked like an angel. According to the text on the cover, this was Pearl Eklund, a "fresh new face in the fashion world." Her name was circled in a green substance that Sam determined to be dried seaweed. Vance turned the cover over to reveal an ad for San Francisco's Fashion Week that announced the participation of the world's top models and designers. But something else caught Sam's eye.

"Look." He pointed to the page. "The girl on the cover is going to be at this event. And that seaweed is around her name again." Sure enough, the same dried seaweed circled "Pearl Eklund." Sam's eyes darted down to the bottom of the page, where the event information was printed, before quickly glancing to the clock on Gladys's wall.

"This is today! Like, right *now*. Do you think—" Sam started to ask.

"Yeah, I think," Vance interjected, standing up. "I haven't the slightest idea why, but that must be where he's headed." The doctor turned to Gladys. "Ms. Hartwicke, thank you. This information could save lives."

Gladys smiled proudly. "That's what I'm here for, Dr. Vantana. And you can be darn sure I'll be keeping these eyes peeled. Maybe I can help you again."

"I hope you won't have to. But thank you kindly. Can I keep this?" Vance asked, holding up the magazine cover.

"Absolutely," Gladys replied. As Sam and Tashi followed the doctor to the door, Gladys suddenly added, "There's one more thing." They all turned back to listen. "Before that man—the selkie—before he ran up the slip, he hid something in the boat locker."

"Boat locker?" Sam asked, confused. Gladys nodded.

"Boaters use them to store their fishing gear, that sort of thing," Vantana explained.

"He broke the lock with his bare hands. Can you imagine?" Gladys said, impressed. "He rummaged around, took some clothes—swimming shorts, I think—and then stuffed something inside before closing it back up." Gladys retrieved her purse and pulled a shimmering piece of gray fabric out of the canvas bag. "I know I shouldn't have taken it, but I just got this urge, like I needed it for some reason, and . . . by the time I had second thoughts and went to put it back, the police were already there. It's unlike any fabric I've ever seen."

Sam noticed that Dr. Vantana appeared instantly unnerved by the item. He tentatively reached out to touch it.

"Mind if I borrow it?" Vance inquired haltingly.

"You can have it," Gladys declared.

"Oh . . . well . . . thank you," Vantana replied, as if surprised by her generosity.

Once they were out of the apartment, Sam followed up on the strange encounter.

"What's with that fabric? You seemed freaked out by it," Sam said.

"It caught me a bit by surprise, to be honest. The person who holds the skin of a selkie controls the fate of that creature. Gladys had this in her possession. To give it up is not something humans have always been willing to do, as the fabric imbues in us an instinct to steal it . . . and keep it."

"It does?" Sam inquired.

The doctor nodded. "Henry—Phylassos—told me some stories," Vantana explained. "Times when creatures were being used by humans for their own, often nefarious, purposes. So to risk all that and leave his skin, like this selkie did, is shocking. It must be somethin' *real* important that got that fish out of water."

"What could be that important?" Sam wondered.

"I haven't the foggiest," the doctor answered.

"We will simply have to ask him," Tashi said. "But if we are going to catch him before he attempts to contact that woman from the picture, we are running out of time."

"The Guardian is right. Let's get moving," Vantana said as he picked up the pace toward the parking garage.

Bay Area news reporter Cynthia Salazar stood poolside on the roof of a high-rise apartment building in downtown San Francisco. This particular building boasted one of the poshest and most expensive penthouses in the country. It was a sixteen-thousand-square-foot condominium that covered two floors and had access to a private rooftop terrace, which was the site of the Couture Showcase, the final event in the city's annual Fashion Week activities. There was a runway consisting of a transparent Plexiglas strip fitted over an infinity pool that was built to the edge of the roof, allowing the models to appear as if they were walking on water, with the skyline a breathtaking backdrop behind them. Although Cynthia felt the "walking on water" bit was a little over-the-top given the context, she couldn't help but recognize that it made for a great visual, a critical element for a story being bumped up to earlier in the evening news lineup.

The reporter wasn't thrilled with having to cover a cadre of beautiful women strutting around in bizarrely designed clothes no normal person would ever be caught dead in, but she gritted her teeth and applied her best fake smile. Cynthia was just thankful she hadn't been assigned to cover the sighting of a man in a seal costume at Pier 39. People were already calling him a merman, which had led a few of her colleagues to make snide remarks about how she should be assigned to it. After all, she had interviewed a woman who'd sworn she saw a gryphon. The declaration made by Gladys Hartwicke that day in Death Valley was reported live by Cynthia and wound up being the most humiliating experience of the news professional's career. She caught flack for that fiasco for weeks. Ever since, Cynthia would find articles about bigfoot on her desk and links to Loch Ness Monster stories in her email.

It might not have seemed like there was a lot of potential for big news at a fashion show, but Cynthia had found an angle. She knew that if there was going to be any real newsworthiness to this segment, it would most assuredly center on the star of the event, a young model named Pearl Eklund. A native of Miami, Florida, Pearl had burst onto the fashion scene just a few months earlier, and her rise to the top had been meteoric. All of the world's top designers were clamoring for her to showcase their latest creations, and everyone marveled at her beauty. They called her exquisite, intoxicating, a modern Helen of Troy. Cynthia chalked it all up to good hair and makeup.

Pearl was not only taking the fashion world by storm, though. She also had become an immensely popular social media personality, as she catalogued—some might say flaunted—her luxurious lifestyle for her adoring fans. It was a lifestyle made possible by her adoptive father, energy magnate Lief Eklund, whose company, Eklund Energy, was one of the world's wealthiest corporations.

Cynthia lobbied for an exclusive interview with Pearl before the event, but Lief, who also acted as Pearl's manager, had declined the invitation. Never someone to take no for an answer, Cynthia had snuck past security earlier that day and headed for Pearl's trailer, with the intent of having a word with the model and maybe even capturing a picture of her sans makeup. Unfortunately, the reporter was turned away by a stern-looking woman dressed in a business suit. She had long black hair that was pulled back off her face and secured in what arguably could have been the tightest, neatest bun Cynthia had ever seen. The woman refused to identify herself and immediately motioned for security to escort the reporter and cameraman from the area.

Now Cynthia was set up on the rooftop terrace, watching the models walk the narrow see-through runway in increasingly outlandish outfits. As the star, Pearl would be the last model out, sporting the latest design from an eccentric Italian designer. When the music was blaring its loudest, the young woman finally emerged from behind the curtain at the far end of the pool. Pearl was wearing a skintight pink bodysuit with blue tiger stripes running up the sides, attached feet like a child's footie pajamas, and, to top it all off, a feathered tiara that extended two feet from the top of her head, colored like a peacock's iridescent plumage. Cynthia's big brown eyes rolled like boulders at the display. Then she noticed something unusual. Pearl hesitated at the start of the runway, as if unnerved by something. Perhaps it didn't appear stable enough, Cynthia speculated. She watched the model glance back toward the woman who had earlier turned the reporter away from Pearl's dressing room and was now standing next to Lief to the side of the curtain. The woman seemed to be nodding encouragement in a firm, unsmiling way. Pearl stepped cautiously onto the runway and walked slowly down the strip. When she was halfway across, a gust of wind nearly blew off her headpiece. Pearl reached up to grab the feathered tiara and secure it, but lost her footing on the glass and tumbled into the pool. The crowd gasped, while Cynthia anxiously eyed her cameraman to make sure he was recording. He responded with a triumphant thumbs-up.

Pearl didn't pop out of the water right away, and when she finally did, she was thrashing about, as if drowning.

"How deep is that pool?" Cynthia asked her cameraman, a slovenly thirtysomething named Lou.

"Four feet where she fell," Lou said with furrowed eyebrows.

That's odd, Cynthia thought.

The poor girl's flailing continued for several seconds, to audible gasps from the crowd, until one of her security guards finally jumped in to rescue her. He pulled her from the water with the help of Lief and the stern-looking woman, who had rushed to the edge of the pool. Pearl was crying and shaking uncontrollably as they whisked her back behind the curtain, away from prying eyes.

"Come on," Cynthia whispered to Lou. "Let's see if we can catch her leaving."

Much to Cynthia's chagrin, she wasn't the only one with that idea. By the time they arrived at the building's rear entrance, there was already a throng of people clamoring outside, anxiously awaiting a glimpse of the ingénue. When the back doors opened and Pearl finally emerged, she was dressed in jeans and a T-shirt, with a Miami Marlins baseball cap fit snugly on her head. She was flanked by two beefy security guards as she made her way to a black SUV that was parked a few yards from the exit. Cynthia wiggled through the crowd to the front, pulling an apathetic Lou along with her. She earned more than a few dirty looks by those she carelessly pushed aside. Once in front, Cynthia immediately understood and appreciated what all the fuss surrounding this girl was about. She was extraordinarily beautiful, but there was also something different about her, something radiant. She was innocent and mysterious and enchanting all at once. Her crystal-blue eyes gleamed in a hypnotic, almost otherworldly kind of way.

Cynthia caught the model's eye and was poised to ask a question, when she was suddenly shoved to the side by a dark-haired man. Lou's camera tumbled to the ground, along with Lou. Cynthia got her bearings and was ready to give their assailant a piece of her mind, until she got a look at him. He was the mystery man whose appearance at Pier 39 had captivated the city. She recognized him from the viral video a colleague had teasingly sent her that morning. Cynthia watched, frozen, as the man reached out for Pearl, grabbed her wrist, and pulled her toward him. A strange bluish mist emanated from their skin on contact. Pearl's eyes went wide at his touch, and she sucked in a breath. One of her security guards attempted to intervene but was pushed away by the man with just one hand. The guard tumbled backward onto the ground, stunned.

"Is it you, Princess?" Cynthia overheard the man ask Pearl. Cynthia craned her neck to catch what he said next. "Come home before it's too late and all is lost."

Pearl yanked her arm back furiously, and the dark-haired man let go with surprise as several more security guards converged. The man quickly maneuvered around them and took off running, disappearing around a corner. Pearl was shuttled to the waiting SUV, with her father and the stern woman following behind. The model was guided into the backseat and quickly driven away. The crowd had been shocked into silence, including Cynthia, who was rarely, if ever, at a loss for words.

"It's not broken," Lou reported, having gotten back to his feet. He was now checking the camera.

"But we don't have the footage," Cynthia reminded him. "And we're live in a few minutes," she added, looking at her watch. Lou shrugged helplessly.

"I guess you'll just have to describe what you saw," he suggested.

But Cynthia couldn't describe it. She had seen the man from Pier 39 up close, and something about him didn't add up. He'd been bare-chested and wearing swim shorts, and the skin on his legs had appeared to be slick and rubbery and had shimmered in the sunlight. Cynthia had also noticed that his fingers were webbed ever so slightly, and she could have sworn she'd seen slits behind his ears, like gills. And then there was the issue of that strange blue mist.

The viewers of the Pier 39 video had dubbed him a merman in jest, but Cynthia began to wonder if they were actually right. It sounded crazy, yet he was awfully odd, though admittedly quite handsome. His eyes were the same crystal blue as Pearl's, and paired with his pitch-black hair, it was a striking combination. The rest of him was chiseled perfection, like a walking Michelangelo's *David*. He possessed an allure and intensity that was almost distracting Cynthia from the dawning realization that she was sitting on what could prove to be the biggest story of her career, if not the biggest in all of human history. But she couldn't say a word about it, could she? She would be risking humiliation once again, and if she was wrong, this time it would have a far more devastating impact on her career. But her curiosity was piqued. First the gryphon sighting and now this? Cynthia Salazar had a story to tell, and she knew she was the only one who could to tell it.

Dr. Vance Vantana parked the SUV at the curb in a neighborhood filled with perfectly manicured trees and pricey high-rise apartment towers. He climbed out of the car along with Sam and Tashi, and the trio headed toward the building hosting the Fashion Week event.

"If the selkie is here for the girl, let me talk to him," Vance said. "He just needs to be reminded of the punishment for violating the gryphon's law. I'm sure he'll come around once—"

Vantana didn't get a chance to finish his thought. A man barreled around the corner and plowed right into the doctor. Vance was instantly floored and momentarily disoriented. Shaking off the hit, he knew this was their creature. Selkies were inhumanly strong, especially outside the water. Tashi and Sam rushed to help Vantana to his feet as he quickly scanned the block and spotted the man sprinting away down the street.

"He's headed for the water," the doctor announced as he took off after him. Sam and Tashi followed, keeping pace with Vance until the Guardian edged ahead. The doctor watched in surprise as the young girl quickly passed him by and pressed on after the selkie. The doctor prided himself on being in top physical shape, but Tashi was making him look slower than molasses going uphill in January.

"She does that to me all the time," Sam yelled, noticing

the doctor's slack-jawed expression. "I have to remind myself she's got the gryphon blood."

That's right, Vance realized. Tashi did have Phylassos's blood pulsing through her veins. It made her physical prowess a little more understandable, though still humbling.

The selkie was barely able to keep a consistent distance between him and his pursuers. Vance reckoned that the sea creature was still getting used to having legs. Regardless, the selkie had the upper hand, as he paid no mind to traffic signals and bounded across a major thoroughfare without hesitating. Cars swerved; drivers slammed on their brakes and honked wildly, narrowly avoiding collisions with the mystery man. The selkie slid over car trunks, leapt over hoods, and plowed through clueless pedestrians strolling along the sidewalk. He peered back briefly to catch a glimpse of his pursuers, before ducking down an alley. By now Tashi was a few yards ahead of Vance, having made it through the intersection, and was gaining on the creature. They were as close as ever, and Vance took the opportunity to yell to him.

"Hold it right there!" the doctor exclaimed. "You are in violation of the gryphon's law." The selkie just kept running, turning the corner at the end of the alleyway and disappearing.

"He doesn't seem to care," Sam huffed out.

Vance grunted in agreement. He was actually a little surprised by the creature's audacity. To risk all this *and* create a public spectacle just didn't add up. Aquatic creatures were rarely an issue for the DMW, especially selkies and the like. The doctor couldn't help but wonder if this one's blatant defiance had something to do with the events in Hérault and the ensuing revelations regarding Phylassos. If so, it was possible this breach was just the beginning of a pattern, but Vance hoped that was not the case. Either way, it was imperative that he capture the creature and question him A-SAP.

When the doctor took the corner in pursuit, he spotted the selkie heading down San Francisco's Lombard Street, a popular landmark known as the world's most crooked street. Cars traveling on Lombard took eight hairpin turns separated by hedges and flowers, all while descending a steep hill. Pedestrians—mostly sightseeing tourists—traversed a flight of stairs that ran alongside the landmark. The selkie didn't bother taking the stairs. He jumped over the hedges and down the hill like a superhuman hurdler. Tashi followed, and while she was impressive, she had less success jumping the giant hedges and quickly lost ground. Vance saw that the stairs were packed with people and decided his best bet was to risk the cars on the street. He flew down the twisting, turning road all the way to the bottom, where Sam caught up to him, completely out of breath.

"I think—I'm go—ing to—be sick," the boy said between ragged gasps for air.

"You can be sick later," the doctor ordered as he kept on after the selkie. They had already lost the distance they'd made up earlier, and the sea creature was nearing the water. The selkie shot down Leavenworth Street, then hooked a right onto Beach Street and made a beeline for Pier 39. Vance, Sam, and Tashi did their best to keep him in their sights.

When they finally reached the pier, the area was teeming with tourists snapping pictures and buying souvenirs, and the trio quickly got separated. Vance maneuvered through the crowd, keeping his eye on the prize. Sam and Tashi could take care of themselves, he concluded—he had a mission to accomplish. The ranger pushed his way through the crowd and headed for the boat slips. Sure enough, he found the selkie crouched down at the boat lockers. One container was open, and the creature appeared agitated as Vance approached cautiously.

"Lookin' for this?" he asked, holding up the selkie's skin. The dark-haired man rose to his feet and stared Vance down, squinting with displeasure. "You've got nothin' to worry about, all right? My name is Vance Vantana; I'm with the Department of Mythical Wildlife. I'm not gonna keep your skin, but you and I need to have ourselves a talk." The selkie remained silent, and Vance stopped a few feet away from him. "What's your name?" he asked, trying a different tack.

The selkie hesitated, then spoke. "I am called Maris," he said in a halting, irritated tone.

"Nice to meet you, Maris. Can you please tell me what all this—" Before Vance could finish his question, Tashi came bounding down the boat slip.

"Dr. Vantana!" the Guardian called out with concern in her voice.

"Where's Sam?" Vance asked, instantly noticing the boy's absence.

"I lost him in the crowd. Come, we must find him!"

"I'm in the middle of something," Vance informed her, gesturing to the selkie. "Sam can find us."

"What if he is in danger?" she asked.

"He's a big boy. I'm sure he's fine. I'll help you look for him as soon as I—"

No doubt sensing a moment of weakness, the selkie snatched the seal skin from Vance's hands, spun around, and dove into the water.

"Aw, nuts!" Vance exclaimed as he watched the selkie disappear into the depths. He turned to Tashi, poised to lose his temper.

"You must improve your grip," she suggested matter-of-factly. Vance wondered if there was cartoon steam coming from his ears. He swallowed his rage and stomped past her, up the boat slip.

After half an hour of searching, Vance finally located Sam in a gift shop. The doctor had already gotten himself into a lather over the situation, and he angrily marched over to the boy, who was clutching a souvenir picture frame that said "San Francisco" in brightly colored letters.

"Sam London!" Vance bellowed. "What are you thinking? You're *shoppin*? We're on a case, kid. You just cost me a suspect—" Sam turned to Vance, and the doctor could see that the boy was as white as a ghost.

"I was trying to get to the boat slip and—and something in the store window caught my eye," the boy stammered, his voice cracking with nerves. "Look—" He showed the frame to Vantana. The picture inside was of a family posing in front of the Golden Gate Bridge. Just a stock photo used to help sell a touristy keepsake.

"I'm looking, but I don't know what I'm supposed to be seeing that would justify you fouling up my capture," the doctor said, his voice rising again in exasperation. "It's a doggone souvenir picture frame—"

"You don't understand," Sam declared. "That man in the photo, Vance . . . He's my father." Tashi looked with a raised eyebrow over Sam's shoulder. Vantana considered the boy's words for a moment.

"All right," the doctor sighed, pressing the pause button on his wrath. "But so what? You said you've never met him before. Maybe he's a model or something," he suggested.

"Maybe," Sam replied. "But that's not the point. His expression, his clothing, it matches the one picture I have of him taken with my mom at Fontana Lake."

"What are you getting at?" Vance asked, trying to make sense of this information.

"I'm saying that I think the only photo I have of my dad, the one that I've stared at for twelve years . . . is fake."

Chapter 4

CASE, INTERRUPTED

The picture Sam London saw in multiple souvenir frames at a gift shop in San Francisco was not, as the old saying goes, "worth a thousand words." Rather, it had spurred a thousand questions and sent Sam's world spinning like a top. Sam forked over the cash for one of the frames without a second thought and exited the store. He sat down on a bench outside and quickly slipped the photo out for a closer look. Vance took the seat next to him and Tashi stood nearby. After a few moments of quiet contemplation, Sam realized what he had to do in light of this shocking turn of events.

"I have to go home," Sam said plainly. He had to talk to his mom about this, and it wasn't like he could just call her up and ask, because what if Nuks was standing right in front of her posing as Sam? That would be problematic, to say the least.

"Because of a picture?" Vance asked.

"Yes, because of a picture. My dad might not be the person I thought he was my entire life, Vance. I need to find out if my mom's been lying to me."

"Just hold on a second," Vance said. "Before we start jumpin' to conclusions like a frog at Calaveras, let's talk this through. How sure are you that this is the same picture? Maybe you're not remembering it exactly right."

"I've seen that picture for as long as I've been alive. I think I remember what it looks like," Sam replied with a huff. It was his favorite picture in the house and was permanently ingrained in his memory. He had never seen his mom look happier than in that photo, and just looking at it always made Sam smile.

"It is the same image of the man," Tashi interjected with certainty. "I have seen it myself."

"See?" Sam followed. "Even Tashi agrees, and she's a Guardian. She probably has supermemory or something."

"I have a memory that is better than the average human," Tashi confirmed. Sam gestured to Vance as if to say *I told you so.*

"Well, what if the company that made that souvenir got ahold of your dad's picture and copied it and put it into that frame," Vantana postulated. "Did you ever think of that?"

"Of course I thought of that," Sam countered.

He considered that theory soon after he spotted the photo and ever since had been trying his best to push aside any thoughts to the contrary—like the fact that the man's image appeared to fit better with the family in the souvenir frame than with his mom in the photo at home, or that his mother was never all that forthcoming about his father or the picture of them together. She always changed the subject when it came up, and Sam just figured it was because the topic made her sad. Now he had to wonder if she had been keeping something from him the whole time. Whatever the case might be, he needed more information.

"I should call the company that made it," Sam concluded. "I could ask them about the models in the photo. Maybe it is just a big coincidence."

"All right. That's a start," Vance said. "But it doesn't take a sharp-shinned hawk to see that your head's not in the game. And as much as I don't want to—'cause I'd love your help—maybe it's best if I take you and Tashi home so you can get to the bottom of all this."

Sam was understandably torn. He didn't want to abandon the case or Dr. Vantana, but he didn't see any other way. He held on to the possibility, however remote, that the photo of his father had been acquired by this company and used in the souvenir frame. That was the cleanest explanation, and one that didn't involve his mom lying to him and faking a picture. Even if she had done so to protect him in some way, it required a particular kind of deviousness that Sam refused to believe his mom possessed.

"C'mon, let's head back to the car," Vance said as he rose to his feet. Three men suddenly emerged from the crowd.

They had large muscular frames and wore dark suits and sunglasses.

"Excuse me," the tallest of the men said to the doctor. "Were you the three who chased the assailant?"

"Assailant?" Vantana replied quizzically.

"The individual who attacked Pearl Eklund," the man explained. "We assumed that was why you went after him."

"Oh, right . . . yeah," Vance said, playing along. "Is Ms. Eklund okay?"

"She's rattled but unharmed," the man said. "Did you see where her attacker went?"

"I'm afraid not," the doctor answered regretfully. "We lost him. You wouldn't happen to know why he went after her like that?"

The man shook his head. "We're not certain, but he was likely just a crazed fan," he said, before abruptly putting his hand up to his ear. Sam noticed a small earpiece like the ones Secret Service officers wear. These men must have been part of Pearl's security detail, Sam concluded as the security guard spoke into a small lapel microphone. "Understood," he said, then released the button and looked to Vance. "My boss would like to speak with you."

"Your boss?" Vantana inquired.

"Lief Eklund."

"Of Eklund Energy?" Vance asked. The guard nodded. "I reckon he's Pearl's worried father?"

"That's correct," the guard answered. "Follow us." The doctor nodded and motioned for Sam and Tashi to come along.

As the trio walked a few steps behind the security guards, Vantana whispered. "I don't buy the crazed fan excuse," he said. "Not with a selkie. Water creatures in general are not fans of humanity. I wonder if the father knows something but doesn't realize it. Or maybe we can talk to the girl. She might have an answer," Vance speculated. "We're going to need a cover story," he added quickly. "Something simple."

"Like what?" Sam asked.

"We'll tell him we're just tourists, in for the day," the doctor suggested. "We came upon the scene, saw the man run, and decided to be good citizens."

"That is the lamest cover story ever," Sam concluded. Even Tashi nodded in agreement.

"Well, we can't exactly be fashion reporters, now, can we?" Vance replied.

"No," Sam said.

"Then tourists it is, unless you have something better."

Sam instantly realized why Dr. Vantana needed him on this case. Cover stories like the one he was proposing would not get them very far, and the information they needed could only come from Pearl Eklund—after all, she was the one the selkie was targeting. But why would she talk to a few tourists about it? Of course, they couldn't pose as law enforcement or reveal that the man who attacked her was a mythical creature, because that would be earth-shattering. But they still needed a cover that fit into Pearl's world. As the three were led to a black SUV, Sam thought about it further. Then—

"I have something better," he announced quietly. "But

Tashi isn't going to like it," he added. Tashi gave Sam a side glance as the doctor leaned in to listen.

*   *   *

The gleaming tower that housed Eklund Energy's San Francisco office was just a short distance from the pier. As Sam, Tashi, and Dr. Vantana were escorted to the lobby, they maneuvered around workers who were moving office furniture into the building, along with a giant Eklund Energy sign that was apparently meant for the lobby. The guard noted that the building had just been purchased by Mr. Eklund a month earlier. Once inside, they were approached by a man in his fifties who looked the part of an old sea captain. He had salt-and-pepper hair, and a beard and mustache that had gone almost entirely gray. He wore an impeccably tailored suit and exuded wealth.

"Thanks for coming. I'm Lief Eklund," the man said.

"The name's Vance Vantana. I'm with the U.S. government. Here acting as a liaison. Part of a cultural exchange," Vance said, offering his hand, which Lief shook heartily.

"Cultural exchange?" Lief inquired curiously.

"That's right." Then, with a flourish of his hand, Vantana announced, "I'd like to introduce Tashi of Tibet, the international fashion phenom." Tashi stood stoically next to the doctor.

Sam nudged her with his elbow, and she smiled faintly and

offered her hand to Lief Eklund. "It is—is an honor," Tashi stuttered, pretending her English was poor. This was a suggestion Sam had given her on the way over to help sell their cover. Lief shook her hand gently.

"A pleasure to make your acquaintance," Lief said, then shifted his attention to Sam. "And you are?"

"I'm Tashi's interpreter," Sam added helpfully.

"A little young to be an interpreter," Lief noted as he eyed Sam skeptically.

"You're right about that," Sam replied with a smile. "But Tashi insisted on having someone her own age speak on her behalf."

Lief leaned over to the ranger. "Is she some sort of child prodigy?" he asked Vance quietly. "I've never heard of her."

"She's exactly that—a child prodigy," Vance began. "And you've never heard of her because . . ." He was searching for an answer, so Sam threw him a lifeline.

"It's why we're—I mean, why she's—here," Sam explained. "Tashi is breaking into the U.S. market and thought your daughter would be—"

"Oh, I see," said Eklund, nodding. "She wants—" he started, then turned and addressed Tashi directly. "You want Pearl to model your designs. To help with exposure."

The Guardian nodded but said nothing. Sam leaned her way.

"Like we talked about," he whispered. Tashi pretended to whisper back, and then Sam turned to Lief, beaming. "Tashi of Tibet says she would be greatly honored to have your daughter model her one-of-a-kind creations. And that she would experience boundless joy if this were to happen."

Lief met Tashi's gaze. She did not seem the type to emote boundless joy. Sam nudged her and Tashi flashed her slight smile. *At least she tried*, Sam thought as the smile vanished as fast as it had appeared.

"I'm afraid these sorts of things are arranged well in advance. We didn't know you would be coming," Lief said.

"Yes, Tashi is aware of this," Vance replied hurriedly. "Unfortunately, we were just informed by the Chinese consulate that her message to Pearl never arrived. We were hoping to deliver the message in person when we saw your daughter get attacked."

"Yes, it's a dangerous world. Who knows what that maniac was capable of. . . . My men tell me you chased him. That was quite brave of you," Lief said, directing his comment to the doctor.

"Tashi was the one who chased him," Sam explained. "We just followed. In her culture, bravery is instilled at a very young age."

"Well, thank you," Lief told her. "I hear he got away."

Vantana nodded gravely. "We lost him at the pier. Did he give any indication as to why he grabbed Pearl?"

Lief shook his head. "Just some fanatic," he said.

Sam nudged Tashi, who pretended to whisper again. Sam played along, nodding, then turned to Lief.

"Tashi is hoping that when Pearl feels up to it, perhaps we

could arrange a meeting. She has traveled a great distance to speak with your daughter."

"I understand completely," Lief said. "And I'd love to make that happen, I would . . . but I sent Pearl home right after the incident. She's on a plane back to Miami as we speak."

"Miami?" Vance asked, startled.

"That's our home. We're in town for Fashion Week, and I had some business to attend to." Lief gestured to his surroundings. "This just became one of our satellite corporate offices."

"Big satellite," Sam said, peering around the expansive lobby.

"An expensive one too," the man added with a smile.

"I'm familiar with your company, Mr. Eklund," the doctor said. "I admire your work in renewable energies. In fact, I just read an article about something called fire ice."

"Methane hydrate," Lief responded, nodding. "We believe it's the future. Leave the earth better than we found it— for the next generation. Which reminds me, I have a launch party for a new drilling ship to plan. Nice to meet you, Tashi. And you two as well," he said to Vance and Sam. "Best of luck. If you're ever in Miami, we'll set up that meeting."

They said their goodbyes, and Lief stepped away to speak with his security detail.

"Great job with the cover story, kid," Dr. Vantana said under his breath.

"Thanks," Sam replied.

"Only problem is, I need to go to Miami to meet with this

girl, and how exactly am I going to do that without you and Tashi?"

"I didn't think about that," Sam admitted. He could clearly see the predicament Vance was in, but he didn't have a solution for him yet. When Lief finished speaking with his security, one of the guards—the tall one from earlier—approached.

"Mr. Eklund would like me to offer you a ride back to your vehicle or wherever you need to go."

"Much appreciated," Vance said. "But it's not too far. We can walk." The guard nodded and was about to walk away when Sam spoke up.

"Excuse me," he said. "You were there when Pearl was attacked, right?"

The guard nodded. "Yes, I tried to take him down," he replied. "Perp was a little stronger than I anticipated."

"And you've been a security guard for a long time?" Sam asked, eyes widening.

"I've been doing this for about eighteen years. Been with the Eklunds for the last two. Why do you ask?"

"It's just . . . in your experience, do you really believe it was a crazed fan?" Sam inquired. "I mean, it seems pretty random."

The guard hesitated, then spoke a touch more quietly. "To be honest, with obsessed fans we usually see warning signs well before they try something like this—"

"And you didn't with this guy?" the doctor followed up.

The guard shook his head. "Not that I've been made aware

of," the guard revealed. "But what he said to her did sound a bit . . . bizarre."

"He said something?" Vantana asked. The guard nodded.

"He called her 'Princess' and said she had to come with him before it was 'too late and all is lost,'" the guard revealed with a half smirk.

"Sounds like a crazed fan to me," Sam agreed.

The trio left the building and headed back to the parking garage. Along the way, Vance speculated on the selkie's motives. "Either this Maris knows something we don't or he's half a bubble off plumb. Whatever the case, I don't think he's going to stop here. He'll try again."

"Dr. Vantana is correct," Tashi said. "I gazed into the selkie's eyes. He is on a mission and will not be stopped so easily."

"Wonderful," the doctor said with a heap of sarcasm.

Sam knew Vance wasn't looking forward to facing this case alone. But he also knew he couldn't possibly concentrate on the case without handling the questions surrounding the souvenir picture frame and his father. The implications for his life were far too great to ignore.

When they climbed into the car and headed for Benicia, Sam looked up the name of the manufacturer he'd found on the picture frame. Unfortunately, the company was headquartered in Atlanta, Georgia, which meant its offices were likely closed already. He called their number anyway and left a few messages on their voice mail, but as it was also a Friday, Sam figured he wouldn't hear anything until Monday at the earliest. That was if they even bothered to call back at all. He would probably have better luck if he went in person. That thought gave him an idea.

"I'll come with you to Miami if we take a detour," Sam offered.

"What kind of detour?" the doctor asked warily.

"Atlanta. I want to go to this company and find out about the man in the picture."

"What happened to just asking your mom?" Vantana replied. "That's why you wanted to go home, isn't it?"

"It is," Sam admitted. "But what if it is just a coincidence? I could find out and wouldn't even have to ask her. Plus, she might wonder why I was at Pier 39 buying a picture frame on a school day."

The doctor considered it and nodded. "All right," Vantana said. "But we go to Miami first. I'm worried Pearl may be in danger—"

"There is nothing speculative about it," Tashi chimed in from the passenger seat. "The girl is most certainly in danger."

"Okay, Miami first, then," Sam capitulated.

In his mind, Sam acknowledged that he was probably avoiding the confrontation with his mom. As much as he wanted to know the truth, he also didn't want to believe she was capable of being dishonest with him, regardless of her motivation. The thought left a gnawing pit in his stomach. He held on to the hope that it was indeed his dad in the picture and there was a simple explanation for the way his father's picture had wound up in hundreds, if not thousands, of souvenir frames.

*   *   *

Dr. Vantana turned the car north to Castle Crags, where they soon hitched a ride on a dvergen subway to Florida. Riding in the centuries-old bullet train built by dwarves was never all that enjoyable, but this trip proved more tolerable for Sam than his first one, probably because they weren't plunging beneath the ocean floor to reach their destination. Instead the group was headed to the only dvergen subway station in the entire state of Florida, which was located in Falling Waters State Park behind the state's highest waterfall—the aptly named Falling Waters Sink. It was a seventy-three-foot-high gentle cascade of water that flowed over a limestone ridge and emptied into a sinkhole. It wasn't mapped yet by humans, but if it had been, they would have discovered one of the largest dvergen stations on the North American continent.

Dr. Vantana regaled Sam and Tashi with the history of how the station acted as a hub, since it was close to two major bodies of water, with the Atlantic Ocean on one side and the Gulf of Mexico on the other. The station had long served as a transfer point for travelers, connecting dwarves to trains that branched out in every possible direction. After only a few minutes, they arrived and stepped off into a cavernous main terminal that reminded Sam of pictures of Grand Central Terminal in New York City. The station featured carvings of dwarven warriors who Dr. Vantana noted were legends in their culture. Sam was in awe of the architectural wonders of the station but saddened by the ancient, abandoned feel of the place.

"I don't understand why the dwarves don't use these subways anymore. They're amazing," Sam said.

"Because it'd be a little conspicuous, don't you think?" the doctor asked rhetorically. "Nope. These were banned for use centuries ago."

"Then how come we get to use them?" Sam inquired.

"Because we're on official business for the gryphon, and that's sort of like a golden ticket," Vantana explained as Sam and Tashi followed him to a spiraling staircase carved into the rock. It led to a stone door, which the doctor activated with a dwarven phrase. The door rumbled and slowly slid open, revealing a small ridge along the limestone wall. The waterfall wasn't the rushing kind. It was more of a trickle that poured into the cylindrical sinkhole. They each stepped carefully onto the ridge and followed it to a narrow embankment that led to level ground. The sun had long ago set on the East Coast, but the moon was full and cast a bright silvery glow on the unlit park. Tashi's shekchen was radiating with energy, which helped provide additional illumination as they headed toward the woods.

"I sent word to our contact to have transportation ready. It should be in the parking lot," the doctor said, before crinkling his nose as if he smelled something bad.

"What's wrong?" Sam asked. Vantana's expression went

from mild disgust to major alarm in an instant. He immediately halted and began dry-heaving, as if he were about to throw up. And then the stench that had hit Vance's enhanced sense of smell reached Sam's nasal passages. It was horrendous. Musky and sweet, with hints of sulfur and sewer and month-old fish left out in the searing hot sun.

"Try to—breathe through—your mouth," Vantana suggested between heaves.

"What—is—it?" Sam asked haltingly, as he too began to feel the urge to puke.

"It can only be one thing. . . ." And then Vance must have made the mistake of taking some of the putrid air through his nostrils. His eyes rolled back and he dropped to the ground with a thud.

"What's going on?" a panicked Sam asked Tashi.

"It is best that you hold your breath, Sam London, or you too will succumb," she said rapid-fire, presumably to save her breath.

"I'm not very good at that," Sam replied, scrunching up his face. He thought about how he didn't consider himself a particularly strong swimmer and had never tried to improve, which meant he was average at best at holding his breath. Of course, how could he have known it was a skill that he'd need to use on land one day to save himself?

"Get good, and quickly. I am done speaking," Tashi announced before sucking in oxygen and holding it. She then fully charged her shekchen, the staff that was a Guardian's weapon of choice. It channeled the energy of Gaia, and Tashi rarely went anywhere without it. Sam took in a breath and held it, as directed. He wondered why the Guardian was readying her weapon. Did the odor signify the presence of some threat? The doctor had said it could only be one thing, but what?

As the need to breathe became increasingly unbearable, Sam spotted a strange green fog rolling in. It was a deep forest green, nearly black, and it crept slowly across the terrain until it surrounded them. Beyond the fog, Sam could see dozens of pairs of red eyes floating in the darkness. Soon, those eyes gave way to creatures that began emerging from the woods. They looked like walking weeping willow trees with dark reddish-brown hair instead of leaves. The bizarre figures lumbered toward Sam and Tashi, and the Guardian quickly took a position in front of Sam to protect him, while Sam stood in front of the fallen doctor. He kneeled down to try to rouse Vance back to consciousness, but the doctor wasn't responding.

The foul-smelling fog began to rise from the ground, and Sam got back to his feet. As the creatures moved closer, Sam could discern more of their features. They were about six feet tall, with apelike faces and arms that were nearly as long as their bodies. Their hands had five pale fingers that peeked out from beneath matted, stringy coats of fur. The creatures opened their mouths, which appeared impossibly large, given the size of their heads. They let out a cry akin to a foghorn. It was overwhelming to Sam's ears, and he quickly covered them with his hands, but the sound was growing in volume. Holding his breath coupled with the stress of the noise was too much. Sam needed oxygen. Tashi could see the weakness in his eyes. She shook her head in warning, but there was nothing he could do. Sam opened his mouth, hoping that it would be better than taking in air through his nose. But the fog that was wafting upward and enveloping Sam was like a poisonous gas. It burned the inside of his mouth and throat. Sam coughed and gagged and clutched at his neck, collapsing to the ground next to Dr. Vantana. As his world turned blurry, he watched Tashi twirl her shekchen, and then everything went black.

Chapter 5
PEARL EKLUND

Vance Vantana's killer sense of smell almost got him killed at Fall-ing Waters State Park in Chipley, Florida. This better-than-average sense was something Vance was born with and had later enhanced through the use of Magnapedaxin 13, otherwise known as the bigfoot blood serum synthesized by Ranger Penelope Naughton of Redwood National Park. The enhancement had served Vance well over the years, enabling him to sniff out danger before it arrived. The doctor had never regretted his decision to heighten his olfactory sense, until the day he traveled with Sam London and the Guardian Tashi to the Sunshine State.

There were very few odors that bothered Vance; after all, when you have such a keen sense of smell, you'd best get accustomed to a wide range of scents. Of course, he didn't enjoy bad odors—they were even worse for him than for anyone else—but he was never driven to sickness by a smell . . . except for the smell of fresh apple pie, that is. That feeling was more a muscle memory than a reaction to the scent itself. When Vance was eight years old, he had challenged his uncle Quinton to a pie-eating contest. Quinton Vantana happened to be the most competitive member of the Vantana clan and accepted the challenge with aplomb. The young Vantana beat his uncle soundly, gobbling up four whole pies in eight minutes flat. Unfortunately for Vance, it took only half that time for the pies to come back up. From that day forward Vance could not eat, look at, or—most importantly—smell an apple pie without feeling sick to his stomach. So it meant a great deal when Vance concluded that he would rather have relived the pie-eating contest than experience the smell that hit his nostrils at Falling Waters State Park.

In fact, this was more than a smell—this was a weapon. A weapon wielded by only one creature: the skunk ape. Although bigfoots and abominable snowmen would deny it, these stinky creatures were distant relatives. They were known to live in the southeastern United States, specifically in the Florida Everglades. They were creatures of the swamp, and for that reason Vance had not been expecting their appearance. Rangers who were assigned to areas inhabited by skunk apes often wore specialized nose plugs to avoid the effects of their legendary scent. The creatures were not known to be aggressive, which made their sudden approach perplexing. But it was the noxious gas they emitted that was the most surprising to Vance. It was as though they were intentionally trying to incapacitate him.

The doctor didn't completely lose consciousness, so he did experience a few lucid moments after passing out from the burning stench. At one point, he spotted Sam unconscious lying next to him and Tashi looming over them. He could hear noises, which he concluded was the Guardian attempting to communicate with the beasts. The next thing he knew, he was being lifted off the ground by one of the skunk apes.

In a hazy stupor, Vance observed the apes forming a single-file line. They appeared to be taking turns jumping into what he concluded was a sinkhole. One by one, the wet, hairy beasts leapt into the hole and disappeared. The doctor knew he was in the clutches of one of these creatures, and it was holding him uncomfortably close to its sticky body. He saw Sam in front, now awake, in the grasp of another skunk ape. Sam's creature took the leap, and Vance could hear Sam scream, before the sound grew too distant to hear. He realized he was next and struggled to free himself, but his body wouldn't respond. The creature holding him jumped and dropped into the hole.

Vance was suddenly sliding through a narrow pitch-black hole at breakneck speed. He imagined this was what riding a mudslide at a hundred miles an hour was like. He could feel the skunk ape raise his knees, and suddenly they hit the bottom. But they weren't done. The ape used its powerful legs to spring upward through an adjacent vertical hole. Now they were shooting up like a geyser.

The doctor could make out faint light at the end of the tunnel. It grew closer and brighter, and then they rocketed out of the hole, rising off the ground a few feet, before plunging into a thick muddy bog. The jolting experience brought Vantana back to reality in an instant. The skunk ape released him and moved away.

"What in the Sam Hill is going on?" the doctor exclaimed. He spotted Sam nearby, caked head to toe in mud.

"Woo-hoo!" the boy called out. "That was the craziest water slide in the history of forever!"

"Dr. Vantana," Tashi interposed as she waded toward him. "How are you feeling?"

"Like I've been chewed up and spit out," Vance replied meekly. "Are you gonna tell me what's going on? I saw you chattin' with those wretched things."

"It was a miscommunication," Tashi said. "They believed they were going to have to subdue us before we would come along."

"Come along where?" Vance asked, glancing around. "This looks an awful lot like the—"

"Everglades!" Sam exclaimed. "We traveled from Falling Waters State Park to here in seconds through a sinkhole."

"That's over five hundred miles," Vance replied. "That's impossible."

"Sam speaks the truth," Tashi said. "The skunk apes use

these sinkholes to travel great distances. It is quite remarkable."

"It was scary at first, but then it was just awesome," Sam said.

"The skunk apes do apologize. They did not wish to harm a ranger with the DMW, so they pulled back their odor the instant they realized their mistake."

"It still smells somethin' awful," Vance responded. He noticed that the skunk apes had retreated a few yards and stood behind a patch of mangrove trees.

"Your bigfoot enhancement made you particularly sensitive. It will take some time for the stench to leave your nostrils," Tashi informed him. Vance grunted his displeasure and began trudging through the waist-deep bog to higher, drier ground.

"So who miscommunicated?" Vance asked the Guardian. She eyed him, unsure of the meaning of his question. "Who sent those hair balls to get us?" he clarified.

"The skunk apes refer to the others as the 'elders' but told me nothing more," Tashi said. The largest of the bunch let loose a foghorn-like call. Tashi looked to the creature and nodded. Vance was growing frustrated.

"What are you nodding about?" Vance asked her.

"They want us to walk to the shoreline up ahead," she explained as she gestured toward a small strip of dry land that led to an inlet. Vance squinted his eyes and wondered what was waiting for them. Sam sprung forward and headed down the path.

"Sam!" both Vance and Tashi yelled out. The boy froze and looked back.

"What?" he asked. "I want to find out who wants to talk to us so badly."

"Too dangerous," Vance replied. "Tashi will go first with the light of her shekchen, you'll take a position on her six, and I'll have our backs." Tashi nodded, then strode ahead and stepped in front of Sam. Vance followed, eager to learn who was behind this so he could give them a piece of his mind. Interfering with a DMW investigation was akin to interfering with Phylassos himself. When the trio reached the shoreline, they found a small lake surrounded by more mangrove trees that opened up a few yards on the opposite side and led to what Vance determined to be the Gulf of Mexico. A few moments passed without any sign of these so-called elders.

"Well?" Vance asked. "We gonna stand out here all night? I need to shower." The waters began to stir.

"Look!" Sam pointed. Two more areas of water whirled, and three creatures emerged. They were five-feet-tall fish with five clawlike fingers in place of their pectoral fins. Their tail fins were appendages similar to human legs but were covered in scales, with flippers instead of feet. The bizarre-looking silvery blue fish had conical heads, making it appear as though they were each wearing a bishop's ceremonial hat. Vance sighed to himself; he knew these creatures. They weren't dangerous, unless you considered being exceedingly annoying a threat to life.

"Who are *they*?" Sam whispered to Vance.

"Bishop Fish," he replied. "The skunk apes called them elders, and that's what they are. Ancient elders of the sea who are among the few creatures still alive that helped negotiate the terms of the gryphon's law."

Creatures of the sea did not usually abide by the same rules as those on land, given the nature of their limited interaction with humanity. The Bishop Fish considered themselves authorities on the subject and were always eager to offer their two cents, whether solicited or not. They always made it a point to not reveal much of what they knew, believing that humans like Vance didn't deserve or need to know what was actually going on.

Their names were Filibert, Feidlimid, and Fridenot. They considered each other equals in every way, which led to a rather irritating form of communication. It was rumored that they were linked telepathically, and because of this they spoke in fragments, with each offering a different portion of their every utterance.

"We will first thank you for," Fridenot began in a gurgling staccato voice.

"Coming," Filibert added in a slightly higher-pitched but still gurgling voice.

"To see us." Feidlimid completed the sentence in his distinctly inquisitive tone.

"We didn't have much choice in the matter," Vance told the trio. "Your skunk apes nearly killed us."

"They are not," Fridenot began.

"Our," continued Filibert.

"Skunk apes," concluded Feidlimid.

"We merely," Fridenot started.

"Asked," Filibert added.

"Them," said Feidlimid.

"To," Fridenot inserted.

"Bring you," Filibert clarified.

"Here," Feidlimid finally finished.

Vance had interacted with the Bishop Fish a few times in previous investigations. This method of communication was slow and inefficient, and Vance didn't have the time or the patience for it right now.

"If you want to talk to us, we can't be here till Christmas," the doctor said. "I understand y'all are equals, and I don't want to upset the apple cart, but can just one of you speak?"

The Bishop Fish appeared shocked by the request.

"You," Fridenot said firmly.

"Offend," Filibert added.

"Us," Feidlimid concluded.

"Sorry 'bout that," Vance offered. "But I'm on official business for Phylassos, and that takes precedence over everything else. If you have anything more to add, I invite you to contact your local DMW office. We best be going." The ranger turned and took a step down the path. He leaned over to Sam and whispered, "Are they talking to each other?" Sam nodded. Vantana winked.

"Wait," the trio said together. Vance hid his smirk and

turned back around. "We have agreed on a compromise for this unique circumstance," the Bishop Fish added in one unified voice.

"Great. Thank you," the doctor responded. "And next time you send skunk apes, try being a little more explicit with your instructions. They're skunk apes."

"Are you implying they are not intelligent, Dr. Vantana?" Tashi asked. Vance glanced over at her, surprised by the question.

"What now?"

"It was not the skunk apes' fault," Tashi said. "They were doing as they were told. This is a language barrier issue, nothing more."

"Right," Vantana replied, placating her. Now was not the time to get into a debate about the IQ level of a foul-smelling swamp monkey.

"The female—she is a Guardian?" the Bishop Fish asked in their unified voice.

"I am Tashi of Kustos," Tashi spoke up.

"Fascinating," the creatures said. "We heard of your departure from Kustos. An unusual development. And therefore, the boy is Sam London, we presume?"

Sam stepped forward, excited to be recognized. "Yes, I am him. I mean, that's me," Sam responded awkwardly. Vance grinned at his youthful enthusiasm. "You heard of me because of what happened with the gryphon's claw?"

"No," the Bishop Fish answered matter-of-factly. Sam was confused by this response, as was Vance. If these creatures hadn't learned about Sam London due to the gryphon's claw mystery, then how *did* they know about him?

"Wait . . . what?" Sam asked. "What do you mean?"

"Your question is immaterial to the situation at hand," the Bishop Fish responded. They shifted their attention back to the doctor. "Tell us what you know about the selkie of San Francisco."

"And why should we share any information with you regarding an ongoing investigation?" Vantana asked.

"Because there are rumblings in the waters. Something is not . . . right," the creatures said, as if concerned.

"You're tellin' me," Vance replied. "But that still isn't a good enough reason."

"According to the gryphon's law, we are entitled to any information regarding a potential violation by an aquatic creature," the Fish explained. "This is stated quite clearly in section—"

"He's after a young woman," Dr. Vantana interrupted, wanting to avoid a dissertation on the arcane legal details of the law.

"A *human* woman?" the Bishop Fish inquired. "Does she possess his skin?"

"Nope, she sure doesn't."

"This defies understanding," they responded. "We require more information. Did the selkie identify himself?"

"He called himself Maris," the doctor told them. The Bishop Fish exchanged curious glances. "You know him?"

They didn't answer; rather, they chattered to each other in their odd gurgling language. The Fish were testing the last remnants of Vance's patience. "Well? What do you know?"

"We will consider this and seek more information," the Fish answered. Vance was just about to yell at the trio but held back at the last moment and took a calmer tone.

"How about you tell me what you know about this selkie before he causes a major problem?"

"Must we recite the gryphon's law aloud?" they asked. Vantana furrowed his brow. He didn't appreciate the lack of cooperation. Sam nudged him, and the doctor leaned over as the boy whispered.

"Is there a part of the law that allows them to withhold information during an investigation?" the boy asked.

"Not entirely," Vance replied. "It just says they don't have to answer to representatives of Phylassos, only to Phylassos himself."

"But what if Maris exposes the existence of his kind to humanity? Isn't that like a really big violation?"

"It sure is," the doctor answered. The question made Vantana think a moment about the law itself. The fish weren't obligated to answer him, but they could be persuaded.

"Must I remind you three that if a creature of the sea interferes with the curse and reveals their existence, that creature would be in breach of the gryphon's law—" Vance began.

The Bishop Fish interrupted. "That is quite elementary, human," they said in a condescending tone.

"Yeah, it is. But what might not be so elementary is that a

violation would allow Phylassos to reevaluate the rules governing all creatures of the sea, and I don't know if you heard about what happened in Hérault, but ol' Phylassos isn't in a very merciful mood. I'm sure you can understand why. So helpin' me in this instance would likely be in your and the rest of your kind's best interests," Vantana said. The Bishop Fish considered Vance's words carefully and quietly deliberated with each other. Then they spoke again.

"The selkie called Maris is of royal lineage," the fish revealed.

"So what? He's like a prince or something?" the doctor asked.

"Or something," they said with snootiness.

"Well, what does a royal selkie want with a human girl?" Vantana followed up. The Bishop Fish again conversed among themselves. "You're as clueless as we are, aren't you?" Vance posited.

"We do not possess all the information we require," the fish answered defensively. The doctor grinned.

"That's a great big 'yes,'" he concluded. The Bishop Fish didn't enjoy the characterization.

"Maybe this will help." Sam moved to hand the creatures the picture of Pearl from the magazine.

"Sam . . . ," Vance cautioned. If the fish were playing their cards close to their scaly chests, why shouldn't the DMW?

"It's worth a shot," Sam said, and shrugged. "We don't have much else to go on, remember?" The boy was probably right, Vantana thought. The ranger nodded his approval, and

Sam handed over the picture. The trio of fish gathered around and studied it intently. They made a few noises as they eyed the picture, mostly "ooo" and "hmmm" as if they were confounded yet intrigued.

"She is the one the selkie seeks?" they asked.

"That's right," Vance confirmed. The fish conferred some more, seeming surprised. "Do you know her?" the doctor inquired.

"It is highly unlikely," they answered. "Highly, but we will need to learn more." At that, the Bishop Fish dropped back into the water with the picture and disappeared.

"There goes that," Vance observed.

"Sorry." Sam shrugged innocently.

"It doesn't matter," Vance told him. "It's time we had a one-on-one with Ms. Pearl Eklund. Something seems mighty . . ." The doctor paused but could think of only one word to finish his sentence, however hard he tried. "Fishy."

Sam groaned. "I saw that coming," the boy quipped.

Current Miami "it" girl Pearl Eklund awoke in a familiar place—the lavishly decorated study in her adoptive father's penthouse apartment at the top of the Eklund Energy building in downtown Miami. She glanced over to see the occasionally friendly but always firm face of psychiatrist Ridley Hawkins. Dr. Hawkins had been working with Pearl ever since she'd come to live with Lief Eklund, helping the girl process her grief in the wake of the loss of her parents. They died in a boating accident several years earlier, when she was only ten years old. Pearl had also nearly drowned but was rescued by Lief, who in light of the awful tragedy had felt a call to adopt her. Doctors believed that the loss of oxygen she suffered while underwater had led to significant memory loss. Subsequently, Pearl had no recollection of her parents or anything before the incident.

Pearl didn't much care for the constant sessions with Dr. Hawkins, but Lief insisted. He believed the doctor was helping her, though Pearl wondered if Lief's judgment was just a touch clouded by the fact that he was attracted to Hawkins. Pearl wasn't surprised. The man was a workaholic with no real social life, and Hawkins was pretty much the only woman in his life other than Pearl. Besides, the doctor seemed like a good catch, even though she could be a little too stiff at times. Pearl's appointments with the psychiatrist often involved hypnosis, which the doctor attempted—unsuccessfully—to use to unlock Pearl's lost memories. Hypnosis was also intended to help train Pearl's mind to deal with life in a productive and confident manner. When it came to this last objective, Pearl couldn't help but conclude that the sessions were effective. She was soaring to the top of the fashion world, and she had yet to experience a single moment of doubt that she deserved all the wonderful things that had come to her, particularly the fame and tremendous wealth.

Although she usually felt refreshed following a session with Dr. Hawkins, this time was different. Ever since that "creepo" guy accosted her in San Francisco, Pearl wasn't feeling like herself. She was tense and out of sorts, and the terrible dreams had returned. They were just like the ones she'd had for several weeks following the boating accident. In these nightmares, Pearl was trapped underwater, flailing for help and taking in large gulps of seawater. Then she would suddenly find herself on the deck of a ship, still thrashing about and gasping for air. It was usually at this moment that she would wake up, drenched in sweat. After several appointments with Dr. Hawkins, Pearl stopped having those terrible dreams, and then years went by. But the evening she returned from San Francisco, she had one again. It was the same nightmare, only this time when she found herself on the boat, the man who'd accosted her in San Francisco was standing over her, his hand reaching out. She could hear him repeating those same words he'd said earlier.

"Come home before it's too late and all is lost."

Pearl clutched her necklace anxiously as the man's strange message echoed in her mind. The red coral pendant that hung on a thin gold chain around Pearl's neck was one of the few items salvaged from her family's boat and had likely belonged to her mother. As such, it never left Pearl's sight and brought her some small comfort after the tragic turn her life had taken. Dr. Hawkins encouraged Pearl to wear it, as she believed it was a therapeutic way for Pearl to remember that even though her parents were gone, they were always close to her heart. Pearl often found herself gripping it in times of stress or worry, and Hawkins must have noticed this pattern.

"Is there something wrong?" the doctor asked as she

peered over the top of her glasses and studied her longtime patient. Pearl was not about to tell her the truth. If she admitted to having the dreams or to still being shaken up by the encounter, it would likely lengthen this appointment and get back to her father. Pearl had no time to waste sitting on a couch talking with Hawkins—she had shopping to do. Lief was holding a party that evening to celebrate Eklund Energy's new state-of-the-art methane drilling ship, and it was going to be attended by a veritable who's who of Miami's elite. The guest list was sure to include a few environmentally conscious Hollywood types, whom Pearl hoped to persuade into giving her a part in their latest projects. In Pearl's mind, the fashion world was merely a stepping stone to greater fame.

"I'm good," Pearl responded, releasing the pendant and flashing her most adorable smile.

"Are you sure?" the doctor asked with a healthy dose of skepticism.

"Totes!" Pearl assured her charmingly before springing to her feet and grabbing her purse. "The girls and I are going to Bal Harbour so I can pick up an outfit for tonight, and I've really got to get going. Daddy said I can spend whatever it takes, and I intend to put his words to the test!"

Minutes later, a company limousine whisked Pearl off to her third shopping spree of the week. At her father's insistence, she was accompanied by two oversized security guards, who would no doubt cramp her style.

Pearl's friends—a coterie of spoiled rich kids and yes-girls who hung on her every word—were waiting patiently at the entrance to the Bal Harbour shops. With her entourage in tow, Pearl paraded into the luxury fashion mall, known for housing some of the most expensive shops in the country. She was immediately recognized, and mallgoers gawked and pointed her way. Pearl just smiled and waved. She was also shadowed by a few paparazzi that had likely been tipped off by a member of her crew, as was customary for their outings.

"Can you tell us what happened in San Francisco?" one of the gossip hounds shouted while snapping pictures.

"Were you hurt falling into that pool?" another barked as he shot video of her. Pearl was miffed at the paparazzi's determination to discuss the incident and ignored the queries. The photographers had served their purpose in snapping her picture, and she didn't want to be bothered with more questions, so with a nod to her security guards, Pearl had the photographers promptly escorted off the premises.

Pearl led her crew to her favorite French couture boutique, traipsed inside, and pointed to a slinky black dress in the window.

"I'd like to try that one on," she told the attendant, who practically leapt to a nearby clothing rack to pull out the right size. But Pearl wasn't done. She gestured to a few others. "And that one. And that one."

"Of course, Ms. Eklund," the woman said excitedly, no doubt sensing a huge commission. Pearl headed into a dressing room, then popped out a few seconds later in the black dress. It fit her like a glove, and she modeled it for her friends in front of a mirror. Her posse nodded their approval and showered her with compliments. She was basking in the attention when something in the mirror caught her eye. Just beyond the door . . . someone was staring her way.

She turned toward the boutique's entrance for a better look and spotted the man from San Francisco! He was standing on the other side of a planter that acted as a central divider for the shopping mall's main thoroughfare. Pearl gasped and cupped her mouth as she felt her heart drop to the floor. Just then a crowd of shoppers strolled in front of the divider, and after they passed by, the man was gone. Pearl stumbled back and nearly fell into the mirror. Her security guard caught her, and she blinked up at him, stunned.

"I want to go home," she told him, her voice cracking with fright.

"Right away, Ms. Eklund," the guard said.

"Just box it all and deliver it to Eklund Energy by five," Pearl told the saleswoman in a daze.

"Of course. Thanks!" The massive purchase had the clerk bursting at the seams with excitement.

*   *   *

On the drive home, Pearl attempted to push the incident out of her mind. She worked to convince herself that she was just seeing things and that the man hadn't actually been in the mall staring at her—it was simply the lingering effects of the encounter in San Francisco. When she got back to the penthouse, she aimed to distract herself and checked her social media profile, where she hadn't posted in a couple of hours. She pulled a quote from her favorite book, *Inspirational Sayings*, and posted it for her fans, whom she had dubbed her "gems." Her gems responded instantly. Her phone vibrated with hundreds of incoming messages as they eagerly liked her post and replied. Most thanked her profusely for her words of wisdom or declared how much they loved her, which she took some comfort in. She enjoyed the attention. It helped her get her mind back to what was most important to her: herself.

With the Hollywood producers coming that evening, she began thinking about ways she could increase her followers, since that would surely help her cause. Maybe she'd surprise some of her fans with personal visits and catch it all on video to post online. Or she could plant a rumor that she was dating Jason Bellamy, a hot new singer her age. She gravitated toward the latter idea, especially since it required the least amount of work. Pearl decided to go through his photos, strategically liking the posts where he was alone. Before Pearl knew it, the party was only an hour away. She sorted through her bags, selected the priciest outfit, refreshed her hair and makeup, and then headed downstairs, determined to not let the events of the past few days affect her.

The soaring sixty-five-story structure of pristine glass and steel that contained Eklund Energy's offices was the tallest building in Miami and took up a full city block on all sides. The lobby featured a courtyard that was open to the tenth floor, with a massive marble staircase leading to the second floor. The courtyard was the perfect space for its centerpiece, one of the largest privately owned freshwater aquariums in the country, featuring a host of exotic sea creatures, many of which Lief had collected on his travels. As the guests milled about and enjoyed their cocktails and hors d'oeuvres, Lief grabbed a microphone and walked halfway up the marble staircase. Pearl strode up to his side, beaming for the crowd and throwing out small waves to various luminaries.

"I want to thank you all for coming tonight and helping us celebrate my crowning achievement," Lief began. "And I don't mean Pearl. She isn't an achievement; she is my *blessing*." Pearl shrugged and smiled back at him; the crowd reacted with a chorus of "aww." Lief continued, "I'm speaking of my— *our*—crowning business achievement, one that could change the world forever. At Eklund Energy, our goal is a clean, renewable energy source, and now that will be made all the more possible with our newest drilling ship. I call her *Pearl* because it will change the world, just as my Pearl has changed mine."

Pearl beamed at this, even as her cheeks flushed. She appreciated Lief's kind words, but he could be embarrassing at times. He made her feel like a little girl, and that was not the kind of persona she wished to project to these particular party-goers. With all eyes back on her, Pearl realized she had better do something in response, so she blew Lief a kiss and stepped back down the stairs. He grinned and winked before shifting his attention back to his audience.

"Most of the people in this room had never even heard of me ten or fifteen years ago. I was just a barge engineer on a drilling platform in the gulf who split his time between fishing and working. But I always had a dream that I could make a difference. From a one-man operation out of my garage to a multibillion-dollar corporation, it's that dream that has brought me here today. It's been a wild ride, but it's not over yet." Hoots and whistles went up in the crowd. "Thank you." Lief paused and smiled. "Tonight we celebrate our achievements—tomorrow we revolutionize the *world*." He raised his glass of champagne, and the guests followed suit. "Cheers!" he saluted, and the crowd took a drink and applauded. He waved and nodded hellos from afar before walking over to join Pearl.

"How are you feeling?" he asked his daughter. She rolled her eyes.

"So much for doctor-patient confidentiality," she volleyed back at him.

"All Ridley—I mean, Dr. Hawkins—said was that you didn't seem like yourself today, and after what happened in San Francisco, can't I be a little concerned?" Lief parried.

"Thanks, but I'm fine," Pearl assured him. "By the way, where is that producer who's supposed to be here?" Her eyes swept the crowd and she primped her hair.

"I don't think he's arrived yet," he said in reply, and chuckled at her focused determination.

"He's not your only Hollywood contact, right? You promised there would be others . . . I need people who can help me break into movies."

Lief nodded, amused. "Don't you worry, sweetheart,

there are others. Let me go find them, and I'll arrange the perfect introduction for Hollywood's next big thing. Now go eat something. You look pale," he told her before being pulled away by his assistant. Pearl sighed and pinched her cheeks, hoping to give them some quick color. She wasn't a fan of mingling and making small talk with relative strangers, unless they could have a direct impact on her career. Meandering through the crowd, she nibbled on crab cakes and sipped a Shirley Temple. And then she heard them: two voices over the din of the crowd. One belonged to a snarky male, the other to a droll-sounding female.

"Would you look at that, Nance? It's a whale in a tuxedo," the man said mockingly, then added, "Wait a second. . . . It's Shamu!"

The female laughed. "Catering can't fry those jalapeño poppers any faster. Moby Dick has already taken down two trays," she added. "I hope that guy next to him isn't named Jonah." The male cackled.

Pearl scanned the room in an attempt to find the people behind these callous remarks. Considering how loud they sounded, she assumed they were nearby, but there was no one close to her. The odd thing was that the other partygoers didn't appear bothered by them. Then she spotted the man they must have been talking about. He was a portly gentleman in an ill-fitting tuxedo who worked in her father's accounting department. She'd met him before, and he seemed like a nice guy, always thanking Pearl for her inspirational social media posts whenever she visited the Eklund offices. He certainly didn't deserve such ridicule, she thought. But the voices weren't finished criticizing the guests.

"Green dress, two o'clock," announced the male. "I've seen starfish with smoother complexions."

"If all those pimples erupt at the same time, her face might give birth to a new island," the woman remarked, to which the man replied with a loud laugh.

Pearl noticed a young woman in the corner with an acne breakout, appearing sheepish. She was no doubt self-conscious about her skin. Now Pearl was getting angry. These people were bullies and needed to be stopped.

"Check out seaweed head at the bar," the woman's voice said, alighting on the next victim.

Pearl's eyes darted over to the bar, where a woman with unruly black curls was chatting with another guest.

"Mer-Medusa," the male said, snickering.

Pearl decided to follow the sound of the voices and found herself in the center of the lobby.

"Great. It's Ms. Loves Herself," the male commented. "Five fish pellets says she's coming over to admire her reflection."

"A guppy wouldn't take that bet," the woman snarked back.

Pearl walked until she stood directly in front of the aquarium that they had guessed she would look at. Then she turned away from the glass to survey the room once more.

"I totally should have taken that bet," the female lamented.

"She has never missed an opportunity to gaze lovingly at herself," the male said. "This is clearly a sign of the apocalypse!" They erupted in hysterics. The voices were at their most audible in this very spot, even though the nearest partygoer was over ten feet away.

"Okay. . . . Wherever you are, I can hear you, and you are being totally rude! I am going to tell my father, and he is going to have you thrown out onto the street!" Pearl declared in a hushed tone. There were a few moments of silence. Then . . .

"Is she talking to us?" the female whispered.

"Seems like it, but that would be impossible," the male responded slowly. "Their kind *can't* hear us."

"Well, I can hear you loud and clear. You two should be ashamed of yourselves!" Pearl scolded them. "Picking on innocent people. Now, where are you?"

"Right behind you," the male answered meekly.

"There's an aquarium behind me," Pearl said. "Try again."

"We're in the aquarium," the female responded dryly.

Pearl turned and gazed into the tank. She found two fish floating at her eye level, just inches from her face. They were discus fish, brightly colored creatures from the Amazon whose finnage made them appear disc-shaped.

"You *really* shouldn't be able to hear us," the turquoise discus fish with black stripes said as he stared directly at Pearl. She could see his mouth moving as he spoke, bubbles slowly making their way to the top of the tank.

"But she *can,* Gary," said the female quietly, a solid red variety. "And she's right. We've been far from nice this evening. I'm so embarrassed."

"Oh, Nance, who cares?" the turquoise fish asked. "They put us in a tank, remember?"

The female fish floated toward Pearl, so that she was now eye to eye with the model. "Ms. Eklund, please forgive us," the fish said as sweetly as she could. Pearl's eyes were saucers by this point. She swallowed, then dropped her drink glass, which shattered on the floor. She also screamed, a scream so loud that the entire party went silent. Even the band stopped playing. Lief came rushing over from across the room.

"Pearl, sweetheart, are you all right?"

"The fish—I can—hear them . . . ," she stammered.

"Excuse me?" he said, peering up at the glass, before shaking his head. "You need some sleep, that's all. Come on. I'll walk you up and we'll call Dr. Hawkins."

"Yeah . . . okay," a rattled Pearl replied.

Lief took his daughter's hand and led her to the elevators. He motioned to the band to keep playing, and soon the murmured concerns of the other partygoers were swallowed up. On the way to the elevator, the two were intercepted by a well-dressed, barrel-chested man in his fifties.

"Eklund! Good to see you! And this must be Pearl," the man said in a booming voice. "Sorry I'm late. Did I miss anything?"

"Not at all, Oliver," Lief answered. "Pearl, this is Oliver Ogilvie of Ogilvie Pictures." Pearl's eyes widened with recognition. This was the producer she wanted to meet. She tried to shake off the recent bizarre turn of events.

"An honor to meet you, Mr. Ogilvie," she said, a bit out of breath. "I adored *A Dusk's Sunset*." That was Ogilvie's latest film, a romantic tragedy based on a series of books that were all the rage at the moment.

"Wait till you see *An Evening's Night*," he responded with a wink.

"I can't wait," Pearl said, flashing her winning smile. Like everyone else Pearl met, Mr. Ogilvie was instantly bowled over by her.

"We just picked up another set of books about a teenage girl who's a samurai in a postapocalyptic future. She's being pursued by three handsome young men: a vampire, an angel, and a genius scientist. We're about to start casting, and I don't know if you're interested in acting, but—"

"I hadn't really thought about it," Pearl said coyly.

"Well, I think you'd be great," Ogilvie said assuredly. "I want you to audition. Just give me a call at . . ." The producer was moving to hand over his business card, when a waiter walked by carrying a crate filled with live lobsters.

"Let us out!" a voice cried from inside the crate.

"We demand a trial!" another voice hollered. Pearl was instantly horrified.

"I'm too young to die!" a third voice announced tearfully.

"Are you all right?" Ogilvie asked, noticing the pained expression on Pearl's face. Her eyes were glued to the path of the waiter. She could see the lobsters inside the semitransparent crate, and she couldn't stand idly by any longer. She rushed over to the waiter, yanked the top of the crate open, and snatched up the crustaceans.

"I'll save you!" she declared as she took off for the entrance of the building, leaving her father and Mr. Ogilvie to stare after her in bewilderment. The guests scattered and watched, stunned, as the most beautiful girl in Miami, if not the world, sprinted to the exit with two live lobsters in her hands and another two tucked under her arms. She burst through the doors, passed the valets, and bolted across the street. Drivers honked and swerved to avoid hitting her. The street ran alongside the Miami River, and Pearl raced to the water's edge and tossed the creatures in. As she did, she could hear one of the lobsters shout, "Thanks, lady!" and then the four plunged into the water.

In the strange, awkward moments that followed, Pearl Eklund realized that her life would never be the same. She was now 100 percent certain she had gone completely and utterly insane.

Chapter 6
MURPHY'S FLAW

Following a seemingly endless day of selkies, sinkholes, skunk apes, and shocking revelations, Sam London welcomed the quiet overnight stay at a ranger cabin in Everglades National Park. Once Sam, Tashi, and Dr. Vantana had settled in, Vance used his DMW badge to contact the Everglades' head ranger, Woodruff Sprite. He was busy on the park's western edge and would be unable to meet up, but he did express his surprise over the encounter with the Bishop Fish, whom he referred to as the "gossip fish."

"Most strange, indeed, Doctor," Sprite said, his words echoing over the badge and through the stale cabin air. He had a dry, whispery voice that Sam noticed would quicken when his interest was piqued, a trait more evident as he spoke of recent events. "I will poke around these parts for any information that might prove useful, although I am curious to hear what the girl has to say. Very curious." The ranger's speech trailed off with such speed that it was difficult to clearly understand all of the words he spoke.

Before they went to bed, Sam decided he should conduct some research into Pearl. He used Sprite's computer to hop onto the internet, where he found newspaper reports related to Pearl's rescue at sea. According to the articles, the model's parents died in a boating accident, which she miraculously survived. The miracle part was in the form of Lief Eklund, who was captain of a fishing boat that happened to be sailing in the area on that day. He pulled Pearl to safety and, as she had no other family to take her in, eventually adopted the orphan girl and raised her as his own child. During that time, Lief went from a humble fisherman to a billionaire energy magnate who showered the young girl with gifts so lavish, they often made the local news. Like the time he bought Pearl her very own zoo, complete with a baby panda, or when he paid to close all the Disney World parks in Orlando for her birthday so that she wouldn't have to wait in any lines.

After perusing a few articles, Sam realized that Pearl's ascent to the forefront of the fashion industry was a relatively new development, and one that appeared to feed the teen's love of attention. This was evident from the strong presence she cultivated on her various social media accounts, where she posted countless videos, photos, and messages, amassing quite the devoted following. Sam couldn't put his finger on it, but there was definitely something unique about Pearl Eklund. She was exceptionally pretty; of that there was no doubt. In fact, he believed she was the most attractive girl he had ever seen—and that included Nerida, who, strangely enough, Pearl reminded him of. He chalked that up to their similar skin tones, hair, and light-colored eyes. Yet it wasn't just Pearl's looks that Sam found so intriguing—she possessed an allure he didn't altogether understand.

Sam wouldn't admit it, but he enjoyed researching Pearl and watching her videos, even if they were on topics like how to achieve a "totes adorbs" hairstyle for prom. Sam was viewing one of her videos on makeup tips when Tashi ambled over.

"Another one who paints her face for foolish reasons?" the Guardian mused.

"My mom and Nerida wear makeup, Tashi, and it doesn't mean they're foolish. It's not a reflection of who they are. It's just something they like to do," Sam said. Tashi nodded but still appeared to be mulling it over.

Sam clicked on a video labeled "Inside Pearl's Shell." It was a Pearl-guided tour of her luxurious home atop the Eklund Energy building in downtown Miami. The place was expansive and had a 360-degree view of the city.

Vance joined Sam and Tashi at the computer and watched a few seconds of the clip before announcing, "Looks like we'll be heading over there in the morning to see if we can make contact." Sam paused the video.

"The sooner the better," he said, and they quickly hashed out a plan for the next day.

That night, as Sam finally lay his tired head on a dusty old pillow, he considered the days that lay ahead. If all went according to plan, Sam London would not only solve the mystery related to Maris and Pearl, but he would possibly learn more about his father. The question remained as to whether that information would prove surprising or not. He still hoped for the latter as he sighed deeply and pulled the covers up to his neck. Now, if only he could sleep, with all of these thoughts of Maris, Pearl, and Bishop Fish swimming in his head.

*   *   *

The next morning the trio headed to Miami, seeking to learn more about Pearl and her connection to the selkie. Per Sam's suggestion, they stopped off at an upscale boutique along the way to find Tashi new clothes to bolster her backstory.

"My friend wants to look really fashionable," Sam told the bubbly salesclerk as Tashi wandered the store, eyeing the clothes with trepidation. "Can you help?" The attendant nodded and flitted around with impassioned purpose. She picked out colorful blue butterfly pants that flared at the ankle, and a blouse with yellow flowers. The clerk seemed to enjoy playing dress-up with the Guardian, especially when it came to accessorizing the ensemble, which included a fake fur stole, a gaudy necklace, and a fedora. When Tashi emerged from the store a half hour later, she was thoroughly irritated with Sam London.

"You look great!" Sam exclaimed. She wasn't buying it.

"I look ridiculous," she huffed, adjusting the stole.

"It's just a disguise. . . . And it will help us stop the selkie," Sam reminded her.

"So be it," Tashi replied with resignation. "But do not dare take a photo of me in this . . . costume . . . ," she added with a steely glare.

"I wouldn't think of it," Sam said, suppressing a smile, though he hoped to snap a picture when she wasn't looking.

Dr. Vantana paid for the clothes and jewelry using cash, which he had in abundance.

"Do you always walk around with that much money?" Sam asked.

"The DMW can't exactly issue a company credit card, if that's what you're gettin' at," he answered.

"That's not, like, taxpayer money, is it?" Sam inquired.

"Of course not," the doctor responded, aghast that Sam had even considered it. "We may be government, but we aren't funded in the traditional manner, given the secretive nature of the department."

"Then where did you . . . ," Sam began, gesturing to the cash.

"Let's just say there are perks to having a gryphon as your boss," Vantana replied.

"Gold," Sam whispered in realization. He remembered the hoard of precious metal in Phylasso's cave in the Himalayan Mountains and recalled that gryphons coveted the metal.

Vance gave a small confirming smile.

When they arrived at the towering Eklund Energy

building, Dr. Vantana promptly headed to the reception desk to speak with a surly-looking security guard, while Tashi and Sam walked over to the massive aquarium that sat in the center of the lobby.

"That's a whole lot of fish," Sam declared as he admired the exotic collection. Tashi suddenly grinned.

"That is funny," she said matter-of-factly.

Sam peered over to the Guardian, confused. "What's funny?"

"The striped one just called you 'Captain Obvious,'" Tashi informed him.

"You can *hear* them?" Sam asked in disbelief.

Tashi nodded. "I hear all animals."

"Oh, right," Sam replied. He kept forgetting that the ability to communicate with animals was a power all Guardians possessed. It no doubt had something to do with the gryphon's blood pulsing through their veins. "Hey, you should ask them if they know anything about Pearl that might help us."

"That is a good idea, Sam London," Tashi noted, and she leaned in toward the clear tempered glass, speaking in a gurgling-like language. But she was so loud, her voice echoed throughout the lobby. Staff and visitors shot them disturbed looks.

"Can you keep it down?" Sam whispered.

"The glass is thick. I was making it easier for them to hear," Tashi explained. "Why are you concerned? Do you suspect someone in the lobby understands their language?"

the Guardian asked, quickly scanning the lobby to see if she could spot the potential eavesdropper.

"No, it's not that," Sam assured her, then added, "Never mind."

Two disc-shaped fish swam up to the glass, and Tashi nodded, as if hearing them explain something.

"According to Nancy and Gary," Tashi began, gesturing to the two fish, "the selkie has not made an appearance. But something interesting has happened with regard to Pearl Eklund."

"Oh?" Sam said, intrigued. That was when Dr. Vantana returned from the front desk.

"They sent the message to Lief's office, but he's in a meeting," Vance reported. Then he nodded his head toward Tashi. "Why were you gurgling like that?" he asked Tashi. "It was creeping all these folks out."

"She's talking to the fish," Sam answered.

"Okay . . . ," Vance replied apprehensively. "And what do they have to say? Are they as insufferably cryptic as the Bishop Fish?"

"Not at all. They are quite forthcoming, actually," Tashi said reprovingly. "Apparently there was a party here last night. Pearl attended, and they claim she could understand their language. She seemed surprised by this ability," Tashi explained. "Nancy and Gary were surprised as well."

"I bet," Vance said slowly, as if deep in thought. "Where is she now?"

Tashi posed the question to the fish, paused for what Sam thought must be an answer, and then turned back to the doctor.

"She left about an hour ago."

"Did she say where she was going?" Sam asked.

"She mentioned going to see a man named Murphy. She said that she was confused and hoped to get some answers," Tashi said. The name sounded familiar to Sam, and then it hit him.

"There was a man named Murphy on the boat with Lief when they rescued Pearl," he recalled. "It was in one of the articles I read last night."

"Interesting," Vantana said. "So where is this Murphy fella now?"

Pearl Eklund's limousine glided up to the curb outside the Shady Gardens Retirement Home in Coral Gables, Florida. She had come to speak with Reginald Murphy, the only man present other than Lief on the night of her accident. She remembered Mr. Murphy visiting often in the months that followed, until his visits grew increasingly less frequent, and then one day he stopped coming altogether. When she'd asked her father what happened to the man she called "Uncle Reggie," he sat her down and explained that Reginald Murphy suffered from a severe mental illness and would no longer be able to visit. Lief promised her he would do everything in his power to help his old friend and even hired Dr. Hawkins to aid in his treatment.

As time passed, Pearl forgot about Uncle Reggie, but the recent incident with the talking fish and the crazed man in San Francisco had her dreaming and thinking back to when she was rescued. She wondered if there was anything about that tragic day that might help explain the recent phenomena. Adding to her curiosity was what Murphy said to her the last day she saw him.

"You don't belong here," an agitated Murphy told twelve-year-old Pearl in a hushed voice. "I'm going to come back . . . and I'm going to rescue you." Pearl reminded him that he'd already rescued her, but he waved her away and hurried off, never to be seen by Pearl again.

A few days later, Lief informed her that he'd had Murphy placed in a special facility where he could get the care he needed. Pearl wrote to him on several occasions but never heard back. She assumed he was dealing with his sickness and that doing so required his full attention. Besides, she was safe and doing quite well—she certainly didn't need any rescuing. But on this morning, she was surprised to learn that the facility she had sent her letters to no longer listed him as a patient. They wouldn't disclose how long that had been the case and referred her to another center, which in turn directed her to Shady Gardens.

This retirement home was a quiet, tranquil place that catered to older people struggling with memory loss and age-related medical issues. Pearl stepped up to the reception area, where an exasperated woman behind the desk was wearing a name tag that read "Joy." Her annoyed expression read differently.

"Hi. I'm Pearl Eklund," Pearl said, smiling, and with a swagger that assumed Joy would recognize her. "I'm here to visit Mr. Reginald Murphy." The nurse eyed her for a long moment.

"Are you family?" she asked in a monotone.

"No," Pearl answered, and then immediately regretted her honesty. "I mean, not exactly," she added quickly. "He's one of the men who rescued me . . . at sea. It's a long story. You probably read about it on the news or saw it on—"

"I'm sorry, miss, but only family is cleared to visit," the nurse interrupted. Joy appeared to take joy in enforcing the rules. Perhaps the name did fit, Pearl concluded.

"Pearl Eklund!" an ecstatic male voice called out from across the room. Pearl looked to the origin and saw another nurse rushing over, a huge smile plastered on his face.

"Are you a gem?" Pearl asked, grinning. The grin wasn't because she was flattered—it was because she instantly knew her fortune had changed. She had come to rely on her gems to always deliver the preferential treatment she craved. Whether it was letting her cut in line for coffee, instantly gaining her entrance to the hottest clubs, or snagging the best table for her at the trendiest restaurants, Pearl's gems were her secret army, positioned throughout the city and ready to fulfill their mission of making Pearl's life extra special.

"Are you kidding?" he responded excitedly. "I'm such a superfan I should have a cape!" Pearl chuckled at this and caught his name on his name tag.

"Well, thank you, Francis." Francis let out a screech.

"You said my name!" he exclaimed. "I can't believe you're standing right in front of me. I love your photos and your videos and everything you do. . . . Do you mind?" Francis gestured to his phone, angling as if to take a photo with her. "I have to get photographic proof of the best day of my life."

"Photos or it didn't happen," she quipped, at which Francis laughed hysterically, as though it were the funniest thing ever said by anyone on earth. He pushed the phone into the desk nurse's hand, draped his lanky arm around Pearl's shoulder, and pulled her closer.

"Say 'Pearl-tacular'!" Francis announced, a reference to a word Pearl had coined that combined her name and "spectacular" and referred to anything that went beyond ordinary description. She often used it when discussing clothes, shoes, and mostly herself. Through big smiles, they both uttered her famous saying, and the reluctant desk nurse snapped the picture. Francis snatched back the phone to ensure that the result was acceptable. "Pearl-tastic," Francis declared a moment later, echoing another of Pearl's words. She secretly hoped they would wind up in the lexicon and further amplify her fame. "What are you doing here?" he asked.

"I'd like to speak with Reginald Murphy. I understand he's a patient here?"

"Crazy Murphy?" he replied quizzically. "He's probably in the rec room playing checkers with himself or talking to the goldfish. Come on. I'll take you to him," he offered.

"Would you?" Pearl replied, smiling. "That would make you one of my brightest gems of all! I'll have to post about this!" Francis was beside himself. Joy, the desk nurse, on the other hand, was not amused.

"That is *not* our policy," she reminded a now-beaming Francis, but he just waved her off and guided Pearl by the hand to the rec room.

"Why do you want to see him?" Francis questioned. "I don't think he's ever had any visitors before. . . ."

"He's—an old family friend," she answered.

"I hear he's been here for years. He's the youngest patient in the facility, but our average age is, like, eighty-five, so . . ." Francis shrugged, trailing off.

"Do you know what's wrong with him?" she inquired.

"Not really, no," Francis said. "I know he used to be a fisherman, but then he started having these hallucinations and now he's deathly afraid of the ocean."

Pearl's smile faltered ever so slightly as she considered that and stepped into the recreation area. It was a long, narrow room with tables and chairs, where residents played cards, read books, or did arts and crafts. Reginald Murphy was at a table all by himself, an untouched checkerboard in front of him. Pearl recognized him instantly but noticed he had aged since she'd last seen him, and he appeared sullen.

"Hey, Mr. Murphy," Francis said as they approached. "You have a very special visitor," the nurse added in a sing-songy voice, like an adult talking to a child. Murphy rolled his eyes in irritation, then peered upward to see his guest. Spotting Pearl, his expression transformed. His face brightened, his eyes widened, and his jaw dropped in disbelief.

"Pearl!" he exclaimed. He stood quickly and pulled her into an embrace she wasn't expecting. He must have thought he crossed a line, because he instantly let her go and apologized. "Sorry—I just—" he stammered.

"It's okay," Pearl told him, touching his shoulder and putting him at ease. "Do you mind?" she said to Francis, indicating that she wanted to speak with Murphy alone.

"Oh, yes. Of course," Francis said, and quickly stepped away.

An animated Murphy motioned to the chair opposite his, and Pearl sat down. Murphy took his seat, a warm smile on his face. "You're just as beautiful as the last time I saw you," he said. "But I guess that shouldn't come as a surprise, considering."

"Considering what?" she asked.

He eyed her a moment. "You still don't remember, do you?" he said, realizing.

Pearl shook her head. "The doctors say my memory loss is due to the trauma and the oxygen deprivation," she explained. "Can you tell me about that day?"

He leaned in and spoke quietly. "You'll think I'm crazy. They all do. But I know the truth. I saw it with my own eyes."

"What truth? What did you see?" Pearl asked, confused. Murphy glanced around nervously. "Please—"

"We weren't supposed to be fishing out there that night," he began. "It was illegal. I told Lief . . . but he didn't care. He needed the money. He was living paycheck to paycheck back then. Can you imagine? And then you came along. . . . I spotted you first. . . ."

"I was floating on a piece of my parents' boat, right?" Pearl asked.

Murphy eyed her and then shook his head.

"Excuse me!" an agitated voice announced. An older man in a suit was barreling toward them, two large orderlies in tow. "You are not cleared to visit Mr. Murphy and must leave at once!"

"But . . . we're just talking," Pearl told the man, flashing her smile. The man shook off the effect of her charm, then gestured for the orderlies to take Murphy away.

"Mr. Murphy is a very disturbed individual, Ms. Eklund," he huffed. "It is not safe for you to—"

Murphy was fighting the orderlies as they dragged him from the rec room, but he caught Pearl's eye and yelled, "A fin! You had a great big beautiful fin!" And then the orderlies yanked Reginald Murphy into another room and slammed the door. Pearl gasped.

"Do you see what I mean? He's delusional. He is not the kind of person you should be speaking with," the man who Pearl assumed was the home's manager said. He added, "I think it would be best if you went on home now."

"Of course. . . . Sorry," she said as she headed for the exit.

Pearl emerged from the facility and walked to her waiting limo. She was still trembling from the jarring experience when she noticed that her chauffeur hadn't arrived to open her door. Glancing around for him, her eye caught something on the driver's side of the vehicle. It was a single black shoe. She stepped around the back of the car to get a closer look and found her chauffeur lying in a lump on the street. She rushed over and leaned down to check on him. Fortunately, he was still breathing, and she quickly pulled out her phone to call for help. A familiar voice cut in from behind her.

"Princess," it said firmly.

Pearl stood and slowly turned to find the man from San Francisco—from her dreams—staring back at her. He reached out to touch Pearl, and she recoiled.

"Do not be afraid. I am here to rescue you," he said.

Pearl's heart skipped several beats, her breath left her body, and she promptly fainted.

Lief Eklund stepped out of the elevator and into the lobby with a group of business associates. As he walked his guests to the exit, he spotted Sam, Tashi, and Vance near the aquarium. He said his goodbyes and walked over.

"I got the message you were waiting down here," he said. "I'm a little surprised to see you all so soon. What brings you to Miami?"

"Tashi is very persistent and did not want to go home until she had a chance to speak with your daughter," Sam explained. "But it looks like we missed her again."

"What do you mean 'missed her'? She's upstairs resting, on doctor's orders," Lief informed them. Sam realized that Pearl must have left without her father's knowledge, and that gave him an idea.

"No, she isn't," Sam corrected him. "She left."

"When?" Lief asked immediately.

"A little while ago. She walked right past us. We tried to speak to her, but she said she was in a hurry to see someone named Murphy."

"Murphy?" Lief replied, concerned. "Thanks for the information," he added, before scrambling off. He grabbed a few of his security people, and they disappeared into the elevator.

"Why did you lie and tell him we saw Pearl?" Tashi asked.

"Because our only lead was the name Murphy, and we had no way of tracking him down, but Lief will lead us right to her."

"Clever," the doctor noted. "Let's go."

* * *

Dr. Vantana trailed a few cars behind Lief's black SUV all the way to the Shady Gardens Retirement Home. The SUV pulled into the rear entrance, while Vance discreetly parked across the street from the front of the facility. It turned out to be the better choice, as Sam spotted Pearl's limo immediately. He also watched in horror as the selkie placed Pearl's limp body in the backseat. Sam leapt out of the car without a second thought and sprinted toward them. He quickly realized this action would upset Tashi no end, but he had to act fast if he was going to catch them. The selkie spotted Sam heading his way and slammed the back door, then raced to get into the driver's seat. After climbing inside, he started up the limo and attempted to make a break for it, but Sam was faster. He got to the limo a second earlier and opened the back door to find an unconscious Pearl slumped on the seat. As the limo began to pull away, Sam had no choice but to jump inside.

"Sam!" he heard Tashi call out through the still-open door. The Guardian was only a few yards behind him and was running after the limo. Sam reached his hand out to help Tashi get inside, but the car picked up speed. Tashi kept pace until she tripped on her blue butterfly pants and tumbled to the ground.

"Vile pants!" the Guardian exclaimed in frustration.

The limo was now hurtling down the street, and just as he had in San Francisco, the selkie ignored all traffic laws. He swerved around other cars, careened into oncoming traffic, and even drove onto sidewalks. Sam was tossed around like a rag doll, and Pearl rolled off the seat, finally coming to.

"Ms. Eklund," Sam said, trying to steady himself and noticing that her eyes had opened. "Are you okay?"

"I think so," she replied groggily. "Who are you?"

"My name's Sam London and I'm here to help," Sam assured her, gripping the seat belts like anchors.

"That man!" she exclaimed, suddenly getting her bearings.

"He's driving," Sam said, gesturing with his chin toward the front seat of the limo. "Did he hurt you?"

Pearl shook her head slowly. "I think I fainted. . . . Who is he? What does he want with me?" she asked with desperation in her voice.

"Just try to hold on. I'll find out what this is all about," Sam told her before letting go of his seat belt and crawling his way up to the front of the compartment. "Excuse me," Sam said through the half-open divider. "It's Maris, right?" The selkie didn't answer. "I'm with the Department of Mythical Wildlife, and you're in—"

"Violation of the gryphon. Except the law does not apply to me or to her," Maris said, gesturing his head backward. "You best get out of this machine before we reach our destination. I am not responsible for your life."

"Destination? Where are you taking us?" Sam asked, instantly unnerved by the implication that his life might be in danger.

"I am not taking *you* anywhere," Maris replied haughtily. "I am returning Princess Iaira to where she belongs."

"Iaira? Her name is Pearl," Sam answered. Maris scoffed at this. "Okay, whatever. Where are you taking Iaira, then?" Sam amended.

"Home," Maris said as he pointed sharply ahead. Sam followed the gesture to see the end of the road approaching rapidly and the ocean just beyond it. Sam's heart raced into overdrive and his mind shifted into fight-or-flight mode. Problem was, he couldn't fly or fight at the moment, so his muscles just seized up and he desperately tried to talk his way out of the situation.

"Listen, Maris, I can help you," Sam pleaded. "If you do this, if you expose yourself again to humans, it would be a major violation. I know you don't think it matters, but it does. The gryphon, Phylassos, would be forced to step in and fix things—did you hear about what happened in Hérault?" Sam asked, hoping to instill some fear in the selkie.

"I heard rumors," the selkie responded flatly.

"Well, I can confirm them. I was there. It *happened*," Sam told him with all the seriousness he could convey. "He will punish all of your people, you and Pearl, and—"

"Iaira," Maris corrected him.

"Iaira," Sam repeated. "You're putting Iaira and others in danger."

"The danger is already upon us," Maris said. "Only she can stop it now." With that, the selkie wrenched the car off the roadway and into a field of overgrown grass. The limo bounded over the uneven terrain, heading toward a short coastal cliff.

"Hold on!" Sam directed Pearl, who had strapped herself in and shut her eyes. Heeding his own advice, he gripped the seat and side console with all his might as the limo launched off the cliff and plummeted into the ocean. Despite his grip, Sam was thrown against the divider. Slam! The car gave a lurch and began to sink quickly. Pearl was screaming, desperately trying to loosen herself from the seat belt, but her hands were trembling in fear and she couldn't calm them enough to unfasten the latch, which only added to her terror. Her screams rose in volume once the ocean water started to seep into the limo's rear compartment.

"Help!" Pearl cried. "Please, help!"

Dazed by the hit against the divider, Sam slowly pulled

himself toward Pearl and unfastened her seat belt. She scrambled out of the restraint, and Sam quickly turned to the door. He tried the handle, but the pressure of the water was just too much for him to overcome.

"We have to stay high—where the air is," Sam instructed her as more water filled the compartment. She nodded amid tears, and they both pushed their faces against the roof of the vehicle. The water level was inching higher and higher with each passing moment, and Sam tried in vain to kick a window out, but the strength of those kicks faded as his legs became fully submerged, dashing any hope of escape. Pearl clutched on to him for dear life as they bobbed at the top of the car. There was nothing Sam London could do to save them.

After one last gulp of breath each, water covered their faces and Pearl's eyes went wide with terror. Maybe it was the lack of oxygen that caused Sam's thoughts to wander at this imperiled moment, but he couldn't help noticing how angelic Pearl looked underwater. It was a comforting observation, considering that her face might be the last Sam would ever see.

Chapter 7

PRINCESS IAIRA

Sam London didn't want the responsibility that was foisted upon him the day he nearly drowned off the coast of Florida. He was certainly not prepared for how it would set in motion a series of events that would transform his entire world. In the biographies of Sam London that had yet to be written, this would be referred to as a turning point, one of the many defining moments in the landscape or seascape of Sam's life.

Trapped in a limousine submerged underwater with Miami "it" girl Pearl Eklund, Sam wasn't aware of the significance of his predicament. He was simply trying to survive . . . and he wasn't doing a very good job of it. Based on the events of late, Sam had grown convinced that Pearl was some sort of mer-creature. This belief instilled in him a hope that she would transform at any moment and rescue him. But as the seconds ticked by, Sam became increasingly aware that it was likely he and Pearl were going to die.

Sam furiously fought the urge to take a breath, and watched helplessly as Pearl thrashed about, gulping down seawater as her body desperately sought oxygen. It wouldn't be long now, he thought, before they both drowned, and his mind raced back to the very first time he had knocked on death's door. His initial brush with mortality happened in the grip of a gargoyle high above the California desert. At the time, he'd wondered if Nuks would continue to masquerade as him to avoid breaking Ettie's heart.

During Sam's time at home, he had received assurances from Nuks that he would continue the ruse for as long as necessary, should anything happen to Sam. The raccoon-dog would have to revert to his animal form now and again as his body demanded, but he could do so during brief periods when Ettie wasn't around or during the night. She might even be happier with Nuks as her son, Sam imagined. After all, the raccoon-dog was affectionate, attentive, and industrious. It was a soothing thought as Sam faced his end in the limousine.

With his vision going spotty, Sam barely glimpsed the selkie pulling the door from the limo as if he were peeling an onion. Next thing Sam knew, Maris was dragging him and Pearl to the surface. When Sam's lips kissed the air, he took the biggest, deepest breath of his life. Pearl was coughing up seawater and clutching the car door, which was now floating in between them. The selkie remained with Sam, an annoyed look on his face.

"She has been surface too long," Maris said, irritated. "I do not know what you humans have done to her, but she has forgotten her natural form."

"Help!" Pearl screamed faintly as she attempted to climb onto the door and use it as a raft. Maris watched her, shaking his head.

"You almost killed us!" Sam exclaimed.

"I warned you," Maris responded. "And I'm not here to kill humans. Not yet, anyway."

Sam was considering that semicomforting notion as he frantically treaded water, barely keeping his head above the surface. His legs soon settled into a calm rhythm, and then his eyes settled on something extraordinary: Maris didn't have legs. He possessed a bifurcated fin like that of a seal. Sam swallowed his surprise and met the selkie's gaze.

"Are you sure you're not mistaken about Pearl? Maybe she just looks like this Princess Iaira," Sam suggested.

"I know my future bride," Maris responded with confidence.

"Bride? You mean you and she—"

"Our families and our kinds were to be united, until she disappeared," the selkie informed him. "But she cannot return to the sea if she is unable to transform."

Sam spotted two U.S. Coast Guard response boats speeding toward the scene. Pearl waved her arms wildly for them to rescue her.

"Over here!" she shouted repeatedly amid the choppy waves.

"Those humans can't be allowed to see you," Sam warned the selkie. "It'd be a disaster."

"Ah yes. The egos of men would be irreparably harmed," Maris said mockingly.

"Please!" Sam pleaded.

"Have no fear, human child. I will continue the gryphon's ruse—"

"Great!" Sam exclaimed with relief.

"But it won't matter when our worlds inevitably collide," the selkie added ominously.

"What do you mean?" Sam asked anxiously.

"The return of the princess is the only way to prevent war. And my failure is your doom."

"War? With who?" Sam inquired. This was sounding worse by the moment.

"A civil war between the mer-creatures and the selkie. Such a conflict will send ripples throughout our oceans . . . and then your lands," Maris informed him. The sound of the Coast Guard boats grew louder, and Sam's stomach churned at the thought that the selkie could be exposed in mere seconds.

"We don't want war. And humans can't know about your kind," Sam said, realizing the stakes had just skyrocketed way above his pay grade. Regardless, Sam knew that the most pressing issue was keeping Maris's existence hidden. They'd deal with the other crisis once this one was resolved. "If she really is who you think she is," Sam told him, "then we'll get her where she needs to go. But you have to get out of sight, right now."

"You are going to return the princess to Ta Cathair?" the selkie asked, amused by the thought.

"Ta Ca-where?" Sam replied.

"Ta Cathair," Maris repeated firmly. "Her home."

"Sure. . . . Just tell me where it is and we'll—"

"I am forbidden to tell you its location. And she won't understand," Maris said with exasperation as he hooked his thumb in Pearl's direction. "But if you are serious—"

"I am," Sam told him.

"There is another way. . . . It is difficult and dangerous and has never been undertaken by man—"

"Quickly!" Sam said as the Coast Guard drew closer.

"The journey to Ta Cathair begins at the first sacred point in the city that never stops. Take this." Maris handed Sam a cylindrical crystal four inches long. It shimmered with an iridescent sheen, and for a brief moment, Sam could have sworn he saw a fractured image of a gleaming city appear in its face. But then the sunlight refracted off the surface and the image disappeared.

"Do you promise to bring her back to me . . . to us?" Maris asked with a sincerity and warmth Sam had not yet heard from the creature. In that moment, Sam could see he truly cared and loved Pearl, who he clearly believed was Princess Iaira. Sam instantly felt the weight of his pledge and nodded apprehensively.

"I do," Sam replied. "Now go."

Maris smiled slightly, as if hopeful for the first time.

"Then may the luck of your gryphon be with you," he said, and dove into the water. His fin broke through the surface and slapped down before disappearing beneath the waves.

Shortly thereafter, the first Coast Guard response boat arrived and fished Pearl out of the water, while the second was hurriedly approaching Sam. They used a long, telescoping pole with a loop at the end to secure him and pull him close before two of the guardsmen grabbed on to Sam, lifted him out of the water, and strapped him onto the boat as it sped toward land.

Several minutes later, Sam was carried to shore and left to rest on a bench, where he huddled under a blanket and sipped a slapdash hot cocoa prepared by the Coast Guard officers. He was woozy and a little nauseous, like he had just ridden the carnival Tilt-A-Whirl ten times in a row after downing a milkshake. It also felt like there was a ten-pound barbell sitting on his chest. He took quick, short breaths to counteract the sensation. But he was alive, and that was the most important thing.

Pearl sat a few yards away, also warming up, though still shivering. Her hair was a tangled, wet mess that she unsuccessfully tried to fix. She glanced over to Sam with a look of fear and uncertainty. Sam didn't know what to say or do—the poor girl had been through quite an ordeal at the hands of Maris. How could he tell her the truth about the selkie? How could Sam even prove to her that it was true? He considered that for a moment, before Lief Eklund's SUV screeched to a stop at the edge of the beach. He leapt out and rushed to Pearl's side.

"I'm sorry, sweetheart. I'm sorry I let this happen," Lief told his adopted daughter while embracing her. Sam could hear Pearl begin to sob quietly. Then Lief addressed the Coast

Guard personnel angrily. "Why hasn't an ambulance been called? Can we get an ambulance here, please? And why aren't you out there looking for that lunatic!"

Sam's attention was pulled away from Lief's tirade when he heard a familiar, albeit aggravated, voice.

"What in the Sam Hill were you thinking!" the person said. Sam had known this would be coming. He peered up to find Tashi and Dr. Vantana looming over him. Both were visibly annoyed—arms folded and eyes glaring. Sam shrugged as best he could under the weight of the wool blanket.

"I wasn't thinking. I just sprang into action," he replied.

"Your springing nearly got you killed, Sam London," Tashi told him sternly.

"I'm thrilled you're okay, kid, but that was absolutely, positively, unequivocally unacceptable. You got that?" Vance said with a fatherly ire.

Sam nodded sheepishly. "Yes, sir. I'm sorry."

The doctor didn't respond, but his expression clearly said, *You should be.*

"You . . ." Sam heard a man call out. Lief Eklund was pointing in his direction and approaching.

"Out of the frying pan," Vance quipped.

"Let me do the talking," Sam insisted.

"Be my guest, kid," Vance replied. "Not sure things could get any worse."

"My Pearl tells me you leapt into that car and rescued her in the nick of time," Lief said to Sam as he reached the trio.

131

"Right place at the right time, I guess," Sam responded humbly.

"Twice in a row is a bit too coincidental, don't you think?" Lief asked, his eyes narrowing. "And I'm not one to believe in coincidence. So how about you tell me who you all really are."

"You're right, it wasn't a coincidence," Sam began. "We owe you an apology, Mr. Eklund, as we haven't been entirely honest with you."

"Sam!" Vance whispered anxiously. "When I said things couldn't get worse, it wasn't a challenge."

Sam waved him off. "It's all right. It's time he knew."

"No, it's *not*," Vance replied firmly.

"Tashi isn't a fashion designer and she didn't come here from Tibet to have Pearl model her clothes," Sam continued as Lief eyed them with newfound suspicion.

"I really don't think—" The doctor made another attempt to intervene.

"Truth is, we're just really big fans of your daughter. Me and Tashi. We follow her on social media, and we totally love her. Isn't that right, Tashi?" The Guardian furrowed her brow in discomfort.

"Totes," she chirped.

Sam grinned. Tashi must have heard that word in one of the videos he had played at the cabin, and he couldn't have been more thankful for her resourcefulness.

"We convinced our dad to bring us to see her, and I cooked up that whole story, hoping to meet Pearl," Sam explained, injecting a mournfulness into his voice. Eklund's attention turned to Dr. Vantana.

"You encouraged this?" he asked Vance. Vantana nodded, feigning shame.

"They were just going on and on about your daughter. Pearl this and Pearl that . . . and I really wanted them to have a chance to meet their idol. This is all my fault," Vance conceded. Eklund considered the new information with surprise, but not disbelief. Sam knew they had him.

"I can understand trying to make your kids happy. They're our everything. And fact is, if it weren't for you people, who knows what would have happened to my Pearl," Eklund said with a slight but forgiving smile. "What can you tell me about this lunatic?" he asked Sam. Sam considered his response carefully.

"Not much. . . . The window between the front and back was closed, so I didn't get a very good look at him."

"That's interesting," Eklund replied. "The Guardsmen said they saw you talking to him."

Sam played it cool. "Me? Talking to the crazy guy who tried to kill us? No way. I was too busy spitting up water and trying not to drown," he told Eklund. "He just swam off."

"All right," Eklund responded, appearing satisfied with Sam's answer. "I have my best people combing the bay looking for him, and when they find him, I'll make sure he pays for what he's done."

"Is Pearl okay?" Sam asked.

"I think so. I'm having her taken to the hospital just in case. What about you?"

"I'm fine. Just a little freaked out," Sam answered.

"That's understandable," Lief said. "Thanks again for what you did . . . and, tell you what, leave your information at the security desk back at my building. I can have Pearl send you an autograph or something."

Sam smiled. "That'd be Pearl-tastic!" he exclaimed. Eklund smiled and nodded before walking away.

"Pearl-tastic?" Vance inquired.

"Long story . . . and I have a way more important one to tell." Sam climbed to his feet and coughed, and suddenly the world spun like he was back on that carnival Tilt-A-Whirl, except now it was on its highest speed, spinning and spinning and spinning until he blacked out.

*　*　*

When Sam opened his eyes again, he was disoriented and groggy. There was a man squinting down at him with scrutinizing eyes. He was small, with shaggy white hair, a bushy mustache, and a beard that framed his worn, leathery face and came to a point right below his chin. His eyes were hazel and his skin was the color of tree bark.

"There you are, Mr. London," the man said, his whispery voice instantly giving away his identity—this was Ranger Woodruff Sprite. Sam's eyes darted around the room. He was lying on a bed in the ranger cabin, surrounded by Sprite, Tashi,

Dr. Vantana, and fellow ranger Penelope Naughton, who was busily checking Sam's vitals. "It is nice to finally make your acquaintance," Sprite added.

"What happened?" Sam asked weakly as he tried to rub the tired from his eyes. It was a feeling Sam compared to sleeping in way too late. A cloudy haze was slowly dissipating from his mind and body.

"You almost drowned," the ranger answered.

"But I didn't," Sam responded.

"That may well be true, but you spent a king's ransom in adrenaline in that car trying not to," Dr. Vantana explained. "It was too much for your body to take, so it shut down for a spell."

"How long is a spell, exactly?"

"One day," Tashi revealed.

"A whole day?" Sam said with surprise. The group nodded in unison. Sam sighed, then looked at Penelope. "Ranger Naughton, what are you doing here?"

"I called her in," Vance explained. "It looks like we might be in need of some gills on this case, and she can make that happen."

Penelope was the Department of Mythical Wildlife's expert on creating serums that enabled humans to not only see mythical creatures, but also acquire some of the creatures' magical abilities. Though whether these serums actually worked on Sam was still an open question. The bigfoot serum that had given Vance his enhanced sense of smell had had no effect on Sam, and no one had a good explanation as to why.

"Where's Trevor?" Sam asked as he glanced around the room, expecting to see Penelope's right-hand man, or right-hand troll, as it were.

"I'm not entirely sure," Penelope answered in a slightly unsettled tone. "He begged me to come along and I finally relented, but then at the last minute he said he had to help a friend and took off in a hurry."

"Oh. Well, you know him and friends," Sam noted.

"You seem right enough to start spilling the beans," Vantana observed.

"Perhaps we should wait on the spilling of beans and have Sam inform us as to what occurred with the selkie," Tashi suggested in all seriousness. "We can all play this game you speak of later." Vance grinned, and Penelope did a poor job of suppressing a chuckle.

"Of course, Tashi. You're absolutely right," Vantana told the Guardian with all sincerity. Sam thought it was a kind gesture on the part of the doctor. No doubt Tashi would have been embarrassed by her misunderstanding. "Go on, Sam," he prodded.

"Well, Maris is convinced that Pearl is a mermaid princess named Iaira, who he's supposed to marry," Sam said.

"Did she transform in the water?" Vantana asked.

Sam shook his head. "I was hoping she would, believe me, but it didn't happen. Maris was pretty annoyed. He said she was 'surface' too long and needed more time."

"That would certainly have an impact on her ability to

transform," Sprite remarked. "Her body would no longer remember. It is similar to what humans experience with muscle memory."

"Is that why Nuks has to return to raccoon-dog form every now and then?" Sam asked.

"Exactly," Vantana replied. "What else did he say?"

"He said if she didn't go home, there would be a war. And it would expose everything to everyone. It sounded serious," Sam revealed.

"It is," Penelope noted. She pulled out a small video device and presented it to Sam. She touched the screen, and a video played. "This is footage from several DMW monitoring buoys positioned throughout the world's oceans."

The video Sam was now watching appeared to have been taken underwater, with the monochromatic, green-tinted look of a night-vision camera. The footage was mostly just fish, but suddenly a swarm of creatures passed by the camera lens.

"Whoa! What are those?" Sam asked in surprise. Penelope paused the image. Sam got a better look at the creatures, and the fins were unmistakable. "Selkies," he concluded. Penelope nodded.

"Hundreds of them," she said. Then she swiped to a video that showed another group of creatures swimming past the lens. She paused it again, and Sam could see that these creatures were less muscular in build and sported a fishlike fin. "And these are mer-creatures. We've seen activity like this in nearly every corner of the world."

"Where are they going?"

"We don't know, but they look like they're being called to something," Penelope suggested.

"War?" Sam posited with concern.

Penelope shrugged. "That's the prevailing theory at head-quarters. We've already had to remove a few videos taken by divers that wound up on the internet, and conspiracy theorists are having a field day. If war does erupt, it might be hard to hide."

"Maris said it would spill over to land," Sam told them.

"It sure would," Vance agreed. "So with all that going on, how did you get him to leave?"

"I promised to return Pearl to her home. A place Maris called Ta Cathair," Sam explained. At the mention of those last two words, Ranger Sprite leaned back in his chair.

"Hmmm," he murmured reflectively. The ranger's hand went to his small, pointy beard and stroked it. "Ta Cathair . . . Are you certain?"

Sam nodded. "Yeah."

"I haven't heard that name since I was a child. My mother spoke of it in bedtime stories," Sprite said.

"So you know it?" Vance asked.

"I know *of* it," Sprite clarified. "It is a legendary place . . . a city of mer-people so secret that even the mighty Phylassos himself does not know where it lies."

"Then how are we supposed to find it?" Tashi wondered.

"Maris said I had to begin my journey in the city that

never stops," Sam informed them. "He said there I would find the—"

"First sacred point," both Sprite and Sam finished in unison.

"Yes," Sam added, surprised the ranger knew. Sprite smirked, as if remembering.

"Of course . . . of course. . . . As the story goes, there are five sacred points positioned throughout the world. Like stepping-stones, these points form a trail that leads to Ta Cathair," Sprite explained. "No one knew where the first point was, and without that first stepping-stone, you could not step to the others in the correct order."

"So the first point is in the city that never stops, but where is *that*?" Sam asked.

"It's Atlantis," Vantana said with a protracted sigh.

"Atlantis? I *knew* it was real!" Sam exclaimed. He couldn't contain his excitement. He loved reading about Atlantis, the fabled lost city that was home to an advanced civilization. According to the myths, the city had been destroyed by a volcano and sank into the ocean, never to be seen again. "This trip is going to be so cool!"

Dr. Vantana scoffed. "Not cool, kid. Not cool. That place isn't exactly welcoming to humans, and it's near impossible to get to."

"But I saw Atlantis on the dvergen map. Can't we just take a subway there?" Sam wondered. On Sam's first-ever ride on a dvergen subway, he'd caught a glimpse of the name "Atlantis" on the globe that acted as the vehicle's navigational system. At the time, Sam had assumed it was the location of the remnants of a once great civilization, not a thriving city.

"Not so simple, I'm afraid," Sprite spoke up. "The map you refer to was no doubt made at a time when Atlantis was still stationary."

"What do you mean 'stationary'?" Sam asked slowly.

"In the wake of the gryphon's law and the increased amount of human seafaring, the Atlanteans—with Phylassos's blessing—concluded that it'd be best if the city didn't stay in one spot for too long," Dr. Vantana explained. "So it's constantly moving—floating, I guess is a more accurate term—around the world, avoiding potential interference with humanity."

Sam's lightbulb finally flickered on. "And that's why it's called the city that never stops." Sprite nodded.

"Now you see the dilemma," Vantana announced. "How does one find a place that is never in the same place? And how are we supposed to find Ta Cathair when just getting to Atlantis is about as easy as puttin' socks on a rooster?" he asked aloud, not expecting an answer. But Sam's haze had now completely lifted, and he remembered something crucial from his encounter with the selkie.

"Maris said this would help." Sam retrieved the strange crystal the selkie had handed him in the water. Ranger Sprite's face lit up like a Christmas tree.

"You are full of surprises, Mr. London. Full of surprises."

"Well, I'll be," Vance whispered as he leaned in for a closer look.

"Is that what I think it is?" Penelope inquired.

Sprite nodded and grinned widely. "An Atlantean crystal," the ranger revealed with an almost religious reverence. "The rarest and most powerful crystalline structure on earth. Legends say they are imbued with a magic so mysterious, not even the great Atlantean elders knew what they were capable of."

Tashi stepped forward to examine the object, and it began to oscillate rapidly. It emitted a low-toned harmonic resonance that reminded Sam of a tuning fork. The crystal also radiated a blue glow that grew in strength and brightness. Vance and Sprite exchanged a concerned glance.

"It wasn't doing this before," Sam said nervously as they all watched in awe. Suddenly energy sprang from the Guardian's shekchen and poured into the crystal. The sapphire-colored stream of energy was being pulled through the staff from the ground and was crawling up through the cracks in the floorboards.

"What's it doing?" Sam shouted over the hum, which was steadily increasing in volume. It was akin in sound and timbre to a human voice singing a protracted "O." The entire cabin rumbled, and Sam could feel his bones vibrate.

"It appears to be using my shekchen as a conductor, pulling upon the energy of Gaia herself," Tashi answered in an emotionless, scientific manner.

"How 'bout you make it stop?" Dr. Vantana asked. "This

doesn't look like it's going to end well." The Guardian nodded, then yanked the shekchen back, breaking the connection with the crystal. But the crystal continued to glow, and now the blue energy was migrating to the tip of the object. "Take cover!" Vance yelled as he plucked the crystal from Sam's hand and pointed it toward the farthest wall. A massive burst of energy shot from the crystal and slammed into the side of the cabin, blowing a three-foot-wide hole in the wall. The blast continued into the surrounding area until it was sucked back into the earth and disappeared. Everyone stood stunned except Tashi, who leaned into Sprite's wide-eyed stare.

"Will that get us to Atlantis?" she asked in a calm, relaxed tone, as though the last few seconds had never happened. Sprite nodded slowly.

"Yes . . . I believe it will."

"If it doesn't blow you all to smithereens before then," Penelope remarked.

"How about I carry that old crystal and you stay five paces away from me at all times," Vantana suggested to the Guardian.

"Excellent idea," Sprite said.

"I concur," Tashi added.

"Awesome possum," Vantana quipped. "Then all we gotta do is convince Pearl Eklund she's a mermaid princess who has to travel with us to the lost city of Atlantis so we can find her mythical underwater home, where she will be marrying a guy she believes is a stalker who's trying to kill her. Is that the short of it?"

"I think so," Sam replied.

"Well, I've had tougher rows to hoe," Vance said, and shrugged. "Where do we start?"

Pearl Eklund had been home for only a few hours, but she was already itching to leave. She was curled up on her bed, clutching her necklace and staring at a picture of her parents. It was the only picture salvaged from the boat, which she later learned had been their home at the time it sank. The odd thing was, no matter how much she stared at these two smiling, average-looking people, they didn't look familiar to her. She tried to see herself in their faces. Maybe she had her mom's eyes . . . or her father's cheekbones . . . but it was honestly hard to say for sure. She had hoped the sessions with Dr. Hawkins would change that feeling in time, but the psychotherapy had failed to spark even a glint of a memory.

Now, after being sent home from the hospital with a clean bill of health, Pearl was reflecting on her first near drowning and trying to make sense of it in relation to Murphy's bizarre outburst, the crazed stalker, and the random boy who had saved her life. Though she couldn't recall exactly how he had saved it. He said his name was Sam London, and her father claimed he was a superfan who happened to be in the right place at the right time to help her, but that seemed too coincidental for Pearl. The boy appeared to know the mystery man from San Francisco, and she could have sworn she heard him say he was with the government. *But isn't he just a kid?*

Is it even possible for him to work for the government? she wondered.

There was also the mystery of the door to the limousine, which had been torn clean off. The police concluded that it had likely been open when the car plunged into the water, and the pressure had caused it to break free from its hinges. Pearl had difficulty accepting this explanation, since she remembered the door being closed when she was in the vehicle. The boy had even tried opening the doors while they were submerged, to no avail. Of course, everything was still a bit fuzzy, and she couldn't be certain of any of her memories. Amid her thoughts, a knock sounded at her bedroom door and a second later the door creaked open. It was Dr. Hawkins.

"I know you want to be alone, Ms. Eklund, but your father insisted I see you," she said in a hushed voice as she approached. Pearl sat up and tucked her knees under her chin.

"I told him I was fine. . . . I just need some time by myself."

"I understand, but you know your dad. He's worried sick out there. And frankly, so am I. May I? Just for a moment?" Hawkins gestured to the bed. Pearl had never seen such concern on the doctor's face before. She nodded permission, and Hawkins sat on the edge.

"How are you doing?" Hawkins asked.

"I'm confused . . . and a little scared," Pearl confessed.

"Feeling scared is perfectly normal, given what you've been through. But the confusion . . . What exactly are you confused about?"

144

"Everything," Pearl answered. "The last few days have been so . . . weird. And I don't know who or what to believe anymore. I started having those dreams again, and I heard the fish in the aquarium talking. . . . Am I going crazy?" Her voice cracked with emotion.

"No. Not at all," the doctor said confidently. "It's actually expected, medically speaking. Whatever is going on is having an impact on your state of mind, which is fragile, especially given your past tragedy. These experiences, the pressure you put on yourself, they're still traumatic enough to cause other manifestations."

"Like what?" Pearl asked.

"Hallucinations, things of that sort. It isn't at all surprising for someone in your condition."

"Hallucinations . . . like when I was younger and saw those creatures?" Pearl inquired.

"Yes. And those went away in time, right?" Hawkins said. Pearl nodded softly. "We'll figure this out, I promise."

"You don't think my father has something to do with this, do you? Something he isn't telling me? About the day he found me?"

Hawkins considered Pearl's question a long moment. "I don't know, Pearl. But I do know he hired me to help you. I know he cares for you a great deal." Pearl thought about it. The doctor was right—Lief did seem to care deeply for her. Why would he lie?

"I think that boy in the car knew the man from San Francisco," Pearl whispered to Hawkins, who raised her eyebrows.

"Interesting. Did he talk to the police?" the doctor asked. Pearl shook her head.

"My dad said he was gone by the time they arrived. He said he'd try to find the boy, but I think he's more concerned with tracking down that crazy guy and locking him up."

"Well, I hope they find them both and get some answers. I know that would be tremendously helpful to you," the doctor said.

"Thank you, Dr. Hawkins."

"You're more than another patient, Pearl. You're a friend." She smiled. "I'm glad we could talk. Get some rest. Doctor's orders." The girl nodded, and Hawkins left.

Now more than ever, Pearl decided it was time for her to take matters into her own hands. The doctor was right—getting answers would be tremendously helpful for her peace of mind. And that meant she had to find Sam London herself. She couldn't depend on her father's help, and even when she found one of her "gems" at the police station, the officer-fan had nothing to offer. Although he did tell her over and over again how "awesome" she was. At one time—probably just yesterday—such compliments had been a vital part of Pearl's self-esteem. But now they had no such effect. She didn't care about being awesome. She just wanted to feel normal again, and normalcy didn't seem possible without figuring out what the heck was going on.

Fortunately, she remembered her father saying that Sam was a superfan. If this was true, there was one possible way to get a message to him. She took out her phone and created a post with two photographs. One of the photos was of the city of London and the other was of a lighthouse on Boca Chita Key in Biscayne National Park. Pearl captioned it "Two Pearl-tastic places at sunset." She pressed the final button to post it and then pocketed her phone.

Pearl was counting on a lot of things to come together in order for this to work, but it was worth the chance. After a quiet lunch with her father, Pearl told him she was going to her room to rest, but instead she snuck downstairs in the servants' private elevator and caught a cab to the docks. She chartered a boat to take her to Boca Chita Key, though the captain voiced his concerns about the inclement weather that appeared to be moving in. She paid the man handsomely for the ride and his silence.

SL002-130-40
SOURCE: PR
DATE: ▮▮▮▮▮▮▮

Biscayne National Park is the largest marine park in the national park system, with 95 percent of it existing underwater. It consists of the bay, a mangrove swamp, a reef, and the keys, which are islands formed by fossilized coral. Boca Chita Key is located in the upper part of the Florida Keys archipelago, a cluster of islands that borders the national park on its eastern edge.

Pearl knew Boca Chita Key like the back of her hand. It was the place she visited when she needed to get away or when she was feeling disconnected and alone. It just happened to be the spot on land closest to the area where Pearl was found by Lief all those years ago. She would often visit the lighthouse that sat on the tip of the island and watch the sunset over the water with the hope that it might help her remember her parents. But today would not be a day to enjoy the view. Just as the boat captain had warned, the clouds darkened and the skies opened up a few minutes after she arrived. The entry to the lighthouse provided Pearl with just enough shelter to avoid getting soaked. The wind was picking up and the seas were much rougher than when she'd come in. She wondered, if Sam had interpreted her message, would he even be able to convince a boater to bring him out to the island? The rain kept coming down, and she peered at her phone, scrolling through her account in case any personal messages—perhaps from someone with "London" in their name—had come through, but though the list was endless, there were no messages bearing that name.

"Pearl?"

Anxiously she looked up and found Sam standing in the storm under an umbrella. The umbrella was being held by a man who appeared to be dressed as a park ranger, and there was also a young girl carrying a staff standing nearby, seemingly unfazed by the downpour.

"You came!" Pearl exclaimed, and ran over to him despite the rain.

"I was hoping those were clues," Sam replied with a smile.

"I had to be vague or my father would have caught on," she explained. "Who are they?" Pearl gestured to his companions.

"This is Dr. Vance Vantana and that's Tashi. They're my friends." Pearl eyed the two, then shifted her gaze back to Sam.

"Thank you for saving my life."

"Don't thank me. It was Maris who rescued us," Sam told her. "If he hadn't torn that door off, we both would have drowned."

"He tore the door off?" she asked.

"Yeah," Sam said.

Pearl considered this new information. "He isn't just some crazed fan, is he?"

Sam shook his head. "No, but I can see why you might think that."

"What does . . . Maris want from me, then? I saw you talking to him."

"It's going to sound a little unbelievable, but I need you to trust me," Sam told her as the rain pelted the island and the wind nearly swept away his umbrella.

"Maybe we should get to some shelter. I don't think this is going to let up," Vantana suggested. "There's a picnic pavilion on the—"

"Dr.—" Tashi interrupted, pointing to his chest.

"The crystal!" Sam shouted over the wind. Pearl's eyes went to the ranger. There was something in his jacket, and it was glowing. Vance peered down, reached inside his jacket, and withdrew a glowing blue crystal.

"Get back, Tashi," Vance instructed. Tashi stepped back a foot.

"It is not my shekchen that is causing this reaction," she noted.

"What is that?" Pearl asked, mesmerized by the object's strange glow. There was something comforting about it. She felt drawn to the crystal. And it was apparently drawn to her as well.

"It's pulling me," Dr. Vantana said. He struggled to keep it in his hand and plant his feet on the ground. Pearl felt compelled to reach out and touch the crystal . . . and that was all it took.

The moment her hand touched the glowing rock, a surge of blue energy shot through her body and launched her high into the air. Up and up she went, until she finally plummeted back down to earth and landed with a splash in the bay. After a few tense seconds, Pearl reemerged, struggling to get her head above the turbulent waters.

"Help! I can't swim!" she screamed. *Not again*, she thought.

Sam and his friends rushed over to the edge of the key, calling her name and reaching out to Pearl to pull her up, but she couldn't hear them. Her head was bombarded with a loud ringing that left her disoriented. And then something swam by her. Something massive.

The creature seemed to be circling, until at last it rose from Biscayne Bay. It was monstrous, easily twice as tall as the Boca Chita lighthouse, with several hulking tentacles and the head of a great white shark. The beast screeched and plucked Sam

London and his friends up in its slimy appendages. Terrified and nearly in shock, Pearl attempted to get away from the creature, but there was something wrong with her legs—they were stuck together and she couldn't separate them, no matter how hard she tried. When she looked down to see what the problem was, she found that they were fusing together. The skin on her legs began to change too, rippling like waves, each wave turning her skin bluer and scalier. Her feet were also growing. They stretched and flattened until she had a fin. A great big beautiful fin! In that moment, it was like a lightning bolt had struck her. Pearl Eklund instantly knew her name was really Iaira and she was a princess—a royal mermaid who reigned over the legendary city of Ta Cathair. But there was no time to ponder this revelation. She had to save Sam and his friends before that monstrous sea creature killed them. She recognized the strange beast as a Lusca.

Protect princess, it repeated in a growling monotone that echoed in her head but, strangely, not in her ears. The Lusca had no doubt heard Iaira scream. She had allies among the creatures of the sea who could sense when her kind was in danger and would come to their rescue.

"Stop!" she yelled, but the creature kept repeating its mantra. Then she remembered that these creatures communicated by thought. She focused on clearing her head until one thought remained: *Release them.* She let it echo in her mind, over and over again. The Lusca's voice suddenly silenced and he dropped his captives into the water. *Go,* she thought. The Lusca caught her eye and appeared to nod with understanding, then slunk back into the water and disappeared. Iaira swam over to Sam and his friends. "Grab on. I'll pull you to the island," she said. The trio did as they were told, and Iaira was surprised by her own strength.

"Thank you," a wet and frazzled Sam said as he climbed back onto land.

"Thank *you*," Iaira told him as she floated up to the water's edge. "I have heard people say that when you die, your life flashes before your eyes. When I touched that crystal, a flicker of a previous life flashed before my eyes. One I never knew existed."

"It's a life you forgot," Sam said.

Princess Iaira nodded. "It is time for me to remember."

"Yes," Sam agreed. "And to return home to your people . . . and your kingdom."

Chapter 8
THE CITY THAT NEVER STOPS

The opportunity to travel to the legendary city of Atlantis did not come often, even for a mythical tree creature over a hundred years old. Ranger Woodruff Sprite was, as his name suggested, a wood sprite—a mythical creature who shared a special kinship with nature, in particular with trees. A spriggen in Celtic lore, a dryad in Greek mythology, sprites were known by various names across different cultures, and they were all technically part tree—a little-known truth that helped explain why the creatures could talk to trees. Woodruff had had wonderful conversations with cypresses and pines in his time at the Everglades park. Because they were stationary, trees were inquisitive about the world outside their realm, and being a gregarious sort, Ranger Sprite loved to regale them with stories from his colorful past. They especially enjoyed his stories of Atlantis, as did Sam London and the Guardian Tashi, whom he briefed about the city on the car ride to the dvergen subway station in Falling Waters State Park.

Vance had dozed off in the passenger seat of the SUV, preparing to take a driving shift halfway through the seven-plus-hour haul to Chipley, while Iaira was sound asleep in the back, no doubt exhausted by the day's events. Fortunately, her fin had reverted to legs a few minutes after being hoisted out of the water in Biscayne Bay.

Even though Iaira had experienced the life-changing epiphany that she was a mermaid princess, her memories were shadowy at best. There was no choice for the group but to try to find Ta Cathair by following the path of the sacred points, starting with the first point—Atlantis.

"The island acts as a kind of neutral zone between mythical creatures of the sea and land," Sprite explained while Vance snored. "The city has a diverse population and many opposing interests, which enabled the Atlantis Assembly, the city's governing body, to negotiate an unusual agreement with Phylassos in the aftermath of the curse. For one, the city not only voluntarily shields itself from humans—"

"What do you mean 'voluntarily shields itself from humans'? It's not invisible because of the curse?" Sam interrupted quietly.

"No, it isn't. Any devices or structures built by mythical creatures fall under the gryphon's curse and are invisible to humanity," Sprite noted. "But Atlantis was built with the help of ancient humans, who worked closely with dwarves."

"The city is a hybrid. Part human, part other—like me," Tashi concluded.

"Correct. And *that* creates inconsistencies. So the leaders agreed to hide the city through the use of an Atlantean fire crystal, which sits in a tower high atop the island."

"Have you ever been there?" Sam inquired.

"A few times," Sprite answered. He had been there three times to be exact—once as a child and twice in his work with the DMW. His second trip was a special errand for Phylassos. On that visit, Sprite recruited an operative to keep an eye on the city and report back with anything that might be of interest.

"What's it like?" Sam asked.

"To be honest, it is much like a town in the Old West, where everyone instantly knows when a stranger shows up," the ranger said with a smirk.

"He means they're paranoid," Sam told Tashi, who he assumed did not understand the analogy.

"Why is that?" she wondered.

"Atlantis was once a nexus of trade and commerce in the ancient world, but now, because it is always moving and difficult to reach, the populace has become isolated and suspicious of visitors."

"How suspicious?" Sam followed up at the end of a yawn.

"Let's just say that although Phylassos ensured that employees of the DMW would be allowed to conduct investigations anywhere the case might lead, we'd best keep a low profile. Atlantis is a wild, unpredictable place where trouble is often unavoidable."

Sprite had no idea if his plan to get them to the mysterious island would work, given how far removed the city made itself from the rest of the world. All he knew was that in ancient times there were places that could be reached only through the use of a special key. This key would be inserted into a slot on the navigation console of a dvergen subway. Given the dwarves' involvement in the building of Atlantis, it was believed that the keys were Atlantean crystals, and this was likely the reason Maris had parted with the object. Of course, this crystal had already sent Iaira soaring into the air and blasted a hole into the side of Sprite's cabin. . . . The question was, would it actually get them to Atlantis in one piece, or just blow them all to pieces? With the fate of the world resting in the balance, Sprite concluded that attempting to use the crystal as a key was a worthwhile gamble.

*　　*　　*

"Why are we picking up speed?" Sam asked as the dvergen subway car shot blindly through the narrow tunnel. They had been traveling for several minutes when the contraption had begun speeding up, which—considering how fast these machines traveled normally—was both impressive and terrifying. Sam remembered it increasing in speed when it was under the spell that had sent him and Vance to Scotland in his first case with the DMW. But this was different. This time the subway was moving even faster.

"I have a working theory, but you're not gonna like it," the doctor announced. His answer was barely audible over the noise of the jets.

"I believe I have the same theory," Sprite added.

"Hold your breath!" Vantana exclaimed. "We're about to get a little wet."

Wet? Sam wondered what the doctor meant as he followed Vantana's request and sucked in a breath. It became clear a moment later when the subway left the track and burst through the seafloor. It shot up to the surface, and Sam was instantly drenched. Then the subway leapt out of the ocean and rocketed into the sky. Iaira and Sam screamed in terror as the car continued its gravity-defying ascent. *Maybe Sprite was wrong about all this,* Sam thought. If he was, it was going to wind up costing them their lives.

Sam noticed that the car wasn't shooting straight up. Rather, it was on an arcing trajectory. That provided a little relief; at least they wouldn't wind up in orbit. And then the car began to descend—more like plummet—back toward the ground. They appeared to be headed for a lush, mountainous island and, more directly, into what appeared to be the mouth of a volcano.

"We're coming in for a landing!" Vantana declared.

"Headfirst into that?" Sam asked incredulously, pointing at the mountain that was zooming ever closer.

"Let's hope it's no longer active," Vance chimed in. Sam swallowed and shut his eyes, praying that he'd live through this to open them again.

As it turned out, the headfirst landing into the volcano was the preferred method of arrival in Atlantis. As soon as Sam felt the subway's momentum begin to slow, he cautiously peeked with one eye and saw that the manner in which the subway car was being stopped was reminiscent of the hooks on aircraft carriers that were used to halt landing jets on short, narrow runways. But this wasn't a hook; it was a metallic net that caught the subway car like a lacrosse ball and deposited it on a track running along a polished stone platform carved out of volcanic rock.

"That was unexpected," Vance remarked as Iaira hurled herself out of the subway car and then hurled her lunch up onto the platform.

When Sam and the others emerged from behind the waterfall that hid the station, they found an overwhelming sight: an island-city unlike any Sam could have ever imagined. The waterfall flowed down from the emerald-green volcano that towered above their heads. It was the center of a small mountain range that skirted the island's southern end. The crystal-turquoise water poured into a narrow river, which wound through a valley of lush jungle and into the city, where it split into canals between buildings. And oh, those buildings . . .

Gleaming towers of blue, green, and white stood more than fifty stories high and fanned out from a central point denoted by a shimmering obelisk that rose higher than all the surrounding structures. It reminded Sam of the Washington Monument on the National Mall in Washington, DC, but there was a niche below the capstone. Inside was a massive blue crystal the size of a truck that gleamed like a beacon in the sun. Sam's awe was interrupted by the sounds of geese. He turned toward the noise and spotted a dozen colorful birds scampering across an open area near the river, but they weren't geese.

"Are those dodo birds?" Sam asked in disbelief. He recognized the flightless birds from a school report on extinct animals he had written in third grade. They were about three feet tall and looked like a cross between a duck and a pigeon, with a long, hooking beak. According to his research for the report, the last known sighting of the creatures had been in the seventeenth century.

"Correct, Sam," answered Sprite.

"Aren't they extinct?" he asked.

"They would have been if not for the great dodo airlift of 1620," Sprite revealed. "Now, that would have been a sight to see—a thousand dodo birds being whisked away to safety on the backs of flying horses. Songs were even written about it." Sprite continued to walk ahead, humming an unfamiliar tune. Sam paused and tried to imagine the fantastical scenario before continuing on. As they approached the city limits, Sprite reiterated, "Remember, if anyone asks, we are on an investigation for Phylassos and that is all you need say." Everyone nodded in agreement.

"Any idea where this first sacred point could be?" Dr. Vantana asked. "I reckon it's mighty easy to get lost in a lost city."

Sprite glanced over to Iaira, who bit her lip while thinking.

"Sorry," she said. "I don't remember."

"That's all right," Sprite told her. "There is another option. It has been some time, but I do know a creature who has a finger on the pulse of this city. If there is anyone who knows where the first sacred point is, it would be her."

"Her?" Vance inquired. Sprite nodded.

"She is a Nuppeppo with a penchant for collecting secrets."

"A Nuppeppo? That's from Japanese mythology, right?" Sam clarified. He recalled stumbling across the name when studying Nuks's history.

"It is," Sprite confirmed.

Sam's attention was pulled away by the presence of Atlanteans going about their business. He saw mythical humanoids and their children playing in a park, alongside cynocephali and other creatures.

Sam and the rest of the group made their way into the city center along a sidewalk that ran the length of the river. The city itself looked like images Sam had seen of Venice, Manhattan, and Tokyo all rolled into one. Billboards advertised strange products, giant screens displayed bizarre sports, and flying contraptions carried creatures high above their heads. But there was something else even more exciting that caught Sam's eye.

The canals of Atlantis were filled with unusual watercraft zipping this way and that, and among those boats were creatures—long-necked aquatic beasts that resembled seals with a giraffe's neck. Sam had seen pictures of what was purported to be the legendary Loch Ness Monster, and these creatures were an uncanny match. Could they be the same kind of creature that had been spotted in Loch Ness, the large lake in the Scottish Highlands? Sightings of the creature dated all the way back to the sixth century, though no human had ever proven the monster's existence.

Sam noticed that the beasts had four giant flippers, which they used to propel themselves rapidly through the water. They also had small square platforms on their backs that were carrying passengers, and that's when Sam suddenly realized that the Loch Ness Monsters were water taxis.

"Are those Loch Ne—" Sam began.

"Don't call them monsters," Vance quickly interjected. "They're sensitive to that."

"Then what are they?" Sam asked.

"They're a species of plesiosaur with a few minor differences."

"Really? What kind of differences?" Sam inquired. Vance pointed to one of the creatures as it made a lane change. It was attempting to get around a giant conch shell that was doubling as a Jet Ski. The Loch Ness plesiosaur shot forward with tremendous speed and whipped in front of the vehicle.

"Whoa! They're quick!" Sam exclaimed.

"Some of the fastest creatures on the planet," Vantana told him. "They have to be to avoid detection. It's an ancient water creature, so it must hide its existence."

When Sprite stopped at the canal's edge, Iaira took the opportunity to sit down and let her legs dangle in the water. She quickly transformed them back into a fin. She was getting the hang of it, Sam noted.

Sprite whistled, and one of the Loch Ness creatures swam up to the walkway. The plesiosaur wore a yellow baseball cap that read "Mesterville Argonauts," which Sam concluded was a local sports team.

"Five of yous?" the creature asked with an accent that sounded strangely Brooklyn-esque.

"That's right. You wouldn't happen to know where Squishy and the Believers are playing tonight?" Sprite asked.

The creature scoffed. "Of course. Everyone knows where Squishy plays. She's got a nightly gig at the Lemurian Lounge in Elasipposton."

"Can you take us there?" Sprite inquired.

"You sure yous wanna go there?" the creature asked. "Squishy is great and all, but why not the new waterfront? They've got crystal-bottomed boats, and the whale Jonah rode in gives rides to tourists. It's pretty popular."

"Is it popular with your wallet as well?" Sprite said, suggesting that the creature received a kickback for his recommendations. The monster sighed.

"All right, all right. Climb on. The name's Niles," he said.

"Nice to meet you," Sprite offered, without giving his name. The omission did not go unnoticed, as the creature's eyes lingered on him for a moment before shifting to Iaira and her fin.

"You—mermaid—you look familiar to me."

"I have that sort of face," Iaira retorted. "You mind if I just swim alongside?"

"No offense, but you couldn't keep up. Grab one of those straps and hold on tight," he said, nudging his head toward two straps attached to the rider platform. They looked like the kind in subway cars that commuters use to hang on. Iaira swam over and grabbed one.

As Tashi climbed on, Niles studied her with squinty eyes. He made a barking sound like a seal. Tashi paused and met his gaze, then turned away. He chuckled.

"Hang on!" Niles warned as he took off through the water. He zoomed in between other vehicles and animals, zipping right and left and right again. Iaira appeared to be having an absolute blast and even shouted an excited "Woo-hoo!"

"Do you think he recognized the princess?" Sam quietly asked Sprite.

"Perhaps. Hopefully he is discreet," the ranger said.

"He doesn't strike me as the discreet type," Vantana added.

"Me neither," said Tashi. "That bark he uttered—in his language it means 'Guardian.' "

"Smart cookie," Vance concluded.

"It is best if we finish our business as quickly as possible and leave this place before rumors start circulating," Sprite suggested.

Niles pulled into a narrow offshoot of one of the city's main thoroughfares. After an abrupt stop, he announced, "Here we are. Tell 'em Niles sent you!" Sprite eyed him.

"Another kickback?" the ranger asked.

"C'mon, pal. I've got a family of eighteen to feed."

Sprite nodded, then pulled out of his pocket several coins that glinted with a reddish-gold hue.

"What are those?" Sam whispered curiously.

"Orichalcum," Sprite told him. "An ancient alloy that originated right here in Atlantis and remains quite valuable." Sprite dropped the coins into a pouch that hung off Niles's neck.

"Very generous," Niles said, his eyes widening. "Very generous. Will you be requirin' any additional transportations? I can wait and take you where yous wanna go."

"That would be welcome, if it's not too much trouble," Sprite told him with a smile.

"No trouble at all. I'll take my dinner break, if it's all right with yous."

"Sure," the ranger agreed as they all stepped off Niles's platform to a set of limestone stairs that led down from the sidewalk and into the water, where the nightclub was partially submerged. Fortunately, it was only about three feet of water. They headed down the steps to the entrance to the club, where a flickering sign at the bottom of the stairway announced: "The Lemurian Lounge Presents Atlantis's Own Squishy and the Believers. Nightly at 5 AT and 7:30 AT." Sam spotted Iaira swimming through a tunnel from the canal to the club's entrance.

"They're very accommodating," the mermaid observed.

"When you're a place that also caters to sea creatures, it's just good business," Sprite said. He glanced up at the sun. "The first show ends in a few minutes; hopefully, I can have a word with Squishy between sets."

"Let's go grab a table in the interim," Vance announced, and started for the door. Sprite put a hand on Vance's shoulder to stop him.

"Perhaps it would be best if I went alone," he suggested. "Squishy can be reticent about land dwellers."

"I appreciate that, Ranger, but heck no," Vance told him. "I'm not splitting us up. Not here. We go together." Sprite nodded but still appeared hesitant.

The Everglades ranger slid the front door open, and they sloshed in, with Iaira swimming alongside. Music filled the venue—it was a slowed-down version of an eighties song Sam had heard before.

"Culture Club." Vance identified the band, amused.

The chorus of the song asked the peculiar question "Do you really want to hurt me?" Sam found it particularly haunting when paired with the singer's voice, which was feminine but deep and raspy. The group made their way to a rounded booth and sat down.

The crowd was sparse and included an eclectic array of mythical creatures, many of which Sam didn't immediately recognize. The waiters appeared to be a sort of humanoid dolphin. Vance must have noticed Sam eyeing them.

"Encantado," he noted. "They're from South American folklore."

They sped around delivering food and drinks, their trays

held a few inches above the water's surface. The tables were both above and below the water, with some patrons eating snacks that consisted of live fish still swimming in bowls. *Gross*, Sam thought. The interior of the club was dark and dank, like a cave. In fact, it appeared to be carved out of the same black volcanic rock as the subway platform.

Sam's eyes finally reached the band on the stage, part of which was also submerged. There was a bevy of strange instruments, including horns made of shells; red coral drums, played by an octopus-man; and string instruments that used thin strands of multicolored seaweed. The singer was one of the oddest creatures Sam had ever seen—in person or in the pages of books. The one they called Squishy was as tall as Vance and three times as wide, with pinkish-white skin. A *lot* of skin. So much that the creature's face was nearly lost in the drooping folds of flab. Stubby appendages stuck out from the body, which were likely its arms and legs. It looked like a melting candle, with a dome-shaped top that finished in a square-shaped bottom. Squishy's eyes were barely visible, but Sam could see they were staring at his table.

"That's her," Sprite informed them.

"Squishy?" Vance verified. The other ranger nodded.

"She's been performing in Atlantis for centuries," he told the group, "and is quite popular and very well networked, which should help us."

When the song ended, there was light applause and Squishy took a sip of a purple liquid from a tall glass on a nearby stool. She used a straw that was a few feet long to avoid having to pick up the drink with her short arms. She finished quenching her thirst, then spoke to the crowd in the same deep, gravelly tone as her singing voice.

"This next song is dedicated to a couple who walked into this club over a decade ago," she said in a Japanese accent. "So very much in love. This was their song. Squishy often wonders what happened to them."

The band kicked in with the song "Happy Together." Sam recalled hearing the tune around the house and in the car with his mom. Ettie called it an "oldie but goodie," and she'd often sing along. This version was slower, more deliberate in its delivery. Oddly, Squishy didn't take her eyes off Sam or his table during the entire performance.

"I prefer the original arrangement," Vance quipped quietly to Sam.

"Me too," Sam agreed.

At the end of the tune, Squishy waved one of her stubby appendages to her audience, who clapped appreciatively. She waddled offstage, where she was met by a yeti that sported two blue-tinged stripes on its head and was easily the largest Sam had yet seen. Sam saw Tashi tense at the sight of the Guardians' mortal enemy.

"Stand down, Guardian," Sprite told her. "He's hired security. Very professional."

"I thought yeti weren't allowed outside their valley," Sam remarked, thinking back to what Vantana had told him. He knew the yeti had rebelled when the gryphon chose the Guardians as protectors of the claw. It had been a new arrangement that ended centuries of yeti protection of Phylassos and spurred tremendous discord. The yeti were subsequently prohibited from leaving their home in the Himalayas.

"Yes, but the prohibition applied only to the yeti who were present in the valley when the edict was put in place," Sprite explained. "They were the ones who organized and launched the rebellion. There were several clans living on Atlantis then, working as security for officials and celebrities. These yeti were allowed to continue their work but were banned from returning home."

"Learn somethin' new every day, huh, Tashi?" Vance said, nudging the Guardian with his elbow. Tashi eyed the doctor curiously.

"I do, Doctor. Often more than one thing," she replied, clearly not catching the sarcasm. Vance just shook his head and chuckled.

"You crack me up, kid."

"Here she comes," Sprite announced. "I will do the talking."

As Squishy approached the table, she eyed the group and slowed to a stop. The yeti guard loomed over her from behind, leveling a steely glance at Sam and the others.

"Woodruff Sprite," Squishy said. "It has been a long time since Squishy has seen your face."

"Yes, it has," Sprite replied with a smile. "The DMW keeps me quite busy. But I'm pleased to see that you sound as wonderful as always and are just as lovely as when last we met."

"Flattering Squishy, are you?" she said with a cynical tone.

"Woodruff Sprite must need something. The DMW does not travel to Atlantis without a purpose."

"My compliments are sincere, I assure you, but you are correct that I come with a purpose. A rather important one. Urgent, even."

"One that could affect the fate of the world, no less?"

"There is that distinct possibility," he responded.

"There always seems to be with you," she replied snarkily.

"What is that smell?" Sam asked Tashi under his breath. It had just now surfaced. The stench was subtle, nearly overwhelmed by a strong flowery scent. But it was there, lingering just beneath the perfumed air. It was best compared to rotting fruit. What was with the pungent odors on this case? Sam wondered. First the skunk apes, and now this.

"What odor?" Tashi replied loudly.

Squishy immediately bristled at Tashi's remark, and Sprite's face changed to one of extreme concern. Iaira must have recognized a faux pas in the making and quickly intervened.

"I think it smells wonderful! Like gardenias," she remarked with her charming smile. Squishy shifted her gaze to the mermaid and appeared to relax.

"Thank you. You smell nice as well," the creature told her, before pivoting back to Sprite. "Squishy is sorry, Woodruff, but she has to prepare for the next performance. Some other time, perhaps? Squishy will check her calendar and get back to you."

"Squishy, I—" Sprite stood up and began to make a plea,

but the yeti held him back with one hand. Squishy waved him away.

"Thanks for coming."

And with that, the creature shuffled off, disappearing through a doorway at the end of the bar. Sprite was dumbstruck.

"I wasn't expecting that sort of response," the ranger admitted. "We have not seen each other in some time, this is true, but I was hoping she'd be willing to at least hear me out."

"Maybe she offended her," Iaira suggested, gesturing toward Tashi.

"Me?" Tashi asked defensively.

Sam interjected. "That was my fault."

"It's possible. She's very self-conscious about her smell," Sprite told them thoughtfully. "Always has been."

"Why's that?" Sam asked.

"Nuppeppos are known to stink somethin' awful," Vance explained. "But I thought she smelled rather nice, considering. Perfumed herself up, I reckon."

"Squishy prizes perfume. That I recall," Sprite said with a smile.

"So what's plan B?" Vance inquired.

"I'm afraid I don't know. We may have to contact the big guy," Sprite posited.

"Phylassos?" Sam asked, to which Sprite nodded.

"That could take days," Vance said. "I've already got a line in to him and I haven't heard a thing."

A moment of silence passed as the five sat considering

their circumstances and options. And then Sam had an idea, or rather, he smelled one.

"Princess?" Sam said, getting Iaira's attention. "Do you have any of your perfume in your bag?"

"Yes," she replied. "It's a perfume that I—I mean, Pearl—helped create. It's sold in boutiques in Miami. You can smell like me. It was pretty popular with all of my gems."

"Can I have it?" Sam asked. Iaira eyed him curiously, then reached into her waterlogged purse and handed him a small glass bottle in the shape of a pearl. The liquid inside was clear, and an etching on the front read "Shimmer by Pearl."

"It's all yours," she said with a smile.

"What's percolating in that head of yours?" Vance asked him.

"Follow me," Sam replied. He slipped out of the booth and led the group to the backstage door. He cracked the door open and noticed the yeti standing guard outside Squishy's dressing room. "Ranger Sprite, do you think you could get his attention?"

Sprite eyed the boy. "I believe so. As long as Tashi has my back."

"I do," Tashi assured him, gripping her shekchen. Sprite swallowed and headed into the hallway.

"Excuse me. Mr. Yeti, I demand an audience with Squishy this instant!" Sprite announced as he marched toward the creature. The yeti turned and met Sprite halfway, blocking his path. "You don't scare me," Sprite told him. He attempted to push past the yeti, but the creature moved to block him. Sam took the opportunity to slip by the two of them and head to the dressing room unnoticed. He could hear Sprite continue to protest as Sam knocked on the partially opened door. Sam peeked inside to find the singer sitting at a dressing table, applying copious amounts of makeup in the mirror.

"Fans are not allow—" Then she paused, spotting him. "*You* again? Squishy thought she made herself clear to Woodruff. Must she call security? He's a yeti, you know. Rumor has it, you had an experience with yetis not too long ago."

"So you know who I am?" Sam inquired with a touch of surprise.

"Of course, Sam London. Everyone knows about you. Some longer than others," Squishy said.

"Oh?" Sam replied, unsure of her meaning. Squishy gazed back into the mirror and continued her regimen.

"Woodruff is well aware that secrets have a cost, and the one you seek is highly valuable, as it puts Squishy in danger."

"You know what we're looking for?" Sam asked her curiously.

"That girl with you . . . she is Princess Iaira, is she not?"

"I don't know what you're talking about," Sam responded, feigning ignorance.

"You're an adorable liar, Sam London," Squishy said. "What is that in your hand?"

"It's a gift for you," Sam told her, holding up the bottle of Pearl's perfume. He added, "Sprite said you like perfume, and we all wanted to give you a gift after you graced us with your wonderful voice."

Squishy eyed Sam, then waddled over with surprising speed, snatched the bottle out of his hand, and returned to her dressing table. Sam was stunned by her quickness. Squishy sprayed herself with the perfume, then closed her eyes and smiled as she breathed in the scent. When her eyes opened again, they were fixed on Sam.

"Squishy likes you, Sam London," she said. "You know how to treat a lady." She gestured for him to come closer, and Sam stepped forward. He was happy she had sprayed the perfume, as it helped mask her true scent. "Squishy does not know for certain the answer to what you seek, but she hears many things," she said just under her breath. "One thing she has heard more than all the others, and so that is the one she believes to be true. The first sacred point is said to lie above the great crystal at the top of the Tower of Atlas."

"You mean the one way up . . ." Sam gestured, and Squishy nodded.

"Iaira's return to Ta Cathair will save lives, but be warned, there are those who do not wish to see her return. Squishy hears many things." Sam nodded, understanding.

"Thank you," he said, then moved to leave.

"Do you know why Squishy did not give Sprite this information?"

"Because he didn't have a gift?" Sam answered earnestly. Squishy shook her head, which shook her entire body.

"Because he did not make good on his promises. Squishy has been keeping a secret for him and the gryphon for twelve years."

"That's as long as I've been alive," Sam told her.

"Of course it is," she said, and smiled. "Perhaps he will tell you this secret. Perhaps you should ask him."

"Okay . . . ," Sam said, uncertain as to why he should but wanting to be agreeable.

"And tell Dr. Vantana Squishy said hello, though he may not remember Squishy," she added. "Memories are fleeting things in his line of work. This reminds Squishy that she has a gift for you as well."

"You do?"

Squishy nodded, and again her whole body moved. She reached into a drawer in her dresser and pulled out a small, wrapped, square-shaped package. "Well, not for you in particular. But for you to give to *someone*. Squishy has been holding on to this for quite a long time. Waiting for the recipient to come along." She handed it over to Sam. "This is to be given to Dr. Vantana when your journey is over, and not a moment before. Do you promise this?"

"Sure. What is it?"

"When the journey is over, Sam London," she repeated. Sam nodded.

As he exited Squishy's dressing room, Sam considered what the creature had said about Vance. He knew from his first case that Penelope Naughton's memory had been erased, and it appeared Squishy was suggesting that Vance had also lost memories of some kind. A discussion for another time, he thought as he exited the club and found the group waiting outside.

"Well, she didn't eat you," Vance quipped. "That's a good sign."

"You assured me she was harmless, Dr. Vantana," Tashi said, annoyed. "I would never have agreed to—"

"It's a joke, Tashi. Relax. He's fine."

"I'm more than fine," Sam announced. "I know where the first sacred point is," he whispered. They all leaned in to hear. "The Tower of Atlas, above the crystal."

"Of course," Sprite said. "Makes perfect sense. Though I am surprised she told you."

"The perfume softened her up," Sam explained. "She claimed you didn't make good on some promise," he then told Sprite. "Something about a secret. And she wanted me to say hello to you, Dr. Vantana."

"Me? I've never met her before," Vance replied.

"She said you might not remember."

"I reckon I'd recall meetin' a Nuppeppo named Squishy," Vance said, puzzled. "What do you make of that, Ranger?"

"Memories can be fleeting things," Sprite replied with a shrug. Before Sam could note that Squishy had spoken the same words, Sprite quickly added, "I best be getting back to the Everglades before the trees start to miss me. You're on the right track now. Good luck." Sprite headed off to the main canal and waved over another taxi.

* * *

On the way to the Tower of Atlas aboard the Loch Ness water taxi, Dr. Vance Vantana reflected upon the fact that he had never been to Atlantis before. Technically speaking, he was barred from traveling to the lost city. It wasn't anything he'd done, per se; rather, it was a request made by Dr. Knox after an incident in the Russian taiga forest more than a decade earlier. Vance's memory of the ordeal was sketchy, given his run-in with a mythical creature known as the Baba Yaga.

As Knox had relayed the story days later, Vance had come to check on his mentor after Knox went to speak with the Maiden Council—a ruling council of swan maidens on Russia's Lake Baikal—regarding human encroachment on the habitats of mythical sea creatures. When Vance didn't hear from the doctor after an agreed-upon time, he hiked into the forest to check on Knox. Unbeknownst to Vance, this was a major violation, and the attack from the Baba Yaga was swift. Vance was knocked out cold and woke up in the care of Knox, who explained that the meeting had not gone well.

Knox subsequently concluded that it'd be best if Vance and other human rangers working with the DMW avoided interactions with creatures of the sea realm. This included visits to Atlantis, given the island-city's preponderance of mythical sea creatures. Fortunately, no investigations had required Vance to travel to the city, so the issue had yet to come up. That is, until now.

It had been years since Knox's edict, and given the urgency of this case, Vance felt it was permissible for him to travel to Atlantis on this occasion. After all, it was a mythical sea creature that had violated the gryphon's law on land, and the DMW was well within its jurisdiction on the matter. He wondered if he should have checked with Phylassos about the decision, but the gryphon had become even more difficult to reach since the events in Hérault. Phylassos was clearly distracted by something, but by what, Vance hadn't a clue. Maybe it was another case that was more critical to the mission of the DMW. Hard to say, but whatever the situation, Vance had little choice but to follow this lead to Atlantis and take his chances.

Vance stepped off Niles's back and onto the city's bustling central plaza, which was filled with all manner of mythical creatures selling their wares or shopping. He stared in awe at the gleaming tower that stood at the plaza's center and represented the very heart of Atlantis, literally and figuratively. This tower held the crystal that powered the entire city, so getting inside would not be an easy task, especially since two stoic scorpion men were guarding the entrance. The humanoid scorpions, complete with tails that could sting with deadly harm, hailed from Mesopotamia, an ancient area of the Middle East.

"How are we going to get inside that place?" Iaira asked.

Before Vance could propose a plan, the massive orichalcum doors opened and a large figure stepped out. He was a broad-shouldered and bare-chested man, wearing a long turquoise robe and a short beige kilt with elaborate colored symbols. He held what appeared to be a kitten in his hands, until he got closer and Vance realized it was actually a tiger.

"Naw, it can't be," Vance thought out loud.

"Who? Who is it?" Sam asked.

"Gilgamesh." They all looked at Vantana blankly. "Seriously? *The Epic of Gilgamesh*? Only happens to be one of the great ancient works of human literature. Y'all need to go to a library when we get back." Of course, the doctor had learned years ago that *The Epic of Gilgamesh* wasn't exactly literature, at least not of the fictional variety. It actually happened. The story told how Gilgamesh was an arrogant king whom the gods sought to punish by sending a wild man to defeat him in battle. But the man and Gilgamesh became lifelong friends. When the wild man died, Gilgamesh was heartbroken and went on a pilgrimage, searching for the secret to eternal life. In the story, he never discovered this secret, but in reality he found it and kept it to himself ever since. Vance had a run-in with Gilgamesh back when the doctor was just starting out with Dr. Knox, and he remembered the former king as being the consummate big-time operator, someone who traded favors like they were currency. Recently Vantana had learned that after a long stint in the Atlantis Assembly, Gilgamesh had ascended to be mayor of the city.

"A meeting with the mayor? I'm guessin' this ain't coincidence," the doctor said with a smile as Gilgamesh walked up. The latter chuckled deeply.

"You'd be surprised how quickly word spreads when continent dwellers are roaming around my island with a long-lost mermaid princess," he replied.

"Nothin' gets past you, huh?" Vance remarked.

Gilgamesh shrugged. "The Bishop Fish are advisors to the Assembly. Iaira, is that really you?" He studied the princess, and a smile broke out across his face that was broader than his shoulders. "By the legend of Sharur, it *is* you! Everyone believes you to be dead," he disclosed.

"We hope to change that," Vantana told him. "Are things as dire as the selkie claimed?"

"From what I've heard, war is looming. Iaira's return could calm the waters, but it will be choppy."

"Then we need to get there A-SAP, but the problem is she doesn't remember where it's at," Vance told him. "So now we're on the path of the five sacred points."

"Let me guess. You believe the first one is at the top of the tower?" a smirking Gilgamesh asked.

The doctor played it cool. "We've heard rumors. We thought we'd go have ourselves a look-see."

"You thought wrong," the mayor informed him. Vance had anticipated this. Gilgamesh was not the type to just roll over because an entire civilization was at risk. He would see this as an opportunity to further his influence. "I will let Iaira pass, because I owe her mother a favor," he said. Then he turned to Tashi. "You can pass because you are a Guardian and I have great respect for those whom Phylassos trusts with his life. But you two may go on only one condition," he told Sam and Vance. "The DMW will owe me a favor. A big one."

"What kind of favor?" Sam asked.

"The only thing I don't know is the future, my boy. You'll find out when I do."

"I know I'm going to regret this, but all right. Let's get on with it," Vance capitulated. Gilgamesh happily nodded his approval and gestured to the entrance of the tower.

"Follow me."

As they stepped through the tower's massive doors, they found the interior pulsating with cables of blue luminescence that snaked down from the top of the tower, along the walls, and to the floor, where it disappeared in every direction. There was an elevator on one of the walls that reached to the tower's peak. It was a simple platform with three railings. Before they climbed on, Gilgamesh turned to Tashi and gestured to her shekchen.

"If what I know about those weapons is true, you may want to leave it down here," he suggested. Tashi glanced over to Vance, who nodded his agreement. She hesitated, then set it on the ground and got onto the platform.

Gilgamesh handed out dark goggles, like something Sam imagined a welder would wear. Everyone put them on, and the platform rose until it reached the crystal's chamber. The brightness was overpowering—without the shades, it would have been impossible to see anything.

"What now?" Iaira asked as they stepped into the chamber.

Sam pointed to the crystal. "She said it was above the crystal. . . . Maybe you have to get closer to see it," he suggested. Iaira looked to Gilgamesh for approval.

"Don't look at me," he said. "I've never been near that thing. I don't think anyone has. *Much* too dangerous."

"Come, I will guide you," Tashi told Iaira, offering her hand. Iaira took it, and the two approached the massive blue crystal. It sat only a few feet off the ground and was positioned directly beneath the capstone. Up close, it seemed to pulse like a beating heart, the light shining strongly, then dimming, then gleaming again. Iaira stretched out her free hand to touch the crystal, as if drawn to it.

"Don't—" Vance warned her.

"I won't," she told him, holding her hand a few inches from the surface. "I learned my lesson. I was just trying to see if—"

There was a sudden and massive surge of blue energy that leapt from the crystal and poured into Iaira's body. The crystal blinked off, and the building went dark as the electricity for the entire city shut down. Iaira's body was instantly illuminated, and she rose several feet off the floor. She appeared to grip Tashi's hand more tightly, and the Guardian's eyes closed, her face grimacing. Then the blue energy shot out of Iaira's mouth and nose and back into the crystal. The current instantly started flowing again, and Vance could hear the distinctive whir of power being restored. Iaira dropped to the floor in a heap. Tashi was thrown backward and slid across the floor. She caught herself just before she went over the edge. Iaira's hair was now standing on end, and she appeared frazzled, pale, and terrified.

"Are you okay?" Sam asked, rushing to Iaira's side. "What happened?"

"It was—in the water—it was raining down—on me," she stammered.

"What was?" Sam responded. She met his gaze and whispered ominously:

"Blood."

Chapter 9
THE ESCAPE

Making the drive in her DMW-issued SUV from the Castle Crags dvergen subway station to her cabin was second nature to Ranger Penelope Naughton, but it hadn't always been that way. Penelope's memory had been erased—or, rather, suppressed—to help Phylassos investigate the threat to the gryphon's claw not that long ago. Though the ranger's memories had since returned in full and she had forgiven the creature for his unconventional methods, Penelope was still unsettled by the idea that her mind had been manipulated by magic without her permission. As the ranger headed home, she thought back on the plight of Pearl Eklund—or Princess Iaira. The young woman was also clearly suffering from a form of memory loss, the cause of which was still unknown.

When Penelope pulled into the parking space in front of

her cabin, she spotted a late-model minivan backing out and a troll behind the wheel. The ranger instantly recognized the driver as Trevor's sister.

"Bernice?" Penelope called out, waving as she climbed out of her car. The troll spotted her and lowered the window.

"Hello there, Ranger Naughton," she said in her signature singsong voice.

"What are you doing here? Is everything okay?" Penelope asked.

"Oh, yes indeedy. I was just bringing the boys up from Benicia," she replied.

"The boys?"

"Sam London and Trevor," Bernice answered.

"But Sam—" Penelope was just about to reveal that Sam was not in Benicia, then quickly thought the better of it and coughed. "They're both in the cabin?"

"That's where they went. I've gotta hustle, darling. Sorry I can't stay and chat. Bye now!" Bernice said with a wave, and pulled out of the lot, throwing up a cloud of dust and gravel in her wake.

A curious Penelope entered the cabin to find Trevor and Sam London sitting on her couch, looking glum. Of course, the Sam she was seeing was Nuks, the shape-shifting raccoon-dog. She was inclined to ask Nuks to shift back into his natural form, but she didn't know what would be stranger—seeing Sam's double talking or seeing a raccoon-dog talking. She went with Sam's double.

"Ranger Naughton!" Trevor exclaimed, standing up

quickly. Nuks followed. "We've been waiting for you to come home," the troll informed her.

"I just caught Bernice outside. . . . She said she drove you two up from Benicia. What were you doing there?" she asked Trevor, then shifted her eyes to Nuks. "And why are you here? You should be keeping up appearances. Wouldn't Sam be in school right now?"

Trevor sighed, and Nuks bit his lip.

"Guys, talk to me," Penelope said. "What's going on?"

"It's about Ettie, Sam's mom," Trevor told her.

"What about her?" Penelope asked. Trevor shifted his eyes to Nuks, who appeared cautious. "Nuks." Penelope glared. "Tell me."

"She was doing her spring thing—Sam said she does it every year, and I was helping. As Sam, of course. And this year she finally got to the attic. Sam said she never gets to the attic, but I was helping and—"

"Nuks, just tell me," Penelope interrupted impatiently.

"She's gone, Ranger Naughton. Just gone," the raccoon-dog revealed in an exasperated tone.

"Gone? Gone where?"

"I don't know. I've looked everywhere. I followed her scent to the door, and then it just disappeared," Nuks said.

"And I reached out to all of my friends, but no one knows anything at *all*," Trevor added. "And that's really weird, 'cause I have a *lot* of friends—"

"Oh no," Penelope exclaimed quietly to herself as she sat down on the couch.

"Do you know what happened?" Trevor asked, hopeful.

"No. Well, I don't know for sure. But I have a theory, and it's not good." She tapped her badge. "Dr. Vantana?" she called out, but no one answered. "I was afraid the badges wouldn't work once the doctor was in Atlantis. Not that it matters. It's not like he could do anything." She exhaled thoughtfully.

"Maybe Carl can help," Trevor suggested.

"I don't think anyone can help now."

Classification 480 (Employee Medical Records)
SUBJ: Tashi of Kustos (SA)
DATE: ▮▮▮▮▮▮▮▮
INTERNAL MEMO

With the cooperation of DMW Special Advisor Tashi, agency medical personnel have learned that Guardians enjoy a unique dreamworld that enhances their physiological and psychological well-being. In contrast, the function of dreams in humans is not entirely understood by scientists. There are many theories as to why humans dream, but nothing is conclusive. For Guardians, the purpose of dreams is to enrich their lives. Given their allegiance to the gryphon, Guardians were never expected to venture beyond their village at the base of Phylassos's mountain cave. Phylassos sought to remedy this isolation by bestowing upon them the power to control their dreams—it was an ability the gryphon himself had mastered.

With Tashi now living outside of Kustos, there is little opportunity for her to train in a manner consistent with Guardian standards. Fortunately, through the power of a Guardian's mind and the magic of the gryphon's blood, Tashi is able to engage in training sessions within her dreamworld. These sessions even have real-world physiological implications on her body. According to the Guardian, she has faced ultra-realistic manifestations of creatures in her dreams that challenge her and help hone her skills. She has also indicated that she can use her dream state to visit her parents or friends, but the difference in time zones seldom allows for such gatherings.

There are rare occasions when Guardians and even Phylassos himself do not have control of their dreamscapes. For instance, the gryphon had no control of his dream when he found himself in Death Valley with Sam London. It is speculated that this was a sign that the universe had stepped in to ensure they meet. Several Guardians, including the Kustos village elder Yeshe, appeared to have experienced this same dream. This was revealed when Sam London entered Kustos on his first case (Case #SL001-180) and the Guardians recognized him as the boy who had met the gryphon in Death Valley.

It should be noted here that just as the gryphon could

Tashi of Kustos did not know where she was, but she knew she was no longer in the Tower of Atlas. She had just witnessed Princess Iaira get hit with a jolt of energy from the Atlantis fire crystal. The energy had surged through Iaira and streamed into Tashi, until suddenly the Guardian was transported into a dreamworld, but it was one she could neither recognize nor control. Tashi took a defensive stance and quickly scanned her surroundings. She appeared to be outside—in a forest—and it was night. She could hear the calls of insects and the flutter of wings of what she imagined to be birds or possibly bats. And then she spotted a figure standing a few feet in front of her. It was Ettie London. But Ettie did not look like herself. Her face was paler than usual, her eyes hollow, her stare directionless.

"Miss—" Tashi tried calling out, but Ettie was instantly swallowed up by the darkness. Tashi awoke on the tower's platform, just catching Iaira saying something about being covered in blood. She also noticed that the crystal was glowing stronger than before.

"Tashi? How are you holding up? You took a mighty big jolt back there," Dr. Vantana said, giving her a once-over.

"I am fine," Tashi responded tentatively. She stood up and regained her bearings. "My body is uniquely equipped to handle energy of that magnitude." She glanced over to Sam and wondered if she should tell him what she had experienced.

"Why are you looking at me like that?" he asked, noticing her eyes on him.

"No reason," she replied. Tashi was not seeking to withhold the truth from Sam, but Guardian dreams were peculiar things and she didn't know what to make of this one quite yet. She decided to follow up with Yeshe as soon as the opportunity presented itself.

"I think I want to go home now," Iaira announced, practically hyperventilating.

"That's where we're headed," Sam reminded her.

"No, the other one. The fun one," she replied with tears in her eyes.

"I'm afraid we can't do that, Princess," Dr. Vantana told her.

"I didn't even touch it!" Iaira declared.

"It reached out and touched you," Gilgamesh remarked.

"Why?" she asked, agitated.

"It is believed the crystal is a living entity that holds the collective knowledge of every species on earth—magical and otherwise," the mayor explained. "It likely knows you're of royal lineage and wanted you to see that which is relevant to your journey."

"Blood?" she replied, disgusted at the thought.

"Was it your blood?" he asked. She considered it.

"I don't know. . . ."

"Well, it's not a ton to go on," Sam said. "Maybe this isn't the place."

"No, Sam," Vantana said, pointing upward. "I reckon this is the place."

The doctor pointed to words that were now revealed on the interior walls of the tower's capstone, and they all gazed up to see them. It seemed as though the words had been there the whole time but were just hidden in the shadows. This must have been why the crystal was brighter now, Tashi concluded. It was intended to *expose* these words. Sam craned his neck to get a better look.

"What language is that?" he asked, staring at the glyphs on the stone surface.

"It appears to be a mer-language of some kind," Vantana answered, squinting his eyes.

"I can read it!" Iaira said with surprise, then recited the words slowly, " 'The path to the kingdom beneath the sea lies beyond the falls in the frozen valley, where the austral waters run blood-red and the golden wolf rears its head, a place where all should fear to tread, for it fills the bravest heart with dread.' "

"Where the waters run blood-red?" Sam wondered aloud. "What does that mean?"

"I've got an idea, and it ain't pretty," Vance replied. Before he could elaborate, the tower shook and the tremor knocked everyone to the ground, except Gilgamesh and Tashi. A Klaxon sounded overhead.

"What the—" Gilgamesh walked to the edge of the tower floor and gazed out onto the city. Tashi followed, with the others close behind. They peered out and saw that the buildings in the city were unfurling massive sections of shimmering fabric along their lengths.

"Are those—" Sam began to ask.

"Sails," confirmed Gilgamesh. "But we're not scheduled to move until evening. Excuse me a moment." He pulled a small cylindrical device out of his pocket and spoke into it. "Why are we sailing?"

"Two human ships off our western coast, sir," a disembodied voice announced through the device. "Avoidance protocols have been automatically initiated."

Gilgamesh quickly turned to Vance. "Did anyone know you were headed here? Could you have been followed?" he asked anxiously.

"No to both questions. We took the dvergen subway."

Gilgamesh considered that for a beat. "Perhaps the loss of power when Iaira touched the crystal shut off the cloaking mechanism."

"But it was so fast," Iaira said.

"Human technology may be good enough to have caught the island. Even if it was just a blip on their radar, it was likely a mighty large blip," Gilgamesh concluded. "Let's hope that it's *just* these ships that are investigating."

"Sounds like it's time for us to get moving, kids," Vantana

announced as he headed to the elevator. But Gilgamesh stepped in front and put up a hand.

"You're not going anywhere, Ranger. Any immediate departures would put the city at risk," Gilgamesh explained. "You and the others will have to wait here for the next few days, perhaps weeks, until we're sure we aren't in any danger of exposing our existence."

"Sorry, but we can't do that, Mr. Mayor," Vance replied. "We're on a case for the gryphon."

"And it was the gryphon who established these rules, remember?" Gilgamesh replied.

"Mayor," a voice called out over Gilgamesh's device. He answered and stepped away.

"We can't stay here!" Sam quietly exclaimed to Dr. Vantana.

"I know that," the doctor told him. "But sometimes you just have to be agreeable, then do what you want when no one's lookin'."

Vance gestured for them to stay quiet and led them to the elevator's platform. They were almost halfway down when the elevator rocked suddenly. Gilgamesh leapt down from the capstone and caught up to them. The jolt knocked Iaira off balance, sending her over the side, arms flailing. Tashi dashed across the platform and grabbed ahold of Iaira's ankle as the rest of the princess's body swung perilously below the lowering elevator. Slowly Tashi pulled the frazzled princess back onto the platform.

"Sneaking off?" an irritated Gilgamesh said to Vantana, pulling himself up and using his height to its fullest advantage.

"Just hear me out," the doctor began, holding his hands up in mock surrender. "If we don't get Princess Iaira back to Ta Cathair, we're all going to have more to contend with than a few broken rules. We don't want a civil war beneath the sea anytime soon, right? So we can do this the easy way or the hard way." The elevator finally reached the floor, and Gilgamesh eyed Vance for a moment.

"Well, when you put it that way, Ranger . . . ," he said, stepping off the platform. He cracked his knuckles as he walked to the entrance of the tower. Then he turned and crouched into a fighting stance. He was grinning. "I'll take the hard way." He gestured for Vantana to come forward. The ranger sighed, clearly displeased by the choice, and moved toward Gilgamesh. Tashi put a hand on the doctor's shoulder, and he froze.

"I will handle this," she said firmly. She walked past Vance, who caught her arm.

"I don't think that's wise. If the stories are true—and trust me, they are—he's the greatest warrior who ever lived."

"All the more reason why *I* should be the one to face him," she said.

"But I can buy all of you some time to get away," the doctor suggested. "Take Sam and Iaira and finish the mission."

"It is unnecessary to risk your life," she said, and then lowered her voice. "Just be ready to leave quickly once I draw him away from the door."

Tashi strode forward, past her staff, which lay on the tower floor.

"At least use your shekchen," Sam exclaimed.

"It is not safe," she responded, thinking back to the blast at the cabin. Trying to draw power from Gaia might backfire now more than ever and in ways she could not possibly predict. It would be best to face Gilgamesh without her weapon and not risk endangering the others.

Tashi stopped a few feet away from Gilgamesh and took her fighting stance. She had fought large adversaries before, most notably the yeti during her escape from their hidden village. The difference was that the yeti were mostly driven by rage, while this opponent was cunning and much more experienced. She narrowed her eyes and nodded her head, signaling she was ready to begin.

"You're going to let a little girl fight your battles, Ranger?" Gilgamesh scoffed.

"Now you went and made her angry," Sam told him.

But Tashi of Kustos didn't get angry, at least not in the traditional human sense of the word. Guardians were taught to never let anger or any other emotion interfere with a fight. Instead of anger, Guardians felt an overwhelming urge to right a wrong. Their motivation was justice, not fury or pride. In this case, the perceived wrong that needed to be immediately righted was this immortal's belief that a Guardian's height or gender had a detrimental impact on his or her abilities as a warrior. Gilgamesh needed to understand that he was sorely mistaken—and Tashi was especially looking forward to the "sorely" part. She sized up her opponent, as she'd been taught, and recognized that he was all muscle. This meant he wasn't very nimble, and that gave her an advantage. Speed, endurance, stamina, were on her side, but she knew her biggest advantage was not physical. It was Gilgamesh's bristling overconfidence.

"This should be quick and easy," Gilgamesh said with a smirk.

"I agree," Tashi replied, before launching her attack on the four-thousand-year-old, undefeated warrior king.

Sam London had never read *The Epic of Gilgamesh*, but he was about to witness the epic fight of Gilgamesh and the Guardian Tashi. He didn't imagine Guardians got nervous, but that was okay. He had enough butterflies in his stomach for the both of them. Iaira gripped Sam's arm, eyeing him with distress, while Sam looked to Vance for his reaction. The doctor sighed heavily and shifted his gaze back toward the impending spectacle.

Tashi didn't waste any time getting started and propelled herself forward into four front flips. She threw her arm out to strike Gilgamesh but managed only to land a glancing blow on his right temple. *A warning shot*, Sam thought.

"Speed will not win the day," Gilgamesh warned. But Tashi was already in front of him again, sliding across the slick stone floor. She moved to strike a second time, and Gilgamesh thrust out an open palm that caught Tashi in the upper chest, sending her staggering back from the force. She shook it off and aimed for Gilgamesh again, successfully dodging a jab from him. But he had anticipated her adjustment.

His other hand hooked in and landed solidly on her back, sending Tashi careening into a wall. Iaira gasped and tightened her grip on Sam's arm. The Guardian deftly flipped herself over and pushed off the wall with her legs. Springing back toward her opponent, she took a shot at his face before spinning in the air and landing back in her fighting stance. This shot had connected hard, and a shocked Gilgamesh rubbed his jaw.

"Let's end this nonsense, Ranger," Gilgamesh said in a frustrated tone. "You will remain here a few days until it is safe to travel. I myself will arrange for your accommodations to stay in our finest hotel."

"As tempting as that sounds, we can't. Not now. Not with what's hanging in the balance," Vance told him.

Gilgamesh pivoted back to Tashi with a determined look. He began to take full advantage of the length of his arms and legs, deflecting the Guardian's attacks and keeping her at bay. Tashi repositioned herself and seemed to be eyeing her opponent more carefully, choosing her moments to move in and take calculated shots. The fight raged on and involved wrestling, boxing, and several martial arts fighting styles, many of which Sam didn't even recognize.

Gilgamesh was the quintessential unmovable object, and Tashi was the unrelenting force. Nothing seemed to faze her for more than a second—she just kept attacking, looking for weaknesses and testing his endurance. They appeared to be perfectly matched, until Tashi hung a spinning kick that nailed Gilgamesh in the face.

Not wasting a moment, the Guardian next came down hard on his foot, smashing it with a fist. Gilgamesh grunted and instinctively pulled his foot up off the floor. Tashi seized the opportunity and swept at the other leg. The big man crashed to the ground, and Tashi pounced, grabbing him in a sleeper hold. Gilgamesh grabbed at her arms, but she was already locked in. He slowly stood up, wavering, and then he began jerking his body this way and that, attempting to shake her loose. It was to no avail; Tashi was simply too strong to be thrown off. Gilgamesh thrust his body backward, hurtling toward the wall to smash Tashi against it, but at the last second she twisted her body around. Gilgamesh took the full brunt of the hit and collapsed into a sagging heap.

"Go!" Tashi exclaimed. Sam looked at the open path to the door. *She did it!* Now was their chance.

"C'mon!" Vance yelled to Sam and Iaira as he led them to the exit. They pushed open the heavy doors and came face to face with a battalion of scorpion men. Tashi looked up to see the group—a momentary loss of focus—but it was all Gilgamesh needed. He pulled her arms off him and flung her aside like a toy. Tashi went sliding across the floor before somersaulting and springing back up to her feet, ready to attack again.

"Now, hold on!" Gilgamesh bellowed, shifting his eyes between the fleeing guests and the indomitable Guardian. The mayor walked over to the door and waved his soldiers back, then leaned over to Vance. "If word spread through the Assembly that I allowed you to leave . . ."

"Oh, I get it now. . . . You're worried about the politics," the ranger realized. Gilgamesh shrugged slightly, raising his eyebrows in a *You caught me* expression.

Sam had a thought. "What's worse, Mr. Mayor, your people knowing you got your butt kicked by a kid a quarter of your size, or them finding out you let us off the island to stop a war?"

"Boy's got a point, Gil," Vantana said. "How about you let us go and everyone gets what they want?" Gilgamesh considered it.

"You have five minutes to get off the island. After that, I turn on the volcanic jets and no one will be allowed to leave," Gilgamesh replied, exasperated.

"We'll be on the subway and off in two," Vance told him.

"No, you won't. The subways won't run if the island is moving."

"Then how are we getting off this floating rock?" Vance asked. Gilgamesh leaned in, his voice quiet.

"You need to get down to the harbor and see Cletus. He's the only one who can get you off the island now . . . for a price, that is. Just don't say I sent you. He hates me. We ran against each other for mayor, and he's convinced he was robbed."

"Why are you telling us this, exactly?" Vantana asked him, skeptical.

"Let's just say I owe you a favor." Before Vance could respond, Gilgamesh added, "It's a long story and don't make me change my mind. Your clock is ticking. My men will secure the dock before the jets fire. You'd better be gone by then."

The mayor stepped away from the door and gestured for them to go. Sam waited for Tashi as the doctor and Iaira exited. The Guardian walked back toward the elevator to retrieve her shekchen before heading toward the entryway. As she was passing Gilgamesh, the mayor placed his hand on her shoulder. Tashi instantly spun like a top, ready for a fight, but Gilgamesh raised the other hand in a calming gesture.

"The fight is over. I merely wish to tell you that you remind me of someone I knew a long time ago. A *friend*. I don't make them easily, but now you have one for life."

Tashi bowed, appearing genuinely honored by the sentiment, and then she joined Sam.

"That was epic!" he told the Guardian excitedly. Tashi smiled ever so slightly.

"Yes, it was, wasn't it?" she said with a hint of pride as they walked out of the tower together.

Niles zipped them through busy canals, while Vance tried to make sense of the information gleaned from their contacts. First Squishy had said she knew him, and now Gilgamesh claimed to owe *him* a favor. . . . It didn't add up, especially considering he had never been to Atlantis. This was something he needed to ask Phylassos about, when the gryphon finally returned his calls, that is.

"We usually have a bit of a warning before the island sets

sail," Niles complained as he struggled against the current and hurtled over the rollicking waves. "But the crystal blinking out may have sped this up. Yous all wouldn't happen to know anything about that, would ya?"

"Can't say we do," Vantana replied, holding on tightly to the side rail of the platform as it rocked wildly. Niles nodded, but the doctor could tell he wasn't buying it.

Minutes later, the now shaky-legged foursome stepped off the water taxi's back onto the Atlantis harbor's boardwalk. It was a surreal version of Pier 39, with bizarrely shaped boats and colorful shops selling unusual wares.

"Where would we find Cletus?" Vance asked Niles.

"End of that dock," he said, nudging his long head in the direction of the main pier. "Can't miss him."

At a sprint they raced down the pier to the very end, but when they reached it, there was no one around.

"I thought Niles said we couldn't miss him," Sam said.

"Cletus?" Vance called out.

"Maybe he's already left?" Sam wondered.

"If he has, then we are—" Before Vance could finish his thought, a massive creature breeched the waters at the end of the pier and dropped its jaw onto the dock. The entire platform shook, and the four of them barely stayed on their feet. It was a whale. A blue whale the size of a small cruise ship.

"Twenty orichalcum for a trip around the bay. Thirty for a trip and a picnic lunch," the creature said in a deep voice. Sam leaned into Vance.

"Is that the whale—"

"I reckon it is," Vantana told him, before addressing the creature. "We're not interested in a trip around the bay. We'd like you to take us off this island right quick."

"Why?" Cletus asked suspiciously.

"We're on a case for Phylassos. We need to get to Cabo de Hornos National Park." Vance retrieved a small pouch of coins. "We've got forty-five orichalcum."

"Too far to go for such a small price," the whale said dismissively. "I'm not a charity. Good luck." He began to shimmy himself off the dock, back into the churning waters.

"Look!" Iaira called out, pointing down the pier. It was a battalion of scorpion men spreading out across the waterfront. Tashi turned toward them, preparing for a possible battle.

"They're securing the area before the jets fire," Vantana said, resigned.

"What are we going to do?" Iaira asked the doctor, who shrugged. He was fresh out of options.

"If Gil was telling us the truth, not much we can do."

"Wait. I think I have an idea," Sam whispered to Vance. "Follow my lead." He began walking away from the end of the dock, where Cletus was just about to slip back into the water. "Aw, well. I guess Gilgamesh wins this round, Dr. Vantana," Sam said in an exaggeratedly loud voice. Vance immediately figured out his play.

"Yeah, you're right. This is going to make that old coot pleased as Punch. I hate it when he wins and, man, he always wins," Vance added. Out of the corner of his eye, the doctor noticed that Cletus had come to a sudden stop at the edge of the dock.

"What do you mean, Gilgamesh will win?" the whale asked.

"He's trying to keep us on the island," Sam explained. "It's complicated, but this is *exactly* what he wants to happen. Don't worry. We'll let the mayor know you helped keep us here. Maybe you'll get a medal or something."

"Taking you from Atlantis will upset Gilgamesh?" Cletus clarified.

"It'll infuriate him," Vance said.

"I've had a change of heart," the whale replied. "Get in and leave those coins in the piggy bank. Hands off the snacks, though. I'm not that generous."

The massive creature's mouth opened wide, and Sam was stunned to see that it was also furnished. There was a bridge made of translucent material that arched over his enormous pink tongue, and in the very middle of the bridge were several movie-theater-style seats, as well as a small metal container that Sam speculated was a refrigerator. The four climbed into the whale's mouth and up the narrow bridge to the seating area. Sam fist-bumped Vance on the way, and the doctor mouthed, "Well done."

"Okay, we're ready!" Sam informed the whale.

Cletus lifted his head slightly and closed his mouth—immediately plunging them into complete darkness. Sam felt the drop from the dock and heard a splash, then sensed forward momentum.

A few moments later, Iaira blurted out in the darkness.

"Are you speaking to me?" she seemingly asked no one. "Oh yeah," she added.

"Who are you talking to?" Vance inquired in a hushed voice.

"Cletus," she replied. "I can hear him in my head. I mean, he can't talk, with us in here, obviously."

"Of course," Sam responded. "Can you mind-text him about the lights, then?"

"He can still hear you."

"Oh, right. Are there any lights?" Sam asked out loud.

"He says, 'Wait for it,'" Iaira responded.

There was a sudden rush of water, and Cletus's mouth was illuminated with blue specks of twinkling light that created an otherworldly gleam inside his mouth.

"Well, I'll be," Vance said. "He just pulled in some of that bioluminescent phytoplankton. It's like the ocean's version of foxfire."

It was still pretty dark, but they could at least vaguely see each other. And then there was a vibration sound, and another light source illuminated the space.

"Is that your phone?" Sam asked incredulously, pointing to Vance's pocket.

"That's odd. I don't ever give out this number," Vance said, baffled, as he pulled it out and hit the talk button. "Hello?" he answered.

"Were you the person who inquired about the model in one of our souvenir frames?" a female voice asked.

"It's for you," he said, handing the phone to Sam. "It's that picture place." It felt like years had passed since Sam had left a message at the souvenir photo frame company about his father's picture.

"Hello?" Sam said anxiously. Vance could hear the woman, as her voice echoed inside Cletus's mouth.

"Sorry for the delay. I wanted—to ge—back t—you," the voice stammered as it began breaking up.

"Yes, hello? Hello?" Sam pleaded into the phone. "I'm losing signal!"

"We're inside a whale deep in the ocean. I don't imagine there's a cell tower in here," Vance said.

"Cletus just texted," Iaira chimed in. "He isn't a fan of passenger cell phone use during trips. It gives him a migraine. Books, on the other hand, are perfectly fine. The paper kind, of course." Sam put his finger to his lips and pressed the phone to his ear, eager to catch anything that might come through. Vantana caught only a jumble of words from the woman on the other end. Something about privacy.

"I just need to know if his name is Marshall London," Sam said loudly. There was no response. He pulled the phone away from his ear, and Vance noticed that the home screen read: "Call Failed."

"Great! Just great!" Sam complained.

"Don't worry, kid," the doctor told him. "We can call back later."

"Sure, whatever," Sam said dejectedly, pushing the phone back into Vance's hand.

"I know it's frustrating, but why don't we all just relax and get some rest. We sure as heck need it. That goes for you too, Tashi," Vance said, sensing the Guardian was about to protest.

"Fine," Sam replied. "But first tell me why we're going to Cabo de Hornos National Park. Is that where the second sacred point is?"

"No. But that's where we can catch a ride to the location of the second sacred point."

"Where is it?" Iaira asked.

"One of the coldest, weirdest places on earth: Blood Falls."

Chapter 10

BLOOD FALLS

SL002–130–50

SOURCE: PR

DATE: ████████

Cabo de Hornos National Park has the distinction of being the southernmost national park in the world. It encompasses a group of islands in Chile at the southern tip of South America. The park plays host to several endangered species, as well as a variety of mythical creatures that originate from surrounding cultures. The area has been designated a Biosphere Reserve, and as such, all of the park's flora and non-magical fauna enjoy special protections.

Although Chile's Ministry of Agriculture employs a

private organization to manage the country's national park system, the true masters of nature in this part of the world are the Ngen, a creature from Mapuche mythology. The Mapuche are an indigenous people of the lower region of South America, also known as Patagonia. The Ngen work secretly inside the parks as rangers and aid in protecting magical and non-magical animals, as well as natural habitats.

Sam London was rattled awake in his seat by a sudden and jolting stop, which was followed by Cletus opening his giant maw. Blinding daylight poured inside, and when Sam's eyes finally adjusted, he saw that the whale had beached itself on a narrow strip of sand. Groggily, Sam stood and walked toward the exit, along with Vance, Tashi, and Iaira.

Once out of Cletus's mouth, they thanked the whale and said their goodbyes. The creature was itching—and shivering—to get back to the warmer waters of Atlantis. Standing on the rocky beach, they watched as Cletus wiggled his way back into the ocean and swam off.

"Well, I can cross riding in the belly of a whale off my bucket list," Vance quipped.

"Are those the austral waters?" Iaira asked, gesturing toward the ocean. Vantana shook his head.

"Not exactly," he replied. "The austral waters are a little farther south."

"Then what are we doing here?" Sam asked.

"I have the same question, Dr. Vantana," a voice said from behind. Tashi spun around, shekchen at the ready.

"He's a friend," Vance said, waving Tashi off.

The "friend" was a tall, slender man in a uniform that resembled those of America's park rangers. He had brown skin, dark eyes, and long dark hair that fell loosely out of his campaign-style hat. Sam noticed there was an ethereal quality to him, as though he were not entirely real. He appeared to shimmer at times, depending on at what angle the sun hit him.

"Antinanco, my apologies for not contacting you earlier," Vance said, stepping forward. He bowed his head; Antinanco did the same.

"An unusual way to travel, that much is certain," the man remarked, motioning to the water.

"You're telling me. We're here because we need your help," Vance told him. "This is Princess Iaira of Ta Cathair and we're trying to get her back home. Unfortunately, the path leads us right through Blood Falls."

"And you require transportation," Antinanco concluded.

"That's the short of it," Vance confirmed.

"And if I discourage you from traveling to that place?" the Chilean ranger asked.

"I appreciate the concern, but we don't have the luxury of choosing our destinations right now," Vance informed him. Antinanco nodded.

"Follow me, then," he said, turning and heading into a densely wooded area.

"I would like to know where we are traveling, Dr. Vantana," Tashi said, standing firm on the shore. "I have a responsibility to protect Sam London, and I cannot do so without knowing where we are going and what dangers we may face when we arrive."

"I understand," Vance replied. "We're going to where the clue directed us, Blood Falls in the austral waters. 'Austral' is another name for the Southern or Antarctic Ocean. The falls flow into Lake Bonney from the Taylor Glacier, so that is our next stop."

"Antarctica?" Sam said, shivering at the thought. Vance nodded.

"Hopefully, the only thing you'll need to protect Sam from is frostbite," he told Tashi. "Now let's get a move on. Antinanco is our ride, and we don't want to keep him waiting." Vance walked ahead with Iaira. Sam looked to Tashi and shrugged, then followed. He peered back to find the Guardian right behind him.

"So *how* are we getting there?" Sam asked Vance curiously, then glanced over at Iaira to explain. "I've been on a subway built by dwarves, on a giant mythical bird, in a sinkhole with skunk apes, on a Loch Ness taxi, and in the mouth of a giant whale. You never know how you're going to get places with Dr. Vantana," Sam told her cheerily. He shifted his eyes back to Vance, who had a wry grin. "So what's it going to be this time, huh? Are we riding on the back of a Mongolian Death Worm?"

"Nope. This time it's a dragon," Vantana replied matter-of-factly.

"A dragon! *Really?*" Sam asked excitedly. The doctor

nodded, and Sam pumped his fist in the air. He had always wanted to see a real dragon. He eyed the clearing ahead, his anticipation growing at what he would soon behold. But when they emerged from the woods, Sam did not see the promised dragon; instead he saw a long, narrow runway and a gray biplane with twin propellers that looked like it should be in a museum. Antinanco was standing beside the aircraft doing what appeared to be a preflight check. Vance was walking that way when Sam caught up with him. "Where's the dragon?" he asked. "Are we taking that plane to it?"

"The plane is it," Vance informed him with a wink. "That there is a de Havilland DH.84 Dragon," he added, gesturing toward the aircraft.

Sam sighed. "We're flying to Antarctica in that? It looks *ancient.*"

"That's one of the originals from 1932. Can you imagine? Still in great shape, considering," Vantana said.

"I've always traveled on private jets. . . . That looks like a death trap," Iaira announced with trepidation.

"It does not fill me with confidence," Tashi added.

"All of you need to just relax," the doctor responded. "It's perfectly safe. Trust me."

"Wait. . . . How far is Blood Falls from here?" Sam asked.

"About three thousand miles, give or take."

"And how fast does that thing go?" Sam followed up.

"About a hundred twenty miles per hour," Vance answered. Sam quickly did the calculations in his head.

"That's like twenty-five hours of flying . . . in *that*?" Sam said, growing increasingly concerned. Vantana didn't respond. He simply smiled and shook his head, then continued to the plane, with Sam trailing behind.

Unlike most propeller-powered biplanes Sam had seen in pictures and movies, this one had a cabin that appeared to be just big enough to fit the four of them plus the pilot. He ran his hand along the fuselage. It looked and felt old, and worse, it didn't appear to be metal.

"What's this made of?" he asked.

"Wood," Antinanco answered.

Sam's eyes immediately went to Dr. Vantana, who was holding the cabin door open, waiting for Sam, Tashi, and Iaira to board.

"We're flying to the South Pole in a plane made of wood?"

"Of course," Vance replied. "Antinanco is a Ngen. They're masters of the forest, so he prefers wood. Now climb aboard; we're killing time."

"I'd rather be killing time down here than getting killed up there," Sam retorted, pointing skyward.

"Like I said, you're just gonna have to trust me," Vance responded. "Now get in."

Sam eyed the doctor for a long while before finally stepping inside the cramped cabin; the others followed his lead. As they strapped themselves into the threadbare seats, the propellers roared to life. Antinanco guided the craft down the runway, picking up speed, and then took to the air. The plane bounced and rocked and tilted as it climbed steadily.

"You see, Sam, we don't need the fastest plane to get

where we're going. We need the slowest," Vance shouted over the engines.

Sam gave him a sideways glance. *What is he talking about?* Sam wondered. The Chilean ranger peered back at Vantana.

"Ready?" Antinanco asked. The doctor gave him a thumbs-up. Sam watched as their pilot took one hand off the yoke and placed it on the cockpit's ceiling. A wave of shimmering energy emerged from his fingertips and rippled through the fuselage like a stone tossed into still water. The sensation that followed was one Sam had never experienced before. The world slowed down until it felt like it stopped completely. The plane was no longer moving. Sam peered out the window to see that the earth below was also motionless. And then, suddenly, the earth began to spin. Quickly. The wind and clouds rushed by the windows at alarming speed, but he could have sworn the plane was still frozen in place.

"What's happening?" Sam asked Vance, the noise of the propellers no longer drowning them out. "Are we moving?"

"The earth's moving, but we're not," the doctor replied. "The Ngen aren't entirely of this world. They're sorta like spirits. As such, the laws of physics don't apply to them. They have a magic that allows this plane to stop in midair."

"So we're floating in the sky and the earth is still rotating beneath us?" Sam asked.

Vance nodded. "The earth and the atmosphere are still traveling at about a thousand miles an hour, but thanks to Antinanco we can just sit tight and let it pass under us."

"We're fast because we're slow?" Sam surmised.

"We're fast because we're still," Vance corrected him.

"This is officially my favorite way to travel," Sam declared. Vance smiled, then tipped his hat over his eyes and tried to get a little rest.

SL002-130-60
SOURCE: PR
DATE: ███████

Tucked within an Antarctic valley is Taylor Glacier, a moving mass of ice that flows into Lake Bonney, an ice-covered lake of salty water. At the junction of these two geological features lies the mysterious Blood Falls. Discovered in 1911, the falls appear exactly as their moniker implies, but the water isn't blood, of course. The color is the result of a scientific phenomenon related to the lake that lies beneath the glacier. It contains a high concentration of iron and salt, the latter of which makes the lake nearly unable to freeze. When the iron-rich salt water hits the oxygen in the atmosphere, oxidation occurs and forms red particles, creating a flow of red water that's made even more striking and ominous by the white expanse that surrounds it.

Antinanco touched his hand to the ceiling and Vance Vantana felt the Dragon rejoin Earth's rotation with a jolt. The propeller noise roared back to life and the plane shook and swayed as the doctor gazed out the small window at the strange frozen landscape below. It was a cold, forbidding place, and Vance hoped their visit here would be both successful and brief. *Tashi was right,* he had to admit to himself. She couldn't do a good job protecting Sam without knowing what to expect, but the problem was that Vantana had no idea what to expect. He felt anxious and uncertain—a feeling akin to walking on ice, and now he would be doing just that.

Antinanco landed the Dragon on the Taylor Glacier with the help of attached skis. Once they were out of the plane, the Ngen opened a duffel and doled out heavy winter parkas with hoods to the group to fend off the extreme cold. Iaira began to protest about the style and color but quickly thought better of it when the icy wind hit her face. Tashi was the only one who appeared at home in this climate, no doubt due to her time in the Himalayas. Though well below freezing, the weather was calm—a positive sign, Vance thought. He loved his omens.

Discreetly Antinanco pulled Vance aside.

"I have heard there is a cavern behind the falls, carved out of the ice by the dvergen when they considered building a subway station," he said. "It was abandoned shortly after construction began."

"Why?" Vantana inquired quietly.

"It is Antarctica," Antinanco replied with a sense of foreboding.

The doctor nodded. He knew exactly what the Ngen was trying to communicate. There were stories about Antarctica, tales of mythical creatures Vance hoped never to encounter. The Japanese culture had suggested the existence of terrifying sea creatures called the Ningen that made this place their home. The DMW catalogued and acknowledged their existence, but no DMW ranger had ever come into contact with the beasts, simply because no ranger had yet to have a reason to travel to Antarctica. It was just one more wild card Vantana had to be on the lookout for on this part of their mission.

"We'll see you in a bit," he said to Antinanco, who nodded and climbed back into the plane to wait for their return. "Let's get in, find the clue to the next point, and blow this oversized Popsicle stand," Vance announced. "We stay close to each other and don't touch anything that doesn't need touchin', got it?" Sam, Iaira, and Tashi nodded in agreement.

They ventured toward the falls, arm in arm, treading cautiously. Glaciers were treacherously slick and often had large crevices that intrepid hikers could fall into. Taylor Glacier was relatively smooth due to its geological origins, but Vance knew that meant its glassy blue-tinged surface was extra slippery. Everyone but Tashi fell down along the way.

After a frosty few minutes, the group reached the falls and Vance faced a new dilemma. Normally dvergen subway station entrances were found behind waterfalls. There were exceptions, of course, but the question was, Where would the dvergen have placed this entrance? This was not a flowing waterfall by any means. It was a slushy, icy stained mass of salt water that oozed down the glacier's surface. He spied a crevice to the right of the falls that appeared to be the right size for a door. Stepping up carefully to the icy wall, he spoke the words of the dvergen, and a door snapped open. Unfortunately, the door wasn't located in the crevice; rather, it was in the center of the falls.

Red seawater drizzled off the ledge above the narrow opening, and as they stepped through one after the other, their hoods and jackets were instantly stained by the rusty liquid. Iaira took the brunt of it, as a chunk of slush sloughed off just as she crossed the threshold, pushing the hood from her head and then showering her with a gush of icy red water. She squealed, and Vance pulled her through the rest of the way. She was shaking, and not from the chill. The vision she'd described in the tower had just come true. Vance caught her eye and tried to console her.

"It's not blood, remember. Just colored water," he said. She nodded and continued forward.

Luckily, it was warmer inside, but not by much. Lights flickered on, and Vance was glad the dvergen had gotten that far with their construction. He led the group down a small hallway to a set of stairs. At the bottom of the stairway they found a large cavern where the subway platform and subway car would normally have been. Though there was a platform, there was no car. The unfinished tunnel was filled with brackish, gritty water that rose almost level with the platform and was likely teeming with minerals and microorganisms.

"What now?" Sam asked, peering around.

"Maybe it has something to do with that." Iaira pointed toward the cavern wall. There was a series of small circular crevices carved into the surface, which appeared to be made of iron. Tashi gestured for everyone to stay back as she approached the wall. She studied the markings, then reached into one of the crevices and pulled out a small brown object.

"What is that?" Vantana asked her, unable to get a good look from his vantage point. Tashi sniffed it, and her eyebrow rose.

"I believe this to be a hazelnut," she said.

"That's weird," Sam remarked. "Do hazelnuts even grow in Antarctica?"

"Nothing grows in Antarctica," the doctor replied. He eyed the crevices, then moved back to get a better look at it. "Does that look fish-shaped to you?" he asked the others. Now that he was gazing at it in its entirety, the crevices appeared to form an outline of a fish.

"Yes, I can see that," Iaira said. "It *is* a fish."

"Are there hazelnuts at each of the points?" Sam asked Tashi. The Guardian nodded.

"It appears that way," she reported.

"Hold on. . . . How many hazelnuts are there?" Vance asked, an idea forming in his head. They all counted at the same time, but Tashi came up with the answer first.

"Nine. There are nine points to this drawing and nine hazelnuts," she revealed. "Is that significant, Dr. Vantana?"

"It sure is," Vance responded. "There's an old folk tale from Irish mythology about a creature who ate nine hazelnuts and got smart. Real smart."

"What kind of creature?" Sam asked.

"The kind the carving indicates," Vance said, gesturing toward the wall.

"A fish?" Iaira supplied.

"A fish," Vantana confirmed. "A salmon, to be exact. The Salmon of Knowledge. And there's only one thing worse than a person who thinks they know everything, and that's a salmon who actually does."

"So the salmon is the third sacred point on the journey?" Sam asked.

The doctor shrugged. "Or he knows where it is. Either way, let's get out of here right quick," Vance said, feeling as if they were being watched. They turned back toward the stairs and were halfway there when Tashi leapt in front of them. She twirled her shekchen and knocked down a long, pointed spear. It fell to the ground with a loud clang that echoed through the chamber. She spun to the source, charged her staff, and prepared for battle, but there was nothing there.

Vantana eyed the spear and noticed that it was gold in color. *Great*, he thought. He had hoped that the message in the Tower of Atlas was more story than warning, especially about the golden wolf. Unfortunately, it wasn't, and that meant things just got mighty complicated . . . and dangerous. So much for a quick getaway.

"Let's talk this out, Millalobo," the doctor announced, to no response.

"Who's Millalobo?" Sam asked. Vantana waved for him to be quiet. He tried again, this time with a slight modification.

"King Millalobo, please grant us an audience." Vance

wasn't one for honorifics, but Millalobo was a king of a royal family of mythical creatures from the Chilote mythology. Sure enough, the title did the trick and the waters began to stir. The creature emerged slowly.

His lower half was sea lion, and his upper was human. However, the creature's face sported long whiskers, black beady eyes, and silvery-gray skin. The rest of his body was covered in short golden-tinged hair, hence his name—Millalobo, or "golden wolf." He considered himself a master of the seas and protector of sea creatures. But unlike Cernunnos, Millalobo was not motivated by his own sense of self-importance or arrogance. He was royalty and, as such, believed he had a responsibility to protect his realm.

"Ranger Vantana." The creature spoke in a voice that sounded as though he were partially gargling. He also held the last syllable of his words a touch too long. "It is a pleasure."

"A pleasure?" Vance replied. "It didn't seem like a pleasure a second ago when you were chuckin' a spear at me."

"I do not wish to harm *you*, Ranger," Millalobo said. "You, the boy, and the Guardian are free to leave this place."

"You forgot Iaira," Vance informed him. "She's coming with us too."

"No," Millalobo said matter-of-factly. "She is a traitor to her people and must be punished." Vance instinctively positioned himself between Iaira and the golden wolf, while Tashi and Sam moved to do the same.

"She was lost . . . forgot who she was," Sam told the king. "We're trying to get her home."

"She abandoned her kingdom and does not deserve to return."

"Now, wait a second," Vance interjected. "She didn't abandon anyone. This is all just a great big misunderstanding."

"Maybe it isn't," a voice spoke up from behind him. It was Iaira.

"What do you mean?" Sam whispered.

"I mean, I think Millalobo is right. I remember . . . swimming away." Iaira appeared confused and contemplative. "I abandoned them."

"She left her city in chaos when they needed her most," Millalobo declared. "Justice must be done."

"Not like this," Vance told him. "We're on a mission for—"

"The gryphon. Yes, I know," the creature replied. "But he does not have jurisdiction *here*. I do, and I find you, Iaira, guilty on all counts. High treason against your kind, high treason against your city, high treason against your queen, the breaking of a royal oath—"

As Millalobo listed Iaira's crimes, Vance realized they were not getting out of this cave without a fight—and it was a fight they likely wouldn't win. But he had an idea. He still had the Atlantean crystal hidden in his pocket. Ever so slowly he slipped it out and positioned it close to Tashi. The Guardian noticed and quickly caught on to the plan, switching her shekchen to her other hand, the one closer to the crystal. Iaira had stepped forward by this point, and Millalobo was busily reciting a laundry list of all the many species of creatures the princess had betrayed. Fortunately, he was too distracted to notice the energy of Gaia entering the shekchen and feeding the crystal. The golden wolf was just finishing up when the crystal reached capacity.

"For your crimes, Iaira of Ta Cathair, you are stripped of your title and sentenced to death!" the creature bellowed, raising his spear.

"I think we're going to appeal," Vance said, aiming the crystal toward Millalobo. The king had no time to react. The energy blasted out of the crystal and slammed into Millalobo. He flew backward, careening hard into the iron wall, then plunged into the water and disappeared beneath the surface. The crystal itself shrunk as it released the energy, until it disappeared completely. *So much for that,* Vance thought. "Come on!" he yelled. Sam and Tashi were moving up the stairs, but Iaira lingered. Vance grabbed her hand. "Let's move, Princess!"

"Why did I swim away?" she asked Vance, distraught over the latest unlocked memory.

"I don't know, but you're not going to find out dead." She nodded slowly, then followed him up the steps.

As they made their way to the station's exit, Vance could hear Millalobo emerging from the waters below. He let out an angry yell, and what was troubling wasn't so much the tenor of his voice as what he said.

"Ningen!" he howled, the noise echoing throughout the cave like the ringing of a bell.

Chapter 11

SWIMMING UPSTREAM

The monsters emerging from the frozen lake beneath Blood Falls were among the creepiest Sam London had ever encountered. As Sam and the others climbed onto the glacier and made a slippery beeline for the aircraft, he caught a fleeting glimpse of the mythical Ningen. They were pure white with black eyes, no mouth, long legs, and arms with thin clawlike fingers. The creatures poured out of the ice surrounding the falls by the dozen and scampered up onto the glacier.

"Start the engines!" Vance hollered toward Antinanco, who was still waiting in the plane, as promised. Sam could see the propellers begin to spin.

The Ningen were already gaining, leaping and sliding on the ice as they hungrily pursued their prey. Tashi shot several jolts from her shekchen back at the beasts, but the hits barely slowed them down. One of the creatures broke away and managed to get alongside Iaira. It was about to pounce, when Tashi lunged and smacked it away with a blast from her staff. The monster got blown back into the horde, causing a pileup of bodies. But the creatures quickly regrouped and continued to give chase. Vance reached the plane and pulled open the cabin door.

"Go! Go! Go!" he yelled to Antinanco.

Antinanco pushed forward on the stick. Sam barely got his hand on the cabin door, and Vance pushed him inside. Iaira tumbled in next, followed swiftly by Tashi. Vantana was still hanging on to the plane when it lifted off the ground. But the Ningen had increased their speed, and at the last second one of the monsters leapt toward the aircraft. The doctor yelped as it grabbed ahold of his foot. He tried kicking it away, but its mouthless face suddenly cracked open to reveal razor-sharp teeth, which it used to bite into Vance's boot, hard.

Sam reached out and grabbed one of the boot's laces. He hurriedly worked to untie one half of the shoe until the boot was loose enough to slip off Vance's foot. Dr. Vantana shook his leg with all his might, and the Ningen plummeted back to earth with a snow boot lodged in its mouth.

"Thanks, kid," the doctor told Sam between breaths.

"You're welcome," he replied proudly.

Antinanco pointed the Dragon to the closest dvergen subway station, which was located in Fiordland National Park in New Zealand. Once they had all collected themselves and the earth was spinning below them, Vance explained the myth behind the Salmon of Knowledge.

"Like I said before, the salmon got his smarts from the hazelnuts," Vance told them. "But that's not the most famous part of the story. A warrior by the name of Fionn mac Cumhaill managed to help catch the salmon. Now, the myth claims he cooked the fish and ate it to gain the creature's knowledge."

"But that's not what happened?" Sam asked. Vance shook his head, and the plane began to descend.

"In reality, the salmon bargained for his life in exchange for sharing all his wisdom with Fionn. It still bristles Sal's scales to no end that not only is he not the sole know-it-all in the world, but he has to share that distinction with a human."

Upon landing in New Zealand, the foursome thanked Antinanco for his help and hopped a dvergen subway to Killarney National Park in Ireland, which was where the salmon supposedly made his home. After exiting the station behind the Torc Waterfall, they hiked along a stream until they reached a large lake, which Vance identified as Muckross Lake. Sam was exhausted by the time they reached the lakeshore, and plopped down on a rock.

"Now what?" he asked. "How do we find this salmon?"

"Well, that depends," Vance replied. "Iaira, can you tell me the percentage of oxygen in the Martian atmosphere?" Sam glanced up at him, confused.

"Excuse me?" she said, equally confounded.

"Can you tell me the percentage of oxygen in the Martian atmosphere?" Vance repeated firmly. "Yes or no?"

"No. But what does that—" she began, before being cut off by Vantana.

"Tashi, what is the name of the horse that won the very first Kentucky Derby?" Tashi stared at him blankly.

"The Kentucky what?" she asked.

"You can't expect her to know that," Sam interjected. Vance waved him off.

"Do you have an answer, Tashi?" He addressed the Guardian.

"No, I do not," she answered dryly.

"And, Sam, do you have any idea what I'd call a group of platypuses?"

"Uh . . . no," he responded. Sam was growing irritated now. After everything they'd been through, the ranger was wasting their time with stupid questions.

"Dr. Vantana, what is the point of asking us questions that we clearly—"

Vance quickly pressed his finger to his lips, shushing Sam. The gesture further infuriated Sam, and he was just about to give the doctor a piece of his mind, when a creature popped out of the water just a few feet from the shore. It was a salmon, about three feet long, floating upright, with a silvery body.

"Point one three percent, Aristides, and a paddle, though platypuses rarely travel in groups, so the use of the term is theoretical, at best," the salmon said in a huffy tone. "Ignorance pains me."

"Hey, Sal, how are you?" Vantana asked, not missing a beat.

"I should have known it was a human," he replied with a huff.

225

"Now, now, let's not be bitter," Vance said. "Just because Fionn tricked you—"

"He didn't trick me. He used me. There is a distinction."

"I'm not here to dredge up bad memories. I've come across some information that says you know where the third sacred point is on the path to Ta Cathair."

"Of course I know it," the salmon replied haughtily. "I am it. I am the only creature who can direct you to the fourth sacred point."

"Great, let's hear it," the doctor said, relieved.

"It is not that easy."

"It never is," Vance remarked. "What's the deal?"

"You must ask me a question I cannot answer," the salmon explained. "And it cannot be about the future."

"You mean we gotta play a game of stump the salmon?" Vantana asked.

"To put it crudely *and* rudely, yes," answered the fish. "Ask a question, and I have to answer. If I can't, then you learn the location of the fourth sacred point."

Vance considered it a moment. "How many questions do we get?" he asked.

"Until I'm bored. Which may be soon. I have a dinner to get to, and this is a futile exercise."

"All right. How many fried pickles did I eat at my tenth birthday party?" he asked quickly.

"Thirty-seven—" the salmon said, and the doctor was just about to protest, when the fish added, "And a half. Gross." Vantana deflated.

226

"Who was the great Guardian warrior who defeated twenty-eight yeti single-handedly?" Tashi inquired.

"Trickery does not suit a Guardian. It was Naljor the Holy and he defeated twenty-nine," the salmon answered without hesitating. "This does not bode well for your success."

"You're really not going to help us?" Vance pleaded.

"There are rules, Dr. Vantana. Unfortunately for you, this is an insurmountable obstacle."

"But it has to be surmountable," Sam said. "It makes no sense to lead us here, just to shut us down."

"Perhaps no one is meant to find Ta Cathair," the salmon suggested. Sam considered that but didn't believe it. There had to be a way. He thought about the hardest question he could ask, but before Sam could settle on it, Iaira spoke up.

"Why did I leave? Why did I swim away from home?"

The salmon turned his attention toward the princess. "Ah, an interesting query, but easily answered. You did not wish to accept your role in the future of the kingdom, especially in its hour of need. You were self-centered, arrogant, and head-strong. Not a pleasant combination in royalty, I must say."

"This role . . . was it my arranged marriage?" she asked.

"That was a part of it," the salmon replied, "a part you saw as regressive and unfair."

"It was and is," she said.

"Indeed, but it was decreed before you were born," the salmon claimed, "and was intended to help keep the peace. Now the peace is as tenuous as ever since the great war."

"The great war?" Sam inquired.

"The war among the selkies, mer-people, and finfolk," the salmon explained. "While the mer-people were a peaceful, matriarchal society, the selkies had a patriarchal, militaristic culture and had been at odds with the mer-people over control of Ta Cathair. The finfolk saw this conflict as an opportunity."

"The finfolk?" Sam clarified.

"They're a species of shape-shifting humanoid fish who use dark magic," answered Vance.

"Why did they care about the selkies or the mer-people?" Sam wondered.

"Because their own home of Finfolkheem had been destroyed in a civil war. They saw Ta Cathair as a way to resurrect their once great kingdom," the salmon said emotionless.

"They invaded . . . ," Iaira said. "They invaded, and with our forces split, the city nearly fell. It's coming back to me in pieces. . . ."

"The selkies and mer-people eventually joined forces to defeat the finfolk. The mer-people were allowed to continue their rule of Ta Cathair."

"Until now," Iaira added.

The salmon nodded. "Over the years, the tensions rose between the mer-people and the selkies. So an agreement was made to keep the peace," the salmon explained.

"I'm guessin' the agreement involved you marrying Maris," Vance concluded. Iaira nodded.

"When I learned of my mother's decision, I got angry and swam away," she said. "I vowed never to return. I don't remember much after that, except for waking up on Lief's fishing boat."

"Now I know why Maris was so determined to get you home," Sam noted.

"Speaking of which, we need to get back to business. The clock is ticking," Vance said. Sam hadn't settled on a question just yet, but Iaira's personal query had gotten him thinking. Whatever he asked, the fish had to answer.

"If you really know everything—" Sam began to ask the salmon.

"Which I do."

Sam pulled the souvenir photo frame out of his backpack and pointed to the model in the picture.

"Is this my father?" he asked.

"Sam, this is not the time—" Vance started.

"No," the salmon responded.

"So my mother lied to me," Sam concluded.

"No," the salmon answered, before adding, "A lie is intentional dishonesty."

"So she thought—"

"We're not here for this, Sam," Vance reminded him. "There's a war brewing. Shakin' your family tree will have to wait."

"Who is my father?" Sam asked the salmon, point-blank, ignoring the doctor's request. Vantana sighed.

"I am forbidden to answer that question," the salmon said. Vance's irritation at Sam's diversion instantly vanished, and the doctor was suddenly very interested in what the salmon had just said.

"Who forbade you?" the doctor asked.

"I am forbidden to say who forbade me," replied the salmon.

"I think you don't know the answer," Sam told him. "It's nothing to be embarrassed about." Vance caught Sam's eye—he knew exactly what the kid was trying to do.

"I know the answer," the salmon said, annoyed.

"Then go on and tell us," Vantana said. "Come on, Sal. You're the Salmon of Knowledge. It's not that tough a question."

"I cannot answer."

"Hold on now. Are you saying that's a question you can't answer?" Vance confirmed.

"Not because I don't know it," the salmon countered.

"That doesn't matter. There are rules, Sal," Sam reminded him. The salmon exhaled, exasperated.

"So be it. I value my existence more than my pride," he conceded. "The fourth sacred point on the path to Ta Cathair is, ironically, with your father, Princess."

"My father?"

"Metaphorically speaking," the salmon clarified. "If he believes you worthy, he will show you the way home." And with that, the Salmon of Knowledge ducked back into the water and disappeared.

"Great job, Sam." Vantana beamed at him. Sam appreciated the figurative pat on the back, but in this moment, he was still reeling from the salmon's words. "I know, kid. You've got more questions than answers. I've never known old Sal to be so cagey. He's a straight shooter. Pompous for sure, but honest. If he says he knows, he knows. And if he says he was forbidden, well—"

"But who could forbid him from telling us something like that?" Sam asked.

"There are few who'd intimidate him, I'll tell you that much," the doctor said.

"What about Phylassos?" Sam inquired.

"He respects the gryphon and would likely honor a request of that sort from him. But why would Phylassos care about your father?" Vance posited, then added, "Look on the sunny side of things—at least you know your mom didn't lie to you."

"That's true," Sam said. He had to admit that knowing his mother hadn't been lying to him this whole time was a huge relief. But there were even more questions that remained. Sam's mind was in overdrive.

"It's time to go," Vantana announced.

"To see my father?" Iaira asked. Vance nodded.

"To see Ika-Tere, the father of all sea creatures."

Chapter 12
MAKER OF GEMS

Despite having learned her true identity, Princess Iaira longed to return to her fake one. After all, things were so much simpler as Pearl Eklund. Not only simpler but fun, carefree, and comfortable. Ever since she'd touched the Atlantean crystal on Boca Chita Key, her world had turned upside down and inside out, and she wasn't exactly thrilled with its new direction. Who would be? She had nearly died on more than one occasion, and she didn't anticipate things getting any better. The know-it-all talking salmon had told her she was selfish, the golden wolf had said she was a traitor . . . and as far as she could remember, they were both right.

Knowing this, how could Iaira ever face her people again? Would they even forgive her? If the warnings were true and the kingdom was on the brink of war, was it already too late for her to make a difference? As the dvergen subway shuttled her and her new companions to the fourth sacred point, she kept to herself, lost in her thoughts. The fact that she was on her way to meet her "metaphorical" father, on top of everything else, was causing her anxiety level to soar and kick off this spiral of introspection. Fortunately, if there was any place in the world that could help assuage her unease, it was this destination.

"Welcome to the National Park of American Samoa," Dr. Vantana announced as they emerged from the station. The falls that hid the dvergen subway station were a cascading stream of clear water that ran against a cliff of jagged black rocks inside a lush, tropical jungle. The sheer beauty of it made everyone reflexively smile. It was truly paradise.

"This is the Amalau Valley. And that's one of the only stations behind an ephemeral waterfall," Vance said as he led them down a narrow trail that ran against the steep cliff side. "The waterfall shows up only when there's a lot of rain, but the dvergen felt its appearance was frequent enough to allow for a station," he explained. "Plus, it's pretty remote. They've got one here and also one behind a waterfall in O Le Pupu-Pu'e National Park on the island-nation of Samoa, which is a different country but all the same culture."

"And this is American Samoa?" Sam clarified.

The doctor nodded. "That's right. This park is the only U.S. national park south of the equator," he added. " 'Samoa' literally means 'sacred earth,' so it makes sense it would be a sacred point. The Samoan culture has a rich mythology, and the creature we are going to see is considered the father of fish. I've never met him, nor do I know anyone who has. He appears only to creatures of the sea. Word is, he can be found in Vai'ava Strait."

The thirty-minute hike followed a coastline of sandy beaches and azure waters that ran adjacent to Vatia Bay. The Vai'ava Strait separated the Samoan island of Tutuila from Pola Island, a group of emerald-topped volcanic land masses with hundred-foot cliffs. When the travelers crossed the beach and reached the end of Tutuila, Dr. Vantana turned back to Iaira.

"This is as far as we go," he said. "You'll have to swim the rest of the way."

"She has to go alone?" Sam asked. Iaira was just about to ask the same question and was appreciative that Sam was concerned for her. The thought of facing this Ika-Tere creature by herself was not at all appealing. Iaira hadn't been separated from her new friends since she'd discovered her true nature, and what if Ika-Tere turned out to be as angry with her as that seal person in Antarctica? She might have just met Sam, the doctor, and Tashi, but she had grown to rely on them. The Guardian had even saved her life twice.

"It's what's required," Dr. Vantana answered. "I wish there were another way."

"What about those injections?" Sam reminded him.

"What injections?" Iaira asked.

"We were given injections so that we could grow gills and go underwater if it became necessary," Sam explained, then added, "Long story, but it has to do with magic and blood. Sounds gross and it sorta is, but—"

"Just because we can have temporary gills doesn't make us creatures of the sea." Vantana cut Sam off with a stern look. "The last thing I want to do is upset him, especially when we need information. Iaira goes alone."

"How do we know he will not harm her?" Tashi inquired.

"Everything I know about this guy tells me he won't," the doctor said. "He wouldn't be in this park if he didn't respect the gryphon and the gryphon's law. Now, I can't force you to go, Iaira, but there's a heck of a lot on the line here, and I'm askin'—no, beggin'—you to go in there and find out where the final point is, so that we can get you home and prevent a war."

"I don't want to go home," Iaira said.

"Excuse me?" replied the doctor.

"I will find out where the last point is, but I'm not going with you," Iaira informed the group. "I think it'll make things worse." The princess had been contemplating not continuing on before she had arrived here. She'd even entertained the idea of running away back in Ireland, but that would have been rude, especially given how much these three strangers—and now friends—had sacrificed. However, this seemed like the perfect moment to separate herself from the journey.

"Now, Iaira, Maris was clear—" the doctor began.

"That's my final decision," she said firmly. "If I go in there and find out where the fifth point is, I get to go home to Miami. Deal?" Vantana sighed, then nodded.

"If that's what you want," he said.

"But, Iaira—" Sam started, but she put her hand up.

"We have shared quite an adventure since our time in that limo, Sam London. And I will miss all of you. But I betrayed my people. Millalobo was right—I'm not a princess. I don't deserve to be." And with that, Iaira walked into the crystal blue waters and dove beneath the surface.

She was quickly surrounded by brightly colored coral and schools of fish. Her legs transformed into a fin, and she moved swiftly toward Pola Island. She never thought she'd get completely used to this ability, but each time she changed, it grew easier and felt more natural. There had been a time when she was afraid of the water, but now it was her oxygen. Before Iaira knew her true form, she often wondered what it would be like to fly like a bird. She had imagined it would be freeing and thrilling at the same time . . . and that was the feeling she had when she swam. Up, down, sideways, looping, dropping, and twirling. She could do anything in an instant, and she loved the way the water slid across her skin, as if it were petting her, as if it cared for her. She wondered how she would handle this back home. She would have to find another outlet for her swimming, and a bathtub wouldn't cut it.

She reminded herself that there were plenty of beautiful underwater sights to see off the coast of Florida, and she'd have the benefit of a rich and rewarding life on land as well. The truth was that she felt more like a princess as Pearl Eklund than she had thus far as Iaira. Her penthouse at the top of a skyscraper was like living in a modern-day castle of glass and steel, and she had millions of loyal subjects in the form of her gems. As she was thinking back on her life in Miami, something caught her eye. There were schools of fish now flanking her on both sides. She stopped for a moment to let the fish continue, but they also paused. Stranger still was that both schools appeared to be formed into the shape of arrows pointing forward.

She knew this wasn't some bizarre coincidence and kept swimming where they directed. They led her toward the end of the island. The fish shifted again, pushing in front of her and forming an arrow pointing left. She followed, and they swam ahead of her, re-forming into an arrow pointing down. Iaira gazed below and noticed an opening beneath the cliff wall where the rock face met the seafloor. It was an archway opening that both schools of fish were waiting in front of. They wiggled their bodies, creating a shimmering effect that made the arrows flash like neon signs. Iaira steeled herself and ventured into the darkness.

Diving beneath the rock, she found herself swimming blindly in a long narrow cave with no light. She continued forward, using her hands on the walls to guide her. Finally she spotted a faint light in the distance. It grew brighter and bigger, until she eventually found herself in an undersea cave filled with bioluminescence generated by a host of sea creatures. Glowing jellyfish, squid, and sea worms lit up the water. Iaira stopped and admired this wondrous sight. Suddenly there was a whoosh of water as the schools of fish who'd led her to this point swam speedily past her. They bunched together, and with the help of some of the other creatures, they formed a face. There were two glowing eel-like worms for lips, a squid nose, and luminous jellyfish eyes. Stunned by the visage, Iaira had never felt so nervous before. It was extraordinary to see and even more extraordinary when the face began to speak.

"Greetings, Princess Iaira," the face said in an ancient voice that sent ripples through the water. She heard the sound, then felt it hit her body a moment later. *Should I say something?* she wondered. *Could I even speak underwater?* "You have yet to discover your voice beneath the sea, have you?" the face asked. Iaira shook her head. "Speak as you would above," he told her. Iaira opened her mouth and gave it a shot.

"H-hello," she said haltingly, her voice a gurgling whisper.

"Do you know who I am?" the face asked. Iaira nodded.

"You are the father of fish, the one they call Ika-Tere," she replied, her voice growing stronger. The face nodded.

"I have followed your journey since the beginning," he told her. "I have been there since your birth, as I am present wherever there are creatures of the sea."

"Then you know why I've come," Iaira said.

"Yes," Ika-Tere said. "Yet you do not wish to complete your journey."

"I don't think I belong there anymore," she told the creature.

"Is that the reason?" he asked skeptically.

"I gave up on them. They won't accept me. They won't trust me. And they shouldn't. I abandoned them, and there is nothing I can do to change that. Now, please, tell me the location of Ta Cathair so that my friends can help my people."

"I cannot," Ika-Tere informed her. "Only when you wish

to return home will you remember where home is. When you think and act as the princess you were born to be, a princess you will become."

"But I'm not that person," Iaira said. The face eyed Iaira for a long moment, as if studying her.

"You remind me of your namesake," he told her.

"There was another Iaira?" she asked. Before Ika-Tere answered, Iaira had a wisp of a memory return. "Of course. The first Princess Iaira. My ancestor," she suddenly recalled.

Ika-Tere nodded. "She was a young woman like yourself. Prideful. Willful. She lived a life of luxury, her every want provided," Ika-Tere explained. "And then war came to her kingdom and threatened her way of life."

"The finfolk. And what did she do?" Iaira asked, her memories still fuzzy.

"She sent her soldiers to fight and they suffered great losses. Her people looked to the palace and saw not leadership but fear. Fear of losing one's power. But if you fear losing power, you never deserved to have it," Ika-Tere said. "Do you know how the finfolk were defeated?"

"The mer-people joined forces with the selkies," she answered.

"Yes, but do you know why these two enemies united?" Ika-Tere asked. Iaira had another fleeting memory.

"The . . . Leviathan?" she said.

"Yes, the Leviathan is a monstrous beast who killed thousands of mer-people and selkies. He was unleashed by the finfolk when they grew impatient with their progress. But the creature alone was not why these two sworn enemies joined together, defeated the finfolk, and made a lasting peace."

"It was Iaira," she realized.

"The finfolk offered her a life of continued luxury if she surrendered and helped them defeat the selkies," he explained. "She was prepared to accept these terms to save herself and her people. And then, from her window she saw something that changed everything. A young mer-boy fighting alongside his father. The father was attempting to protect his son and family, until he was mortally wounded by the Leviathan. Undeterred, the boy took hold of his father's weapon and—with tears flowing from his eyes—continued to fight against a creature he could not possibly defeat. So moved by the father's sacrifice and the boy's courage, Iaira rejected the finfolk's offer. She climbed atop her prized sea horse and led the Leviathan into a cavern close to the city, and ordered her soldiers to cause a cave-in. They did as she demanded and trapped the creature for eternity . . . but Iaira did not escape in time. Inspired and humbled by the princess's sacrifice, the selkies put aside their differences with the mer-people and united against their common foe. Without the Leviathan, the finfolk were soundly defeated and were sent retreating into obscurity, never to be heard from again."

"This is the legend they tell schoolchildren," Iaira said. "To make them proud."

"It is not a legend, Iaira. It is the truth. I saw it happen."

"Maybe, but it doesn't change what I've done."

"You were a child when you left. Now you have a chance to return and show your people the woman you have become, to prove that you truly are of Iaira's blood. A chance to show your people that you serve a purpose greater than yourself."

"And if I don't?" she asked him.

"Then you don't. Only you can accept your calling," Ika-Tere said. "But I wonder . . . what is it that stops you from accepting yours?"

"Like I told you, I betrayed them," she said. "And now I am trying to protect them from the truth that their princess is not the one they deserve."

"I'm far too old to be fooled so easily. You do this to protect yourself. To avoid facing the pain of your past. Your refusal is not altruistic. It is selfish. And isn't selfishness what drove you to leave them in the first place?"

Iaira had often heard the phrase "The truth hurts," and now she understood its meaning. Ika-Tere had found the truth inside her reasoning, and she felt the shame that came with it.

"They would be better off. Please just tell me where it is—"

"No. Your people shall simply have to go on believing you abandoned them. There will be no chance for redemption, no cowardly way out," Ika-Tere told her.

"And what if there is a war?" she asked. "You are the father of fish. Don't you care?"

"Of course, but even I cannot change the tides," he said. "Or the creatures who swim against them. I'd hoped that you had changed, but I still see that scared child who swam away from her responsibilities. And perhaps you are right. Your people would be better off without that Iaira. Farewell."

Before the princess could protest, the school of fish scattered and the other creatures that had made up Ika-Tere's visage receded into the darkness of the cavern. The father of fish was gone. Iaira swam back through the opening with her failure weighing heavily on her mind. She had brought Sam, Dr. Vantana, and Tashi across vast distances, risking their lives, to what end?

Ika-Tere had told her that the only way she would recall the location of the final point was if she wished to return, but she didn't. She couldn't fake something that wasn't in her heart. She was fearful of facing her people, and terrified by the reality of her responsibility. How could she want to return to such an unknown when the known was so much easier, so much simpler, so much more gratifying? There was no need to seek validation from the people she'd abandoned. How could her presence make things better? Or stop a war, for that matter? It wouldn't, she concluded confidently. It was time for her to return to Miami and say goodbye to Iaira forever.

When she reached the shore and climbed out of the water to tell her friends the bad news, she didn't see them right away. Her legs transformed, and she began walking toward the sand, scanning the shore. She finally spotted Sam London waving his hands frantically, not as if he were saying hello but as if in warning. His mouth was moving, but Iaira couldn't make out what he was saying. And then she felt a terrible pain in her torso. She peered down to see a bleeding wound and then felt a similar burning sensation on her back. She spun around to find a mass of creatures swarming her. Hundreds of flying fish attacking without mercy, biting her repeatedly. Overwhelmed, Iaira collapsed into the water.

There was heavier splashing nearby, and then she was quickly pulled out and carried to the sand. Through bleary eyes, she saw Dr. Vantana and Sam London holding her, and beyond them was Tashi, using her weapon to shoot at the fish. A shadow fell across her vision and she found ground underneath her again. They were now behind a group of rocks that covered them on three sides from the onslaught.

Iaira convulsed in agony, and Vance tried in vain to hold her steady. It felt like her blood was on fire—a wildfire that was spreading throughout her body, even to the very tips of her toes. Poison, she concluded, her head pounding. As her heart fluttered and the world dimmed around her, Iaira knew it would be only a matter of time before she lost this battle, and with it her life.

Unlike the moment when she'd touched the crystal in Biscayne National Park, it wasn't the life she didn't know that flashed before her eyes; rather, it was the life she did. The life she hoped to return to. The charmed life of Pearl Eklund. And when it passed in front of her, she saw that existence for what it was: fleeting and empty. Iaira instantly understood what her namesake had realized watching the young boy and his father so many ages ago. Her ancestor's power had been an illusion, just like Pearl Eklund's fame and status. If Iaira died on this beach, the world would go on spinning, unaffected by her absence. Having had no real impact on the world, she would be forgotten in time. All of the fame that Pearl enjoyed, all of the fans, all of the perks, all of the splendor, hadn't made a difference in the world, and it certainly wouldn't stop a war. Her life in Miami was shallow and superficial, and it would come to an end here on a remote island beach . . . for nothing. In that moment Iaira wanted to return home and fulfill her purpose more than anything she had ever wanted before. But if it was too late for her, perhaps Sam, Vance, and Tashi could make the difference on her behalf.

Just as Ika-Tere had promised, the moment her heart wished for home, Princess Iaira remembered the location of the final point. All of her memories rushed back to her on the beach as she fought death, and through the pain, she saw that the answer she was seeking had been right in front of her the whole time.

She grabbed Vance Vantana's arm firmly and spoke with what felt like her last breath.

"Ta Cathair is in Ratnakara, the maker of gems."

Chapter 13
TA CATHAIR

After all these years, it was a snooty talking salmon who pulled the patriarchal rug out from under Sam London. As Sam waited for Iaira to reemerge from the water off the coast of American Samoa, he mulled over the admission from the Salmon of Knowledge regarding the identity of his father. He wondered—if the salmon had been ordered by the gryphon to not divulge this information, did that mean it was dangerous in some way? But how could knowing such basic information about his life be harmful? And when did the gryphon order the salmon not to discuss it? Was it before or after Sam met Phylassos in Death Valley? He was trying in vain to make sense of it all when his eyes caught sight of a rainbow, and Sam London just happened to love rainbows. In fact, he always made it a point to try to spot them in the skies over Benicia on rainy days. He would even attempt to persuade his mom to chase the rainbows, which she would do on occasion. He was fascinated by them, especially when there was more than one visible at the same time. His personal record was a triple rainbow, though his mom claimed he was counting a second rainbow twice.

The rainbow in American Samoa appeared to end just a few hundred yards off the shore and happened to be the most brilliant and colorful Sam had ever laid eyes on. Strange thing was, rainbows were the result of light refracting on rain droplets, hence why they accompanied storms, but there wasn't a cloud in the sky.

"Check out the supercool rainbow!" Sam exclaimed to Vance and Tashi. Vantana looked up, but instead of displaying an expression of wonder, he was instantly alarmed.

"Get down!" he wailed, and hurled himself on top of Sam, flattening them both on the sand. Sam took in a mouthful of grit and was about to protest angrily, when he noticed Tashi crouching, her shekchen charged and at the ready.

"What? What is it?" Sam asked.

"That," the doctor said, motioning out toward the water. Sam followed Vantana's gesture and saw a creature riding down the rainbow, as though it was surfing the colored band of light. It splashed into the ocean, then sprang back up. The rainbow disappeared, and the creature who was now standing on the water's surface was monstrous. It was a humanoid fish with dark grayish-green scales instead of skin; a dorsal fin on its head like that of a shark; and a long serrated bill instead of a nose, akin to the beak of a swordfish. Whatever the creature was, it must have been over six feet tall and had legs that were lined with fins . . . and it wasn't alone. There were dark-colored fish leaping up and down from the water behind the creature, whose hand was raised, as if he intended to give a signal.

"We need to find shelter, A-SAP!" Vance ordered.

"You think it's going to attack us?" Sam asked, a hint of disappointment coloring his words at the thought of the rainbow surfer being dangerous. Vantana flashed him an incredulous glance. "I mean, maybe we need to talk to it, tell it we're on a mission for Phylassos," Sam suggested hopefully.

"That 'it' out there is an Adaro from the Solomon Islands," the doctor informed him. Sam still didn't understand what that meant. "He didn't come all this way to bake cookies and make friendship bracelets. He means business, and unfortunately for us, his business is death."

"I will keep him at bay," Tashi offered. "Get Sam to safety."

"I appreciate that, but you see those fish behind him?" Vance asked. "They're poisonous flying fish that he commands like an army. There's not enough energy of Gaia surging through your shekchen to take care of all them critters."

"Poisonous. Flying. Fish?" Sam asked in disbelief. "Like venomous snakes?"

"Worse," Vantana replied. "This poison is magical in nature. It will kill, and we know of no antidote."

"Of course," Sam said, his brow furrowing. "What are we going to do when Iaira comes out of the ocean?"

"She already is." Tashi pointed. Sam looked to the water and saw the unthinkable. Iaira was emerging from the ocean, oblivious to the danger lurking just feet behind her.

"Aw, nuts!" Vance exclaimed.

"She doesn't see him!" Sam cried, and started frantically waving his arms. "Go back under the water!" he yelled again and again, but it was too late. The creature swung his hand forward, and the swarm of flying fish leapt out of the water, attacking the mermaid with ferocity. It was like something out of a horror movie.

"Tashi, give us cover fire!" Vantana ordered the Guardian. "Distract that monster! C'mon, Sam—"

Tashi stood and let loose with her shekchen, firing multiple bursts of energy at the creature. Sam followed the doctor to the water, where they waded in and grabbed Iaira, then pulled her to the shore. Sam could already see that her face and body were covered in bites. But these bites didn't bleed; they glowed red and black. Crooked lines webbed out from the wounds and crawled across her skin. Vance led them to a rocky outcropping, where they all hunkered down. Once there, Iaira latched on to Vance's arm and spoke, but Sam couldn't make out her words. Her breathing was labored and her voice was nearly a whisper. Vance nodded, as if understanding.

"Thank you," he told her.

"What did she say?" Sam asked.

"The final point is in the Indian Ocean," Vance revealed. "The Sanskrit name is Ratnakara, which means 'maker of gems.'"

"Is she . . . ?" Sam began, but didn't have the heart to finish. Vance confirmed her fate with a nod. "Tashi could try to heal her," Sam suggested. The Guardian did have the ability to heal, which she had used to save Sam's life in Kustos on his first case. She absorbed his wounds and, because she was a Guardian of the gryphon's claw, could then heal herself. Sam hoped this same magic could be applied to Iaira.

"I don't know if that would work," Vance told him. "But we can't even try. We need Tashi shooting down those fish or we're all goners."

Vance was right. Tashi was already struggling just to keep the hordes of fish at bay. If she tried to heal Iaira—never mind whether it would work or not—it wouldn't help their predicament one bit. They would all wind up like Iaira. It was an impossible situation. As Sam wondered what their fate would be, he heard Iaira whispering again and again, repeating a series of words. Sam leaned in to listen.

"Ika-Tere . . . father of the seas . . . I beg of you . . . help us . . . ," she said, barely audible. She continued for a while, and then suddenly she stopped. A slight smile crept over her wounded face. "Thank you," she murmured.

Sam wondered if the mermaid was hallucinating. Perhaps the poison was affecting her brain now. Why was she thanking Ika-Tere? Their situation was just as dire as it had been moments ago.

"What the—" Vance said in surprise as something flew overhead, casting a shadow over the beach. Sam peeked over the rock to get a better look.

"What is it?" Sam asked.

"More like, Who is it?" Vance corrected him. Tashi was smiling broadly. This was the first time Sam had ever seen a smile this big on the Guardian's face—not counting the tanuki who had taken her place in the school library, of course.

"Nafuana!" Tashi exclaimed, her excitement boiling over.

There was a woman now standing on the beach. She had long dark hair and was dressed in a wood-colored cloth with a fringed hem. She sported several tattoos that consisted of geometric shapes and intricate lines. She gripped an ax-like weapon that hooked on one side. Upon her arrival, the flying fish suddenly ceased their attack and retreated back to the Adaro, swirling in the air above him—no doubt waiting for their next command.

"And she is . . . ?" Sam asked.

"A guardian," Tashi said, beaming. "But not like me. She is a guardian of her people, a warrior princess I studied in my schooling in Kustos. Her ax is known as the Tafesilafa'i and she built it herself," Tashi added, pointing to Nafuana's weapon.

"She's a popular figure in Samoan mythology," Vance added. "And luckily for us, she's also a force to be reckoned with."

"But he has an army," Sam reminded them.

"She *is* an army," Tashi contended. Nafuana stared down the Adaro unflinchingly, then glanced back toward the rock Sam and the group were hiding behind.

"Guardian," Nafuana commanded. Sam looked to Tashi, who appeared frozen in place. He nudged her.

"I think she's talking to you," Sam told her. His friend snapped out of her stupor.

"Yes, Nafuana. How may I be of aid?" Tashi asked, bowing her head.

"You are formidable and have kept your friends alive, but I am here to help defeat this vile creature, so that you may do what is needed to save Iaira." Tashi bowed again.

"Thank you," she said, before turning toward Iaira and crouching down next to her. "I will try to heal your wounds," Tashi told the princess.

Tashi placed her hands on Iaira's shoulders. A second later she jerked her body and gripped the mermaid tightly. She closed her eyes, and Sam could see a few of the bite marks on Iaira's body begin to close up, the blood that had trickled out was pulled back inside, and the black lines that had branched out disappeared. The wounds were then mirrored on Tashi's body, cropping up in the same spots where they had been on Iaira. Sam stared, wide-eyed, until the wounds on Tashi also began disappearing. It was working, Sam concluded. He felt a giant sense of relief, until he turned to look back at the water.

The Adaro had amassed an even larger swarm of flying fish. With a wave of his arm, the poisonous mass rocketed toward the shoreline, but Nafuana remained stoic. She didn't even raise her weapon. Sam wondered how she would defend herself against so many creatures.

"*Pe'a vao!*" the Samoan warrior cried out. The trees began to shake, and the cracking of branches could be heard. Multiple shadows passed overhead, and Sam gazed upward. These shadows were enormous and moving. Giant black-winged creatures launched from the trees of the adjacent jungle and descended on the beach.

"Are those bats?" Sam asked.

"Yep. They call them the Samoan flying fox," Vance explained.

These bats had wingspans of at least three feet, and they swooped down onto the flying fish, quickly cutting them to shreds.

"Woo-hoo!" Sam exclaimed. Nafuana glanced back with a smirk, then turned her attention to the Adaro, who was already preparing for his next onslaught. This time he had even more beasts at his disposal, and he was walking toward the group. Nafuana took a defensive stance. The Adaro charged, with his monsters in tow. The bats descended once more and drove back the swarming creatures, while Nafuana slashed at the Adaro, then booted him in his scaly chest. He flipped backward several times from the force of her hit and grasped at the open wound on his torso. The Adaro snarled, clearly unhappy with his results, and gazed up at the sky. He made a series of ominous clicks and whistles like a blend of dolphin sounds and the clatter of a rattlesnake tail. A second later, Sam spotted another rainbow . . . and another . . . and another.

At any other time in Sam's life the sight of multiple rainbows at the same time would have been thrilling beyond words. He would have bragged to complete strangers about it and marveled in its wonder for years after the last one had faded away. But now these extraordinary bands of color were not conjuring smiles or happy thoughts; they were instilling sheer terror. An Adaro creature sailed down each of the rainbows, bringing its own small army of flying fish.

"And the hits just keep on comin'," Vance quipped. "Millalobo was trying to prevent Iaira from returning home because he believed she needed to be punished for her betrayal. I didn't agree with him on that, but I could understand the logic. These monsters, on the other hand, don't have any moral code. Something else must be motivating them to have a throwdown like this."

"Like what?" Sam asked. Vance shrugged.

"I don't know. Maybe they want a war," he replied. "We'll get to the bottom of it, but first we have to get past them."

"There are so many!" Sam exclaimed.

"She doesn't look too worried," Vantana remarked, gesturing toward Nafuana. He was right. Much to Sam's surprise, Nafuana was completely unfazed by the creature's newly arrived reinforcements.

Peering back to check on Tashi and Iaira, Sam found that the Guardian was clearly fighting the pain Iaira's wounds had inflicted, while the mermaid appeared to be completely healed, though still unconscious.

"There is a problem," Tashi said.

"What problem?" the doctor asked.

"Observe," Tashi said. As she removed her hands from Iaira's body, the wounds began to return. Sam spotted a bite materializing on Iaira's leg.

"She's not healing?" Sam inquired. Tashi shook her head.

"I can heal her, but it doesn't last. Once I lift my hands, her wounds return," Tashi explained. "We must find a cure."

"I was afraid of this," Vance told them. "It's the magic—it's too strong."

"Ta Cathair," Iaira whispered. She was barely conscious, but talking. "The healers in my city . . . they can cure this. . . ."

"Which means we gotta get you out of here pronto," Vantana said. He turned back to talk to Nafuana, who was engaged in a pitched battle with the Adaro creatures. She spun, dodging jabs from one Adaro, to then punch another, before drop-kicking a third. Sam understood why Tashi revered her so much—she was unstoppable. Problem was, the Adaro did not appear to be stopping either. The fight might last hours, maybe even days, and as strong as Tashi was, keeping Iaira alive for that long seemed unlikely.

"Nafuana!" Vance called out to her. She managed to glance back while continuing to fight. "We need to get the princess home. Do you think we'll make it to the falls if we hug the cliff side?"

"Not all would survive that journey," she replied, before dodging a few more strikes. "But there may be another way. Warrior?" she called out to Tashi. "Keep a strong hold on Iaira." Tashi nodded and wrapped her arms around Iaira from behind as Nafuana cried out, *"Pe'a vao!"*

Three of the flying foxes that were battling the poisonous flying fish instantly changed direction and headed for the shore. They dove down and hovered above the group. "Go!

Tofa Soifua," Nafuana said, before turning back to the marauding Adaro.

The flying foxes snatched each of them by the backs of their shirts. Tashi held on tight to Iaira as one scooped both of them up. Sam's fox had a solid grip on him, but he reached up to hold on to the creature's short legs for extra security. The Adaro creatures spotted the attempted escape, though, and concentrated their fish on the group. As the bats made their ascent, a few of the flying fish came within inches of biting Sam and Vance but were quickly dispatched by other flying foxes. With the Adaro creatures redirecting their attack and leaving themselves vulnerable, Sam watched with delight as Nafuana drove the monsters back into the water.

Before long, the group was soaring over the National Park of American Samoa toward the ephemeral falls and the dvergen subway station. Sam glanced over to Tashi and noticed the Guardian wincing, no doubt from the pain of healing Iaira's wounds. As long as Iaira was hurt, Tashi would be unable to defend the group from potential threats. Considering the dangers they had confronted of late, Sam couldn't help but feel anxious about the journey ahead.

Tashi of Kustos was worried. It was a sense of foreboding, which was not a familiar feeling for the Guardian. And it didn't stem from her concern about the dangerous creatures who might attempt to sabotage their mission, nor was it due to the toll the healings were having on her body. Tashi was concerned about Sam London. She needed to speak to Dr. Vantana about her unease but had yet to have a moment alone with the ranger to do so. When they arrived in Sri Venkateswara National Park in Andhra Pradesh, India, via the dvergen subway, Iaira was again nearly covered with bites. Tashi healed her once more in the station that was hidden behind Talakona falls, before venturing outside. While Tashi regained her strength, Dr. Vantana and Sam placed Iaira on an elephant with the help of Dandak, the park's forest officer from the Mythical Wildlife Institute of India.

"Can you take us to the coast?" Iaira asked Dandak, who nodded. "I can summon help to get us the rest of the way home."

Once Sam began walking ahead with the new ranger and Iaira, Tashi was finally able to approach Vance in private.

"Dr. Vantana?" she said quietly.

"I know what you're gonna say, Tashi," he replied.

"You do?" she asked, surprised.

"Of course, and you're right," Vantana added.

"I am?" she followed, still caught off guard by the doctor's response.

"You bet," he said. "We've been putting ourselves in a heck of a lot of danger, and—"

"That goes without saying, but that is not what I wish to talk with you about," Tashi interrupted before Vance could continue any further. He had tried to anticipate her concern and had completely missed the mark. "There is something that has been troubling me, and the closer we get to the coast, the more concerned I become."

"To trouble you, it must be mighty troublin'," Vance remarked. "What's up?"

"We will be breathing underwater with the injections Ranger Naughton provided, correct?"

"Yeah, that's right. Our bodies will react to the lack of breathable oxygen, and the serum's properties will kick in, giving us the means to breathe like an aquatic creature. I've done it before. You grow gills for a little bit—it's no big deal. Although, it's freaky at first as your—"

"You misunderstand my reason for bringing this up," she interjected. "I am not worried about growing gills. I am worried about Sam—"

"He'll be fine," Vance tried to assure her. Tashi really wished this human would stop trying to predict her intentions.

"I'm sure he would be, but he did not receive the same serum that you did," she pressed. Vance eyed the Guardian, suddenly serious.

"What do you mean?"

"I mean, I watched Ranger Naughton give you the injection in Sprite's cabin. It was light blue in color, but the one given to Sam when he was still unconscious appeared dark blue, nearly black."

"Well, he had problems with the effectiveness of the bigfoot serum, so maybe it was a stronger dose," he suggested.

"A dose like my own?" she asked. Vance looked at her sideways, uncertain of her meaning. She continued, "The dosage he received was the same as the one I received. And, as you know, my blood is rather unique."

"Yeah, I know," Vance told her. "But all I can tell you is that while I'm not totally familiar with Ranger Naughton's methods, they work. Penelope wouldn't do anything to harm Sam. We'll know straightaway if the serum isn't working, and we'll cross that bridge when we get there." He winked at Tashi and continued ahead, but the Guardian hung back for a moment. She didn't doubt that Ranger Naughton knew what she was doing; quite the contrary. Tashi believed the ranger was extremely adept at this science, and that is why the situation confounded Tashi. She wondered if there was something that Ranger Naughton was hiding, something about Sam London that she knew but no one else did.

"Tashi!" Sam yelled back with an arm in the air. Iaira's wounds must have returned, Tashi concluded, and she raced ahead to heal the mermaid's body once again.

By the time they reached the shoreline, Iaira had already undergone two additional healings. They were increasingly losing their effectiveness, and Tashi knew it would not be long before the healings ceased working altogether.

Upon Iaira's request, they carried her to the water's edge, where she dipped her hand in the ocean.

"Makara," she whispered with her hand submerged. A few moments later, a mass of bubbles appeared on the water's surface and a creature emerged. Dandak bowed almost immediately.

"What is that?" Sam asked.

"That, my friend, is the Makara. An ancient creature whose name is derived from the Sanskrit for 'sea monster,'" Dandak explained. "It is associated with Ganga and Varuna, two legendary beings from my culture's mythology."

Tashi found the creature's appearance to be, in a word, confusing. It was as large as an elephant and had an elephant's trunk, but its lower jaw jutted out and was lined with sharp teeth, like that of a crocodile. Its two front legs were also like those of a crocodile, but its hind legs were flippers, and its tail was that of a walrus. It sat in the water and waited as Dandak and Dr. Vantana placed Iaira on its back.

"He is one of the protectors of Ta Cathair," Iaira said softly. "He can take us to the city's edge. Everyone, climb on."

One by one, Tashi, Sam, and Dr. Vantana mounted the creature. Tashi took a place behind Iaira and in front of Sam, so that she could heal one and stay close to the other.

"Please tell the Makara that we will need to adjust to the water," Vance informed Iaira. "It might take a few moments for us to develop the gills necessary to breathe."

"He is now aware," the princess replied. "Hold on."

The Makara dove into the ocean, and Tashi instinctively held her breath. Vantana nudged her and Sam. He pointed to his mouth—which was closed—and shook his head. He opened his lips and breathed out the remaining oxygen in his lungs. It bubbled up to the surface. Closing his eyes, the doctor took in a gulp of water. His body began convulsing immediately, desperate for air. Sam appeared horrified by the display, so Tashi reached out and grabbed his hand to comfort him.

She pointed to Vance's neck, right below his ears—the skin was opening up. Three slits appeared on both sides and began to open and close, taking in water. A moment later, Vantana opened his eyes and gave a thumbs-up.

"You should be able to hear me," the doctor said. He looked to be speaking normally, but his voice sounded different, as if it had vibrato. Tashi knew she could hold her breath for much longer than Sam but decided it would be best if she made her transition before him so that she could concentrate on his reaction to the serum. She released the oxygen still in her lungs, and her body demanded a breath. The Guardian took in the ocean water, and her body spasmed, trying to reject the liquid now filling her lungs. A wave of warmth rippled over her skin, followed by a stinging pain below her ears. Her skin split open and gills formed. Tashi suddenly had control of her body once again and was relieved to have the unpleasant experience behind her. Turning her attention to Sam, she waited for his transformation. Sam's eyes were wide, and Vance put a hand on his shoulder.

"It's gonna be okay," the doctor told him. "You got this."

Sam exhaled, and the ocean water rushed inside his body. Just like Tashi and Vance, the boy convulsed. His expression was one of sheer terror. Sam's body continued to shudder, and Tashi grew concerned.

"Maybe we should bring him back to the surface," she told Vantana.

"Just give it another moment," he suggested. Sam's head hung down on his chest, his body still shaking. The Guardian eyed the doctor.

"This is not right," she said. "I will return him to—"

"I'm fine!" she heard a voice exclaim. She peered back to Sam to see that he was exactly that—fine. There were gills forming below his ears, and Tashi noticed a twinkle in his eyes when they had finished—a sparkle of light that she had not seen in Vantana's. She caught the eye of the doctor, who shrugged, as if to say, *I guess it worked.*

"This is the coolest thing ever!" Sam announced, the water rippling from the sound waves he created. Perhaps she had just been overconcerned, the Guardian concluded.

With all of them transformed, the Makara dove deeper into the water. The last glimmer of light from the surface above winked out, and darkness enveloped them. Fortunately for Tashi, her eyes were sensitive enough to see in the darkness, and she surmised that Ranger Naughton's injection might have also helped enhance this ability. There wasn't much to see at this depth—she'd occasionally spot a fish or two, but otherwise it was barren. Every time it appeared they had reached the seafloor, the Makara somehow managed to find another crevice or valley that would take them even farther down. After a few minutes of this continuous dive, Tashi spotted what she thought might be the end of the journey. There was a faint light in the distance that was becoming less faint by the moment. When they got closer, the Guardian could see it was a ring of iridescent coral that was at the mouth of a tunnel, lined with the same phosphorescent material.

"The entrance to the city," Iaira told the group in a labored voice. Tashi noticed that the princess's wounds had returned in full. The marks from the bites on her face made her hardly recognizable anymore. But the worst part was, the Guardian had her hands on the princess the entire time. As Tashi suspected, her healings could no longer come fast enough. She had seen this young woman transform before her very eyes— and she wasn't talking about her fin. Just days earlier, the princess had been basking in her wealth and fame. She'd been consumed with vanity and materialistic pursuits and obsessed with her own popularity. She'd sought the approval of complete strangers, her gems, and had cared only for herself. But through this journey, the Guardian had watched these last vestiges of Pearl Eklund fade away. Now Tashi hoped they would reach the city with enough time to save Princess Iaira.

The Makara entered the coral tunnel, and the twinkling colors passed by them with such speed that the colors began to blend and blur together. The group was zooming through a portal, twisting and turning and dropping deeper.

"No worries now, Princess," Sam assured her. "We'll get you cured."

They shot out of the tunnel like a rocket and into a massive cavern. Tashi simply assumed it was a cavern, given the manner in which they arrived, but she could not see the walls in any direction except for the spot where they had emerged. Sitting in front of them, though, was a city unlike any Tashi had ever seen—an undersea kingdom that made Atlantis seem dull and lifeless. Surrounding the city were farms of multicolored seaweed and glowing aquatic plants and flowers. There were aquatic animals that Tashi did not recognize, including a creature that appeared to be a full-sized cow with flippers and birdlike fish with colorful fins that resembled wings, among others. Beyond these fields was the city itself—a coral and crystal metropolis that sparkled and glittered in the bluish bioluminescent light that emanated from the city's streets and buildings. She could hear the roar of a crowd in the distance, and Iaira perked up.

"Of course," she muttered. "Take us, Makara. . . ." The Makara shifted direction and headed toward the noise. The origin was the most illuminated spot in the city—an undersea arena that reminded Tashi of the ancient Colosseum in Rome, Italy.

The Makara let them off in a field of seaweed on the outskirts of the kingdom. Tashi could see crowds of mer-people and selkies entering the arena. Skirmishes broke out between the groups, and security officials swooped in to break the two species apart.

"What event is that?" Sam asked.

"It's the Seahorse 5000," Iaira replied. "It's an annual race, and the sport is our most popular pastime."

"Looks like the fans can get pretty rowdy," Vance said.

"I don't ever remember it being like that," Iaira told him.

One of the security officials—a large male selkie—was suddenly upon them.

"Who are you creatures, and what are you doing in this zone?" he asked gruffly.

"Zone?" Iaira responded, confused.

"This is a selkie-only zone. I could arrest the lot of you for trespassing without wearing the proper permits."

"My name is Dr. Vance Vantana of the Department of Mythical Wildlife. We're here on an errand for Phylassos."

"Isn't the gryphon from the over-earth?" the officer asked.

"That's right," Vance replied. "And this is Princess Iaira. We've come to bring her home." The security officer took one look at Iaira's discolored, pockmarked face and grimaced.

"She's the long-lost princess of Ta Cathair?" he asked, incredulous.

"Absolutely, she is," Sam asserted, annoyed by the selkie's tone. "And we can prove it. We just need to see the queen."

"Take your proof to the mer-side of the city and get in line behind all of the other would-be Iairas. There's at least one a day claiming to be the heir. Now move along to the neutral zone," he said, gesturing toward the arena. Tashi pulled Iaira to the designated area, with Sam and Vance following.

"It's like Anastasia," Vance remarked. "She was a Russian princess from a long while back who was thought to be dead, but when they couldn't find her remains, several women came forward claiming to be her. Unfortunately, we don't have the time to try to convince a bunch of bureaucrats."

"I agree," Tashi said. "I can no longer keep Iaira healed. The magic is growing stronger."

"We do have another way to meet the queen," Iaira whispered. She closed her eyes and called out in a weakened voice, "Rosi."

"Who is Rosi?" Sam asked. Before he got his answer, there was a commotion in front of the arena. Mer-people and selkies dove this way and that, scrambling out of the way of a giant seahorse as it charged toward the group. The Guardian took an immediate protective posture.

"It's okay, Tashi," Iaira whispered. "He's a friend."

The creature darted straight for the princess. It was a majestic beast, about the size of a land horse but with blue shimmering skin, front legs with fins insteads of hooves, and a long curved tail. The creature leaned down to Iaira and nuzzled her neck.

"You remember me," she said, petting the seahorse's head. The animal nodded. "I was the reigning champion when I left," she relayed to the others. "There was no one faster than Iaira and Rosi." She smirked, as best she could, and added, "I always found it ironic that the most coveted prize for winning was meeting my mother, whom I was always trying to avoid."

"You mean, if you win the race—" Sam began.

"You meet the queen," Iaira replied.

"You're in *no* shape to race, Princess," Vance told her.

"I'm not going to. Sam is."

Chapter 14

THE SEAHORSE 5000

Of all the unusual experiences Sam London had had in his time with the DMW, sitting at the starting line of the Seahorse 5000 atop a jet-powered seahorse in a majestic undersea kingdom was one of the strangest. When Iaira had suggested the strategy of meeting her mother by winning what appeared to be the underwater equivalent of a NASCAR race, both Tashi and Dr. Vantana immediately voiced their opposition. After all, Sam had zero experience riding one of these creatures, let alone at death-defying speeds. It was much too dangerous. But Iaira insisted, reminding them they had no other options and her time was running out.

The Guardian couldn't ride, since she needed to keep the princess alive until they got her help, and Dr. Vantana was too large to give them their best shot at winning. Professional seahorse riders were on the short side, as it was less of a burden on the seahorse and made the duo more streamlined. Shorter fin lengths were also ideal for riding with the attached jet engines and was one of the reasons why Iaira had been so successful as a child.

Though Sam may have been the right size, he wasn't the right species. The seahorse's saddle was designed for a creature with a fin, not legs. That meant he had to straddle the seahorse and bend his knees, as if kneeling. It wasn't very comfortable, but it was necessary to combat drag and keep his legs from getting burned by the jets once they were ignited.

Just thinking about those jets unnerved him. His thumb hovered anxiously above the special button on the reins that initiated the jet propulsion and provided the extreme amount of thrust that made the race famous. The key would be knowing when to use it, as using too much too early would mean running out of fuel, but not using enough would mean losing badly. It was a delicate balance that Iaira said Rosi would help maintain by tugging on the reins to signal to Sam when to hit the button. Iaira had also suggested a good five-second blast off the starting line to break away from the pack and ensure he wouldn't be playing catch-up for the entire race, which, Sam learned, only partially took place in the arena. Much of it followed a path through the city. No doubt a way to lengthen the event and provide more viewing opportunities for the many fans.

As Sam waited anxiously for the sound of the coral horn that was the undersea race's version of a starting pistol, he glanced around at the other racers. Each seahorse and its rider was unique, but all had one common trait: a steely-eyed determination. It was a mix of mer-people and selkies, and the contrast of styles was clearly evident. The selkie riders appeared much more aggressive. They were dressed in clothing fit for a warrior going into battle. The creatures wore black tunics with arm gauntlets and thigh guards. They each had a silver chest plate with shoulder pads that curved back in an aerodynamic design. Their seahorses snorted angrily, while the selkie riders yanked on the reins to keep them from starting before the signal.

The mermen and mermaids were calmer in their dispositions, as were their steeds. They were dressed in sleeker outfits that hugged their bodies and were lightly colored. They ducked down behind the seahorses' necks and remained perfectly still. As the time until the start of the race ticked away, Sam could feel an increasing number of eyes on him. The occasional curious glances his way became more frequent. And then he spotted a selkie race official near the starting line conversing with a merman rider who was gesturing wildly and pointing at Sam. He quickly concluded that this merman was Rosi's designated rider—the one she had knocked off to meet up with Iaira. Fortunately, before the merman could reclaim his seahorse, the coral horn was blown and the race was on.

Sam immediately hit the thrust button on the reins, as Iaira had instructed him to do. The jets lit up with a bluish-red flame, and Sam could instantly feel the rush of heat on his legs. Rosi rocketed off the starting line with more velocity than a dvergen subway, which was extraordinary, considering they were in liquid.

Sam instantly took the lead, but quickly realized he applied way too much thrust and was moving too fast as he took the first turn on his way out of the stadium. As the racers charged out of the arena and on toward the city, Sam lost his grip on the reins, slipped off Rosi, and went barreling into a field of seaweed. He regained his bearings and spotted Rosi racing to pick him up. Out of the corner of his eye Sam saw the other riders zooming past and realized he would be playing catch-up for the rest of the race.

"Sorry about that," he told Rosi as he climbed back on. She snorted and shot back onto the track. They were in the middle of the pack now, but holding steady. The racers were kicking at each other and smashing into their opponents as if it were a demolition derby. Luckily, they didn't pay Sam any mind, probably because he didn't appear to be enough of a threat, he surmised.

On their way to the city center, the course wound through what Sam concluded was the Grand Canyon of the ocean floor. It was a deep valley of colorful seaweed and glimmering coral reefs. Vents in the bottom of the canyon occasionally erupted with bursts of boiling water, suggesting an underwater volcano. Thankfully, Rosi seemed to know exactly where these spots were and deftly avoided them.

The riders were becoming increasingly packed together, and Sam found himself surrounded on all sides, as well as above and below. The fiery discharge from the jets of the riders in front of him created a distortion to the water and heated it up. Not only was he having trouble seeing the path ahead, but Sam could feel the burn of the water as it passed quickly over his skin. The canyon course ended a short distance from the city, and the riders continued the rest of the way along seaweed pastures. Though Sam was moving at quite a clip, he could appreciate the splendor of the kingdom as he approached. There were crystalline towers, buildings made of brightly colored coral, streets of pearl, and seaweed gardens.

The palace was visible at the far end of the city, and there were government buildings lining the street along the way. The racers' path took a sharp turn right in front of the palace, and Sam could see that the building was constructed of a gleaming sapphire-colored glass and decorated with thousands of precious gems. Sam noted giant pearls, turquoise, opals, and emeralds, as well as purple and red jewels he didn't recognize. He also noticed a massive armed presence in this area of the city. Mermen soldiers stood with long gun-shaped weapons on one side of the thoroughfare, while selkie soldiers were positioned on the opposite side. Both groups had vehicles that were akin to tanks, but with jets similar to the ones used on the seahorses. The two armies sounded like they were trying to out-cheer the other as the seahorses zoomed by. Seeing the soldiers segregated made Sam realize just how much of a threat there was for armed conflict. With so much depending upon the outcome of this race and which rider won, he could practically feel the weight of this underwater world on his shoulders.

Coming up another straightaway, Rosi signaled to Sam to use the throttle and he did. He was cautious and determined, and was avoiding any nasty skirmishes with his competitors. Sam knew he needed to win to meet the queen. He needed to win to save Princess Iaira's life. He needed to win to stop a war. Unfortunately, Sam London didn't win. In fact, he didn't even come close.

He tried in vain to power his way through the tightly knit mass of racers, using his thrust, but he was blocked at every attempt. When Rosi finally shot across the finish line, she did so ahead of only one other racer. Sam patted the dejected seahorse on the head. He appreciated the faith Iaira had placed in him and was disappointed that he'd let the princess down. Sam London likely would have preferred that the case file exaggerate his seahorse racing prowess, but the fact was, he was a twelve-year-old boy who had no experience riding a jet-powered aquatic equine at mind-boggling speeds, not to mention competing against seasoned professionals. He chalked this up as another sport he wasn't particularly skilled at. However, even though Sam may not have been a champion seahorse racer, he was crafty . . . and he had a plan B.

Sam spotted Queen Muiria high atop the arena in a luxury box that featured 360-degree views, which allowed her to follow the action from both inside and outside the stadium. A raven-haired replica of her daughter and dressed in a shimmering gown, Muiria stood toward the front of the box, applauding as the results board replayed the race's thrilling finish.

Back on the arena's floor, rings of colorful seaweed were

lofted onto the winning seahorse by a pair of ushers as an announcer's voice boomed through the arena, naming the victor: a selkie called Niallas. Sam recognized him as one of the most aggressive racers on the course.

The crowd cheered as the queen floated down from her box toward the floor, surrounded by security, to meet Niallas near the podium. Muiria's guards allowed him to approach, but the selkie refused to kneel before the queen. Her security attempted to force him onto his knees, but she waved them off, unfazed. She handed him the glistening, prized trophy, which was adorned with countless precious gemstones, and he lifted it high above his head.

"This is for the selkie!" he declared. Then he added, "And the true ruler of Ta Cathair, General Searus!" Half the crowd went totally wild with applause, while the other half howled in disagreement. The guards moved in to punish Niallas, and Sam saw his moment.

He had not used all of the thrust left in his jets. As the realization that he would not win had crystallized, Sam thought he better keep a little fuel in the tanks just in case he had to make a quick getaway; after all, there were officials who knew he didn't belong and they might have been waiting at the finish line to confront him. Sam realized that what he was about to do was risky, but he also knew it was his only shot. And it was the very least he could do to save Iaira from an awful fate. Steering Rosi, he positioned the seahorse toward the winner's circle and hit the throttle. The smidgen of fuel left ignited the jets and sent the duo hurtling toward the queen. A surprised Rosi reared back, but there was little the seahorse could do to stop her forward momentum. Sam was instantly in front of Queen Muiria, and was just as instantly surrounded by soldiers, their weapons trained on him and Rosi. The crowd gasped, and Sam quickly put up his hands.

"Please don't shoot!" he exclaimed. "I'm human, and I just need to speak with the queen." Sam's voice echoed throughout the arena, and he realized this entire incident was being broadcast live on giant screens around the venue. The soldiers yanked him from Rosi and threw him to the seafloor.

"If you are human, how are you breathing with gills?" one of the soldiers asked angrily. "Get the queen to safety," he said to two of the other soldiers. "We'll deal with this assassin." They pulled Sam to his feet, and he spotted the queen's security attempting to rush her to safety.

"Please! I'm here with Princess Iaira. The real Iaira," Sam cried out. "I was sent by Maris, the selkie, to bring her home. I'm with the Department of Mythical Wildlife. We work with Phylassos—"

"How dare you insult the queen with your claims," a soldier said, lifting his weapon and bearing down on Sam.

"Wait," Queen Muiria ordered the soldier, stopping with her security detail to look back. The soldier halted, as ordered. "Explain your gills," she said.

"It's a little complicated, but I received a serum that enables me to breathe underwater," Sam explained.

"And why should I believe you?" she asked. "Do you know how many others have come here with similar claims, in a vicious attempt to gain passage to the throne through false hope and lies? What makes you any different from those piranhas?"

"Like I said, I'm human," Sam told her. "Please, come see her and you'll know I'm telling the truth."

"It could be a trap, Your Majesty," one of her advisor's warned.

"It's not a trap. We have to hurry. She's dying. If she doesn't get help, she won't survive," Sam revealed.

The queen moved closer. "Why is she dying?"

"An Adaro—his flying fish poisoned her," Sam explained.

"And what was she doing with an Adaro?"

"We were following the five sacred points after Maris gave us a crystal and we went to Atlantis and then wound up in Samoa with Ika-Tere and the Adaro attacked. I'd love to explain it all, Your Majesty, but we're—she's—running out of time."

The queen considered his words, then nodded.

* * *

With all eyes on him, Sam London led the queen of Ta Cathair and her heavily armed entourage out of the arena and to the spot where he'd left Vance, Tashi, and Iaira. The arena crowd was dead silent, as this entire event was still being broadcast on the jumbo screens. Even the selkies watched and listened intently. Sam swam ahead when he spotted the group and saw

Iaira lying down with her eyes closed. Tashi had her hands on the princess, but it didn't appear to be having any effect. Vantana smiled as Sam approached.

"Good save, kid," he said. "We saw the whole thing." He pointed to a large screen outside the arena that had been broadcasting the race and was now airing the live scene with Muiria.

The queen froze when she saw Iaira in the Guardian's arms.

"That is her?" Muiria asked tentatively.

Sam nodded. "Yes, Your Majesty," he replied. "We've come a long way. Tashi is a Guardian. She has been able to heal Iaira just enough to keep her alive, but the magic is too strong."

"May I—" The queen gestured that she wished to approach.

"By all means," Dr. Vantana said.

Queen Muiria swam to Iaira, and her guards remained close. Tashi offered her the princess, who looked to be barely breathing.

"There is no more I can do for her," Tashi informed the queen. "Only your healers can help her now." Muiria nodded as she lifted Iaira up and cradled her child in her arms. She brushed the hair from Iaira's wounded face. The princess's eyes opened, but just slightly.

"Mother?" she said in a whisper. "Forgive me . . . ," she pleaded as she began to cry. Her dark sapphire tears floated up and out of her eyes. Muiria embraced her tightly.

"Bring my doctors," she ordered her guards.

"But, Your Majesty, how can we be sure—" an advisor began to say.

"I know how it feels to hold my baby," Muiria said, clearly emotional. "Bring my doctors now!" she said firmly. "I lost her once. I will not lose her again."

As Dr. Vance Vantana waited with Tashi and Iaira outside the arena during the Seahorse 5000, he tried to glean any information he could regarding the political situation in Ta Cathair. He got ahold of two of the city's newspapers, which appeared to be printed on a thin organic material that was stiff yet flexible in the water. The newspapers told two very different stories about the state of the city, with one clearly written from a selkie perspective and the other from the mer-people point of view. The two headlines read "Extremists Push for War!" and "Selkie Freedom Under Attack!" Given the polarizing language, it was no surprise that the city was in crisis and why Maris was so intent on returning Iaira. He must have seen their union as a last-ditch effort to prevent a civil war.

This day's newspaper editions were predominantly focused on the queen's decision to allow the Seahorse 5000 race to continue as planned. According to the papers, the prior year's race had a disastrous ending, in which one of the leading mermen racers was killed in an accident after bumping against a selkie competitor known for his illegal tactics. The merman was thrown into the path of a volcanic vent and died instantly. The selkie racer responsible for the hit was banned forever from competing.

Given the tensions in the city, Vance was thrilled to see Sam emerge unscathed from the race rather than feeling disappointed he'd lost, especially after the stunt he'd pulled at the end. Sam's move to meet the queen could have been seen as an attack, but surprisingly, it had worked out for the best. The scene that unfolded was seen by millions of Ta Cathair's citizens. The silence of both the selkie and the mer-people in the arena and surrounding areas was a testament to just how moving the reunion was between mother and daughter.

* * *

A little over an hour later, Vance, Sam, and Tashi were sitting at a table in a grand dining room in the palace of Ta Cathair. Though the thought of sitting in a chair underwater seemed unusual, Vantana noted that the ocean water felt thin and light at this depth—like liquid air. He wondered if that was the water's true nature or if Ranger Naughton's injection was responsible for the sensation. A variety of edible sea plants had just been brought out on silver platters, and the doctor couldn't remember the last time he'd eaten. He stabbed at one of the purple plants and popped it into his mouth. It was chewy and tasted like licorice. Eating while submerged in water was a strange feeling, but Vance was hungry enough that he got used to it quickly. He was constantly swallowing water with every bite, and somehow this excess water would leave his body through his gills. Both Tashi and Sam were eating too, especially the Guardian, who had expended a great deal of energy healing Iaira. The last time they saw the princess was outside the arena when the queen's medical team had arrived and whisked her off to the city's best hospital.

Vance was briefing Sam and Tashi on what he'd learned from the newspapers about the state of the city, when the doors to the dining area opened and Queen Muiria swam in. They all rose to a standing position in deference.

"Please, be seated," she said. They settled back into their chairs.

"How's Iaira?" Sam asked anxiously. The queen smiled.

"The doctors believe she will survive, and I have all of you to thank for it," she said, then looked to Vantana. "Sam said you were associated with Phylassos?"

Vance nodded. "That's right. I'm part of an organization that helps ensure that Phylassos's law is followed and enforced. This case was unusual in that the jurisdiction wasn't clear-cut. It originated on land but led here." The queen nodded her understanding.

"I never thought I'd see her again," she told them. "I believed she had died, but I always held out a little hope that she would return home. When Maris came to me with a picture of a young woman in a human magazine, I told him it wasn't her. It couldn't be. But he insisted."

"He was quite determined, that's for sure," Vantana said. "Fortunately, he gave us an Atlantean crystal that helped Iaira transform and led us to the first sacred point. She had no memory of her life here. She didn't know who she was."

"She thought her name was Pearl Eklund," Sam added. "And she was pretty famous where I come from. Still living like royalty, in a way."

"Iaira never had a problem acting the part," Muiria said with a smile. "It was the actual duty that accompanied the title that she disliked."

"I know the city is in a bit of an upheaval right now," Vance started.

"That is putting it mildly," Muiria admitted dryly. "The selkies view Iaira's abandonment as a rebuke of their kind. Her actions were just more evidence that we mer-folk believe ourselves to be superior. In the years that followed her disappearance, violent clashes became the norm and a political solution seemed unattainable. So I divided the city into segregated areas to try to ease the tensions."

"And that made things worse?" the doctor asked.

"Much worse. It separated us. Exposed our base instincts of fear and distrust. The selkies insisted on having their own government. They believe Ta Cathair is their city and are threatening to take it back by force. I believe it's only a matter of time before the war erupts."

"Who is General Searus?" Sam asked. "I heard Niallas mention him when he got his trophy."

"He is a selkie military leader with a royal lineage. The selkies see him as their king, and he has pushed for my abdication of the throne based on Iaira's violation of the peace treaty."

"The marriage," Sam concluded. Muiria nodded.

"Yes. That was part of the agreement. It would allow for joint governance by linking our kinds in a sacred union."

"Well, hopefully Iaira's return can help calm things down," Vance told her. "But there is something you should know about our journey here. I believe there are forces who were actively trying to prevent her return."

"I see," Muiria replied thoughtfully.

"Maybe the selkies are—"

"The selkies are the least of my worries," Muiria interrupted. "Please, come with me."

Muiria and her guards led the trio out of the palace and to an area on the outskirts of the city. Vantana spotted hundreds of mer-people and selkies streaming down from an opening above them in the cavern. They were being processed by government officials and watched by soldiers.

"Refugees," Muiria explained as she gestured to the crowd. "They come from our many colonies around the world."

"That must be what we saw in the videos from the buoys," Sam quietly suggested to Vance.

"For sure," the doctor agreed, then shifted back to Muiria. "Why are they fleeing their homes?" he asked.

"Because of you," a deep voice bellowed. They turned to find a silver-haired selkie approaching with his own group of guards. He was an older creature, but just as muscular as Maris.

"General Searus," Muiria acknowledged him. "I did not know you would be gracing us with your presence."

"This is a selkie issue as much as it is an issue for your people," he remarked with irritation.

"Hold on a minute," Vance interjected. "Why is this because of *us*?"

"Like Ta Cathair, the Syrenis, Gorgonas, and Vannari colonies are built above energy sources," the queen revealed. "It is what powers our civilization. We call it the silver fire. And it appears humanity has discovered it and has begun to exploit it."

"Silver fire?" Sam wondered aloud. "That sorta sounds like—"

"Fire ice," Vantana concluded. Tashi leaned in.

"Perhaps Lief Eklund knows more than he claims," she suggested.

"We'll get to the bottom of this. I promise you that," the doctor assured Muiria and Searus.

"Where's Maris?" Sam asked. "I didn't see him at the arena. I want him to know I made good on my promise."

"We were hoping you would be able to tell us where the general's son is," the queen replied.

"The general's—" Vance suddenly realized Maris was Searus's son. It all made sense now. "Why would we know where he is?" he asked.

Searus responded in an incriminating tone. "Because he never returned from your over-world."

Chapter 15

FIRE ICE

SL002-130-70

SUBJ: Methane Hydrate

SOURCE: PR

DATE: ▮▮▮▮▮▮▮

For the purposes of context within the case file
SL002-130, it is relevant to understand the energy
source referred to as "fire ice." The substance, known
as methane hydrate, is made up of methane gas contained
inside water molecules that form a crystalline solid.
Formed biogenically or geologically, methane hydrate
deposits are found beneath the ocean floor and Arctic
permafrost. Once extracted, the crystalline structures
can be burned to generate significant amounts of
energy. In fact, one cubic meter of methane hydrate is

equal to 164 cubic meters of natural gas. The potential energy that lies in known deposits of methane hydrate theoretically exceeds the energy of all other fossil fuels combined. When methane hydrate is ignited, the crystalline appears to be on fire, giving the illusion of flammable ice, hence the term "fire ice."

Although Iaira's return and the reunion with Muiria that was broadcast in the arena and on video devices across the city had helped to ease the tensions between the selkies and mer-people, the events had not eliminated the tensions entirely. For a large percentage of selkies, the disappearance of Maris—the beloved son of General Searus—was met with skepticism and suspicion. Sam knew it was imperative that the DMW do what was needed to help avert a war. This included investigating the possible link between Lief Eklund and the drilling for methane hydrate beneath the mer-people and selkie colonies, as well as looking into the disappearance of Maris. Dr. Vantana, Sam, and Tashi were preparing to leave via a special selkie-built submersible that Muiria and the general led them to, when a familiar voice made them all stop on the boarding ramp.

"You're not going anywhere without me," Iaira said from behind them. Sam turned and could see that the mermaid was still healing—she moved much more slowly than she had in Atlantis, but her condition was still cause for celebration.

"You're already swimming?" Sam observed with a grin.

"Our physicians were able to reverse the magic," she said.

"I'm not a hundred percent, but I'm getting there." A frantic merman in a blue uniform was rapidly swimming toward the princess.

"I tried to stop her, Your Majesty," the exasperated merman told the queen, who stood beside the sub.

"It is okay, Doctor. She is quite willful," the queen said. "You may go." Relieved, the doctor nodded and swam off. "What are you doing here? You *should* be resting," Muiria told her daughter.

"There is no time to rest. I have to go with them," Iaira said with certainty.

"Now, hold on, Princess," Vance piped in. "We just got you home, and we all nearly died doing it. You especially. Stay here with your people."

"I agree," the queen said firmly.

"I second it," Sam added, then nudged Tashi.

"I third it?" the Guardian said, unsure if she was using the correct verbiage. Sam gave her a confirming nod.

"Maris risked so much to try to save me and our kingdom. I must return the favor," Iaira explained. "My father—I mean, my pretend father—was determined to find him after the limousine accident. If he did, who knows what happened? Plus, I have to find out if Lief is behind these incidents at our colonies and why he never told me the truth about who I was." She swam toward the submersible, then stopped when she noticed no one was following her. "Isn't there anyone who understands why I must go? General Searus, you have not offered your thoughts. He is your son."

"I believe I speak for all of my people when I say we would be very appreciative of this gesture, Princess. It would be looked on kindly. And, perhaps more importantly, it is quite courageous." Iaira grinned.

"Then it's settled," she declared.

Vance and Queen Muiria hemmed and hawed a few minutes more, but they eventually had to bend to the princess's will. The reunited foursome boarded the submersible and headed to the ocean's surface.

When they reached land, the transition to breathing air was, to put it mildly, unpleasant. While growing gills had been a frightening experience, returning to pure human form was painful and disgusting. The gills disappeared fast, and then the lungs began to expel water. In other words, Sam threw up over and over again, along with Tashi and Vance. Though most of the expulsion of liquid was done in India, Sam didn't completely stop coughing up ocean until they reached Miami. If there was one positive, it was that Sam had never felt so light on his feet. Moving through water for so long had gotten his body accustomed to the constant resistance; now he felt like he was practically floating. He was excited that Ranger Naughton's injection had worked and was eager to see if there were any other abilities he might be able to try out for future cases.

Before they all boarded the subway back to Florida, Vance reached out to Ranger Woodruff Sprite to inform him of their return. He tapped his DMW badge and called Woodruff's name, but there was no answer. He tried again, and this time a strange voice responded.

"Ranger Sprite is unavailable. May I be of service, Ranger Vantana?" It was a nasally, slightly high-pitched male voice.

"Who is this?" the doctor asked, his brow furrowed.

"This is Bob," the voice replied.

"Bob who?"

"Ferguson. Bob Ferguson," the man named Bob answered. "We met at last year's holiday party in the DC office. I thought maybe you'd just remember me as Bob, but I guess that was a while ago and—"

"Where's Ranger Sprite?" Vance interjected, sensing that Bob might ramble on.

"He is on a special mission for Phylassos and out of communication range. But how can I be of service?"

"What kind of special mission?" Vantana inquired, growing more impatient by the second.

"I'm not authorized to say," Ferguson replied.

"Oh, c'mon, Bob," the doctor said in a friendlier tone. "I thought we were friends. We had a nice chat at that holiday party, didn't we?"

"We just said hello to each other," Ferguson revealed. "I was at the name-tag table, and I recognized you and . . ."

"But it was a real friendly hello," Vance told him. "Like long-lost pals. Help me out, buddy. I'm on a real important mission here myself." Sam had to smile at the doctor's attempt to manipulate Bob Ferguson. He also couldn't help but think that he had rubbed off a little on the ranger.

"Ranger Vantana—" Ferguson began.

"Call me Vance," Vance interrupted.

"Vance . . ." Ferguson paused a moment, then, "I honestly don't know what mission Ranger Sprite and Naughton are on, but—"

"Hold up, Bob," Vantana said. "Ranger Naughton is on the same special mission?" There was a longer pause.

"I'm not authorized to say, Vance," Ferguson replied nervously.

"That's all right. I understand. Now I do need your help if it's not too much trouble."

"Sure, Vance," Bob replied. "That's what I'm here for. You need an extra hand in the field? I'm not supposed to leave the office, but if this is an emer—"

"No need, buddy," the doctor interjected. "I just need some wheels waiting for me at Falling Waters. Can you handle that?"

"Of course," Ferguson responded, his voice betraying a hint of disappointment there wasn't more required of him.

"Thanks. See you at the next party," Vantana said, before motioning for the group to join him in the subway.

After the conversation with Ferguson, Sam could tell the doctor was deep in thought. No doubt trying to figure out what kind of mission Sprite and Naughton might be on.

"Didn't you say you have been trying to contact Phylassos for some time?" Sam inquired.

"That's right," Vance confirmed. "Considering everything that's going on, I'm surprised I didn't receive a heads-up." He was annoyed by the oversight, and Sam could understand why. This case and the events surrounding it were growing more baffling by the moment.

The Pearl Eklund who returned to Miami was as different as the Iaira who had left Ta Cathair. The princess had spent a great deal of time away from her prized social accounts and didn't appear all that interested in seeing what reaction her sudden absence had caused. Rather, Iaira was itching to find Maris and get answers to her many burning questions regarding Lief and the fire ice drilling beneath the colonies.

Among all the memories that had returned to her about her previous life in Ta Cathair was the memory of Maris himself. They weren't strangers. They had been classmates in a private school attended by the children of government officials. At first, Iaira had a crush on Maris—he was, after all, the most handsome of all the selkie boys—but he teased her mercilessly. He would often pull her fin and call her "Fishface." Muiria claimed it was a sign that he liked her, and looking back, Iaira realized her mother was probably right, but her ten-year-old self did not appreciate it, not one bit. The day she learned he was the boy she would have to marry, she was mortified. Maris came to see her after getting the same news from his father and apologized for his past behavior, promising to change and asking for her forgiveness. Iaira refused to listen. She begged her mother to change the law, but Muiria couldn't—too much was riding on the treaty. Though Muiria did remind Iaira that the marriage was still several years away. Perhaps she would feel differently in time, or maybe the political climate would change and they could renegotiate the terms of the peace. Iaira would not accept this consolation.

The princess locked herself in her room. Not only would she have to devote her life to serving as queen and never have a chance to travel to the over-world (a lifelong wish that wouldn't be granted due to security reasons), but she would have to do so married to Maris. It was too much for her to bear, and so she packed a few belongings and fled the city. She believed that running away would show everyone she meant business and maybe, just maybe, convince them to change the law. If they didn't care about her wishes, why should she care about theirs, she reasoned? Of course, her absence only worsened the situation and she was nearly lost forever. The details of her rescue remained the only fuzzy part of her memory now. And that made her wonder about Lief and his true intentions.

Iaira knew, based on her recent conversation with Murphy, that she was in mermaid form when she was rescued. This meant Lief was aware of her abilities, yet he had kept her in the dark. Why? He'd even made up a story about her parents being killed in a boating accident and actively hid the truth from her ever since. That didn't make much sense, especially when he appeared to genuinely care for her. Was it all for show? Or was there another, more sympathetic explanation for his actions? Maybe he had told her the story about her parents and kept her identity secret to somehow protect her. After all, he must have realized that discovering such a creature would be world-changing. If everyone had known, she would likely have been exploited or studied for science. Lief could have made a fortune quite easily, taking advantage of her in that way. But he had chosen to keep this information to himself and treat her like a daughter instead. She had also always felt loved, and that puzzled her. As for the fire ice, if it was Eklund Energy that was behind the drilling at the colonies, could it have simply been a coincidence? That seemed like the least likeliest idea, and that threw everything else she knew about Lief into doubt. With all the possible scenarios, her mind was darting in a thousand different directions. It was a storm of thoughts and feelings, and she knew of only one way to clear her head.

"I think we should go straight to the Eklund Energy building," Iaira suggested upon their arrival in Florida. "I'll talk to Lief and get to the bottom of all of this."

"That's way too risky," Vance told her. "There are a lot of moving parts, and we need more information before we make our move. Let's hunker down someplace, investigate Maris's disappearance, and make a plan." Iaira nodded, reluctantly. The storm in her head raged on.

They wound up in a cabin in Everglades National Park, where they gathered around the computer and started their search. According to online news sites, Pearl Eklund wasn't missing. Lief had released a statement claiming she was on a mission helping the less fortunate in a far-off country that would remain nameless for the sake of privacy. However, his announcement had come in the wake of news reports about Iaira's breakdown at the party, as well as reports of the limousine incident. By now there was all sorts of speculation from her gems on fan sites regarding these unusual events. Some believed she was in a rehabilitation center dealing with anxiety, while others concluded it must all be part of a publicity stunt to snag a reality-television-show contract. Surprisingly, Iaira found that her following had actually grown in the last few days. She appeared to be more popular when she was missing.

In addition to looking into the stories swirling around Pearl, they checked the news for any leads related to Maris. Unfortunately, there was no mention of the mystery man from the accident in the bay. Iaira called up her contact at the police department to see if she could glean any information that wasn't being reported.

"Pearl, is it really you?" the gem answered skeptically.

"Of course it's me! Who'd you think it'd be, silly?" Iaira cooed as Pearl.

"This is Pearl-tastic! I was so worried. Is everything okay?" the officer said, all in one breath.

"Yeah. You know. They say absence makes the heart grow fonder, and I'm just trying to drum up some excitement for this new TV show I'm working on. But that's a secret, so please don't tell!" Iaira begged.

"I wouldn't dream of it," he assured her in a hushed voice.

"Oh, you're one of my brightest gems!" she said, and

heard him giggle. "I was wondering, did you ever hear anything more about the man who kidnapped me? How freaky was that, right?"

"Very freaky. And, I'm sorry to say, we never found anything more," the officer told her. "The trail went ice-cold. I even tried to push my superiors to add more resources to the investigation, but they said they couldn't spare the extra personnel."

"What about my dad?" Iaira asked. "He was super-obsessed with finding him."

"Yeah, I thought so too," the gem replied. "That's why I reached out to his office and requested he put some pressure on my captain, but he never returned my call."

"I see," said Iaira. That was a strange development, she thought. Why would Lief suddenly stop searching for Maris? "And there were no other sightings? Not even rumors?"

"Nope, nothing at all."

"Well, thank you. You did a Pearl-rific job," she told the officer, who chuckled giddily on the other end.

Hanging up the phone, Iaira relayed the conversation to the others. They were all equally baffled as to why Lief had lost interest in searching for the selkie, especially given Iaira's disappearance.

"If they didn't find him and then you suddenly went missing, I would think that Lief would have been even more invested in trying to track him down," Sam concluded.

"I agree," Iaira replied.

"Unless Lief found him after you went missing," Tashi suggested.

"Before the police got their chance to," Vance speculated. "Maybe he's got him hidden away, trying to figure out ways to exploit him. Plus, we know there are creatures out there who didn't want you to return home. Perhaps they don't want Maris to either."

"So what's next?" Iaira asked.

"We have to get into Eklund Energy and have a look around your father's office," Vantana told her. "See what we can dig up."

"And when do I get to talk to him?" she inquired.

"When we have more to go on," he answered. "Seeing him will only complicate things. If he knew you were a mermaid, now that he's lost you, he might try to expose you." Iaira nodded with understanding.

"How are we planning to get into his office?" Tashi asked Vance. "Last time we were at the building, I took note of the security detail. It is quite robust. There are more than a dozen guards stationed around the lobby alone. Perhaps even more if Mr. Eklund's intentions are indeed nefarious. We should assume his people have instructions to alert him if they see you."

"Good point. We could enter through the staff entrance in the parking garage," Iaira suggested. "I—I mean, Pearl—used to sneak out that way all the time when the guard wasn't looking."

"Well, he'll no doubt be looking now," Vance said.

"We could try using Lief's own cover story," Sam suggested. "If he lied to the press, he probably lied to his own people, right? They might think she's away on some mission. Dr. Vantana could pose as a driver or something—maybe bringing Pearl home from the airport. And if the guards get too curious, Tashi can just come up from behind and shock them out cold."

"From behind?" Tashi asked. "That does not sound very honorable."

"We don't have time for honorable," Sam declared. "We have a kingdom to save."

Vance Vantana was in his full ranger uniform when he escorted Princess Iaira into the parking garage beneath the Eklund Energy building. He thought it would give him more credibility if he appeared to be a law enforcement official, rather than a driver, as Sam had initially suggested. The doctor had his arm draped around Iaira in a protective manner, and she had her head down, her face hidden with a scarf, as if trying to avoid the prying cameras of the paparazzi. As they approached the service elevator, which was in a corner beyond the main bank of elevators, Vantana spotted not one but two security guards.

"I guess Tashi was right," Vance whispered. "Looks like Lief beefed up security." This was definitely a red flag for the doctor and potentially disastrous for the Department of Mythical Wildlife. They were walking right into the hands of a very wealthy and powerful individual who knew Iaira's true nature and might have been exploiting her for his own benefit. As they arrived at the service elevator, Vantana just hoped it wasn't too late to stop Lief from exposing Iaira and her kind.

"This isn't a public entrance," the taller of the two guards said. "The building's main elevators are behind you."

"We'd love to use them," Vance told him, "but we can't risk her being spotted." With that, Iaira removed the scarf and revealed herself. The guards were stunned.

"Ms.—Ms. Eklund?" the other guard stammered.

"I've come back from my mission earlier than planned," she explained. "I was hoping to surprise my father. Thankfully, this lovely park ranger helped whisk me away from some reporters who were staking out the airport. They must have been tipped off."

"Good to see you," the tall guard said cautiously. "Call it in," he told his partner. Then he turned back to Iaira to explain. "We have orders to contact your father as soon as you return home."

"Well, that's weird," Iaira replied. "He knows I'm on a mission . . . unless he already knows I'm coming to surprise him and he's got something planned. Like a party." She pretended to be excited at the thought. The guards looked at her blankly.

"Mr. Eklund isn't here," the other guard said. "He's on an expedition aboard the new drilling ship."

"Right, of course," Iaira responded, as if she'd just remembered.

"Hold on. Aren't you that guy from San Francisco?" the

tall guard said to Vance as he eyed the ranger more closely. *Uh-oh,* the doctor thought. The tall guard's demeanor changed and he reached for his earpiece.

"I'm calling this in," the guard announced.

"Enough chitchat," Vantana said. "Tashi?"

"Who's Tashi?" the other guard asked.

"I am," the Guardian proclaimed. The guards spun around as Tashi bowed. Then she leapt up, delivering a flying kick to the tall guard's face. When she landed on the floor, she twirled her shekchen and touched the tip to the other guard. He took a massive jolt and dropped like a rock. "Sam?" Tashi called out. Sam popped up from behind a parked car, and the four made a beeline into the service elevator.

"I think it best that we split up and look around before those guards wake up or someone finds them sleeping on the job," Vance told the others, who nodded their agreement as the elevator neared the Eklund penthouse. "If you find anything, holler."

The doors opened, and they all went off in opposite directions. The penthouse that Pearl had called home was easily the most luxurious apartment Vance had ever seen. It was eight thousand immaculately appointed square feet filled with priceless art and furniture, located atop one of Miami's tallest buildings. Once outside the elevator, Vance headed to his right through a foyer that acted as a connector to the various rooms at the far end of the penthouse. This foyer contained an aquarium so large, it could have been a diving tank. He stepped quickly past it and through a doorway into what turned out to be a study.

Like the rest of the penthouse, the room was beautifully furnished and contained a fainting couch, two chairs, a large mahogany desk, and a matching built-in bookcase with cabinets and drawers, as well as shelves filled with photographs and books. Vance walked to the drawers behind the desk and began looking for clues. The first drawer he pulled open contained letterhead and envelopes, but the second had a digital recorder, pads with handwritten notes, and a stack of memory cards. The cards were in plastic cases that were labeled with the words "Syrenis," "Gorgonas," and "Vannari." Vance instantly recognized them as the names of the mer-people colonies that had been compromised by the methane hydrate drilling. Lief's connection to the plight of the mer-people and selkies was looking more incriminating by the minute. He slipped one of the memory cards into the recorder and pressed play. But instead of Lief, Vantana heard a woman's voice.

"Pearl? Can you hear my voice?" the woman said. *That must be the Dr. Hawkins that Iaira mentioned*, Vance concluded.

"Yes," Iaira answered robotically. The princess sounded as if she were in a trance. Her response came out in a monotone, staccato fashion.

"Good. I need you to think back, back to before your boating accident," Hawkins said. "Can you do that for me?"

"Yes."

"Your real home . . . do you remember it?" the psychiatrist asked.

"Ta Cathair . . . ," Iaira said wistfully.

"I need you to tell me where it is. . . . I need to take you back there. Where is it, Iaira?"

"I don't know," she replied.

"I have asked you countless times, Iaira," Dr. Hawkins said. "You will upset your father if you again refuse to tell me."

"I don't know," the girl replied once more, her voice cracking as if she were pained.

"Tell me now!" Hawkins declared angrily, her voice deep and menacing. Vantana could hear Iaira crying softly on the recording.

"I don't know," she said meekly through tears.

"Fine," the woman told her in a suddenly calm, sweet demeanor. "I will ask again later and I won't tell your father you refused. You do want to make him happy, don't you?"

"I do," Iaira responded.

"Good. Fortunately, I have another way for you to please him. He wishes to know where he can find a place called Syrenis." There was a long pause, before Hawkins added, "It is just a colony. Surely you can tell me where it lies."

"Syrenis . . . is in the Middle Sea in the Calypso Deep. . . ." Vance clicked off the recording, having heard more than enough to make him sick to his stomach. Iaira had confessed the locations to Dr. Hawkins, who must have been working for Lief. The psychiatrist was not intending to help Iaira deal with the fake loss of her parents—she was trying to procure information from Iaira through hypnosis. But something still felt off. How did the psychiatrist know Iaira's real name, as well as the existence of Ta Cathair and the colonies? It was possible that Iaira had talked about them in earlier sessions and revealed their abundance of methane hydrate, Vance postulated, running his finger along the memory cards. Whatever the case, it was clear that these humans were exploiting the princess for their own personal gain.

The doctor gathered up the cards, notes, and recorder and headed out of the study. As he stepped back into the foyer, Vantana got a better look at the massive aquarium that sat close to the wall and took up most of the space. This time he took note of the horrendous quality of the water. It appeared as though the tank hadn't been cleaned in quite a while. *Did the filter break?* he wondered. Lief clearly loved fish, yet this aquarium didn't appear to house any. The water was murky and seemingly devoid of life.

"Dr. Vantana?" Vance heard Tashi call. He glanced over to see the Guardian approaching from one of the other rooms.

"What's up?"

"I believe I have found a secret room in the library. It is behind the bookshelves," she revealed. "Though, I have not determined how to enter."

"Interesting. I found something too. Looks like Doc Hawkins wasn't on the up-and-up," Vantana informed her. "We should talk to Iaira," he added. Then he eyed the aquarium once more. "Tashi, does it strike you as strange that there's a big ol' aquarium in this room with no fish in it?"

"How can you see there are no fish?" she asked. It was a valid point, but no fish had swum close to the glass for the entire time Vance had been staring at it. Surely he would have seen one or two. "What does occur to me as strange, however, is that there are stairs behind it, leading up to the top of the tank." Vance raised an eyebrow and moved to the rear of the aquarium to get a look. As Tashi had indicated, there was a steep set of wooden stairs that had been pushed up against the back of it.

"Maybe Lief uses it to practice diving," Vance suggested. He climbed the stairs and gazed down into the forest-green liquid. The water appeared to be covered with green algae. Vance kneeled down for a better look, then leaned over and sniffed the water. It had a strong scent of rotting fish. He grimaced as the putrid stench entered his nostrils. Then he thought he saw a flicker. A fish, perhaps? In *this* muck? He eyed the water for another sign. Without warning, a webbed hand with long, thin fingers sprang from the water, clutched Vance Vantana's face, and pulled him in.

Chapter 16
THE FINFOLK

Sam London didn't care for surprises. He didn't even care for the idea of surprise birthday parties. In fact, he made his mother promise to never surprise him with one. The thought of having a bunch of people jump out and scare the living daylights out of the honoree of the party was not appealing in the least. Birthday parties were something to look forward to, not to be lied to about. Of course, there were exceptions to Sam's surprise aversion, including surprise gifts, treats, and trips to the amusement park. But surprises meant to shock or stun an individual were not his cup of cocoa. Case in point, the surprise he received on the day he returned to Eklund Energy.

Sam London had already torn apart Lief's master bedroom searching for any clues regarding the energy magnate's involvement with Maris's disappearance or the drilling beneath Ta Cathair's colonies. Unfortunately, he'd had no luck on either of those fronts, so he decided to check on how Tashi and Vance were faring. Approaching the north side of the apartment, he looked ahead to the foyer and saw a puddle of water beside a massive aquarium. *Was that puddle there before?* he wondered. As he went to take a closer look, he heard two female voices from the other room—one was unfamiliar to him, but the other was definitely Iaira's. He turned and headed toward the living room. Rounding the corner, he spotted the princess on the couch, staring straight ahead, and a woman standing beside her.

"Sam London, is it?" the woman inquired, but didn't wait for an answer. "I'm Dr. Hawkins. A pleasure to meet you." She reached out her hand to shake Sam's, but he shifted his eyes to Iaira, who appeared to be in a trance.

"What's wrong with her?"

"Iaira and I were just having a little chat," Dr. Hawkins explained. Sam's heart took a trip to his throat.

"Did you just say 'Iaira'?" Sam asked. How would Hawkins have known that was Pearl's real name?

The doctor let out a long, slow, menacing laugh, and that was when Sam noticed a trail of water that led from the puddle near the aquarium all the way to the doctor's feet. He looked back to find that the doctor's face was now pulsating as she laughed. Her skin bubbled up and began to disappear, as though it were being absorbed back into her body, leaving just a scaly, slimy surface behind. Her eyes moved farther apart across her face, then grew larger into vertical oval shapes that turned yellow as Sam watched in horror.

"Surprise!" Dr. Hawkins said with a monstrous smile. Sam's eyes turned to saucers. "Mr. London. I want to thank you for all of your help. I will have to kill you, of course. But I did want to express my appreciation."

Sam didn't have a weapon to fight off the creature, but he did have reflexes, and quick ones, at that. There was a tall, circular glass table in front of him. It had a large—likely priceless—vase on it. He pushed the table as hard as he could toward the monster, who leapt back to avoid it. The vase and table shattered on the floor, and the noise was enough to snap Iaira from her trance.

She spotted the creature and screamed, "Finfolk!"

"C'mon!" Sam yelled, grabbing Iaira's hand and pulling her off the couch. They ran toward the study. "We have to warn Vance and Tashi."

"There's nowhere to run," the monster chided with an evil snarl as she stalked after the pair.

When they reached the study, they found Vance and Tashi soaking wet and unconscious on the floor. Their hands and feet were bound in seaweed. Sam could hear the creature walking toward them, her wet webbed feet slapping against the marble floor like suction cups.

"Wake up!" Sam yelled as he shook Vance, but there was no response.

"They can't help you now," the monster sneered. She stood in the entryway near the aquarium. Sam and Iaira took off down the other hallway, and the creature tracked them from a parallel hall, effectively blocking their access to the exit. As they reached the south end of the apartment, the fin-folk leapt out in front of them. Iaira screamed, and Sam pulled her into the nearest room and slammed the door shut. It was Iaira's bedroom, and the two began pushing the furniture in front of the door. A nightstand, table, chairs—anything they could find and had the strength to move.

"This is not going to hold that thing!" Iaira cried as a snarl reverberated from the hall. "The finfolk are very strong . . . and they have magic. We can't fight it."

"I know," Sam told her. "We need a plan."

"Can we call the police?" she asked.

"And tell them what? We're being chased by a mythical sea monster? Even if they did come, who knows what that creature is capable of. She could shape-shift and convince them of anything."

Thwack! The monster banged against the door.

"Come out, and I'll let one of you live," she said. "On second thought . . ." She banged again, but this time the wood splintered and the door buckled. They had a minute, maybe less, before it was curtains for them. Sam quickly scanned the room and spotted a laptop on the desk, and a lightbulb blinked on in his head.

"We need reinforcements. And I know just where to find them."

Vance Vantana had wrestled a few alligators in his youth, but that was literal and figurative child's play compared to the creature that pulled him into the aquarium in the Eklund penthouse. Of course, he was caught completely off guard and didn't have a chance to take in a full breath. Stopping to form gills would have taken him out of the fight completely, so he held what little air he had in his lungs and struggled against the monster in the water—a monster he couldn't see. The water was so thick with algae and other debris that he was unable to get his eyes on his opponent, but he could certainly feel the beast. Scaly hands were on him, pushing him downward, no doubt expecting him to drown. The doctor felt a rush of water—Tashi dove in to help. But the creature was unfazed by the Guardian's attempt and grabbed both of them by their necks, before leaping out of the aquarium. The monster landed just outside the tank and threw the two onto the floor like sacks of potatoes. It quickly raised its hands and made a clawing gesture. Vantana felt his body freeze, but the sensation wasn't like the paralysis he'd experienced with a banshee. That was a neurological seizing up, and this felt like being physically held down by an invisible force.

Vance immediately recognized the creature standing before them as finfolk. They were a legendary race of magical, shape-shifting sea creatures from Orkney mythology. Until this moment he had assumed they had all died out. No one had seen the finfolk for centuries. According to mer-people and selkie history, the creatures disappeared after their defeat at Ta Cathair. But here one stood. The doctor struggled against the enchantment that was keeping him from moving, but to no avail. Tashi was attempting to break free as well, with no luck.

"Human . . . as weak as all the others of your kind," the creature said to Vance, before shifting her eyes to Tashi. She appeared amused by the Guardian's inability to overcome the enchantment. "I expected more from you. But it appears the gryphon did not give you much magical protection. Oh, he made you formidable. Strong and immortal, if the rumors are true. But you can be stopped quite easily." Vantana instantly recognized her voice as the one on the digital recordings. This creature must have shape-shifted and posed as Iaira's therapist all this time in order to extract information. Before Vance could say a word, the finfolk suddenly clenched her fists and hissed. Vance's eyes closed against his will and he lost consciousness.

* * *

Vance couldn't tell how long he had been out, but when he awoke, things had changed—and not for the better. He was sitting on the floor, propped up against the wall of the study. His hands and feet were bound in seaweed, and the creature loomed over him.

"Oh good, you're awake," she said in a mocking tone. "I brought you some friends." Vance glanced to his right to find an alert Sam and Iaira sitting next to him, tied up as well. Tashi was on his other side, also awake.

"Everyone okay?" Vance asked.

"Not exactly," Sam answered.

"I'm so sorry," Iaira said. "It was all my fault. All of it."

"She used dark magic on you, Iaira," Vance reminded her. "There was *nothing* you could do."

"I betrayed my people by abandoning them, and then I betrayed them again by exposing them," Iaira said.

"You sealed their fate, as well as your own," the creature remarked with a slimy grin.

"So you're working with Lief? Helping the very humans you despise?" Vance asked.

"He works for *me*. Does my bidding. Weak-minded fool," the finfolk sneered. "When my allies in the oceans told me of your escape from Ta Cathair, I began tracking your movements. I was mere moments away from capturing you when you got caught in that net and those primitives pulled you aboard."

"I remember it all now," Iaira said. "I was being chased by something, I didn't know what. And I raced into the bay but got caught up in the fishing net and hit my head on Lief's boat, trying to get loose. Then I woke up on the deck. And I remembered who I was. I told Lief, and he promised to return me home and keep my secret. But then—"

"I changed the plan," the finfolk interjected. "And I saw a need that only the human could fill. Thankfully, you were very forthcoming with the locations of the colonies, and that helped me make Lief a very wealthy man."

"But you wanted to know about Ta Cathair . . . and I never told you," Iaira said. "No matter what you tried, your magic couldn't get it out of me."

"Not then, that is true. But it eventually did."

"What do you mean?" Iaira said, suddenly unnerved. The creature leaned down and ripped the coral pendant necklace off Iaira's neck.

"The only remnant of your parents' shipwreck. Your pretend parents, of course. And the pretend shipwreck. You were so sentimental that you never took it off."

"It was enchanted," Iaira realized with a heavy sigh.

The monster grinned. "I could hear and see everything."

"The ships at Atlantis were yours," Vance concluded.

The finfolk nodded. "I instructed Lief to follow you there, but it was simply the first sacred point. So we kept following until you led us right to Ta Cathair."

"What will you do, creature?" Tashi asked. "Attack the city single-handedly? Even if you have brethren, your kind was defeated before—you will be defeated again."

"I don't think so," the finfolk replied. "You see, Lief is above Ta Cathair right now, aboard the *Pearl*. The ship named after you will be the tool of your kingdom's destruction. I designed it myself. Ironic, don't you think?"

"The drill," Sam blurted out. "That's why you made Lief rich. You needed him to build a ship powerful enough to—"

"Free the Leviathan," Iaira said, completing Sam's thought.

"And the drill is moving beneath Ta Cathair as we speak," the finfolk told them. "The Leviathan will rise up and kill your people. All of your people."

"Just like you killed Maris?" Vance interjected, baiting the creature.

"Not yet," she responded. "I kept him alive, just in case he proved useful. But now that you're here and Ta Cathair is under attack, I can eliminate him. After I eliminate all of you, of course."

"But the Leviathan can't be controlled," Iaira reminded her. "You'll be dooming the *world*."

"I'll be dooming *humanity*, and they deserve it," the finfolk responded angrily. "They pollute our life's blood, and we must hide and cower? They deserve their destruction. Starting with these two." The monster moved toward Sam and Vance.

Now, this is quite a pickle, Vance thought. He didn't have a backup plan. And with Sprite and Penelope on some special errand for Phylassos, there was no cavalry coming. He racked his brain for a way out, but none appeared. The finfolk stood over Vantana and gestured with her hands. The ranger knew a spell being cast when he saw one, and given her recent declaration, it probably wasn't going to make him more handsome. Sure enough, the air suddenly left his lungs in a whoosh. He felt his chest tighten as though he were being slowly suffocated by a boa constrictor. His body seized up, and the lack of oxygen was no doubt going to turn his brain into jelly. He could feel death closing in, when Sam suddenly cried out.

"Wait!"

The monster paused. Vantana inhaled as much air as he could.

"Kill me first," the boy demanded.

"Sam!" Vance, Tashi, and Iaira exclaimed all at once.

"I'm serious," Sam told them. "If we're all going to die, according to the fish-woman here—"

"Finfolk," the creature corrected him, irritated.

"Whatever. The point is, I want to go first. I love to go first. I love riding in the front of the roller coaster or being in the front on the log ride at the water park; you know, the one who gets drenched. I even like the first day of school and the first day after vacation. I like it when the teacher calls on me first. I actually try to be the first guest at any party I go to."

Vantana had gotten to know Sam London well enough to know that he was stalling. But why? What was he waiting for? Was he simply trying to prolong the inevitable, or did he know something Vance didn't? Whatever the case, the doctor knew when there was a time to pile on, and this was it.

"Now, hold on a minute," Vance demanded, just as the finfolk had begun to shift toward Sam. "Don't I get a say in this? I've competed my whole life in all kinds of things. From apple-pie-eating contests to bog snorkeling, and I never ever came in second place. I'm not going to start now."

"How about I kill you both at the same time?" the creature suggested in a huff. She raised her hands again, and Sam interrupted.

"Can I choose?" he asked.

"Choose what?" the finfolk responded, growing increasingly more impatient.

"The way you kill me. Like the method or spell you use."

"No," it replied.

"Seriously? I mean, it doesn't seem like that much to ask," Sam said. "I'd just like to be able to pick how I bite it."

"It doesn't work that way," the monster said, exasperated.

"Oh, I get it. That's the only death spell you know," Sam concluded.

"I think you hit the nail on the head, Sam," Vance added. "If this finfolk here was an ice cream store, instead of thirty-one flavors on the sign outside, it'd just be a big fat one."

"Yeah," Sam chuckled. "A flavor called 'Lame.'" They both laughed. That really upset the creature.

"Shut up and die!" it snarled, and raised its hands, preparing to unleash its magic.

"Finfolk, I too have a question," Tashi chimed in. The creature eyed the Guardian. "How are you going to kill me, exactly?" Tashi must have spotted Vance and Sam's strategy and decided to get in on the action, the ranger surmised.

"I haven't decided," the monster told her.

"But you have a plan?"

"What does it matter?"

"I am very hard to kill. Perhaps impossible," Tashi said. "So I was wondering how you would do it. That way, if I knew it wouldn't work, I could tell you now and we'd save a lot of time on trial and error."

"Maybe I'll just keep you as a pet," the finfolk said.

"She'd make a terrible pet," Sam told the creature.

"I'd be a great pet," Tashi retorted, feigning offense.

"She would not," Sam mouthed to the monster, then said,

311

"But I'd love to take the pet option. Not ideal, but given the choice . . ."

"I agree," Vance said. "I'll take the pet option as well."

"I wouldn't mind the pet option," Iaira chimed in.

"Enough!" the creature exclaimed, now thoroughly annoyed. "There is no pet option!" They all started to vocally complain, but the finfolk was done listening. She raised her hands again, and a swirl of bluish fire began to form on her fingertips. *This is it,* Vance thought. And then a male voice echoed through the penthouse.

"Hello?"

"Is she here? Do you see her?" a girl's voice asked. The creature froze and narrowed her big fish eyes.

"Who is that?" she asked with equal parts suspicion and irritation.

"Sounds like we have guests," Sam remarked with a wry grin.

Chapter 17

INTO THE CAVE

SL002-130-80

SUBJ: Gomez, Francis

SOURCE: WS, BG

DATE: ▉▉▉▉▉▉

When Francis Gomez spotted the new post on Pearl Eklund's social media page, his heart soared. There had been no word from his favorite celebrity for what seemed like an eternity but was actually just a few days. Francis was still coming off cloud nine from his surprise meeting with Pearl at the retirement home, where he worked as a nurse. Formerly worked, that is. He'd been fired for allowing Pearl to speak with one of the patients—a guy everyone called "Crazy Murphy." Murphy had appeared to know Pearl and had announced that she had a fin like a mermaid.

Even though he was fired, Francis considered that day to be his best ever. Pearl was as perfect in real life as he imagined her to be. But her disappearance had left him in a lurch. Searching for a new job had given him a lot of downtime. Downtime that would have normally been spent obsessing over Pearl's latest posts or reading news about her from various fan sites. But the stories had dwindled and people began to lose interest after her father's announcement that Pearl was on a humanitarian mission. This new message from the Miami "it" girl could not have come at a better time.

He had been in the midst of preparing for a job interview when his phone emitted the special chime he'd programmed to correspond with Pearl Eklund's social media page. He nearly dropped the phone as he juggled it to bring up the message. Her new post was unlike any she had ever posted. It was a video, and Francis couldn't click the play button fast enough. Pearl didn't appear as made-up as she always did, but maybe this was a new, more natural look for her, he concluded. Whatever the case, she still looked Pearl-tacular. He turned up the volume and listened, intently.

"Hello, my shiny little gems. Long time, no chat. I've been super-busy doing a reality television show. . . . Yay! In the episode we're shooting right now, I'm pretending to get captured by a hideous sea monster. Gross! But guess what? Whoever gets up here to my penthouse and rescues me gets to hang out with yours

truly and party! How Pearl-tastic is that? My passcode
to get inside is 4-2-4-7-2. Don't pay any attention to
the security guards; they have to pretend to not be in on
it. It's all part of the show. There are hidden cameras
everywhere capturing the action. So you have a chance to
be a star, just like me! But you need to hurry if you're
going to win the ultimate prize. Good luck, my gems. I'm
counting on you!"

Francis watched it a few more times on his phone
as he rushed out of his house and headed downtown to
the Eklund Energy building. The job interview would have
to wait.

SL002-130-81
SUBJ: Bradley, Wanda
SOURCE: WS, BG
DATE: ███████

Wanda Bradley had been following Pearl Eklund's rise to
fame from the very beginning. She saw Pearl in her first
fashion show at a local mall and became an instant fan.
She met the model a few times since then at various
appearances that the social media star held around
town. Wanda belonged to the Precious Gems Fan Club, an
elite group of Pearl Eklund fans who were highly active

on social media and often received replies from Pearl herself—which indicated that the star actually read their posts. This made Wanda a minor celebrity in her high school. She even received a handmade gift from Pearl the previous Christmas that included an autographed picture of the star, as well as a blanket and pillow that Wanda used every night.

Wanda styled her hair like Pearl's, which was no small feat, considering the star changed her hairstyle weekly. Wanda also did her makeup like Pearl—agonizing over internet videos to ensure it matched perfectly. When she tried to dress like the model, her parents told her they couldn't afford it. But Wanda was not easily stopped when it came to her idol, so she went out and bought fabric, learned how to sew, and created her best duplicate outfits for a quarter of the price. She was obsessed with all things Pearl Eklund and was devastated by the star's recent disappearance. No one had seen or heard from Pearl in the fan community for days, though her dad claimed she was on a mission helping the poor. That was Pearl, Wanda thought. Always so generous and selfless. Wanda's parents generally disagreed with their daughter's rosy assessment, and that led to a few arguments around the dinner table about vanity and arrogance. But her parents were just jealous, Wanda concluded. Without Pearl's presence, Wanda felt like she had lost her best friend. She couldn't stop refreshing the pages of Pearl-related sites and the star's own social media wall to get the latest update. And then it happened. A video appeared from Pearl. She was back and she was in trouble.

Not real trouble, of course, but trouble cooked up in the context of a television show. Now she was inviting her fans to help save her. This was the moment Wanda had been waiting for. She would not only be in the presence of her idol once again, but she would also be on television! Maybe she'd become as famous as Pearl. Her daydreams were growing more elaborate by the second, until she refocused herself, slipped out of the house, and headed to downtown Miami. She didn't even bother calling her friends. If they didn't already know, it would mean less competition. She was determined to be the heroine and save her absolute favorite damsel in distress.

When Francis Gomez appeared in the doorway to the study in Pearl Eklund's penthouse, Sam London knew his plan had worked. Then Wanda Bradley followed, and Sam smiled in quiet celebration.

"Oh my God! She's in here, everyone! It's really her!" Francis exclaimed.

"Pearl!" Wanda squealed in delight as more voices echoed in the foyer, and then the two were joined by half a dozen more kids who made a beeline for Iaira. The fans pushed the finfolk aside, as if the monster were a plastic prop on a movie set, and converged on the star.

317

"What is this? Who are you people?" the creature snarled.

"They're my gems. The fans you helped me create to distract me from my true purpose, to make me forget where I belong," Iaira replied gleefully.

Within minutes, the place was mobbed with people. Francis and Wanda insisted on unbinding Iaira together, since they'd been the first to arrive on scene. Iaira asked them to untie her friends, which they gladly did. As soon as Tashi was loose, the Guardian retrieved her shekchen and searched for the finfolk, but it appeared to have been swallowed up by the crowd, which had now surrounded Iaira, snapping photos and getting autographs.

"Where did the creature go?" Tashi asked.

"She could have shape-shifted into anyone and slipped out undetected," Vance told her. "Well done, Sam," the doctor added.

"Thanks!" Sam replied. He knew the plan was risky. What if no one showed up or just a few wandered in and the finfolk attacked? He was counting on a big display of support to help overpower the creature. It actually wound up being a much bigger showing than he had imagined, and the penthouse was packed to the hilt.

"We need to clear these people out," Vantana yelled to Iaira. She nodded—amid the camera flashes, personal questions, and general adoration as her gems stared in awe at Pearl's penthouse furnishings.

* * *

An hour later, Sam, Vance, and Tashi had helped Iaira and the Eklund security guards herd most of the fans into the living room—the overflow was being corralled in the lobby. Sam noticed the Guardian tightly gripping her shekchen and keeping a close eye on Pearl's gems. She was no doubt concerned that the finfolk could still be lurking about in disguise, and Sam motioned for Tashi, Vance, and Iaira to meet him in the study.

"I'm going to have to return to Miami at some point to deliver on that promised reward, Sam," Iaira said once they were all in the room.

"Sorry." Sam shrugged; he hadn't thought that far ahead.

"Not a problem," Iaira replied, smiling. "I'm happy to do it. They saved our lives. Only problem is, we didn't get a chance to find out where the finfolk is holding Maris."

"That is true, but I believe I may know," Tashi revealed. "Before we were attacked by the creature, I found a secret room behind a bookshelf in the library. I didn't have a chance to get inside."

"Let's have a look," Vance said, gesturing to Tashi, who led them into the library and stepped toward the central bookcase. The room was floor-to-ceiling shelves filled with hundreds of books. Tashi slid her finger between two of the shelving units.

"I believe this is where it opens," she said. "There has to be a release somewhere."

They began pulling on books, and even tried the light fixtures on the walls, like they were in some old movie with a spooky house. Sam's eyes eventually fell upon the book he immediately knew was the switch: Hans Christian Andersen's "The Little Mermaid." He pulled on it and heard a *click*.

"You found it!" Iaira exclaimed.

Tashi opened the door, and they all rushed inside. The room was constructed of steel, and in the center was a chair. It resembled a dentist's chair, but with clamps for binding wrists and ankles. Maris was fastened to the chair, and he looked awful. Pale, gaunt, and unconscious.

"Maris!" Iaira exclaimed, dashing to his side. "Maris?" she said more quietly, and nudged him. His eyes squinted open. "I am here to bring you home. Our kingdom needs you," she told him softly.

"Our kingdom?" he asked. His eyes closed, then reopened. "Who are you?"

"It's me. Fish-face. Remember?" she said with a smile. He eyed her, still unsure.

"He's been out of the water too long," Vance concluded. "He's starting to lose his memory."

"Maybe this will help." Iaira leaned in and kissed Maris gently on the forehead. There was something magical about it, and not just romantic magic but actual magic. A blue spark flashed as Iaira's lips touched his skin, and Sam could see the energy spread throughout the selkie's body. It rejuvenated him just enough to bring him back from the brink. Vance unfastened the clamps and helped the selkie to his feet. He held on to Vance for support.

"Finfolk," Maris announced.

"We know. And she's attacking Ta Cathair," Iaira informed him. "She's releasing the Leviathan." His face went grim.

"We must stop it!" Maris exclaimed.

"And we will, right after we free another prisoner of that vile creature," Iaira declared.

Tashi of Kustos did not want Sam London returning to Ta Cathair. After all, according to the finfolk, the city would be under siege by a legendary creature that could end all of humanity. Sam had no reason to accompany Tashi and the others into such a dangerous situation, but he refused all entreaties to convince him otherwise. To make matters even worse, Iaira insisted on bringing another human along—Murphy, who she claimed might have some helpful knowledge of the drilling technology that could stop the ship and foil the finfolk's plan.

While they were readying to leave the penthouse, Iaira recruited Francis Gomez to help rescue Murphy. Gomez agreed, still believing he was taking part in a reality show. Thanks to the low-level security at the retirement home, Francis easily smuggled Murphy out of the building in a laundry bin.

On the way to Falling Waters State Park in a DMW-issued SUV, Vance caught the old fisherman up on the state of mythical creatures in the world, and Murphy agreed to assist in stopping Lief's ship from releasing the Leviathan. He didn't understand what that meant entirely, but he understood it was important to Iaira, and that was enough. Exposing Murphy to the truth was an unorthodox move, Tashi thought, but Vance believed it was necessary, given the time-sensitive situation, and Vance hoped Murphy proved useful in the hours ahead. Just prior to boarding the dvergen subway, Vantana made another split-second decision and contacted Bob Ferguson in the DMW's Washington, DC, office.

"Initiate Protocol Two," Vance ordered.

"Excuse me?" Bob replied, surprised by the request.

"You heard me, Bob. Protocol Two."

"But—but Protocol Two is only for emergencies, Dr. Vantana," Ferguson said nervously. "It can be authorized only if there is an imminent threat of exposure."

"There is. You have to inform the world's leaders to pull back all shipping, military, and surveillance activity in the Indian Ocean and the surrounding areas."

"I can't just ring up world leaders like I'm calling a friend. It would require approval by Dr. Knox."

"Knox is unreachable, and this is an impending crisis with catastrophic potential," Vance told him firmly. "You gotta do it, Bob. Unless you want to be responsible for the single largest breach in the history of the gryphon's law." A few seconds of silence elapsed before Bob came back over the badge.

"Do you know how many rules I'd be breaking if I did this?" he asked quietly. Vance smiled—he had him now.

"Don't look at it as breaking the rules, Bobby. We're just going to bend them a lot before they snap. Like an old carrot."

With the DC office no doubt awhirl with activity, the group hopped aboard the subway and arrived at Sri Venkateswara

National Park in India a short time later, heading to the coast, where Iaira called on the Makara.

After climbing onto the creature again, they were shuttled out into the open sea, where they quickly spotted Lief's drilling ship, the *Pearl*, looming in the distance. The seven-hundred-foot-long vessel included a helipad, cranes, and a derrick that reached a hundred feet high. Although the group on the Makara was still a good distance from the ship, Tashi could determine that there were a little over thirty crew members aboard, helping to sail the ship and operate the rig.

"That ship is a floating drilling platform," Murphy explained. "It's capable of pushing down through several hundred feet of seabed to expose methane hydrate deposits. A well is created that pumps up the fire ice to the ship in the form of gas. But the thing is, that process can loosen the surrounding bedrock. In some cases it can trigger landslides, cause tsunamis—"

"And free Leviathans," Tashi added. Murphy shrugged.

"I guess so."

"So now we are dealing with two possible catastrophes," Tashi concluded.

"Good times," Vance added.

"I don't believe they've succeeded in releasing the creature yet," Tashi noted. "We would no doubt already see the consequences."

"Agreed. That gives us some time to try to stop him," Vance said. "Mr. Murphy, do you think you can turn off that drill if we get you onto that ship?"

"I can turn it off, sure, but I don't think they'd let me," Murphy replied.

"Leave that to me and Tashi," the doctor assured him. "I have an idea."

"I will remain with Sam London," Tashi informed Vantana.

"It is best if he comes with us," Iaira contended. "He can help get my people to safety. I promise, I will protect his life with my own."

"If we do manage to stop this thing, the safest place for him might be in that city," Vance added. The Guardian considered this information. If she could stop the threat on the ship, Vantana was right. And bringing Sam onto the ship with them would prove dangerous.

"I'm going with Iaira," Sam said, interrupting the Guardian's thoughts. Tashi eyed him and then nodded her approval.

"Be mindful of your surroundings," she said.

"Always," he chirped, but Tashi gave him a look that said otherwise.

The Makara snuck up to the drilling ship, and Tashi, Vance, and Murphy disembarked. The creature then dove into the water with the others still on its back. Vance led Tashi and Murphy to a ladder at the rear of the vessel.

"I'm new to all this. Do we have a plan of some sort?" Murphy asked.

"You bet," Vance told him. "We have to get to Lief."

"That is a mission, not a plan," Tashi noted.

"We know Lief is under the influence of the finfolk's dark

magic, right?" Vance asked. Tashi nodded her agreement. "Well, the only way we can get the crew to help us stop this thing is to have Lief on our side. So we have to break the spell first."

"How do you suppose we do that?" the Guardian asked.

"Easy as pie. You're gonna shoot him with your shekchen," Vance said. Of course, Tashi realized. Her shekchen had the ability to disrupt magic. It's why Dr. Knox had been forced to transform into Phylassos in Hérault during Sam London's first case.

"Excellent idea, Dr. Vantana," Tashi complimented the ranger. "Now, where can I find Mr. Eklund."

"He'll likely be on the bridge," Murphy said. "Follow me."

Vance and Tashi headed up the ladder behind Murphy and slipped aboard undetected. The drill sounded like it was working overtime, emitting a loud, sustained squeal and making the deck plates vibrate like chattering teeth. The trio moved stealthily along the side of the ship, hiding behind equipment when needed, to avoid being spotted. As they climbed a set of metal stairs and headed down a gangway toward the bridge, a hatch door opened and Lief Eklund emerged. They froze in place and then quietly crept after him onto the bridge. There were three crew members working the ship's controls, but they appeared oblivious to their new guests. Lief headed to the captain's chair, and Vance nudged Tashi, indicating that she should let him have it.

"Excuse me, Mr. Eklund," Tashi whispered—she really didn't care for striking people behind their backs. As soon as he turned, she leveled her shekchen and shot a bolt at him. Lief convulsed as he took the charge, then fell toward the ground, and Vantana caught him. The Guardian quickly placed a hand on his shoulder. She closed her eyes, helping him return to consciousness.

"Who are you?" Lief asked, still dazed. Taking in his surroundings, his eyes went wide. "Murphy?"

"Hey, pal," the fisherman said. "Your head clearer?" Lief grabbed his head reflexively.

"Where's Pearl?" Eklund asked. The crew had turned from their stations and were shooting looks at each other and the visitors.

"Everyone just calm down. I'm with the U.S. government. We're here to prevent a disaster," Vance announced hastily as he flashed his badge. He then looked to Tashi. "Does he remember what happened?"

"Are you aware of the events that have transpired since the night you found the mermaid in Biscayne Bay?" the Guardian asked Lief.

"Yes . . . but it's like a dream," Lief replied. And then he suddenly blurted out, "Oh no! Hawkins . . . she's not human. She wants to—we have to stop that drill!" Lief climbed to his feet and rushed to the navigation controls. He began frantically inputting commands into a touch screen.

"I think we're too late," Murphy said, gesturing to an overhead monitor. The screen showed an infrared night-vision image of the drill's point of contact with the seabed. The earth had a massive fissure, and a creature swam out of the opening—it was the finfolk known as Hawkins. And she wasn't alone. She was followed out of the crevice by something so large that the camera lens went black.

"The Leviathan is loose!" Tashi announced.

"And it looks like we've got more fish to fry," Vance added as he gestured toward the crew members on the bridge. They were approaching . . . and transforming into finfolk!

Tashi aimed and fired off a short burst of blue energy at each of the creatures. They convulsed and dropped to the deck.

"How many crew are on this ship?" Vance asked.

"Thirty-five . . . well, thirty-two," Lief replied, factoring in the unconscious bridge crew.

"The question is, how many are finfolk in disguise?" Tashi posited.

"All of them," Murphy said, pointing out the bridge window at the crew now gathering together and heading toward the bridge. They were transforming en masse.

"How much charge do you have left on that?" Vance asked, motioning to the shekchen.

"None," Tashi answered. Vance sighed.

"Great. We have to get ourselves off this ship, pronto," Vance said. "I take it you have lifeboats on this thing?" he asked Lief.

"Yes, of course. Follow me."

Lief led the way out of the bridge and onto the gangway, but when they turned toward the rear of the vessel, they saw finfolk heading right for them. They spun around to move the other way, but the creatures were approaching from that side as well. With two escape routes blocked, they went the only way they could—up. The four climbed the metal stairs to the helipad, but there was no helicopter waiting to help them get away. They quickly found themselves standing in the center of the pad surrounded on all sides by snarling finfolk.

"No way you can charge that shekchen?" Vance confirmed while unsheathing his knife and preparing for battle.

"I must have a connection to Gaia. Water will not work," Tashi clarified. "But I can fight them without it."

"Maybe you can, maybe I can, but they can't," Vance said, gesturing to Murphy and Lief.

"What is Gaia?" Murphy asked.

"It is the earth," Tashi answered. "I must be linked to it directly to draw on its energy."

"You already are," Murphy replied. "The drill is connected to the ship, and it's driving straight down into the earth." Tashi and Vance exchanged a look of realization. Without saying another word, the Guardian touched the shekchen to the helipad and waited.

"It might take a moment," she told them.

"We're fresh out of moments," Vance observed.

The finfolk converged. Vantana slashed at them with his knife, while Murphy and Lief stood back-to-back, fists raised. It was easy to see that this was not going to end well. Fortunately, the creatures were distracted by the blue energy of Gaia crawling up over the deck and across the helipad. They followed the trail, which led to Tashi's shekchen, but by the time they realized what was happening, it was too late. The shekchen was charged and ready. The Guardian stood tall and leveled her weapon.

"Get down!" she ordered. Vance pushed both of the men to the deck and dropped onto his belly. Tashi spun like a top, firing off her shekchen like a Gatling gun. One by one, the finfolk were hit by devastating bolts of energy. The creatures collapsed, convulsed, and quickly lost consciousness. Within seconds, the entire crew had been taken care of, but there was no time to celebrate. The ship was rocked by a massive wave caused by an even more massive creature. The monstrous beast breached the surface, giving Tashi and the others their first full view of the legendary Leviathan.

The creature was a horrifying amalgam of dragon and whale—a hideous beast that sported flipperlike appendages where a dragon's wings would be, and a mane of sharp, spiky fins that ran the length of its elongated body. It had two rows of serrated teeth, narrow slits for eyes, and a whale's tail that was the size of Cletus. It roared as it shot out of the water, and the Guardian ran down the side of the ship toward the front.

"Tashi!" Vance yelled, but she wasn't listening. She knew what needed to be done. She leapt over the railing, just as the Leviathan dove back into the water.

Once beneath the water's surface, the Guardian's gills formed quickly. She swam toward the creature and grabbed hold of one of its spiky fins as it turned. She climbed on and spotted the finfolk known as Hawkins riding the beast's neck, likely guiding it with dark magic. The Leviathan shot through the tunnel that led to Ta Cathair, and Tashi knew there wasn't much time left to stop Hawkins before the monster laid waste to the undersea kingdom. The Guardian crept stealthily along the creature's body toward the finfolk. When they emerged outside the city, Tashi could see that a mass evacuation was still under way. Thousands of selkies and mer-people were swimming for the arena. The kingdom's entire army was positioned just beyond the tunnel's opening, awaiting the Leviathan's appearance. They opened fire with their specialized weapons, which appeared to emit a strong, focused blast of energy that pushed the water at destructive speed. But their efforts had no effect. The beast just barreled right through them and headed straight for the city.

The finfolk guided the creature right down the city's main thoroughfare, causing massive destruction. The Leviathan's spiky fins ripped up the roadway, sending chunks soaring through the water, and its tail plowed through buildings, which crumbled and collapsed. Tashi was directly behind the finfolk and was ready to pounce, when she spotted the unthinkable: Sam London was riding Rosi the seahorse just ahead of the Leviathan! The Guardian was thunderstruck. She had no idea what the boy was up to, until she noticed a large group of Ta Cathair's soldiers positioned on a mountainside in the distance. They were armed with larger versions of their wave weapons, all of which were aimed toward a cave at the end of a canyon. Tashi quickly concluded that Sam was attempting to lure the Leviathan inside the cave so that the soldiers could cause a cave-in that would trap the beast. But how would he escape in time to avoid the same fate? It was clear—she had to stop the creature herself to save Sam from what was sure to be a suicide mission. Tashi didn't know what led him to take up this cause and regretted ever allowing the boy to leave her side.

With no time to waste, Tashi stabbed the Leviathan with her shekchen and released the remaining energy. A deafening groan echoed through the kingdom as the creature hit the seafloor and slid along the pearl-paved streets of Ta Cathair. The energy also poured into the finfolk, who convulsed from the charge, before lunging at the Guardian and knocking the shekchen away. Without Tashi's hand gripping the weapon, the flow of energy immediately ceased. The finfolk was wily in the water, as the ocean was her natural environment. She gestured with her hands toward Tashi, attempting magic, but nothing happened. The finfolk tried again, but still nothing. The Guardian smirked—the energy of the shekchen had disrupted the finfolk's ability to manipulate magic. Though this was likely a temporary phenomenon, it gave Tashi a chance at stopping the creature and saving the day.

Without the energy of the shekchen pulsing through its body, the Leviathan let out a screeching growl and continued its path of destruction. The creature nipped at Rosi's tail as it followed Sam into the canyon—the same one that had been part of the Seahorse 5000 route. The sudden movement knocked both the Guardian and the finfolk off balance. They fell from the Leviathan's back, but each was able to grab hold of a fin and hang on.

With one fluid move, the finfolk hurled herself up onto

the Leviathan's back, and Tashi joined her. The pair faced off before the finfolk made the first move. Its speed and dexterity in the water put the Guardian at a significant disadvantage. The creature charged and pinned Tashi to the Leviathan's back. She gripped Tashi's neck with her clawlike hand and attempted to impale the Guardian's head on one of the Leviathan's spiky fins. Tashi strained against the pressure, but was losing ground. Her face hit the tip of the spike, which drew blood, and then Tashi saw the finfolk's eyes light up—she had her magic back. She smiled and raised her arm to cast a spell, but she never got the chance.

A fin—a mermaid fin—swatted at the finfolk, disorienting it. Iaira was suddenly beside them on a seahorse, and she whacked the creature a second and third time until the finfolk lost her hold on the Leviathan. She tumbled back, directly into the path of a thermal vent. The creature melted into nothing in seconds. But the Leviathan was unfazed by the loss of its master. The monster took a sharp corner, and its body slammed into the side of the canyon, causing a small avalanche. Tashi was thrown from the beast, and Iaira dove and caught her before the Guardian could meet the same fate as the finfolk. The Leviathan zoomed ahead in pursuit of Sam, leaving Tashi and Iaira far behind.

"We must tell those soldiers to hold their fire!" the Guardian shouted. But there wasn't any time. The Leviathan entered the cave after Sam, and the soldiers immediately fired on the opening. There was an earth-shattering rumble. Iaira and

Tashi were tossed backward by the impact waves as the cave began to collapse on itself.

"I'm going in!" Iaira announced, triggering the seahorse's jets and racing ahead.

When the princess was halfway to the cave, the rock around the opening buckled and collapsed completely. A horrible sound reverberated throughout the canyon, and a huge plume of sand whirled upward, blinding Tashi and sending Iaira reeling back.

"No!" she screamed.

The dust settled, and the screech of the Leviathan waned as the beast became permanently trapped beneath thousands of tons of rock. Tashi felt her heart sink. There was no sign of Sam . . . and no way he would have survived the cave-in. She felt an immediate and powerful emotion that was entirely alien to her: the one Sam called sadness. Guardians dealt with death in a celebratory way. Given their immortality, death had always been a choice. But this was not Sam's choice—it was a devastating tragedy.

Dr. Vance Vantana arrived with General Searus and Queen Muiria, taking in the collapse and the look on Tashi's face.

"Where is he?" the doctor asked, as though he had already deduced the answer. Iaira limply gestured to the cave-in.

"Sam London sacrificed himself to save our people," she said.

"Tashi?" Vance eyed the Guardian, hoping for another answer. But the Guardian couldn't oblige. Not this time. She was just about to nod, when she spotted a glimmer in the distance amid the cave-in rocks. Something—or, rather, someone—was emerging from the rubble.

"Who's that?" Iaira asked.

Tashi could discern the seahorse Rosi approaching. Sam was lying across its back, and there was another creature leading it. It appeared to be a sea creature, but not a mermaid or selkie or even finfolk. The hands had webbed fingers, the feet were flippers, the ears pointy and finlike. It was a sea nymph, or Nereid, Tashi concluded. As the creature drew closer, Tashi slowly realized that this wasn't a random sea nymph that had rescued Sam. Much to the Guardian's surprise, Tashi knew this sea nymph . . . and so did Sam London.

Chapter 18
THE MAIDEN COUNCIL

When Sam finally passed through the cave's entrance with the
Leviathan nipping at his heels, he still had no plan for escape.
He hadn't thought that far ahead. He was shocked he had gotten this far with the creature remaining on his tail. Leading
the Leviathan into the cave at the end of Atargatis canyon
and trapping it with a massive cave-in wasn't even his idea.
It was Princess Iaira who'd insisted on executing this insane
plan, despite all objections, and Sam was supposed to just retrieve Rosi from the stables. But by the time he returned with
the seahorse, the Leviathan had entered the city limits and
debris was raining down from the monster's destruction. Ta
Cathair became an instant war zone, and Sam's ears rang with
the screams of the wounded and calls for help. As the princess
barked orders to her soldiers and rushed to aid the injured,
Sam realized that her people couldn't lose her again. Not when

their whole world was crumbling around them. He informed Rosi of the change in plans, the seahorse snorted her approval, and then they took off toward the Leviathan.

It seemed like such an easy decision at the time, except now he was faced with the prospect of being buried alive with the beast for all eternity. He knew Iaira had intended to rocket her way out of the cave by using the seahorse's jets, and he did have some fuel left in the tanks, but he still needed to lure the monster deep enough inside the cave to ensure it would be trapped. Luckily, Sam spotted a narrow cavity toward the back of the cave and directed Rosi to swim for it. The cavity was beyond a web of stalactites and stalagmites, and Sam was betting on the Leviathan getting itself lodged between the cavern wall and the icicle-like rock formations.

Everything was going according to his hastily devised plan. The Leviathan pushed through the cavity and became stuck, but only its upper body was trapped. Sam heard the soldiers begin to open fire and knew he had only seconds to spare. He hit the thrusters, and the seahorse shot forward, hurtling toward the exit, just as the roof of the opening began to crumble.

But the Leviathan wouldn't go down so easily. As the beast struggled to break free, its massive tail sliced back and forth through the water. Sam veered right in an attempt to dodge the fin, but the tip caught him in the chest. He was knocked hard off Rosi and sent careening into the cave wall. Sam slammed into the rock and dropped to a small ledge right below. He was barely conscious and suffering from the intense pain of what was likely several broken bones, including a cracked rib or two. Rosi rushed to his side and nudged him with her muzzle, but he couldn't move, his injuries having effectively paralyzed him. Even worse, he could see the Leviathan moving—it was nearly free. The cave was collapsing and time had run out.

"Go!" Sam told the seahorse. Rosi whined and tried again to help him climb on, but it was no use. "It's okay. . . ."

As the world grew darker for Sam London, he could have sworn he saw an angel approaching. He wasn't sure he could trust his eyes anymore—they pulsed with pain. Everything seemed to have a halo, and maybe this angelic figure was simply a hallucination—something to help him transition to the other side. The figure got closer and reached out with webbed fingers. Sam's eyes moved from the fingers to the face of his rescuer and he immediately concluded that he had to be hallucinating. After all, what else could explain the fact that this angelic figure appeared to be a student at Benicia Middle School? And not just any student, but the girl who had her locker next to his. The one who always missed Fish Fridays.

"Time to get you out of here, Sam London," Nerida Nyx said. "We have school tomorrow."

* * *

Sam awoke on the beach with a gasp and a cough. He reflexively moved backward, unsure where he was or what had happened. Tashi knelt in front of him, her hands out, and he presumed that she must have healed him.

"Glad to see you're okay, buddy," Vance said. Sam spotted

Dr. Vantana standing nearby, along with another figure—the angel from the cave. The one who had apparently saved him from certain death.

"Nerida?" he said, and gaped in complete shock. Could it be? The girl he saw every day . . . his crush for as long as he could remember?

"Hi, Sam," she said with a small smile. "Sorry I couldn't tell you the truth about what I really am, but—"

"You're a mermaid?" Sam asked.

"No . . . I'm a Nereid, a sea nymph."

Sam grinned, then suddenly remembered—"What happened to the . . . ," he began, rubbing his aching head.

"Leviathan? He's trapped under a great big pile of rock, hopefully forever," Vance informed him. "You saved everyone, *and* you almost got yourself killed in the process. I want you to promise you won't do anything that stupid again, but you probably will." Sam shrugged sheepishly and looked back to Nerida.

"How did you know I was here?" he asked, confused.

"I received an urgent message from Rangers Sprite and Naughton."

"And they sent you here to help me?" Sam asked. That didn't make much sense, he thought. How would they have known he needed help? Weren't they on some secret mission? Why send Nerida?

"No, Sam," she replied. "That was just good timing. They sent me here to deliver some news about your mother."

"My mother? Is she okay?" He sat up straighter.

"She's in trouble. A great deal of trouble," Nerida said gravely. Then she became more contemplative. "We should have been more vigilant with regard to our mission. I'm so sorry."

"What mission? What trouble?" Sam was becoming increasingly concerned with Nerida's tone.

"My mom and I were assigned to keep an eye on Odette in Benicia—"

"Assigned by whom?" Sam pleaded.

"Phylassos," answered Nerida. Sam immediately looked to Vance, who shrugged.

"First I'm hearing of it, kid," he said.

"The day the selkie made an appearance in San Francisco, we were called to our ancestral home to determine the impact of his actions on the mythical communities beneath the sea. Because of this, we weren't there when it happened."

"When what happened?"

"When your mom found her feathers," she replied.

"Excuse me?" Sam said.

"Feathers?" Vance interjected with sudden interest. "You mean . . ." Nerida eyed the ranger and nodded. Vance's face fell.

"Will someone please tell me what's going on?" Sam exclaimed.

"There is something you don't know about your mother," Nerida began. "Something you were never supposed to know, but now it appears you must. She is not human, Sam. She is a swan maiden."

"You're joking," Sam said, half-laughing at the ridiculous claim. He knew his mom better than anyone else, and she was no swan maiden. Ettie was just a mom, an occasionally goofy, embarrassingly overly affectionate mom.

"I'm afraid it's true," Nerida told him with a seriousness he had never heard before from his longtime friend. "I know it's hard to believe. Without her feathers, she looks and acts human and believes herself to be human. But when she found them—"

"She was called home," Vance concluded, and Nerida confirmed with a solemn nod. "Aw, nuts."

"What do you mean, 'Aw, nuts'?" Sam quickly asked. "Where is she?"

"Lake Baikal?" Vance asked Nerida.

"Yes. And she is to face judgment in front of the Maiden Council."

"Judgment?" Sam repeated nervously.

"She will be punished for her crimes," Nerida told him, her voice cracking. "I'm breaking laws by telling you this, but you're my dearest friend. And you must try to save her before it's too late."

When Lynnae of Lake Baikal heard whispers that the council was once again meeting with strangers, her unquenchable curiosity led her to risk further punishment by heading to the shore to see firsthand what was happening. Ever since the green man visited the maiden sanctuary, Lynnae couldn't stop wondering why the council appeared so concerned by the news he brought. She was caught by Caer that night and simply given a stern talking-to. She found the lack of significant punishment surprising, coming from the ultra-strict disciplinarian. In fact, following the green man's visit, Lynnae had noticed a change in all of the members of the council. They seemed pensive and anxious, as well as kinder to her and her fellow maidens, who were now given more privileges that translated to less work maintaining the beauty of the sanctuary and extra time to frolic and swim. She was convinced it all had something to do with what the green man had said about a human boy named Sam London, but she didn't understand why. What was it about him that seemed to so greatly disturb them?

When she arrived at the council's gathering place and tucked herself behind another set of honeysuckle bushes, she spied two visitors. One was a wood sprite, and the other was a human female. They stood at the shoreline as the Maiden Council approached. Melusine was the first to speak.

"You are not Phylassos," she said plainly. The sprite half-smiled.

"I am Ranger Woodruff Sprite, and this is Ranger Penelope Naughton of the U.S. Department of Mythical Wildlife. We are emissaries of Phylassos."

"Where is he?" Faye asked impatiently.

"He is on his way," answered Sprite. "Where is Ettie London?"

"We do not recognize that name here," Melior, the teacher maiden, said in her studious tone.

"My apologies," said Sprite. "May we see the maiden Odette?"

Palatina nodded, and a maiden Lynnae had never seen before stepped out from beyond the trees. She wore a white dress and had two magnificent white wings that fanned out behind her. Lynnae had heard rumors of a maiden who had escaped the lake, but they were never actually believed to be true. The council had made it clear that such actions were impossible, given the Baba Yaga's guard. But could this be the rumored maiden herself?

"May we speak to Odette?" the human female named Penelope asked.

"No," replied Manto, the maiden who assigned tasks and managed the maidens' lives.

"We permitted you entrance into our sanctuary because you assured us the gryphon would come, but we do not see him," Palatina said.

"The judgment will be made without his presence," Sibyl announced.

"Please," Penelope implored. "Can we discuss this all before you render your decision?"

"The time for discussion is over," answered Caer. "She has her feathers. She is no longer of your world. You have no jurisdiction in this place. It is time for you to leave our—"

The wind suddenly kicked up, the sand whirled, and the waters surged. But it was not weather causing this disturbance. Lynnae gazed upward to see a magnificent sight: a gryphon. The legendary Phylassos had arrived. Lynnae thought back to what Caer had just said about jurisdiction. Lynnae knew of the curse and Phylassos's law, but swan maidens were unique in their relation to the gryphon's edict. Though they lived on or near water, they were not sea creatures. They also had their own authority in the Maiden Council and had arranged for autonomy from the gryphon's law and curse. Their ability to shape-shift was another reason why they did not fall under the curse's magic. She was shocked to see him here in the sanctuary. So shocked, she audibly gasped and instantly revealed herself.

"Lynnae, return to your nest at once or you will be punished," Caer said, her eyes trained on the bushes the maiden was hiding behind. "And I assure you it will prove far worse than the previous consequences."

Without wasting a moment, Lynnae popped up out of the bushes and ran off as fast as she could. She was so frightened at being caught, she just kept running and inadvertently wound up overshooting her nesting place. Thankfully, she stopped herself before she crossed the sanctuary's boundary. If she had crossed the thin, glittering line of foxfire that surrounded her home, the Baba Yaga would have dragged her back to the council for judgment. They would have immediately concluded that she was trying to escape, which is an unforgivable violation of the rules that govern the maidens. Lynnae had no intention of ever breaking that particular rule. She turned back toward the nest and was just about to head over, when she heard rustling in the forest, followed by voices.

"We can't just barge in there," a male voice announced.

"Why not?" a younger male voice asked.

"'Cause I told you—the Baba Yaga is not to be messed with. Trust me on this."

"Tashi can shoot her," the second voice asserted. He was answered by a different voice, one that also sounded young, but of a higher pitch.

"I do not attack a creature simply because it is carrying out its sworn duty," the voice maintained. "She does have a right to do so, Doctor, am I correct?"

"You are. . . . The gryphon allows it because of the sensitive nature of the maidens' existence."

"Then how will we get in?" another voice asked. "We need to find her."

"Hello?" Lynnae called out.

"Did you guys hear that?" the boy asked.

"I'm over here," the maiden said. "But do not cross the boundary, or she will come for all of us." Four figures emerged from the woods and stepped into a small clearing on the other side of the sanctuary's border.

"Are you a swan maiden?" the tall man asked.

"Yes," she answered. "Are you human?"

The man nodded. "My name is Vance. This is Tashi, Nerida, and Sam—"

"Sam? Sam London?" Lynnae asked excitedly.

"Yes," the boy said, surprised by her reaction. "Do you know me?"

"I've heard of you."

"Have you seen another human, a female?" Sam asked her.

"He means a swan maiden named Odette," Nerida clarified.

"She's my mother," the boy added hopefully.

"Your mother?" Lynnae replied slowly. So that was why the council had spoken of Sam—the maiden who was facing judgment had a child. This was all too extraordinary for Lynnae to fathom. "Of course," she said. "You are the maiden's son. The maiden who escaped."

Sam nodded. "Can you take us to see her?" he asked.

"I would, but if you cross the boundary, she *will* attack," Lynnae reminded them.

"We're going to have to find another way," Vance said. "We can't risk it."

"There is no time for another way," Sam asserted. "We have to help her now!"

At that moment, the young female named Tashi stepped across the boundary. The entire forest went silent. Every bird or animal that had been making noise ceased instantly. The result was an eerie foreboding hush.

"Tashi!" Sam exclaimed. "What are you doing?"

"Breaking the rules," she said. "Go find your mother, Sam."

A gust of wind roared through the forest and into the clearing. It sounded like a terrifying scream as it wound its way through the trees. Leaves were pulled from their branches and sent swirling into the air.

"She's coming!" Lynnae cried.

But the Baba Yaga was already there. The creature swooped

down toward the Guardian, and everyone ducked. Tashi took the full brunt of the hit and was sent hurtling through the air. Her body slammed so hard into a tree, it split the trunk. The Guardian tumbled to the ground, and the tree followed, collapsing on top of her. Sam gasped.

"No!"

His exclamation immediately drew the attention of the creature. Lynnae had never seen the Baba Yaga before—to do so would have meant violating the rules. But now she could see the creature was every bit as hideous as the stories claimed. The Baba Yaga was inhumanly thin, with skin that barely covered her bones. Her face had a long nose, sunken eyes, and iron teeth that chattered like rattling chains. A mass of stringy white hair sprouted from the creature's head in all directions.

"The sanctuary has been breached!" she snarled in a deep, gravelly voice. She lengthened that last word for several seconds and pointed at Lynnae with a bony finger that peeked out from her tattered sleeve. "Return to the sanctuary, Maiden, or you shall be—"

Before the creature could finish her sentence, she was blasted by a bolt of blue energy and propelled into the forest. Tashi had managed to crawl out from under the tree and was pointing her shekchen toward the creature.

"Go, quickly!" she ordered. "I will handle this!"

"Thank you!" Sam said, then turned to Lynnae. "Take us, please."

The maiden nodded and headed back toward the council's meeting place. The others followed closely as Lynnae led the three all the way to the shore. The maiden hung back and gestured for the others to continue on, while she took cover behind her favorite honeysuckle bushes. She could hear the gryphon speaking, but he instantly quieted when Vance, Sam, and Nerida stepped onto the sand. She was counting on their presence to distract the council enough to help her avoid detection. There was no way she was going to miss this historic event. The other maidens were not pleased by the arrival of the new strangers.

"These creatures were not permitted to enter the sanctuary!" Faye declared angrily. "You violated our trust . . . our code!"

"I did no such thing," Phylassos replied.

"Now, hang on a hot minute. We came here on our own, Council," Vance informed them. "The gryphon here had nothing to do with it, I assure you."

"And the Baba Yaga?" Sibyl asked.

"She attacked, as is her duty," Vance replied. "But she's tusslin' with a Guardian of the gryphon's claw right now and is a little busy."

Sam suddenly spotted his mother standing near a patch of trees.

"Mom!" he exclaimed. He tried to run to her, but the sand grabbed ahold of his feet, instantly immobilizing him. Lynnae had seen the council do this before with the sand, for fellow maidens who had violated the rules or defied them.

"She is not your mother any longer," Caer told him. "She is a maiden who has returned home to her sanctuary. And she will be punished for her crimes."

"What crimes?" Sam asked, bewildered. "Let me go!" He struggled against the hardened sand.

"Odette left her home, she fell in love, and she had a child," answered Manto.

"And that is a crime?"

"It is in our world," Melusine told the boy.

"When she escaped with your father, she violated our most sacred covenant," said Palatina.

"My father . . . ," Sam whispered. He stopped struggling and felt the sands relax around his feet. He turned his attention to the council. "I know that the man in the photo my mom has isn't my dad. The Salmon of Knowledge told me, but he said he couldn't reveal my father's identity. That it was a promise he made to you." Sam shifted his gaze to Phylassos.

"It was necessary, Sam," Phylassos answered. "For everyone's protection."

"I don't understand. . . . If that man in the photo isn't him, then who is?"

"He is wasting our time with these questions," Faye huffed.

"He is trying to distract us," Caer added.

"We do not look kindly on being mocked," said Palatina sternly.

"I'm not mocking anyone or distracting," Sam argued. "I just want to know the truth. Who is my dad? Is he still alive? Is he even human?"

The maidens appeared confounded and looked to the gryphon for an explanation.

"Per our agreement, Odette's memory was adjusted, as was the human's," Phylassos told the maidens.

"*What* human?" Sam asked, thoroughly exasperated.

"All right. Now, I don't have the first clue as to what this is all about, but could we just stop the mind-numbin' subterfuge and tell the kid who his father is?" Vantana declared. "He *deserves* to know."

"You both do," the gryphon replied.

"What?" the doctor said, confused.

"It's you, Vance," Phylassos revealed. "You're Sam's father."

Chapter 19
NEVER SAY GOODBYE

Vance Vantana was in his early twenties when he was writing his dissertation for his PhD at a cabin in Crater Lake National Park. He sat himself smack-dab in front of the only window because it offered a breathtaking view of Crater Lake, which is located in southern Oregon and is the deepest lake in the United States, having been formed by a collapsed volcano. He'd prefer being outside on a case, of course, but it was tranquil and relaxing here and was Vance's all-time favorite spot to work. He happened to be taking a break from his studies and staring out onto the lake one late spring day when the cabin phone rang.

"Ranger Vantana?" A grim-sounding familiar voice could be heard on the other end. Vance recognized it as Orry Avskogen, his old friend, a park ranger at Great Smoky Mountains National Park.

"Orry? You sound about as cheery as a funeral march. What's the trouble?"

"It's Rupert. He is in his final days."

Vance exhaled. Rupert the Bigfoot was the creature who had led Vance to discover the truth about mythical creatures, the DMW, and Dr. Knox. He was mighty special to Vance, and to hear this news was heartbreaking.

"He's requesting to see Henry, Vance," Orry added. "He says it's very important. Says he has information for Phylassos. He won't tell me what it is, and I tried reaching Dr. Knox directly but—"

"He's in Russia," Vantana quickly informed the ranger. Just two days earlier, Dr. Henry Knox had notified Vance that he would be traveling to Russia's Lake Baikal for a meeting with the Maiden Council, the governing body of swan maidens whose sanctuary was critically important to maintaining a balance with nature. It had been theorized, though never confirmed, that the sanctuary was the magical lifeblood of all the beauty of Gaia. The swan maidens committed their entire lives to nurturing the sanctuary and were not allowed beyond its borders. The council had called the meeting after growing displeased with human encroachment on their habitat and was concerned the environmental poisons being introduced by humans could damage the sanctuary.

"Can you get a message to him?" Orry followed up.

"I'm afraid that's impossible," Vantana answered. The Maiden Council was extremely protective, and no creatures were ever allowed inside the sanctuary's boundaries without express permission, especially human males. Knox had secured passage due to his relationship with Phylassos, but he had been prohibited from bringing anyone else.

"I see," Orry replied, disappointed. "I will let Rupert know and will hope that this errand of the doctor's is completed before . . ." Orry didn't finish his sentence, but he didn't have to. Vance understood the implications.

When the young ranger hung up the phone, he thought at length about this sudden and unforeseen circumstance. Given Knox and Rupert's longtime friendship, he felt an obligation to fulfill the bigfoot's final wish, but to do so would be a clear violation of protocol. Vance had always tried to live his life by an old adage from his ancestor, American frontiersman Davy Crockett, which said: "Be always sure you're right—then go ahead!" In this instance, Vantana reckoned he likely wasn't right, but he went ahead anyway. He hopped a dvergen subway to Russia to retrieve the doctor before it was too late.

Vance approached Lake Baikal several hours later and treaded carefully toward the sanctuary. Through his studies, he had come to know of the Baba Yaga, the creature sworn to protect the sanctuary and the maidens from any trespassers. Though no one had confirmed the Baba Yaga's existence, Vantana had learned in his line of work to always err on the side of assuming that myths were true. As such, he stopped at the boundary of the sanctuary and considered his options. If he ran as fast as he could through the sanctuary and found Knox before the creature found him, he might just be able to convince the council to call off the creature in time for him to deliver his message. But that plan was risky and could potentially jeopardize any negotiations taking place between Knox and the council. Vance had to get the message to Knox without crossing the boundary and therefore quickly concluded that the only way to do so would be to recruit a maiden to help him. Of course, revealing his presence to a maiden might send her running off to inform the council of danger, or worse, to alert the Baba Yaga. This strategy was risky as well, but he believed it was significantly less so than his previous plan.

He had spent most of his young life in the wilderness, so camping out near the sanctuary was second nature. He watched and waited, remaining stone silent to avoid detection. After a few days, Vance determined the schedule of several maidens who left their nesting area to visit a small pond located near the boundary—the closest they came to the edge of the sanctuary. They visited this spot on a daily basis, and Vance found that the maidens were as beautiful as the legends claimed, but one maiden in particular caught his eye. Though Vantana knew he had a plan to stick to, he couldn't help but become distracted when this auburn-haired maiden joined her sisters at the pond. There was something about her, he thought. Something that set her apart, beyond just her beauty. There was a gentleness and an energy that always—without fail—made him smile every time she entered his view.

Vance's plan to attract the attention of a maiden was simple: he would throw a small rock from his hiding place into the sanctuary. He did this once for every time the maidens visited the pond. Most of the maidens became frightened by the sound and ran off. Yet one always remained—the auburn-haired maiden. Unafraid, she looked toward the sound with great interest, until her fellow maidens pulled her away. And then one day she visited the pond alone. Vantana tossed the stone as he had before, the maiden looked toward where the pebble had come from, and instead of running off, she walked toward it.

"Hello?" she called out in a soft, fearless voice. "You can come out and show yourself. I don't bite."

Vance peeked his head out from behind a tree. "You're not scared I might?"

The maiden laughed at this. "I'm standing on the other side of the boundary," she noted. "If you tried, you wouldn't live long."

"Right. The Baba Yaga," Vance said. "So the stories are true?"

"Do you wish to find out for certain?" she asked with a smirk.

"Nah," he replied playfully.

"Wise choice. So who are you? Besides someone who likes to throw stones and scare off maidens, of course."

"The name's Vance. And what do they call you?"

"Odette."

"Pretty name," he said.

"It's all right," she replied flatly.

Vance grinned. "Not a fan, huh?"

She shrugged.

"Okay. Then how about I call you . . . Ettie. That better?"

She smiled and nodded. "I like that."

SPECIAL NOTE

Given the nature of the meeting between Odette the swan maiden and Vance Vantana, the files in the DMW archives include few details regarding their interaction. For this reason, I have asked Dr. Vantana to provide a personal statement describing the events as he now remembers them. The following is in his own words.

—T.C.G.

Once I had established a rapport with Ettie, I explained what had brought me to the sanctuary. I asked if she'd be willing to tell Dr. Knox that I was there and needed to speak with him immediately. She agreed, but when she came back a few hours later she said she wasn't able to get close to the council's meeting place. They were apparently engaged in a secret discussion, and the area was protected by some sort of magical barrier. I decided to stick around a few more days until the meeting was completed or there was a break, during which she could possibly get a message to Knox. Although I have to admit that I would have probably given up on the whole thing if it hadn't been for Ettie.

Nearly every minute of my time waiting was spent with her. The council was so caught up in their meeting they didn't notice that she was sneaking away from her nesting place. And before

I realized it, I began to have less and less interest in seeing Knox and delivering the news regarding Rupert. It no longer felt important to me.... What was important now was seeing Ettie. It wasn't long before I just stopped asking about the council and Knox, and Ettie stopped telling me what she saw or heard from her fellow maidens. We were both much too busy learning about each other. I wanted to know all about her life in the sanctuary, and Ettie wanted to know all about my life beyond it.

Ettie and I filled our days with conversation and laughter. There were no awkward silences, as we never ran out of things to talk about. At night, we'd lie on the ground as close as possible without crossing the boundary. Inches away yet worlds apart. With this invisible wall separating the two of us, we'd stare up at the stars and share our dreams. Ettie's dream was pretty simple—she showed me a poster that had washed up on the lakeshore, which advertised a production of Swan Lake. She wanted to go to the place called London on the poster and see this ballet, which was clearly about her kind. I felt a little bad having to explain that the date on the play meant it had been performed quite a long time ago, so it could not be seen as advertised. But I suggested that there might be another version we could see together. Ettie liked that idea very much.

I had been so singularly focused on my studies and my work with the DMW under the guidance of Henry Knox that I rarely had any leisure time and never sought relationships. I prioritized work, and everything else fell by the wayside. Yet spending time with Ettie had become my new singular focus. I think we both realized our time together was fleeting and that made our interaction all the more intense. Every second that passed was one less second we had remaining. And then one day it all came crashing down.

She was showing me a few of the rare flowers that grew alongside the boundary within the sanctuary. I had never seen or smelled flowers like these before. One of them smelled like chocolate—honest to goodness—another like root beer, and the roses bloomed in colors that spanned the spectrum. Ettie was particularly fond of a rose that appeared to change color depending on the angle the sunlight hit it. She was going on and on about its beauty when I suggested she wear it in her hair. She just blushed and shook her head, but I insisted. She finally gave in and attempted to remove a rose from the vine but was pricked by a thorn. My protective instinct kicked in and I reached out to grab her hand; but the moment we touched, everything changed.

I had a sudden and swift realization about my feelings for Ettie: I was in love with her. And from the way she looked at me, I reckoned at the time the feeling was mutual. Unfortunately, the happiness we experienced by recognizing this love was short-lived. The wind howled and the trees swayed. The Baba Yaga had sensed the breach of the sanctuary's boundary and came looking for a fight. I quickly took up a stance in front of Ettie, but the Baba Yaga paid her no mind—the creature set her sights on yours truly. She tossed me around like a rag doll while Ettie pleaded for her to stop. I was hurting something awful and barely conscious, but I could hear the Baba Yaga demand that Ettie return to her nesting place. She refused.

Through swollen eyes, I could see her standing between the Baba Yaga and me, telling the creature that she would have to go through her. Of course, the monster simply pushed her aside and came at me once more.

I took one look at Ettie—a look I honestly believed would be my last. I smiled at her, as best I could. Fortunately for me, she wasn't ready to say goodbye just yet. She stood up, spread her wings, and flew right toward me. She swooped down in front of the Baba Yaga, scooped me up, and took off. The Baba Yaga chased us for a good while, but Ettie never slowed or stopped. We flew for what must have been hours, possibly days, until the Baba Yaga finally stopped her pursuit. We collapsed somewhere in the Great Smoky Mountains. Ettie tended to my wounds and nursed me back to health.

As I healed, we talked at length about our unusual circumstances. I realized this was beyond forbidden and would cost me my career with the DMW. Poor Ettie was too terrified to even think about the consequences of her actions. The only thing we were certain about was that we wanted to be together, despite the overwhelming odds against us. To make that happen we had to disappear . . . to go someplace where we couldn't be found. But that seemed impossible. We needed help, and so I reached out to Rupert the Bigfoot. We went to meet with him and found that he was in his final hours.

Old Rupert begged us to return to the sanctuary, apologize, and ask for mercy, but he realized right quick this was not an option we were willing to consider. Rupert then suggested another possibility: Atlantis. After all, it was not under the gryphon's law, nor did it fall under the authority of the Maiden Council. It was a neutral place that became a haven for displaced mythical creatures. The bigfoot believed the city could keep the two of us safe from punishment. I agreed and persuaded Ettie that Atlantis represented our best hope. Rupert contacted a ranger from the Everglades National Park who I did not know at the time. His name was Woodruff Sprite, and he could smuggle us to Atlantis and help secure us new identities. Sprite had been a trusted friend to Rupert for over a hundred years and, though surprised by the bigfoot's request, even he could clearly see that the feelings Ettie and I shared were the real deal. He committed to helping us, despite the danger.

Reaching out to a Nuppeppo lounge singer named Squishy, Sprite arranged passage to the mysterious island. Once there, we were directed to meet with Squishy, and the singer managed to get us a place to stay, even finding me a job in the administrative offices of the island's park service. Ettie and I took on different names and were married. Though everything seemed to be going well, Squishy was worried. She believed that as strangers on the island, we could not avoid being noticed, and this would draw unwanted scrutiny. But Sprite wanted us to wait it out while he contacted Knox to discuss how this might all be remedied. Unfortunately, Squishy's instincts were correct and we never had a chance.

Gilgamesh, who was working as the head of the Atlantis security forces at the time, learned of our presence and used us as leverage to propel himself to a powerful seat in the Atlantis Assembly. As a result, Ettie and I were arrested and sent back to Lake Baikal, where we were brought before the Maiden Council.

The council decided that Ettie's punishment would be a return to Gaia, but there was one small hiccup: Ettie was pregnant. The Maiden Council found itself in a sticky situation. They couldn't return an innocent child to Gaia, so they couldn't carry out the sentence. It was then that Phylassos stepped in. I had never seen the creature in person before that and was surprised it chose to get involved.

The gryphon managed to negotiate an agreement that satisfied the council and didn't require anyone to be returned to Gaia. Phylassos would use his powers to ensure that Ettie and I didn't remember any of the past several weeks. Our memories of the events that transpired would be completely different from reality. Ettie would be relocated somewhere far from the sanctuary, and we'd have no further contact. She would be permitted to have and raise her child, but neither she nor her child would ever know the truth about me. The council could inform the other maidens that Odette was returned to Gaia for her crimes, and none would be the wiser. Life would go on, and this unfortunate episode would be forgotten.

The Maiden Council consented to the gryphon's proposal, but had one condition that was nonnegotiable: Ettie's feathers would have to be placed somewhere close to her, so she might find them once again and return home. Phylassos didn't like this idea, but the Maiden Council's autonomy had to be respected, and this was the only way to keep both me and Ettie alive. Of course, I didn't see it that way. I protested, vigorously, and held Ettie as

long as I could until those awful magical sands pulled us apart.
Next thing I knew, I woke up in the forest outside the boundary
of the sanctuary with no recollection of what occurred.

—V.V.

Sam London stood on the shore of the lake in front of the Maiden Council. He saw his mother with wings and had just learned the identity of his father: Dr. Vance Vantana—the man who had become his closest friend since his first case with the Department of Mythical Wildlife. The same man he once imagined dating his mother and perhaps becoming his stepfather—he was his dad all along. It seemed so crazy. But Squishy knew, Sam realized. She had hinted at it, practically even said it.

When Phylassos revealed the truth, Vantana's eyes went wide. He looked at Sam, then at Ettie, and nodded softly, as if suddenly understanding.

"I remember now . . . ," he said. "I've been here before. In front of this council."

"Yes, you have," Phylassos confirmed.

"You helped us, Sprite," Vance said to Ranger Sprite, who was standing off to the side with Ranger Naughton.

"I tried . . . and failed," Sprite replied sheepishly.

"How is this possible?" Sam asked. "You just met my mom in Benicia when we came back from Hérault."

"That wasn't the first time, Sam," Vantana told him. "The first time was before you were born, right beyond the boundary of this sanctuary." Vance then turned to face Phylassos and squinted his eyes with anger. "I did not agree to it. You did this without my permission."

"I had little choice," Phylassos responded.

"I lost twelve years . . . twelve years getting to know my son. Seeing him grow up. Being a part of his life. Moments I didn't get to have—to enjoy—because of you."

"He would not have had a life if I had not agreed to the terms the council presented," the gryphon reminded him. Vantana shifted his ire to the council.

"Y'all should be ashamed of yourselves for what you've done."

"You will cease this impertinence at once," said Faye.

"Or what? You're gonna punish me? Her? Haven't you already done that?"

"No, we haven't," said Caer matter-of-factly. She eyed Phylassos. "The agreement is null and void. A new judgment shall be passed. Are the maidens of the council prepared to render a verdict?" The maidens nodded.

"Guilty," they each said in turn. Sam's heart sank lower and lower as they repeated it over and over again, until all nine had spoken. He didn't want to think about what it might mean—what this punishment could possibly be.

"The verdict is unanimous," Caer declared. "All three violators shall face sentences for this crime."

"No, they won't," Phylassos said firmly.

"The time for negotiation is over," Palatina asserted.

"I am not negotiating, simply stating the obvious. If we

are to declare the previous agreement null and void, as Caer stipulated, then we must proceed as we would have prior to the agreement," Phylassos countered.

"What are you saying?" Sam asked. Phylassos did not answer. The maidens conferred before turning back to the shoreline.

Palatina spoke for the group. "We shall agree to these terms out of respect for you, mighty Phylassos." The gryphon nodded once in acknowledgment.

"What did you do? What just happened?" Sam exclaimed. He was quickly concluding that the terms weren't favorable and was terrified of the result.

"The child and the human shall be spared," Melusine said. "The maiden known as Odette shall be returned to Gaia at once."

"What? No!" Vance yelled.

"You can't! She's my mom. She didn't do anything wrong! Phylassos, please! Do something!"

"The gryphon has agreed to this sentence. There is nothing more to discuss," Caer said. "Odette? It is your time. Your life on the lake is complete. You shall return to the waters from whence you came."

Sam raced down to the shore, but Caer put up her hand and the sand gripped Sam's feet once again and stopped him cold. When Vance made the attempt, she put up her other hand, and he quickly halted. Sam watched helplessly. The swan maiden known as Odette and known to him as his mother stepped into the lake.

"Mom!" Sam cried out. Odette peered toward his voice, her face expressionless, and then turned back to the lake, continuing on.

The moment Odette the swan maiden disappeared beneath the still waters of Lake Baikal, the dawn sun broke against the horizon. Everyone—human and otherwise—shielded their eyes from the blinding light. Vance grabbed Sam by the shoulders, as tears ran down his cheeks.

"I'm so sorry, Son. I'm so sorry." He embraced Sam and kept repeating those words, as if it were all his fault. Sam couldn't process any of it. He could not—would not—believe she was gone.

"The punishment has been carried out according to the law," Manto said. "We ask that you leave our sanctuary and do not return."

Sam London collapsed on the sand. The tears could not be stopped. The pain could not be quelled. He could hear Nerida and Penelope, Sprite and Tashi, all trying to console him. And he could hear his father whispering as he held Sam in his arms and squeezed him with all his might.

"It's going to be okay, Sam. . . . I've got you. . . . It's going to be okay. . . ."

But Sam London knew it would never be okay again.

Chapter 20
CASE CLOSED?

SL002-130
FINAL CASE NOTES
DATE: ██████████

In the days that followed the completion of DMW case SL002-130, aka "The Selkie of San Francisco," the city of Ta Cathair underwent major social and political upheaval. The Leviathan had taken a heavy toll on the infrastructure of the city and left many of its residents homeless, which now included the influx of refugees from the evacuated colonies. With the creature now buried beneath the seafloor—thanks to the near-fatal sacrifice of the DMW's own Sam London—and the surviving finfolk creatures imprisoned, the population and government of Ta Cathair moved forward with the Herculean task of rebuilding, both the city's physical structures and its social underpinnings.

Queen Muiria announced her abdication of the throne four days after the Leviathan's attack, to enable her daughter, Iaira, to take her place. According to Muiria's statement to the DMW, the queen sensed a need for a new generation of leaders and recognized the overwhelming popularity of her daughter following her dramatic homecoming and efforts to save her people. The treaty requiring Iaira to marry a selkie was amended at the request of Maris, with the support of his father, General Searus, who'd been the initial force behind the edict.

In her first act as queen, Iaira successfully persuaded the mer-people to form a coalition government that would ensure that the selkies had equal representation. She also invited Maris to jointly govern by her side and return the city to its former glory. In light of these changes, General Searus stepped down from his post, and the newly formed government chose a successor who was well liked by both the selkies and mer-people.

Against her counsel's objections, Queen Iaira took a secret trip back to Miami, Florida, a few days into her reign to tie up the loose ends of her life as Pearl and to help her gems find closure regarding her disappearance. She also owed Francis Gomez and Wanda Bradley a thank-you for rescuing her and her friends from the finfolk. Maris supported Iaira's wish to return to the over-world for a brief and—what he hoped would be—final visit but insisted on accompanying her, for security reasons.

A party that was open to her most loyal gems was held in the lobby of Eklund Environmental's headquarters. In the wake of Lief's experiences with Iaira, the finfolk, and Ta Cathair, the billionaire abandoned the energy-seeking aspects of the company and focused its efforts on cleaning up the world's oceans, as well as finding eco-friendly, renewable sources of energy that would not displace mythical sea creatures (the existence of whom he pledged to keep secret).

With Lief's help, Iaira convinced her gems that she was devoting her life to helping her father with his environmental work. Her new focus would preclude her from engaging on social media or pursuing film and television roles. She encouraged her gems to follow her example and get involved in their communities, working to make a difference for the better. Lief had the drilling ship *Pearl* stripped of its drilling equipment and fitted with the latest technology for cleaning oil spills and garbage from the seas. Once the work was complete, he renamed the ship *Iaira*.

Before Iaira and Maris returned to Ta Cathair, they were met outside the Eklund Environmental building by San Francisco news reporter Cynthia Salazar, who asked about the day when Maris confronted Iaira at the fashion show. Iaira became concerned that the reporter was connecting the dots and might already know too much about the mythical world. When Ms. Salazar inquired as to whether Iaira had ever seen a gryphon or knew a boy named Sam London, the queen abruptly ended the interview and climbed into a waiting limousine with Maris. Ms. Salazar attempted to follow the two as they headed to Falling Waters State Park, but the limo driver was able to lose her along the way.

Back in Ta Cathair, the close working relationship Iaira had with Maris further developed the bond the two had already shared as a result of the events that had begun in San Francisco. Iaira came to greatly appreciate the risk Maris had taken to come and find her. It demonstrated true concern for her and all of the city's inhabitants. Witnessing his good heart in action and his charming manner—and likely recognizing he was hesitant to make the first move, given their history—Iaira eventually asked Maris out to dinner. She recognized her people's extreme interest in the pair and decided to do something that had never been done in the undersea world—she live-streamed their first date. Working with the technologists of Ta Cathair, Iaira helped launch the kingdom's own version of a social media platform as a way for citizens to interact with their leaders, as well as each other.

Exposing the people to their courtship, coupled with this new form of communication, played a major role in continuing to break down the cultural barriers that had been growing more fortified between the two races over the centuries. At the time of the filing of this report, Iaira and Maris were engaged to be married.

As for Murphy, the old fisherman and friend of Lief was offered the chance to start a new life in Ta Cathair. He was given an injection synthesized from Maris's blood, and utilized a prosthetic fin to help fit in. He enjoyed his time in the city, became a bit of a celebrity, and sparked up a wonderful friendship with Muiria.

The kingdom of Ta Cathair dedicated the new Seahorse 5000 stadium exactly one year, to the day, after the Leviathan's attack. It would forever be known as Sam London Arena, in honor of his actions that day, and a new plaque at the entrance of the facility featured a likeness of Sam with an inscription that read: "Dedicated to Sam London. The human boy who saved us all."

An emotional trifecta of anger, sadness, and despair consumed Sam London as he stood motionless on the shore of Lake Baikal. Even though the enchanted sands had released their hold, Sam felt helpless to budge from the spot where he had watched his mother return to Gaia. His heart felt like it had been ripped from him. . . . He couldn't even feel it beating anymore. He felt hollow and sick to his stomach. Although the maidens were responsible for carrying out the sentence, Sam placed all of the blame for this horrible turn of events on one creature. He glared at the gryphon with contempt.

"How could you?" Sam asked angrily.

"I am sorry, Sam," Phylassos answered. "There was nothing more that could be done."

"You lied to me and you let them do this," Sam declared as he motioned toward the Maiden Council, its members already receding back into the lake.

"I hope you will come to understand the difficulty of my predicament."

"I won't," Sam replied defiantly.

"You need time," Phylassos contended, then looked to the others. "Please see him home." They nodded, and Phylassos took flight, disappearing over the mountains. Vance placed a hand on Sam's shoulder.

"C'mon, Sam. It's time to go."

Nerida reached out, grabbed his hand, and clutched it tightly as she led him from the shore. He appreciated the gesture and thought how much he would have enjoyed it under different circumstances. Now it was just a reminder that he was being consoled for tragic, awful reasons. He half-expected Tashi to start telling him about the wonderful nature of returning to Gaia, but the Guardian no doubt sensed that now was not a good time for a discussion on mythical death.

Everyone silently left the sanctuary, shell-shocked by what they had witnessed. They boarded a dvergen subway and traveled back to the United States. Trevor and Nuks were waiting on the platform at the Castle Crags station. Ranger Naughton must have let them know that the group would be returning, and given the duo's solemn expressions, she likely had informed the two of Ettie's fate. As the travelers disembarked from the subway car, Ranger Sprite tapped Sam on the shoulder. Sam turned, and Sprite kneeled down on the platform, so that he could meet Sam eye to eye.

"I have to return to the Everglades, but I want you to know that I understand how hard this is for you," the ranger told him. "Harder than anything you have ever experienced. And there are no words, Sam. No words I can say to make sense of this or lessen the pain in your heart. All I can do is be a friend to you, always. Here whenever you need me." Sprite embraced a now teary-eyed Sam.

"Thank you," the boy whispered.

The group stopped at Penelope's cabin to drop Trevor and the ranger off. The two said their goodbyes to Sam, with Ranger Naughton having a hard time letting him go from her hug and Trevor acting surprisingly subdued. The troll simply kept expressing his condolences until Ranger Naughton pulled him away. Before they left, Vance took Penelope aside to talk, and Sam overheard the conversation.

"I'll be taking some time away from the department," he told her.

"Of course," she replied.

"I've got some catching up to do."

"Any idea when you might—"

"I haven't a clue," Vantana said. "To be honest, Pen, I'm not even sure I'm coming back." Ranger Naughton appeared surprised to hear this but tried her best to hide it.

"I understand," she replied half-heartedly. "I'm here if you need me, Vance. You or Sam." He nodded, and the two embraced.

The drive back to Benicia was initially spent in silence. Sam sat in the passenger seat and stared out the window. Occasionally Vance would reach over and put his hand on Sam's leg in a consoling gesture. Sam didn't acknowledge it, and Vance would simply retract it after a few seconds. Sam didn't mean to be rude, but there was just so much to process, and he didn't know where to begin. His mind was racing with thoughts. Thoughts about the truth regarding his mother, his father, Nerida, and himself. He now knew that he wasn't entirely human. This was a major revelation in the life of Sam London, and he had no idea what the implications were. He had so many questions.

But there was one specific question that kept pushing its way to the very front of this crowd of thoughts. A question that he wanted to know the answer to more than all the others combined. Fortunately, the only person who could answer it was sitting right next to him.

"Vance?" Sam said. The doctor quickly glanced over.

"Yeah, Sam?"

"How did you meet her?" he asked.

Vantana smirked. "It's a long story."

"We have a long drive. And I want to hear everything. I want the *whole* story," Sam insisted.

"All right. My memory is still a touch spotty, but I'll do my best."

"Please," the boy said.

For the remainder of the drive home, Vance told Sam, Tashi, Nuks, and Nerida the tale that had led them all to that fateful moment in the sanctuary. Sam loved hearing about his mother in a way that he'd never known her. It was comforting to him. He also enjoyed learning a bit more about his father at the same time. It was an escape into the past that helped him forget the present.

"Tell it again," Sam demanded when Vance had finished the story.

"The whole thing?" Vantana asked.

"The whole thing," Sam confirmed.

The doctor complied, and this diversion eased the pain for a spell, at least until they arrived at Sam's house. Walking inside the home he had shared with his mother brought him instantly back to the present moment and the reality of the life that now lay before him. Like Sam, the house felt empty inside. He immediately dropped his backpack and retreated to his room.

In the days that followed, Nerida would frequently stop by and try to persuade Sam to go outside and play. Tashi offered to help train him in various fighting styles—something he had badgered her about—but Sam remained uninterested. The only person who could truly understand his sorrow was Vance. And he was taking it just as hard.

"We're quite a pair, you and I," Vance quipped over a dinner that Miss Bastifal had prepared for them. "Misery loves company. Add to it that I already enjoy your company, kiddo, and we've got ourselves a perfect storm of self-pity."

Nuks had a particularly difficult time with the loss. The raccoon-dog was convinced it was all his fault. He was the one who'd made it possible for Ettie to clean the attic and find her feathers. If it wasn't for him, she'd still be alive, he contended. No matter how much Sam tried to explain that he shouldn't blame himself, Nuks was racked with guilt. Finally Sam had to order the creature to forgive himself and explained that if he wanted to make Sam happy, he wouldn't mention it ever again. Nuks obliged. The raccoon-dog was continuing to go to school as Sam, which eventually prompted Tashi to complain to Vantana directly, after Sam ignored her pleas to return.

"We gotta move on," the doctor told him unconvincingly one night before bed. "You can't be sendin' Nuks out in your place. You gotta live your life. That's what she would have wanted." Sam nodded numbly. "I've directed Nuks not to indulge you any further. It's time you had a normal day and went back to school."

"I guess," Sam said reluctantly, turning toward the stairs. He was just about to head back to his room, when he thought of a question for Vance. One that felt strange to ask. "I always called you Dr. Vantana or Vance, but now—"

"Yeah, I know," he replied. "What would you like to call me?"

"Dad," Sam said matter-of-factly. Vance smiled.

"I'd like that very much, Son. I'd like that very much."

Sam grabbed his book bag and then suddenly remembered—

"Wait. I've got a gift for you," he said.

Vantana looked to him, surprised. "A gift?"

Sam retrieved the square package given to him by Squishy and handed it over.

"Squishy said I was supposed to give this to you when our journey was over," Sam explained. Vance unwrapped it and stumbled back a step in shock. His face lit up and his eyes watered.

"I'll be darned," he said. Sam leaned in to take a look and immediately understood why his dad was now grinning from ear to ear. It was a picture of Vance and Ettie on their wedding day. They stood with Woodruff Sprite and Squishy. Everyone looked a little younger, except for Sprite, who appeared exactly the same.

"I have the perfect place for it," Sam said as he took the photo from Vance and set it on the mantel in place of the one with his fake dad and Ettie in front of the lake, which Vance snatched up and examined.

"I know this image—not the guy, of course. He wasn't there when I took it."

"You took it?" Sam asked.

"From what I can remember . . . it's where we went after the sanctuary. Your mom never had her picture taken before, so I took one," Vance revealed. "Maybe we can have that other guy removed or somethin'."

"I'm sure we could," Sam said as a loud bang was heard coming from upstairs. Sam rolled his eyes. "I better go see what Nuks has broken now."

"School in the morning," Vance reminded him. Sam nodded, and Vance pulled him into a hug.

"Good night, Son."

"Good night, Dad," Sam replied. Saying that made him smile, and smiles were hard to come by.

When Sam entered his room, he was surprised to find that it wasn't Nuks who had made the noise. Rather, it was Dr. Henry Knox. Sam hadn't been expecting to see the gryphon in human form so soon after the events at Lake Baikal, but there he was sitting in a chair at Sam's computer desk, dressed in a sweater and tweed jacket, his signature hat resting on the desktop.

"Hi, Sam."

"What are you doing here?" Sam asked him harshly.

"I wanted to check in and see how you were."

"How do you think I am?" Sam replied, irritated.

"I did not come to argue with you about what is done. I am here because I imagine you have questions only I can answer."

Sam eyed him a long moment. "What does it mean to be half swan maiden?" he asked.

"It means you're a hybrid creature."

"Does it mean I have powers?"

"Yes."

"What are they?"

"Only Gaia knows, but I can speculate that they will likely involve shape-shifting." Sam considered that. And then he concentrated on his hand, trying to make it change into a flipper. Knox chuckled. "It is not that easy. Hybrids are unpredictable creatures, but I would surmise that whatever the magic, it won't appear until you mature." Sam dropped his hand to his side, suddenly feeling silly. "How's Vance?" Knox asked.

"He lost the love of his life twice and found out he had a son he never knew. Not great, but we've got each other now, right?" Sam answered sarcastically.

"I really hope you eventually come to understand—"

"You didn't have a choice, I know," Sam quickly replied. "But I did."

"What do you mean?"

"I mean I could have stayed home . . . never boarded that bus to Death Valley. I guess the name of that place was a hint, huh?"

"You had a destiny, Sam," Knox told him. "It was unavoidable."

"Well, then I wish I'd never met you, never had that dream, never known any of this. . . . I'd still have my mom." Sam retreated to the window of his room, turning his back on Knox.

"Sam . . . please—" Knox began.

"Just go away. I never want to see you again," Sam demanded. "And here." He tossed Knox his DMW badge and turned back toward the window. Knox sighed heavily. As Sam gazed out the window of his room, the tears returned. What would become of his life now? How would he go on without his mom? Knowing that Vance was his dad was great and all, but it didn't fix this—it didn't even come close. He wanted his whole family intact. The way it was supposed to be. The way he deserved it to be. In the emotional cage match that was taking place in Sam's head, anger was soundly defeating sadness.

Sam wanted to hit something, scream, kick—anything to get this fury out of him. He was mad. More furious than he'd even thought possible. He could hardly see straight. . . . And then something caught his eye—movement outside on the street below. It was his neighbor from across the way—his teacher Christopher Canis. He was simply fetching his mail, but Sam suddenly saw in him the one thing he needed now more than ever: hope. Sam spun back to Knox, who was just about to leave.

"Is she still alive?" Sam asked with renewed determination. Knox eyed him. "But she's someone else now, right? She doesn't remember who she was?" Seeing Mr. Canis had reminded Sam that his new teacher had once been a mythical creature: a cynocephalus named Chriscanis who was returned to Gaia after a fight with the Beast of Gevaudan. Sam had thought then that his friend was gone forever, until a human bearing a striking resemblance to Chriscanis moved in across the street. The teacher didn't remember his former self, but Sam *knew* that Gaia had granted the creature his wish to be human.

"Sam . . . I do not control Gaia. And to even discuss this is a violation of—"

"Please," Sam pleaded. "Just tell me if it's possible."

"I'm sorry," Knox said.

All the hope Sam had briefly felt began to drain from his body, until Dr. Henry Knox met Sam London's eye and did something that changed everything.

He winked.

EPILOGUE

Wes Jenkins's diner was a local favorite, known for its large por-
tions, cheap but tasty breakfasts, coffee strong enough to keep
a farmer farming from dawn till dusk, and Sunday dinners like
Mom used to make—only better. It was a busy place, but for
a small town like this, "busy" was relative. Wes's wife, Charlotte, did all the baking, and he did all the cooking, except for
Sundays, when Charlotte insisted on making the meals. It reminded her of Sundays with their kids, who had all moved
away and relegated the tradition to the holidays.

Though retirement was out of the question, Wes and his
wife were getting older and—despite his outward denials—
needed help running the restaurant. This was why Wes was
so thrilled that his new hire was working out so well. She was
a hard worker, kind and conscientious, even though she remained a bit of a mystery. Wes had been out fishing when he'd

come upon her sitting on the lakeshore staring out at the water. The woman didn't say much about herself, except that she was looking for work and a place to live. He could tell that she was good people, just maybe a little down on her luck. So he offered up their guest room and then gave her a job at the diner waiting tables. The woman took to it like a duck to water, and the customers loved her. She was always exceedingly positive, but Wes sensed there was something missing from her life. He would frequently catch her staring off into the distance between the breakfast and lunch rushes. She never discussed her past but would talk a lot about wanting to travel, and London was an often-mentioned destination. The woman didn't say why, just that she felt like she really needed to visit there.

Another oddity—if you could even call it that—was her enjoyment of a particular song on Wes's antique jukebox. Whenever it came on, she'd smile bigger and there was more bounce in her step. He suspected she'd been using her tip change to keep the tune in rotation, but he didn't mind. It was an oldie but goodie from a group called the Turtles. The song's name was "Happy Together."

* * *

Sam London will return in *Search for the Swan Maiden*.

GLOSSARY OF MYTHICAL CREATURES

Memorandum

Date: ███████████

To: DMW Rangers & Administrative Personnel

From: Dr. Vance Vantana

Subj: Creatures linked to Case SL002

The following is a list of the mythical wildlife connected to Sam London's second case. At my request, the department's forensic arts division has provided illustrations for reference.

Adaro

Origin: Solomon Islands

Known Abilities: Controls poisonous fish

Favorite Food: Filet of soul

Comments: They ruined rainbows.

Bishop Fish

Origin: Somewhere annoying

Known Abilities: Being annoying

Favorite Food: Something annoying

Comments: See above

Finfolk

Origin: Orkney Islands

Known Abilities: Shape-shifting, sorcery

Favorite Food: Seahorse

Comments: Zero sense of humor

Loch Ness Monster

Origin: Scotland

Known Abilities: Super speed

Favorite Food: Fast food

Comments: Hang on for dear life.

Lusca

Origin: The Bahamas

Known Abilities: Camouflage

Favorite Foods: Crustaceans and/or humans

Comments: Shark + Octopus = Run!

Makara

Origin: India

Known Abilities: Unknown

Favorite Food: Gulab jamun

Comments: One strange-lookin' critter

Ningen

Origin: Antarctica

Known Abilities: Transmogrification

Favorite Food: Snow cones

Comments: Avoid Antarctica, please.

Nuppeppo

Origin: Japan

Known Abilities: Unknown

Favorite Food: Ōtoro (extrafatty tuna)

Comments: Bring perfume.

Scorpion Men

Origin: Mesopotamia

Known Abilities: Venomous sting

Favorite Food: They don't play favorites.

Comments: A tail as old as time

Skunk Ape

Origin: Florida Everglades

Known Abilities: Poisonous odor

Favorite Food: Stinkbugs

Comments: Try not to hurl.

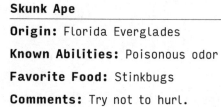

Additional creatures (pending verification):

–

–

TRANSMISSION INCOMPLETE.

DMW FILE
CLASSIFICATION

DMW case files are presented in the following format: #XXXXX-XXX-XX.X. This ten- or eleven-digit code consists of both letters and numbers.

The initial series of letters and numbers represents the investigating ranger and the case number involving that ranger. These particular files are associated with Sam London (SL). As this is Sam London's second case, the files are designated as 002.

The second series of three numbers indicates the applicable DMW offense code. In this instance, offense code 130 is used, which is broadly defined as a "creature-involved incident." Although this particular case involves several types of violations of Phylassos's law, the catalyst for these additional crimes was a single creature-involved incident.

The final number pertains to the section of the file for those files with multiple sections. Numbers that appear after the section and are separated by a period indicate subsections.

SUBJ: This is the subject or subjects of the section.

SOURCE: This notes the source or sources of the information included in a particular section. These sources are designated by an abbreviation. Below is a list of relevant abbreviations:

> **SA:** Special Advisor
> **MC:** Mythical Creature
> **ODB:** Operational Debriefing
> **MR:** Medical Records
> **SR:** Surveillance Records
> **BG:** Background Investigation
> **WS:** Witness Statement
> **PR:** Public Record

DATE: This is the date on which the incident or inquiry took place.

FORMS: In some instances, case files include forms used by DMW personnel to record information from witnesses or intelligence sources related to an investigation. For example, FD-11 is an Activity Report that draws on information procured from witnesses, informants, and surveillance to monitor important persons related to a case.

SPECIAL CLASSIFICATIONS: Files that are administrative in nature are given a classification code in the 400s. For example, classification 470 is reserved for personnel records and 480 for employee medical records. Specific file numbers of these records have been withheld due to privacy concerns.

PARKS TO VISIT

National Park of American Samoa

American Samoa

nps.gov/npsa/index.htm

Biscayne National Park

Florida

nps.gov/bisc/index.htm

Crater Lake National Park

Oregon

nps.gov/crla/index.htm

Everglades National Park

Florida

nps.gov/ever/index.htm

Falling Waters State Park

Florida

floridastateparks.org/park/Falling-Waters

Great Smoky Mountains National Park

North Carolina, Tennessee

nps.gov/grsm/index.htm

Redwood National Park

California

nps.gov/redw/index.htm

Cabo de Hornos National Park

Chile

chile.travel/en/intereses-destacados/national-parks-
and-reserves/cabo-hornos-national-park

Fiordland National Park

New Zealand

doc.govt.nz/parks-and-recreation/places-to-go
/fiordland/places/fiordland-national-park

Killarney National Park

Ireland

killarneynationalpark.ie

Sri Venkateswara National Park

India

http://www.forests.ap.gov.in/WL%20svnp.htm

Support America's National Parks

National Park Foundation

Official Charity of America's National Parks

nationalparks.org

ACKNOWLEDGMENTS

This is that page in the back of the book where I thank everyone who helped make this possible, but could never have enough room on the page or words to thank them enough.

Dolores & Billy for having me.

Tiffany for encouraging me.

Valentina for laughing at me.

Lacy Lalene Lynch and Dabney Rice at Dupree/Miller & Associates for believing in me.

Random House, Delacorte Press, and Beverly Horowitz for trusting me.

Monica Jean for guiding me.

Bara MacNeill and Colleen Fellingham for correcting me.

Sarah Hokanson, Kevin Keele, Chris McClary, and Julius Camenzind for sharing their artistry with me.

Monkey Max for always grinning at me.

And to everyone else who knows who they are and will wonder why they aren't specifically named, thank you for humoring, inspiring, and supporting me.

ABOUT THE AUTHOR

When he's not hammering out the next Sam London novel on his 1935 Royal Deluxe typewriter, Todd Calgi Gallicano is a ███████████████████. Despite pressure from the media and the government, Todd remains tight-lipped when it comes to questions about the Department of Mythical Wildlife and his sources within the secret organization. He lives with his wife in ███████████, where he helps raise his daughter and tries to steer clear of gargoyles, chupacabras, and other nefarious creatures.

For more top-secret information, visit mythicalwildlife.com and follow @TheDMW on Twitter and @MythicalWildlife on Facebook. Also, look for the first Sam London adventure, *Guardians of the Gryphon's Claw,* available from Delacorte Press.